30p

A LOVELY ILLUSION

A LOVELY ILLUSION

Tessa Barclay

This first world edition published in Great Britain 2001 by
SEVERN HOUSE PUBLISHERS LTD of
9–15 High Street, Sutton, Surrey SM1 1DF.
This first world edition published in the USA 2001 by
SEVERN HOUSE PUBLISHERS INC. of
595 Madison Avenue, New York, NY 10022.

British Library Cataloguing in Publication Data

Barclay, Tessa
  A lovely illusion
  1. Swindlers and swindling
  2. Love stories
  I. Title
  823.9'14 [F]

ISBN 0–7278–5639–1

Typeset by Palimpsest Book Production Limited,
Polmont, Stirlingshire, Scotland.
Printed and bound in Great Britain by
MPG Books Ltd, Bodmin, Cornwall.

One

The last part of the journey to the island was always the part Erica liked best. London Airport and the flight to Greece were penalties to be endured, but once aboard the north-south ferry from Piraeus she could relax. There was the fun of watching for the church of Agios Chrysostomos to appear above the white rim of Kimolos, its rounded dome perhaps gleaming in morning sunlight. Then hurrying down the gangway to the quay, crossing to the familiar little café for a cup of reviving coffee while boatmen drifted in to barter for the final crossing to Parigos.

This morning the sun was warm through the thin cotton shirt on her back as she stood waiting to step down into the fishing boat. Old Giorgiou knew her by sight, giving her a cheery toothless grin and a 'Good morning, Kyria' as he helped her aboard. In her halting Greek Erica began a conversation – about the weather, the fishing, the matters that interested him. But what she was longing to ask was: 'Has Kyrios Townley arrived yet?'

For she was going to meet her lover.

How many times had she come to this rendezvous in its far corner of the Mediterranean? Well, why should she pretend she couldn't recall – each visit was precious, remembered in every detail during the long months when she and Willard Townley could meet only infrequently in London. This was her sixth trip to Parigos, the sixth time she could look forward to a few blessed days of relaxation, happiness, and love.

'It makes sense to have a place where we can just be together,' Willard had said when he first suggested it. 'If we're seen about too much in London, the whole of the art world tends to sit up and takes notice.'

1

'Oh, Willard . . . We're not really as famous as all that!'

He shook his dark head at her. 'Not famous, but notable. Buying and selling paintings is big business these days, Erica. Of course other dealers keep an eye on what I'm doing – and if we're seen together too much people begin to think I'm going to sell you something for a lot of money, or vice versa.'

Erica wasn't entirely convinced. But why argue? Why protest against the idea of occasional idyllic sojourns on an almost unknown island in the Cyclades?

Parigos had once been practically uninhabited, except by goats and a few herders. But an eccentric shipping tycoon had decided to buy it as a hideaway for himself and his family. He turned the goat tracks into passable roads for small cars and vans, built generators and water storage tanks and houses – a series of cool, airy, perfect houses for himself and his relations, a scattering of lesser cottages for staff.

Then, after a few years, he had grown tired of it. He couldn't moor his great motor-yacht at the little quay, he had to be ferried to the quayside in a powered dinghy. It was undignified, inconvenient. So he abandoned the place, leaving it to his agent to recoup some of the money he'd spent.

Now a small and motley group owned the houses he'd built. Willard had one of the places intended for boat crew, on the western side of the island and somewhat closer to the sea than the others. At its big windows Erica and Willard would stand, arms about each other, to watch the spectacular island sunsets. And in the morning it was only a few steps to a rocky pool where they could bathe and splash, cool water against sleep-warm skin – a perfect start to any day.

They never travelled together to Parigos. In the first place there was the wish to keep their relationship under wraps. Then Willard liked to go by sea, using his cabin cruiser. 'I like to potter round the Med,' he explained. 'It's amazing what you can pick up in little galleries here and there – even in resorts like Nice, there are back streets where a little shop might be showing something from somebody's attic.'

Erica never asked to go with him on these trips. In the first place, she didn't have so much time at her disposal.

Willard was his own boss, and so could take off whenever he wanted to and stay away as long as he liked. Erica, for all her prestigious title of 'gallery curator', was after all just a council employee. Though she had great responsibilities, and considerable freedom of judgement when it came to acquiring paintings, she was nevertheless bound in a way that Willard was not.

For instance, she was only free now on this late October day because the autumn exhibition at the Corie Gallery of Modern Art in Gratesford was safely under way. The year had its seasons: there had to be an educational series in January and February with lecturers in the afternoon, then by Easter some fresh view of the collection with perhaps a few important borrowings from bigger galleries. Summer had to have something a little startling, to attract tourists to Gratesford. There had always been a small flow of visitors because the town had a fine old abbey and a history of straw-hat making – enough to make it worth the day trip from London. But the town council wanted to increase the tourist income so Erica had to invent themes for exhibitions that would get media coverage.

Autumn was usually easier. A new selection of the gallery's legacy of Impressionists would be brought forth, with special emphasis on one particular painter – this year it was Sisley, for whom the town's benefactor, Benjamin Corie, had had a special liking. While she was planning the autumn exhibition Erica would get on with ideas for Christmas. This year the theme was 'snow paintings' of which, heaven knows, there are plenty.

She loved her work. And one of the reasons she loved Willard was that he had helped her get the post of curator to the Corie Gallery.

As the elderly fishing boat nosed its sedate way across the few miles to Parigos, Erica let herself savour once again the great day when she'd been told she'd landed the job. The head of the Arts and Leisure Department of Gratesford Council had invited her for a late-morning interview, the second in the process of applying for the curatorship.

'I must say your qualifications are very suitable, Miss

Pencarreth – yes, yes, entirely suitable, in fact, more than that, quite impressive. And then, you know' – a little smile of complicity – 'you being your mother's daughter is no drawback.'

Inwardly Erica had sighed. She didn't want to win the post because her mother was a famous painter. She wanted it on her own merits. But she'd learned to stifle this reaction. Jobs in the art world were hard to come by. Competition was fierce and the art colleges turned out dozens of new applicants every year. She, then twenty-eight, had learned the hard way. Use whatever advantages you could and be thankful you had them.

But then Mr Dulliver had surprised her by saying, 'But what the committee liked most was the special recommendation from Willard Townley. You know, old Benjamin Corie bought some of his Impressionists from Townley's – Willard Townley's – great-uncle, he must have been, I think. So the name means something in this town, you'll understand. And then of course he's so well known for his particular interest in the Impressionists, so when he says you're an expert on that period, you'll understand we're impressed – yes, very impressed.'

What a wonderful day that had been! And then once her contract was agreed, to be taken to the big old house in Gratesford High Street to inspect Benjamin Corie's legacy to his home town.

On every wall, paintings from the great period of French art, beginning with Degas and showing examples of Manet, Cézanne, Renoir and Monet. In the carefully air-conditioned cellars, yet more: Sisley in all his styles, Berthe Morisot in several of her unfinished attempts, Boudin, Pissarro . . .

It was overwhelming. Glorious, wonderful, inspiring – and she owed it all to Willard. Just because at university she'd specialised in the late nineteenth century and the Impressionists, and had been useful to him in authenticating a drawing or two of John Singer Sargent's, he gathered a good impression of her. It was generous and, she felt sure, impartial, based only on the fact that her knowledge of the subject had pleased him.

Of course the new post had been hard work. Supervising the final alterations to the house to make it fit for displaying the collection to the public, seeing to the cleaning and restoration of some of the works, trading those she felt she should part with for some she thought were under-represented . . . But within a year Benjamin Corie's bequest to Gratesford had had its grand opening, with reporters and correspondents attending from all over Europe and even one or two from the United States. Because of that success, the town council increased her grant for staging exhibitions. Tourism increased by a verifiable eighteen per cent in the first year.

And now, into her third year, she felt she was accepted by her colleagues in the British art world. Not as a painter – never that, for a short spell as an artist in her teens had taught her that she hadn't inherited her mother's talent. But as an arbiter, an expert, a source of information and knowledge, she felt she had found her place.

Old Giorgiou was glad the foreign lady had drifted off into her own thoughts. These people from the north spoke a version of mainland Greek that made you want to laugh – and of course that would be disrespectful, especially as they were all so rich. Well, perhaps this one didn't seem so very rich, at least not compared with those gilded butterflies who used to flutter around that foolish old shipping millionaire.

No, her shirt and jeans were good but nothing special. Her travel bag was quite worn. And she herself wasn't the type to spend much time having her eyelids frosted nor her fingernails inset with mother of pearl. A slender girl, with short light-brown hair and eyes an unexpected dark blue – you never saw anything like that among the womenfolk of Kimolos but perhaps in her homeland it was quite usual. And a nice smile – thoughtful, appealing.

One could understand, thought Giorgiou, why Kyrios Townley liked her. Now Kyrios Townley, he was rich – he owned that neat, well-kept cabin cruiser, he'd bought one of the houses built by the millionaire and he seemed to have nothing to do but please himself, so that meant money in the bank. The clothes of Kyrios Townley had cost a lot

– Giorgiou envied him his fine polo shirts of black knitted silk that went so well with his black hair and black eyes. A handsome man. No wonder the blue-eyed foreign lady was so eager to reach Parigos.

Ah, love, thought Giorgiou. He was past all that now but he remembered the heat rising in the blood at the thought of meeting again, the ferocity of that first kiss . . .

The cabin cruiser with the funny name that Giorgiou couldn't read was tied up to a buoy a few yards off the jetty. That of course meant that Kyrios Townley was already here. Giorgiou smiled and nodded as the lady thrust some money into his hands, seized her travel bag and, jumping ashore, set off up the steep path to the cliff top.

Erica's heart was beating fast as she crossed the stony expanse that passed for a garden to the boatman's cottage. The sound of her footsteps brought Willard to the door. He threw up an arm in salute then hurried to meet her. They hugged and kissed, teetering to and fro in a momentary loss of balance. She felt his cheek against hers, the pressure of his hand against her spine. 'Oh, darling,' she murmured in an almost voiceless greeting.

'So here you are at last,' he said, and urged her towards the house.

It was almost two months since they'd had time to themselves. Their meetings had been in public, at exhibition openings, auctions, special showings. Little short glimpses, meaningless kissings on the cheek . . . Tiny moments that made them hungrier for this meeting.

By mutual consent they went into the shady bedroom of the cottage and, wrapped in each other's arms, fell upon the bed. Troublesome clothing was quickly shed. They made love with an unchecked ardour made all the sweeter because they knew that on the next occasion they could be gentler, slower, full of consideration for each other's wishes. But now they let themselves be selfish, rough, quickly roused and quickly satisfied.

Willard pulled himself up on an elbow to look down at her. 'As I was saying,' he remarked with a smile, 'so here you are at last.'

'When did you get in?'

'In the early hours of the morning. Yesterday was a bit rough so I delayed leaving Poliegos until the wind had gone down. That made me a bit late but I wanted to be here before you, to welcome you home.'

'Home,' she echoed. She brushed back damp hair from her forehead and laughed a little. 'No, home for me always seems to mean my mother's place in Cornwall. This is different – a sort of dream world.'

'Let's have something to drink.' He got up, found a towelling robe and put it on. 'I bought some highly recommended wine in Italy, let's see if it lives up to its reputation.'

She picked up the loose black silk shirt he'd left over a chair and slipped it on. In the kitchen he was looking for the corkscrew. 'Red or white?'

'It's too early in the day for wine, Will,' she protested. 'Is the water turned on? I'll make some coffee.'

The cottage had simple equipment but it functioned so long as the elderly odd-job man obeyed instructions telephoned in advance. Sometimes Willard had to use the moped for the trip to the office area where facilities such as water and electricity were hired, but in general services were kept up, the baker's boy called as soon as they were in residence, fishermen would come with the morning's catch, supplies such as cheese and goat's milk could be obtained from the two or three herdsmen's families.

But on the whole the cottage was a lonely place – and this suited Erica and Willard perfectly. Erica could never stay very long, so each day was precious. They would bathe and rest in the shade of the olive tree at the garden's verge. They would go island-hopping in Willard's boat, the *Connoisseur*. They would read – each would bring some important new book on art, a monograph about the work of some painter or a heavy catalogue from some important art sale.

Watching her lying prone in her skimpy bikini with a book propped against the tree trunk, Willard would marvel at how different she seemed here on the island. This relaxed, peaceful creature was unknown to her colleagues in the art world. There she was always somewhat on guard, for she was young to have gained so much prestige and so of course she was the target of envy.

Although he would never have admitted it, Willard Townley had 'collected' Erica. Introduced to her at an opening, he'd recognised her name as author of an extremely perceptive article on the Impressionists' use of nineteenth-century machines in their paintings, featured in a very worthy international art magazine. She was then assistant curator of art at the Beltrane Museum in Sheffield but a few minutes' walk around the display of that evening had convinced him she had a superb 'eye' – that special talent, perhaps an inborn instinct, which could tell true from false, good from bad, genius from mere talent. Such people were rare, and in the world of art dealing were worth their weight in gold.

Erica, however, had shown no wish to go into the buying and selling of art. Perhaps without knowing it, she was influenced by her mother. The famous Lisbet Pencarreth was contemptuous of dealers: 'Always hoping we'll die soon so that we'll become "rare" and let them put the prices up,' was her scornful verdict.

But Willard had been unwilling to let Erica go. He added her to his list of 'useful' contacts, troubled himself enough to be helpful to her in her career, and throughout all this, somehow found himself becoming fonder of her than he'd intended. Moreover, there was a side to her that had been quite unsuspected. He'd thought her idealistic, a little naïve, too hard-working for her own good – in short, a bit too seemly for his taste. But there was passion there, turbulent, tempestuous, answering his demands with a fervour he found captivating. These short holidays on Parigos were indeed a sort of dream world, and all the more magical because she could so seldom come to him here.

He found himself studying her now, admiring the unconscious charm of her appearance in the soft silk of the black shirt, barefoot, all her attention on the business of making coffee. If he himself had had any talent as a painter, this would have been a picture worth making: the shaded light of the island sunshine through the rattan blind, the dark brown of the coffee in the cafetière, the shimmer of the silk against her pale skin . . .

Today he would make her happy. No, he added inwardly with a suppressed grin, not by making love to her again, although that too would happen. But he had what was almost a present for her. Something that would delight her, intrigue her, capture both her interest and her admiration.

But not just yet. She'd arrived a little earlier than he'd expected. They would go for a swim – that first swim, always so enjoyable. Then they would eat, and perhaps rest in the shade or read. And while she wasn't watching, he would arrange the surprise.

Footsteps from a heavy-booted foot could be heard on the crumpled rock outside. Erica scuttled through the door into the interior of the cottage, aware of how her appearance would shock the conventional islanders. Willard opened the door to find the baker's boy with his basket. Really, it was like some kind of bush telegraph – before you'd even had time to unpack, the locals knew you'd arrived.

He bought bread and honey-cake from the boy. As he put his purchases on the kitchen table Erica reappeared in a swimsuit. So the normal routine of their holiday visit took over; they went for a swim in 'their' rock pool and afterwards lay sunbathing on the *choma*, the hard white chalky surface which formed the island and was quarried for export elsewhere in the Cyclades.

So the day wore on. In the late afternoon Erica was drowsing over a copy of *Whistler and his Influence from 1890 to 1903* by a learned but boring writer. She was roused by the sound of Willard whispering in her ear.

'Come and look at what I brought with me.'

'Wha-at?' she said, still half in a dream.

'Get up, sleepyhead. There's something very interesting in the living-room.'

She allowed herself to be pulled to her feet and padded indoors after him, round the side of the house and in at the french windows. In the centre of the living-room stood an easel, and on the easel was a canvas covered for the moment by a large bath towel. Beneath it was a rectangle about a metre in breadth and less in depth.

'You've been shopping again?' She was smiling. Willard could almost never walk along a street where there were paintings in the window without going in to inspect the wares – and more often than not he came out with something under his arm.

His gallery in London, Townley & Co, was very well known. It had been founded in the 1860s by some moustached ancestor who had had the good luck to befriend Monet and Pissarro when they came to Britain to escape being called up in the Franco-Prussian War of 1870. Old Morland Townley had bought paintings from the hard-up Frenchies, thereby laying the foundations of a firm that flourished to this day. Although Willard bought and sold twentieth-century paintings and drawings, and was always on the look-out for some undiscovered Old Master (as who was not?), it was when Impressionist paintings changed hands that he was called upon as agent. The firm's name was somehow linked in the public's mind with the Impressionists.

Erica moved up to the easel and took hold of a corner of the bath towel. She hesitated, glancing back at Willard.

'Go ahead,' he urged.

She twitched the gaudy towel off the rectangle.

Because the room faced north, a cooler light streamed in through the windows. Yet the canvas on the easel seemed to radiate with a strange umber glow. The paint on its surface was like dark gold, thickly laid on, an arc of tawny fire across a darker background.

Erica stared. Then, half thinking she was dreaming, she rubbed her eyes. But no, she was awake, and she was looking at something she'd seen represented many times before.

It was the Japanese bridge over a pool in a garden, painted as the artist saw it in the later years of his life while his eyesight was damaged by cataracts.

She was looking at a painting by the most famous of the Impressionists, Claude Monet.

Two

A long silence. She could hear Willard's breathing, the cicada in the olive tree, the faint crack of the roof beams as they contracted in the waning heat of the day.

'Well?' he asked at length, unable to bear the suspense. For her opinion was vital. If she refused to acknowledge it as a Monet, his hopes were gone for ever.

'Where did you get it?'

'In a little curio shop in Istanbul.'

'*Istanbul?* What on earth would a Monet be doing in a shop in Istanbul?'

So . . . She was thinking of it as a Monet. He said nothing, biding his time. Unable to resist, she came close to the easel, narrowing her gaze, taking it in little by little.

It was a dark painting. Yes, dark, because it came from a dark period in the painter's life. What is so important to a painter as his eyesight? And Monet had been losing his, slowly seeing the world grow dim around him as his cataracts thickened.

She pulled herself together. 'Come on, Will. You know as well as I do that it probably isn't genuine.'

'Don't say that until you've really examined it.' At the suggestion she put out her hands as if to take the painting from the stand, but hesitated. 'Yes, go on – pick it up.'

She took hold of it, as experts do, with straightened fingers merely holding it by the edges. She took it over to the french windows.

The painting wasn't in good condition. An area of darkness in the left-hand upper corner which she'd taken to be brown paint now looked odd. She turned the canvas over, and drew in a surprised breath.

The painting had been burned. The stretchers were tinged

11

with scorch marks and those at the angle of the upper corner were charred almost black. They'd been inexpertly strengthened with thin strips of wood glued on top. The back of the canvas was somewhat damaged by heat and smoke but only the upper corner was seared – she could imagine the painting lying in a fireplace with only one corner seriously beginning to catch fire.

She shook her head in dismay. 'How could this happen?'

'I can give you a complete provenance,' Willard said. 'Take a look.' From a side table he picked up a leather document case. Unzipping it, he offered her a sheaf of paper. Rather unwillingly, she took it.

'Let's be clear, Will. Are you saying . . . Are you *claiming* this as a Monet?'

'Yes.'

'From a curio shop in Istanbul.'

'Yes. Read the documents, Erica. You'll see.'

The top document was handwritten and in Turkish. She flipped over pages until she came to a typewritten version but once again it was in Turkish. 'Go on,' Willard urged. Three or four pages later she came to a translation typed in English, with the heading of a legal firm in Istanbul and a certificate from a courthouse translator.

> I, Yamin Emin, antique dealer of Kazneri Sokak 53, Istanbul, hereby affirm that I have agreed the sale to Willard Townley of London, England, for the sum of £1,500 sterling, of the painting herein described as *Bridge after the style of Monet* and acquired by me with the attached authentication. The painting was formerly the property of Sergei Piotrovitch of Yalta whose family sent it for sale with other personal belongings after the fall of the Communist government of Russia. His family believe he obtained it in 1945 from a house in Hamburg. The house was probably the home of Hauptmann Andreas Loebletz. Herr Loebletz bought *Bridge after the style of Monet* in 1943, from Aristide Curacie, for the sum of Fr 800 (Occupation currency – bill of sale herewith).

I believe this bill has been kept with the painting ever since it was first sold. I found it in an envelope attached to the back of the canvas (envelope also supplied). I can say nothing as to the bill of sale's authenticity but believe it proves the painting originally came from the district near Paris where Claude Monet lived. I am not an expert of European painting, being more knowledgeable about Middle Eastern *objets d'art*, but have sold *Bridge after the style of Monet* under the belief that though badly damaged it is very likely the work of the said Claude Monet himself.

The next two pages were a somewhat rambling and self-laudatory account of how Yamin Emin had singled out the painting from the cardboard carton of goods sent to him by the Piotrovitch family – two 'dark paintings' of harbours and sailing boats, a silver salver and ornate gilt cup engraved in German, candlesticks of various metals, a French carriage clock, medals of several eras including one Iron Cross – all of it, Erica thought, sounding very like loot taken by a young Russian officer from a house during the advance of the Russian army across Germany at the end of World War II.

She skipped through all this, eager to get to the bill of sale given to the German captain in 1943. Her imagination, running away from her, was summoning up a picture of some Frenchman, weary of privation under the German occupation, selling something to an art-conscious young military man stationed in his area.

The bill of sale was in a glassine envelope between two pieces of card held together by elastic bands. She took off the bands, and the glassine envelope offered the words of the bill of sale to her sight. They were in French, written in the cramped hand of someone not much accustomed to putting pen to paper.

I, Aristide Curacie of Rue du Portier No 6, Epte-Rouet, Deptmt Seine, accept payment of Fr 800 for a painting rescued by me from a bonfire in the winter of 1923 in the garden of the house of Mr Claude Monet at Giverny. At the request of the purchaser I give an explanation. I was at that time gardener's boy, employed to do rough work such as moving barrows of soil and disposing of rubbish. For reasons I do not understand M Monet decided to burn several of his paintings. I tended the fire on which they were thrown. This brown painting displeased him so much that he threw it on and walked away. I thought it a pity, pulled it off with a rake and took it home when it had cooled. I remember I cycled the four miles home with the painting tied to my handlebars with a piece of string. My mother told me I was a fool because it was an ugly painting and put it in the cellar, where it has been ever since. Attested to and signed, Aristide Curacie, nursery gardener, aged 35, Official Registration DS 4018116 Classification Essential Occupation.

Erica stood staring at the page with a sensation of height-giddiness. Nothing seemed firm around her. Her breathing was unsteady, perspiration broke out on her forehead.

Could she really be looking at proof that an unknown Monet existed?

It was so entirely possible.

Claude Monet had noticed his eyesight was changing in 1908 but chose to do nothing about it. 'What I see is what I see,' he was reported to have said to a friend. Pride in his own 'vision of life' prevented him from seeking medical advice for fourteen years. Erica remembered being told that when in the end he agreed to have an operation he was said to be choosing colours to paint with from the labels on the tubes – the colours themselves had been almost indistinguishable on his brush.

A cataract operation was an awesome undertaking in the 1920s, Erica recalled from accounts she'd read. No movement of the head was permitted for ten days. Eyes covered in bandages, the cranium held immobile with sandbags, the patient had to lie unmoving, flat on his back. She could imagine the terror with which the painter had approached the moment when the bandages were removed in a darkened room. He would have been aware that a famous illustrator, Honoré Daumier, had had unsuccessful surgery for cataracts – in fact had been blinded by it.

But for Monet, things went well – though not as well as he had hoped and longed for. He was given glasses but couldn't focus with them. Gradually the lenses were corrected and at last Zeiss produced a pair of spectacles which catered for the restored vision in one eye while mitigating the cataract that still remained in the other.

In a rage of productivity Monet began to paint again. When he compared his new canvases with those he'd painted before the operation, he was seized with something like angry shame. He knew that because of the cataracts he'd been unable to see colour correctly, painting as brown and yellow plants which were green and flowers that were blue. But he had had no idea how totally wrong his colours had been.

And so, he told some of his friends, he destroyed many of those paintings.

Perhaps this was one of them, rescued by a lad of fifteen from the flames about to consume it.

True, it was a 'faulty' painting. It showed the Japanese bridge in the garden at Giverny as a swirling arc of brown, ochre, vermilion, cadmium, and sepia. There was no visual truth in it. But the energy, the engagement with the subject through the painter's brush! It was as if he wanted to leap into the space between his easel and the little bridge, trapping the light he could distinguish so dimly within a whirlwind of colour strong enough to hold it in place for ever.

Erica had never fallen so entirely into adoration of Monet as some of her colleagues. She admired and approved him, yet she didn't succumb to him totally. But at this moment she felt a surge of emotion – sharing across the gulf of years the desperation that had driven him as he thrust the paint on to the canvas. She honoured him, she felt pity, fellowship, something approaching wonder. Here was an artist who utterly refused to be beaten. He would paint as long as his hand could hold a brush, as long as his failing eyes could distinguish form. He would fight, he would never give in.

She started out of her reverie as Willard touched her shoulder. 'What do you think?' he asked in a low voice.

'It's . . . it has a strange effect . . .'

15

'Everything we have here' – he touched the folder of documents – 'says it's a Monet.'

She nodded agreement.

'So what do *you* say?'

'At this moment – I'm so overwhelmed with the surprise and feeling – oh, I don't know, sort of *weepy* thinking of what Monet must have gone through . . .'

'Thinking what?'

'Perhaps it is a Monet, Willard.'

He threw his clenched fists in the air. *'Yes,'* he shouted.

She laughed, putting her arms around him and hugging him. 'It would be wonderful for you, wouldn't it? To find a new Monet.'

'Think of the glory! Think of the respect!' He too laughed and added, 'Think of the money!'

'Ye-es . . . But Will, it would have to be examined, and studied, and authenticated before you could offer it.'

'Of course, of course! X-rays, chemical comparisons, examination of the *toile* – of course, all that. But you agree, Erica – you do agree – it's by Claude Monet!'

She hesitated a long moment. But she was still in the grip of the experience, that moment when she'd felt herself standing in the artist's place, brush in hand and the canvas on the easel, trying to put down what she saw.

And Willard was watching her, dark eyes aglow with delight and enthusiasm – and he was a good judge, he too felt it was a genuine Monet.

She gave a slow, thoughtful nod of the head.

'That's my girl!' He swung her round, lifting her off her feet, kissing her hard on the lips, holding her so close against him she could feel the thud of his heart through the thin shirt.

They lost their balance and collapsed on the sofa, laughing and exultant. 'Oh, God,' cried Willard, 'thank you, thank you for sending me to that alley! Think of it, Erica – I could have walked the other way, I could have gone to the market to buy spices . . .' He jumped up. 'We have to celebrate! How about some of that wine you didn't want this morning? We ought to drink a toast – to Monet, to Aristide Curacie who didn't want to see his work burned, to – well, we won't drink to the

Hauptmann who paid him a few francs for what he thought was going to earn him a fortune—'

'Oh, Will,' she reproached, 'never mind the Hauptmann, what about you and that Turkish shopkeeper? Fifteen hundred sterling for what you thought was a Monet?'

'Ducky, he was delighted. He's not the sort of man to understand anything about restoring a painting. He thought of that canvas as a load of old burned-up rubbish only saleable because it might once have belonged to someone famous – it was as if he was selling me Monet's watch or his inkwell. He expected to get a couple of hundred for it. In fact, we'd almost agreed on six hundred when he remembered to look in the envelope again and realised the German captain had thought it important. Then he began hesitating and saying he thought he ought to get it appraised by an expert before he parted with it. So I pretended I was going to walk out, and he called me back and said "Two thousand?" and I beat him down to fifteen hundred. Honestly, darling, he was pleased as punch.'

He was hurrying into the kitchen as he spoke, talking to her over one black-clad shoulder, snatching up glasses from the draining board and setting them on the kitchen table. From the refrigerator he produced an unopened bottle of the Italian wine, found the corkscrew, and proceeded to open it.

She couldn't help smiling to herself at his exuberance. He was sparkling with pleasure and triumph. Quite understandably – because it was the dream of every art dealer to find a great new talent or discover a lost treasure.

Willard Townley was well thought of in the art world, the descendant of a long line of worthy experts whose name still graced the gallery in Mayfair. He could be relied on to search out a piece of work for a client adding to his collection, he would be called upon to assess the authenticity of some minor drawing or sketch by a master – he was by no means a negligible player in the buying and selling that had become such big business these days.

Yet this was something different. His name would appear in all the art magazines, and probably in the broadsheets too.

From having a good reputation he would ascend to fame. And fame brought the big players, the museums endowed by great legacies and the collectors who would employ him to bid fantastic sums at auction. Erica could understand how his mind was reeling with the possibilities of the future.

He offered her a glass of wine. As she took it, he raised his own. 'To the provenance of the new Monet,' he toasted. 'To all the people who are going to want to own it – the lottery winners trying to make themselves look important by collecting great paintings, the Internet tycoons whose wives are proving how cultured they are, the trust fund managers looking for safe investments – come one and come all, I'm waiting for you!'

She shook her head at him. 'Now, now, calm down. There's a long way to go before anyone is going to buy. First there's the tests – and then you know, Will, as badly damaged as it is, it's not going to fetch a stupendous price.'

'But I'll have it restored, of course.'

'Really?' She was surprised. 'It would be a difficult task, even if it should be done.'

'Should be done? Of course it should be done.'

'Do you think so?'

'Well, for heaven's sake, why not?' He was staring at her in bewilderment.

'Well, historically . . . Don't you think the fact that Monet himself threw it on a bonfire and walked away makes the damage historically important?'

'Don't be idiotic! The damage will still have happened – *historically* – even after it's been restored. We've got Aristide's evidence – a *historical* document – what more do you want?'

She could see her opinion had shaken him. She didn't want to spoil his mood so said rather diffidently, 'But to a museum – the damaged picture would be so striking—'

'If you think I'm going to let some museum buy that picture for a song and then put it up for sale in a year or two when they've had it restored . . .'

'There's no reason to think they'd—'

'Oh, you're such an idealist!' he exclaimed in exasperation. 'Of course a museum would sell if they needed money. After all, it's not the only version of the Japanese bridge he painted while he was seeing everything in red and brown. That one in the Minneapolis Institute is very like ours.'

'But that's just what I'm saying, Will. The thing that makes it unique is the fact that it's burnt.'

'All right, so a museum might find that interesting. But what about all these people with new money, the Silicon Valley millionaires, the lottery winners – do you really think they're going to want to hang a burnt painting on their walls?'

'But it's not to them that you'd be hoping to sell.'

'It certainly is!' he riposted. 'What puts a man at the top of the list these days in the art world? It's the price you can get for a painting. The chap that sold that Modigliani last year for nine million dollars – he's *somebody* now! And the chances of getting a big price for a Monet are just as good, so long as it's what a collector would want to show off. And sooty paintings aren't in that category, Erica my pet!'

She heard the ambition in his voice and so made no further argument. One of the things she loved about him was the enthusiasm that drove him on. And of course, she trusted his judgement in matters of finance. It was true she was 'idealistic' – naïve, perhaps, was a better word. One of the things she was learning in her role as curator of the Corie Gallery was that having paintings worth showing came down, in the end, to hard cash.

'I suppose if the restoration work was done by someone really good . . .'

'That's where you come in, ducky.'

'What? Oh – you mean you'd want to ask Pritchett to do it?' Pritchett was the restorer who'd dealt with problems in the Corie collection. When she'd brought the rows of wrapped paintings up out of the cellar she'd found inevitable damage, even though the conditions in which they'd been stored were reasonably good. Some slight damp decay, a patch on a Renoir where a green fungus had taken residence, a gash in one of the Morisots . . . Pritchett was still at work on the Morisot – painstakingly, lovingly at work, because he was a perfectionist.

'You'd ask him for me, wouldn't you? That stuff he's doing for the Corie – it's not urgent, after all.'

'I suppose not.'

'I'd pay double his usual rate, Erica. I'd want to have that in the publicity hand-out – that the restoration was going to be done by the best restorer of Impressionists in Britain.'

'Well, I could ask him.' They both knew that even if Erica asked him, he might still say no. An old and difficult man, he had to be approached in just the right way.

'Would you speak to him? Coax him into it? Oh, Erica, it's going to be so absolutely fantastic!' He seized her round the shoulders to hug her fiercely, planted a kiss on top of her head, then held her off to address her as if she were an audience. 'The BBC, my friends and colleagues, will do a TV feature on it – showing Pritchett at work, camera close-ups of picture detail – one of those late-night programmes where the critics sit round a table and show off about how much they know. And the Sunday supplements too – they'll go for it, they're all still nuts about Monet. And then, people, always remember, there's all the usual guff about my great-great-grandfather and how he befriended the exiles in 1870 and ancient photographs of him and Monet standing next to each other in those terrible tall hats . . . Can't you just see it?'

She could indeed. It was just the kind of thing to excite interest – treasure trove, a little something about the Occupation during World War II, another little something about the miseries of Russian society after the fall of Communism, which had brought families to the point of selling their possessions, and so on. Enough to make a couple of columns on the Arts page, and to tempt an editor to send a photographer for a weekend spread in the supplement.

They discussed the possibilities over the wine, and then it was time to decide what to do in the evening. Generally they had a last dip in the rock pool, then showered in fresh water and changed before sitting down to a simple meal.

But today Willard was too much aflame with excitement to submit to anything so tame. He declared they had to go out to dinner. Since there was really nowhere to go on Parigos – only a taverna patronised by the few herders and fishermen still remaining on the island, or a sort of ice-cream parlour installed for the offspring of the eccentric millionaire and still visited by the children of new residents – they decided to make the short boat trip to Kimolos, where there were a few cafés in the main square of the village at the top of the *choma*.

Willard insisted they dress up for the occasion, which meant changing into designer jeans and, for him, a different black shirt with gold buttons. Someone had once nicknamed him 'Hidalgo' for his dark, almost Spanish good looks, and he freely admitted he played up to the name. 'It's my trademark,' he told Erica. 'When some ignoramus wants to hire a dealer to look for a painting, they can say "that foreign-looking joker in black" if they've forgotten my name.'

Erica chose the best of the summer tops she'd brought with her, a sleeveless wisp in a rich violet shade that had the effect of a T-shirt without the cling. Her jeans were from a less chic source than Willard's but they fitted sleekly against her slender hips. She brushed her short brown hair into a glossy cap, touched her eyelids with shadow, and added lip colour recently bought from a very expensive boutique.

She was pleased to see admiration in Willard's eyes as she turned from the mirror for his inspection.

'You look gorgeous,' he exclaimed. 'Why is it that at home you always have a sort of prim effect?'

'That's to counteract the memory of my Dizzy Days,' she laughed. 'There are still folk out there in the art world who remember me as a teenager with pink hair and bare dirty feet.'

'Dizzy Days' was rather an understatement for the time she meant. For almost two years Erica had gone completely off the rails. It was a period she looked back on now with regret and distaste, because she knew it was wasted time,

21

time spent in being full of rage and rebellion when she could have been doing something useful.

It had been an almost unbearable moment when shortly after her seventeenth birthday she finally let herself know that she was never going to be a great painter. A good painter, yes. A passable landscape artist with the opportunity of making at least a living from the kind of thing interior decorators liked – tasteful, rather handsome views of the Cornish cliffs, the Somerset meadows . . . A quick-sketch artist with the ability to catch a likeness on paper, but without the perception or the inborn urge to set down on canvas the inner life of the sitter.

Art college became a nonsense. What was the point of going on when all she ever produced was adequacy? Where was the fire, the power that her mother had? Lisbet Pencarreth could put down four or five lines on a canvas and at once the soul of the countryside was there, breathing and evolving. Let her daughter Erica do the same and all you saw was four or five lines that were an outline of a view, nothing more.

She dropped out of college, took herself off to New York, lived in a squat, drank too much and ate too little, sold her personal belongings bit by bit until she was penniless. The next step was to sell herself for enough to live on – but something prevented her from doing that. The other girls in the squat did it, and the men who partnered them lived off the proceeds without thinking it shameful. Erica's then partner, the third in the succession, was quite happy for her to follow the trend. He'd even picked out the street corner where she might offer her wares.

But she could not. And it caused disputes. And she began to see her fellow rebels as less pleasing. Free spirits – oh yes, free to turn themselves into zombies or trollops – where was the freedom in that?

After about four days of self-questioning she went to the half-wrecked bathroom in the decaying tenement where she was living, and stood for a long time under the shower – cold, rust-stained water pouring down on her thin body still in its torn jeans and halter top. When she got back to the living area a few of the group were there, sharing a bottle of cheap wine. They stared at her. 'You're all wet!' And then they laughed, because the expression could also mean, 'You've got things wrong.'

'I've been baptising myself,' she said.

'Taking a new name?'

'Taking a new life.'

She changed into the only other item of clothing she still possessed, a print dress that had come from a well-known Knightsbridge store and had been bought for her by her mother as a seventeenth birthday present. She went out to find a pay phone, put through a reversed-charge call to Lisbet Pencarreth, and asked for enough money to come home.

'You sound strange, love. Are you ill?' her mother asked, suppressing both her anxiety and the joy she felt at this unexpected call.

'I think I've been ill. But I'm recovering.'

Lisbet told her to go to her agent in Manhattan where she'd be given money and anything else she needed. She telephoned the agent beforehand to warn him that a strange girl – perhaps looking like a vagabond – would shortly be arriving and begged him to treat her kindly.

About two weeks later, improved somewhat in health and certainly better dressed, Erica flew home. Lisbet met her at Heathrow. She was driven straight to Cornwall. For a couple of months she pottered about in her mother's house, helping to clean up the studio, to prepare canvases, to run errands, but saying very little.

In the end it was Lisbet who took the first step. 'What do you intend to do with the rest of your life, kiddo?'

'I don't know, Mamma.'

'You can't stay here for ever.'

'You don't want me here?' Erica's eyes filled with tears, as they tended to do these days over almost nothing.

Her mother's dark brows came together in a frown of irritation. 'Don't ask silly questions,' she reproved. Lisbet Pencarreth had no time for fools. 'You know you're welcome here any time you like. But you surely don't intend to go on wandering around picking things up then putting them down and staring into space. What do you foresee for yourself? A new start in something completely different? D'you want to stay in the art world or get out of it? D'you want some money to start a business? What?'

'I don't know,' her daughter mumbled.

'Huh!'

Nothing more was said at the time, but Erica began to think about the future. Until then she'd spent most of her time mourning over the past.

She said to Lisbet, 'I don't know anything about anything except art. I've lived and breathed it since I was born. Here at home, at school where I was singled out as talented and given special lessons, at art college . . .'

'And so what?' Lisbet demanded.

'So I think I ought to try for something connected with art. Not painting,' she put in hastily, 'because we both know that would be a stupidity.'

'Go on.'

'I was wondering . . . I know it means asking you for more money and I hate doing that—'

'Oh, pouf, don't talk rubbish,' said Lisbet. 'Money's only paper stuff that buys things. What do you want it for?'

'I thought I'd go to university and study History of Art.'

'Umm . . .' Lisbet didn't know what to make of it. She'd never thought of her daughter as an academic. 'What would be the purpose of this notion?'

'Well, I . . . I can't paint, we both know that . . . but I can't really bear to be away from painting. Even when I was at . . . my lowest point . . . you know, while I was in New York . . . I used to smarten myself up and go into the Guggenheim . . .' She swallowed a lump that seemed determined to close up her throat. 'I thought if I got a decent degree, I might get a job in a gallery.'

'Selling paintings?' Lisbet said, with only half-concealed contempt. Although of course paintings had to be sold if a painter wanted to make a living, she had a low opinion of art dealers. They went in for tricks: they tried to hoodwink buyers, they offered 'exclusives' to reporters and journalists, they gave you silly advice about hoarding canvases so as to increase prices . . . They never seemed to understand that painting was about *communication*. What was the point of trying to say something on canvas if nobody saw it? Hoarding was silly, and chicanery about prices was silly, and building up a false image in the newspapers was silly, and she would be seriously, *seriously* displeased if Erica wanted to go into art dealing.

But no, her daughter wanted to get qualifications so as to work in a museum. And work in a museum she did, after studying at the Academie des Beaux Arts and then spending two years in Florence as dogsbody to one of the finest art scholars in Europe.

The Dizzy Days seemed a long way behind her. Yet she always wanted to dissociate herself from them. The person who had earned some regard as an expert on turn-of-the-nineteenth-century paintings was a totally different one from the silly girl who had nearly thrown herself away in New York. This person, who now accepted the admiration of Willard Townley, could allow herself to smile, and be exultantly happy at her life at this moment – on an island in the fabled Cyclades with the man she adored, sharing with him the marvellous secret of a newly discovered work by a master, about to go out by boat to an evening of carefree enjoyment.

'Ah!' said Willard as they crossed the little living-room on their way out. 'Before we go . . .' He laughed. 'We must bury our little treasure.'

He took the Monet from the easel, laying it momentarily on a side table. Going back into the bedroom, he took from his travel bag the special corrugated cardboard in which he'd wrapped the painting. Because older works of art were so vulnerable, special packing materials were available in which to transport them – chemical-free, smooth-surfaced, evolved in the modern age to avoid any snick or catch to the precious surface of paint. Presumably he carried a supply aboard the boat, Erica thought, in case he found anything worth buying in his leisurely trips around the Mediterranean.

She helped him tie the package. He placed it carefully on a shelf in a cupboard in the living-room, locked the cupboard with its flimsy key and hid the key in a vase. 'There! That's as safe as we can make it here.'

'Sweetheart, anybody could open that cupboard with a teaspoon!'

He had to nod in agreement. 'But then, nobody knows it's there but us!'

Arm in arm, laughing at the glorious absurdity of it all, they made their way down to the jetty for their trip to Kimolos. In an unpretentious restaurant they had one of those long, intermittently served meals of Greece – food was brought when it was cooked, and it could only be cooked in small portions because cooking facilities were limited – a grill over an open charcoal fire. But the coarse local wine was there to fill the waiting time, and they had things to say to each other, so they had no complaints.

It was very late indeed when they set off back to Parigos. Willard stood at the wheel with one arm around Erica. She loved their closeness, loved the intimacy that their shared secret seemed to enhance. The moon behind gauzy clouds touched the dark waters with silver lace. Except for the sound of the boat's engine and the whisper of the sea passing along the side, there was a trancelike silence.

When they reached the mooring place a few yards from the island's jetty, Willard cut the engine. Erica tied up the boat to the little buoy. As she straightened from the task, she found him close behind her. He took her in his arms.

The cottage seemed far away up on the cliff top – too far, too long to wait. Without a word needed between them they went into the cabin which served him as stateroom and bedroom. They drew each other down on the bed and gave themselves up to the joy to which the whole evening had been the prelude.

Happy lovers, free from the restrictions of their London life, rocked to sleep at last by the gentle sway of the boat in the lingering warmth of the October night.

Three

The cruise liner had nosed into its berth at Southampton in the middle of the night. Most of the passengers were asleep, worn out by the last-night party. A few light sleepers heard the movement of mooring and running out gangways, but by now they were so accustomed to the everyday routine of the crew's activity that they simply turned over and counted a few more sheep.

Alexander McNaughton moved quietly about the stateroom, picking up his overnight bag and his briefcase. The bulk of his luggage would be brought ashore later; for the moment he needed to take only enough to freshen up later in the London hotel, and the usual paraphernalia of a business meeting – organiser, palm-top computer, the file of faxed documents.

The steward waiting outside the door conducted him to the deck from which he could disembark. The purser went down the gangway with him. 'Don't you worry, Mr McNaughton, we'll see to everything. By the time you get back it'll be mostly quiet here so Customs and baggage retrieval will be quick and easy.'

Nodding acknowledgement, Zan McNaughton went into the Arrivals building. There a minor official from New Zealand House was waiting, a brief display of his passport was all that was required, and he was soon out into the chilly, rainy October night of England. A limousine and chauffeur, hired through the hotel, were awaiting him, the passenger door already open. He sank into the back seat, and allowed himself to snooze as the car took him on to the motorway for London.

Somewhere about Godalming he roused, stretched, and

took a look about him. He looked for the mechanism that lowered the glass partition between him and the driver. 'Anywhere around here you can get a cup of tea?' he inquired.

'There's a service station, sir.' But it was said in an uncertain tone, for passengers in limousines very seldom wanted to go into such workaday places.

'Great, let's stop there. My mouth's as dry as a professor's lecture.'

Smothering a laugh, the chauffeur took the off-ramp for the service area, found a parking space without difficulty since it was still so early, hopped out, and opened the passenger door for Mr McNaughton to get out. He was taking his place again in the driving seat when Zan turned back.

'Don't you want a cup?' he inquired in surprise.

'Me?'

'What's wrong? Is the tea rotten here?'

'Well, er . . . No, I think it's about average. But, er . . .'

'You're not thirsty?'

'As a matter of fact . . . Well . . . Passengers don't usually invite me to drink cups of tea with them.'

'Oh, come on, stop being a daftie.'

Now Bert Allgood had to debate with himself. Would it offend this eccentric if he said no? Should he say, 'It's against the rules?' But was it, in fact, against the rules?

Aw, what the heck, he could do with a cuppa. He got out, locked the doors with the electronic gizmo, and followed the rangy figure in the rather new-looking suit into the restaurant.

Once inside, he found he had to guide his passenger through the routine of discovering which counter you wanted and making the machines work. 'We've got places like this back home,' said Zan, watching the tap send scalding water into the little teapot, 'but I don't go into them much. You got to admit it's clever, though.'

Once they were seated, Bert found out that 'back home' was New Zealand. 'We've been on our way to England for weeks,' Zan confided. 'Took cruise ships, you see – that way you don't suffer from jet lag and Nyree got a chance to have another look at Sydney and see Kuala Lumpur – places like that, you'd never see them if you went by air, but it takes ages, of course. Still, Egypt was interesting – we stopped off there for a week, saw the temples and everything.'

'My missus did a Nile cruise a couple of years ago,' offered Bert. 'I didn't go. I'm not much of a one for culture.'

'Me neither. But you know, you can always find something interesting to see while the ladies go round the museums and stuff. That agriculture in Egypt – that's really clever, getting water from one channel to another so that in the end it feeds all the crops.'

Bert had noticed that, though his client had an expensive suit and could afford a hired limousine, he had hard skin on his hands. 'You interested in agriculture, then, sir?'

'Grapes,' said Zan. 'We grow grapes. It's spring now where I come from – the vines'll be putting out their first leaves now.'

There was regret in his voice. It was clear he wished he was there to see the young growth unfolding to the sun on the south-facing slopes of his land.

Bert had chauffeured enough passengers to have some general knowledge about climates and homelands. 'Unusual, isn't it, sir, to be coming to Britain in the winter? Generally folks coming on holiday from your part of the world leave home when it's your winter and come to our so-called summer.'

'This is no holiday,' sighed Zan.

'Oh, I see – business.'

'Uh-huh. That, and something else.' He fell silent. Bert was sorry he'd mentioned the holiday idea. It seemed to have depressed his passenger.

They finished their tea to the accompaniment of a discussion about rugby. Zan was glad not to have to think about the reasons for coming to Britain. Once back in the car, they made good time, and he was delivered to the Mayfair Rialto Hotel while London was still waking up to the day's work.

The suite at the hotel was warm and welcoming. Fresh flowers in both the bedrooms, a basket of fruit on the table in the lounge, softly glowing lamps to lighten every corner. The mini-bar, however, drew his chief attention. He opened the refrigerator to find it well stocked with spirits, wine and soft drinks. He picked up one of the bottles of wine, took it to the lamp to examine the label.

French, of course. Not a bad château, might be worth tasting later in the day. He sighed inwardly. There was a lot of hard work still ahead, despite the fact that wines from outside Europe were gaining in popularity. McNaughton's Hill . . . One day a hotel resident would find McNaughton's Hill in the mini-bar of his suite and feel only pleasure, not surprise . . .

This wasn't Zan's first London trip. But it was likely to be the most important. He was here for two reasons, and one of them was to conclude deals with two of the major outlets for wine in the UK. One was a prestigious store in Oxford Street, the other was a big supermarket chain. The first would bring McNaughton wines to both London shoppers and to the many families who bought from the store's catalogue. This was an outlet for the superior vintages, which of course were pricey.

The second outlet would put his wines on the shelves of supermarket branches throughout the British Isles, and though these would be the more run-of-the-mill labels, they were good enough to please the educated palate and were likely to bring in much greater profits than the sales through the department store.

The whole thing had been in negotiation since last year. Included in the deal was a big promotion of the wine by the supermarket chain, accompanied by wine tastings and visits by TV stars to the shops.

McNaughton's were by no means amateurs in the field. Years ago they had diversified from wine producing into the provisions market; in New Zealand and Australia they owned shares in one of the big supermarket chains. But the vineyard had always been the dearest inheritance of the family. His brothers and cousins and everyone else connected with the vineyard shared Zan's ambition – to put McNaughton's up there alongside Château Mouton Rothschild and Château Latour.

So that was the business he was here for, to finalise the deals and sign the contracts. He glanced at his watch. Time to get ready for the meetings of the morning.

He showered and shaved, then while still in his bathrobe ate the breakfast he'd ordered. He read the financial pages of the newspaper that came with it. Then he washed his hands to get rid of the printer's ink before putting on a clean shirt. He wore the same suit, the one Nyree had insisted he had made in Hong Kong.

Looking at himself in the mirror as he tied his tie, he grinned a little at his reflection – a long, tanned face topped by fairish short-cropped hair, grey eyes with a good many lines around them from having to work in the sun. He thought it was the kind of face that looked more comfortable above an open-necked shirt and chinos – but you could hardly go to a meeting involving big money looking like a hick.

The HQ of the supermarket chain was quite close to his Mayfair hotel. He borrowed an umbrella from the hotel doorman then set off on foot. He liked to do this when he was abroad, getting the feel of the workaday life of the place. His path took him through streets where exclusive boutiques were just coming to life, and he watched with interest as handsome doors were flung open, safety curtains were raised, and smartly dressed girls began to move about in the shining interiors. He came soon to Bond Street.

Bond Street. Nyree would be here as soon as she could make it, credit card at the ready. She'd be trying on dresses in those shops, shopping for fiddly things like handbags and headbands. Why she should want them was a mystery because back home at McNaughton's Hill there was hardly ever any opportunity to show them off. But so what, if it pleased her . . .

Townley & Co was just coming to life as he passed. The chief salesperson, a young man with an aristocratic manner, was pressing buttons to raise the sun-proof blinds and release the safety locks. He and his two assistants were in a state of some expectation. The boss had rung them to say he was bringing something special to show them.

Willard had been back from his Mediterranean trip for

two days. They had expected him to have something to show – he seldom came back empty-handed. But this time he had seemed almost elated. Since no one ever came art shopping at an early hour on a Tuesday, they were to have a special coffee break at ten thirty when the new treasure would be unveiled. They paused for a moment in their morning chores to speculate on the possibilities. If they saw Zan McNaughton go by, they thought him just another businessman hurrying under his black umbrella to some boring meeting.

Erica too was getting ready to open for the day. She'd been back for a week now, and had resumed the usual tenor of her life. The Corie Gallery didn't open until ten a.m. and Tuesday was normally a slack day, but today there was a school visit. She always made special preparations for this because she hoped to fire one of the youngsters with enthusiasm for painting, but today she made a little extra effort because the visitors were the sixth form of the local high school. In her experience, teenagers either showed a determined indifference, or else asked questions she was hard put to it to answer.

She'd already spoken to Gerald Pritchett about restoration work on *Bridge after the style of Monet*. The old man had been irritated by the enquiry. 'What're you saying, girl? You want me to restore a painting by some art student copying Monet?'

'That's its provisional title. We think . . . well . . . wait till you see it.'

'Ah?' The wise old face wrinkled in amusement. '"We" being you and your boyfriend, I suppose. What's he done now – discovered an unknown masterpiece?'

It was impossible to talk to Pritchett when he was in this kind of mood. She shrugged. 'Never mind, then.'

'I'm busy, you know. I haven't time to spare for larks.'

'But will you at least look at it?'

'We'll see.'

And that was as much as she could achieve for the present.

She knew Willard was taking the painting to the gallery

today. She wondered what the staff would say to it. She tried to conjure it up before her inner eye, but as always it eluded her. Ever since she'd left Parigos the image she saw seemed always to be merging with the studies of the Japanese bridge she'd assessed and appraised in the great collections.

This evening she and Willard would meet at his Mayfair gallery. She'd hear what his colleagues had to say, learn what he planned to do next, and report to him Pritchett's tepid reaction over a possible restoration. She knew that would annoy him. He'd hoped for an enthusiastic undertaking to work on the Monet so that he could start off any publicity campaign with the news that the greatest expert on restoring damaged Impressionists was on his team.

Big money was involved all along the line. The restoration in itself would be an expensive business, and then there would probably be a launch party, an important occasion when the rich and famous would be given the first view of the painting. Then there was the printing of the brochures giving provenance and the usual survey of the life of the artist and his work. And the insurance – since he was hoping to sell the painting somewhere up in the millions, the insurance would have to be commensurate.

And of course there were the fees of all the experts who would examine the actual texture of the painting. Scientists with specialised knowledge and specialised equipment – they didn't come cheap. And fees to scholars for their opinion on placing the picture in the artist's career – had it been painted in 1918? 1920? Later, earlier?

It was exciting. But it was frightening too. If anything went wrong – if Pritchett by any chance damaged the work, if one of the scientists said something derogatory . . . But no, that couldn't happen.

By the time she was changing for her evening in town with Willard, Erica was exhausted. The sixth-formers had been great fun but tiring, and then in the afternoon an unexpected coachload of tourists had descended on the gallery. They were as full of questions as any teenager and the limited gallery staff had had to call on Erica for answers. Then, of course, the café had run out of food; she and her secretary had been making emergency phone calls for an hour.

When at five the doors were closed, she had scarcely enough energy to walk the half-mile to her flat in Gratesford. She'd have liked nothing better than a bath, a snack on a tray, and early bed.

But she was going to see Willard. The thought reinvigorated her. She showered and changed into a crimson silk chiffon blouse from Emma Willis, last year's big fashion buy and intended to last out for special occasions at least until the end of this year. With it she wore navy poplin trews, topping it off with a navy pea jacket against the chill of the evening. It had become an axiom with her, that she must never wear black when she was going to see Willard – for black was Willard's trademark and must be left to him alone.

When she got to the Townley Gallery he was waiting to unlock the security system and let her in. He hugged her in greeting, took her jacket and ushered her into his office. On a little side table stood an opened bottle of champagne.

'We had a bottle or two this morning, in celebration,' he explained. 'Everybody was so excited and enthusiastic, it seemed only right that we should drink to it. Would you like some? It's been in the fridge until now.'

She accepted a glass, looking round for the painting.

'Oh no,' he said at once, understanding the inquiry. 'It's in the security room. I'm taking no risks with it! News will get round – it always does, doesn't it?'

'Well, nobody could ever accuse the art world of being close-mouthed,' she agreed.

'Did you speak to Pritchett? What did he say?'

This was the question she'd been rather dreading. 'He's less than enthusiastic. You know how he can be.'

'He's a cantankerous old nuisance!' Willard cried. 'But I *do* want him to do the job. The more so since – wait till I tell you! – on the way home I anchored overnight at Nice and went to see Polly.'

'You didn't talk to Polly about the Monet!' Her heart sank. Polly was Cyril Polmeche, a Mr Fixit, one of the many who made a living on the periphery of art circles. He sold information, arranged introductions, and kept a watchful eye on the health of great-grandmamas in continental families whose death might disclose an array of minor masters. The minute he saw an obituary, he was at the house offering condolences and spying out the land, so as to be first with the news to the dealers. He wasn't exactly dishonest but he wasn't Snow White either.

Willard was explaining why he'd chosen to confide in Polly. 'You know he has these great contacts among the American museums,' he began.

'Oh, I *see*!' She was pleased. Willard had decided after all to treat the Monet as a museum piece.

'It occurred to me,' he went on without regarding her exclamation, 'that the cost of the restoration is going to be enormous. I mean, that upper left-hand corner is really a mess, the burn mark gives no idea of how the colours were laid on. So Polly has arranged for two of the biggies to finance part of the cost. That means no matter what Pritchett and his team want to charge, we can accept it.'

This would inevitably mean that once the restoration was done, the investors in the restoration would get first sight of the result. They would therefore have a much better idea of whether to recommend its purchase to the finance committee of their city.

Some American museums had great financial freedom but on the whole it was the city art galleries with big private endowments that would put in the biggest bids. Early knowledge of how the restoration work had turned out would be an advantage. Even if the curators themselves couldn't bid, they would earn goodwill by passing on their knowledge to favoured friends. Erica knew from personal experience that unless gallery curators helped each other, great works could fall into the hands of avid private collectors, never to be seen again by the ordinary gallery visitor.

Willard was waiting for her response. As she hesitated he said, 'Don't be cross, Erica. It's by a great artist – we must do him justice.'

'I'm not cross.' But inwardly she was, a little. Forming syndicates was something she disapproved of, and this had some of the earmarks of a syndicate, a little club to gain advantage over others. 'So what's the plan now? Shall I get Pritchett to come and take a look?'

'No. What I'm going to do is . . . I'm going to hold a special viewing.'

'Of what?' she asked, momentarily puzzled.

'Of the Monet.'

'What – in its present state?'

'Yes, so that everyone can see how much work needs to be done. Perhaps another investor will put something in the pot towards the restoration.'

She tried to think it through, to understand what he intended to achieve. No viewing could take place quickly if he wanted important people to attend – three weeks at least, and by that time the news of the Monet's discovery would be common knowledge. Was that what he wanted? Celebrity? That was understandable enough, because the more his reputation was enhanced the more business he would do. But he need only wait six months or a year, and when the Monet was restored and sold, he would have all the fame he deserved.

But the money was important too. Banks would make big advances for the kind of work the Monet needed, but they tended to be interfering, troublesome – and of course they charged interest. If Willard could put together a syndicate which would finance the entire restoration, there would be much less of a drain on his own resources, that was self-evident. Perhaps she shouldn't be so critical of his motives. After all, he was working in the commercial market. Erica's experience had all been in the public sector where, although she had to keep balancing the books, the money was a fixed asset, always available unless the town council made budget cuts.

She listened to his plans, her criticism waning. When they went out to a meal at a local restaurant she was more or less convinced that it would all turn out well. She helped devise a guest list for the intended viewing, looked over a draft of the announcement that would go out to the press, and couldn't help but agree it would be a very interesting event.

*   *   *

The special viewing of the newly discovered Monet was held in the Townley Gallery. The year had turned to November, so it was no great loss to move out the paintings that usually hung on the walls. November was the month when Townley & Co put on a kind of Christmas sale: small paintings by undiscovered but talented artists, limited-edition prints of greater artists, lithographs, and sketches – nothing over a hundred pounds, presents suitable for art-loving aunts and young couples setting up home. Now this easily moved stock lay in the warehouse, waiting to be brought out and put up. The walls, for the moment, were empty.

Except for the furthermost wall of the furthermost room of the gallery. There the Monet hung in all its angry splendour. Lit by specially angled lamps, it glowed. The crowd that stared at it were clad in evening dress and held glasses of expensive wine. The viewing had been scheduled for nine p.m. and for once, most of the guests had not arrived late.

There were press people here, but they were mostly gossip columnists. The art journalists had been invited for the early afternoon so that their columns could be ready for next morning's papers. The gossip columnists were studying the women's clothes and identifying their companions rather than assessing the painting.

Erica, swept along by the excitement aroused by the viewing, had gone a little mad and bought herself a glittery blue dress at Matthew Williamson. When she would ever wear it again, she couldn't imagine. But she didn't care – this was Willard's evening, and she wanted to do him credit among the crowd of eminent and rich people.

His gallery staff were there too, all in their party clothes and incandescent with delight at the success of the event. They were wearing gilt badges identifying them as staff members and Erica too had agreed to wear one just for the occasion, so that anyone who wanted background could consult her. After all, who apart from Willard himself knew more about the painting than she did? She had been his first confidante, and her heart was singing with the pleasure of it.

A tall, angular man approached her, someone she'd never seen before at an art gathering – but then there were many new faces tonight, experts who had flown in from all over the world.

'Could I have a word?' he ventured.

'Certainly. How can I help?'

'This' – he held up the brochure that had gone out with invitations – 'says you can give information about the painting.'

'Exactly. The provenance is available on that table over there—'

'Yes, I read that, and I read the snippets in the papers the other day. The word is, this is a great discovery, a Monet never seen before, but it looks in a very bad state. Right?'

'Right.' She was amused. His manner was nothing like the usual let-me-show-you-how-clever-I-am from art experts she had known.

'And it's for sale.'

'Yes. Mr Townley will be offering it some time next year.'

'So how much is it likely to cost?'

'Oh . . . Once it's restored . . . Say, eight million pounds?'

The inquirer accepted the estimate in silence. He seemed deep in thought. After a moment he said, 'It's a funny-looking painting.'

'Yes, you could say that. You understand it's because Monet's eyesight—'

'Yes, yes, I read all that. He was feeling a tremendous surge of . . . something . . . when he slung that on a bonfire, you'd think.'

Erica said softly, 'And when he painted it. It leaps off the canvas at you – "I want to *see*" – the determination not to give up.'

'Yes.' From his taller viewpoint he glanced around the room. 'Is that the gallery owner, him in the black gear?'

'Yes, that's Willard Townley.'

'Could you introduce me to him?'

'Of course I will. And you are?'

'Alexander McNaughton. I'm in London on a business trip.'

'To do with paintings?' she asked as she ushered him through the throng.

He gave a laugh. 'No, until a few days ago I never thought about paintings.'

She stopped. She was making a big mistake. 'Then how did you get an invitation to the viewing?' He was some sort of party crasher, a celebrity seeker perhaps.

'The hotel got it for me,' he said, 'the Mayfair Rialto.' Then, understanding her hesitation, he added, 'Ring them if you like – the manager's Joaquin Talez.'

It would be a problem to do that. She would have to get to the office to use the phone, and if it turned out he was a genuine guest she would have to apologise abjectly. Better to take him to Willard, who was quite capable of freezing any interloper with a look.

Willard was chatting with a couple from Texas, very rich and very acquisitive but not the greatest fun in the world. He looked round with relief when Erica appeared at his elbow.

'Will, this is Mr McNaughton who got his invitation through the manager of the Mayfair Rialto.' Yes or no – the unknown would live or die at this point.

'Ah, yes, I remember – Joaquin said you were very keen to come. How are you, Mr McNaughton? From New Zealand, I believe?'

'Yes, I produce wine there – McNaughton's Hill.'

'Really?' said Willard politely. He himself never drank anything but French or German wine. He covered his lack of enthusiasm by introducing the Texans.

'You'll be seeing the label around a lot more from now on. It'll be in all the supermarkets,' offered Mr McNaughton. 'That's one of the reasons I'm in London, to sort that out. But I want to talk to you about the painting.'

Mr and Mrs Texan evinced some interest in this. Coming themselves from a country that was still building its reputation as a wine producer, they had a slight fellow feeling for this guy from the Antipodes.

Willard exchanged a glance with Erica, a glance that no one else could have read. It was saying, Why on earth have you brought this nincompoop to me?

39

She said hastily, 'Mr McNaughton was asking me about the possible selling price.' Her message was, Even men who make deals with supermarkets might want to buy paintings.

'Ah yes.' Willard had already discussed this with the two Texans so rather than bore them with the same information, he moved a little aside, to a corner of the room that offered some slight seclusion. 'Well now, about the Monet. As you can see, it's very badly damaged. It's going to take a lot of work to restore it. Several people are interested in putting up the money for the work, on the understanding that it gives them some priority in bidding for it ultimately. If you'd like to take part in that, we can discuss it?'

'Restore it? That would change it a lot, surely.'

'Oh, of course. It would look like – well, one can't quite say it would look like new, but it would look like other Monets.'

'I was telling Mr McNaughton,' Erica put in, 'that the likely cost for the restored painting would be in the region of eight million—'

'And of course if it goes to auction, who knows how high,' Willard concluded.

Zan McNaughton had come to the viewing with quite a different game plan from the one the gallery owner was putting forward. He didn't have time for all this long-term stuff. He looked at Willard and drew in a breath.

'Let me make you an offer,' he said.

Despite himself, Willard was surprised. 'Now? Before it's restored?'

'Two million and it never goes to the restorer,' said Zan.

Four

The shock wave took some time to disperse. Willard, generally so composed, seemed almost dumbfounded. It was Erica who restarted the conversation.

'You must forgive us if we seem taken aback, Mr McNaughton. The painting is on view this evening to let art lovers see how much damage has been done. This is so that if they want to, they can take part in subsidising the repair work.'

'I'm not interested in that.'

'You're interested in buying the painting as it is now?'

'That's the general idea.'

Willard found his voice. 'Usually, prospective buyers don't make their offers so brusquely—'

'Oh, you mean there's an etiquette or something? Sorry – I'm new at this.'

'That's partly the problem, Mr McNaughton. I know nothing about you. Forgive me for saying so, but I've no way of knowing whether you're serious.'

'I can have a certified cheque in your hands in two days.'

For two million pounds? Erica could see that the offer had a lot of attraction for Willard. Because this thought worried her, she said quickly, 'What exactly would you think of doing with the painting, Mr McNaughton?'

'That's *my* business.'

'You say you're new at this? Are you starting a private collection?'

He shrugged. 'Who knows?'

'But you're interested in art?' she persisted. 'You have paintings at home?'

'Ma bought a few while she was alive – but not like that one – landscapes, mostly, and by New Zealanders.'

'Doris Lusk? Colin McCahon?' she suggested.

'Oh, nobody famous. Mostly local fellas. To encourage them, you know.'

'But you haven't bought any yourself?'

'Not till now.'

'So how did you arrive at the price you offered?' Willard demanded. 'If you know nothing about paintings?'

'I saw all those bits in the papers, making guesses at what the Monet might fetch, comparing its chances with what other things had brought in at auction. They mentioned one in New York that went for fourteen million dollars at auction. That's about nine million sterling. But that was for a perfect painting, of course.'

'So you subtracted what you thought was a good discount and came up with two million.'

'You seem a bit huffy,' said the prospective buyer, with a puzzled frown. 'I'm sorry if I've offended against convention but the fact is, I've been here about half an hour and *everybody* seems to be talking about money. I've heard one or two blokes discussing the cost of the restoration and it seemed a lot to me. I thought you might like to sell without having all that hassle.'

Willard could see he'd been tactless in mentioning a discount. But it had been put into his head by this extra-ordinary man himself – talking about selling his wine to supermarkets . . . Was he really being asked to sell his Monet to a man in the grocery trade?

Erica moved in to soothe ruffled feathers. 'It's just that we're so surprised, Mr McNaughton,' she murmured. 'And of course, we feel a responsibility to the painting. It's a newly discovered addition to the life work of a master – we'd want to be sure it was falling into good hands.'

'Well, I can understand that.' He gave Erica a sudden brief smile. 'I'd be willing to take advice about how to look after it, and all that.'

'From whom? Do you know anybody in the profession?' asked Willard.

'No, but it wouldn't be hard to find somebody, now would it? This is a famous painting already – I'm sure I'd get a lot of people showing an interest.'

This was only too true. 'But how would you know who was bona fide?'

McNaughton sighed. 'Does everybody that wants to buy a painting have to go through this third degree?' he enquired, with a quizzical turn to his expression. 'Look, I've made you an offer. You say it's taken you by surprise. Well, think it over, Mr Townley, and call me at my hotel in the morning with your verdict. I'm at the Mayfair Rialto – well, you know that. I'll be there till about ten and then I have to go out, but they'll take a message, of course. Oh, and here's my mobile, if you'd rather ring me direct.' He gave Willard a card, obviously newly printed since his arrival in London. Willard, impressed despite himself, took it and murmured that he'd be in touch, and with a cool nod at them both, the customer left.

Willard and Erica exchanged glances. 'Now wasn't that just *weird*,' he exclaimed. 'Walks in off the street and makes an offer of two mill?'

'I've certainly never heard of it happening recently. In the old days, tycoons used to do it, but nowadays . . .'

'Do you think he really has two million?'

'Probably. He gave the impression of straight talking. I don't think he'd waste his time discussing the Monet unless he was genuinely interested.'

'But *why* is he interested?' Willard exclaimed, baffled.

But at that moment one of his staff came to say that Sir John wanted a word, so that Willard had to reserve consideration of Alexander McNaughton until later.

After the guests departed and Willard had locked up, they went to his flat in Hampstead. In the taxi Willard said, 'That chap . . . I think I know what he's after.'

'Mr McNaughton, you mean?'

'Maybe he's not so weird after all. You heard him your-self, talking about his business affairs. I think he sees the Monet as a way of making a profit.'

'Oh, I didn't get that impression—'

'I bet he's telling himself he can get the Monet at a knock-down price in its present state and then have it restored himself and sell it for millions.'

'But you heard him say – he wasn't interested in the restoration idea—'

'Sweetest, if you believe that, you must have been hatched in an incubator yesterday. The man's into buying and selling – supermarket stuff—'

'All he said was that he'd made a deal to sell his wine through supermarkets. He's a wine maker, Will.'

'But a wine maker with his eye on the main chance. Yes, I think I've got him sussed out.'

She decided not to waste any more time on defending McNaughton, who after all was a totally unknown quantity. It seemed to her that if Willard kept to his view, he wouldn't want to sell the Monet to McNaughton, which would be in Erica's view a good thing. McNaughton seemed to have no motive except to possess the painting – to buy it and keep it for himself. Whereas Erica wanted it to be available to the general public in either a museum or a gallery.

Although there had been food at the gallery it had been of the canapé-and-nibbles variety. At home in Willard's flat, they found provisions for a snack in the larder. Over sandwiches and coffee they chatted about the other clients who had come to the viewing. Some of them had expressed a muted interest in being part of the group financing the restoration. They would undoubtedly be in touch next day. Then there were the experts who had given opinions on the painting. For the most part they were intrigued and supportive.

In the early hours of the morning they went to bed, and so tired were they from the agitations of the evening that they merely lay with arms around each other until they fell asleep.

Next day Erica was in the store-room finalising the choices for her Christmas exhibition of 'snow scenes' when her secretary came to her with a smile on her dark face. 'There's a man on the phone asking if he can come and speak to you – a Mr McNaughton.'

'Oh?' Erica was a little taken aback. 'When does he want to come?'

Suzi's smile widened. 'He's on his way now on a train, calling on his mobile. But he says if it's inconvenient he can get out at King's Cross and come some other time.'

'Oh! Oh, well, then . . . Tell him it's OK.'

Suzi laughed. 'I thought you'd say that. I think my boyfriend would say you've been snookered.'

Erica couldn't disagree. She shrugged and smiled and went back to her task, allowing herself a little time to wash and freshen up before going to her office. She rang the gallery café to ask for afternoon tea to be sent over. Then she rang Willard.

'Will, that Mr McNaughton is coming to see me. What's it about?'

'Oh . . . Erica . . . I was going to get in touch . . . Yes, well . . . The long and short of it is, I've made the sale to McNaughton.'

'What?'

She heard Willard draw in a weary breath. 'I thought it over, Erica. After all, it's money in the bank. And he was right – getting the Monet repaired is going to be a hassle, and what if something went wrong and it didn't come out well?'

'But Will – he's going to keep it on the other side of the world where nobody can see it.'

'We don't know that. Perhaps he wants to give it to a museum in Wellington or wherever it is—'

'Did you ask him if he was thinking of donating it?'

'No, I . . . well . . . we had a long talk but somehow we never got around to things like that. But after all, Erica, it *is* my painting and I can sell it to who I like.'

'And the people who were going to finance the restoration – what about them?'

'There was never anything in writing, Erica. We hadn't got to that stage yet.'

She couldn't find any words for a reply. There was a pause and then Willard said, 'Well, it's done now. I signed a letter of intention and I get the cheque in a couple of days.'

45

'I see.'

'You think I've done the wrong thing.'

She hesitated before saying, 'It's not what I would have done.'

'But you don't have a gallery that isn't making much money and a huge rent for Mayfair premises and a staff to pay and—'

'All right, love,' she intervened. She didn't want to hear him lowering himself to commercial justifications – and at that thought she was shocked and told herself she had no right to be so patronising. She herself was cushioned from the kind of problem that Willard had to wrestle with on a daily basis. 'All right,' she repeated in a gentler tone. 'I understand.'

About five minutes later the doorman came through on the gallery intercom to say that a Mr McNaughton had arrived. She asked her secretary to go and bring him to the office. 'Can't wait,' said Suzi, and hurried off.

Erica too was greatly intrigued. What could he possibly want with her?

When Zan McNaughton walked in he saw a different creature from the previous night. Instead of the girl in the glitzy dress and strappy high heels, he found a quiet-looking young woman in jeans and a blue sweater. She came to greet him and shake hands.

'Thank you for agreeing to see me,' he said. He glanced around. Quite a come-down from Townley's office in Mayfair – a room with a desk and a couple of chairs and cupboards, handsome enough in an old-fashioned way but making no claim to designer status. Paintings stood about, propped on a display shelf or with their faces to the wall.

'Would you like some tea?' she enquired, ushering him to one of the chairs.

'I certainly would.'

'How do you like it? Milk? Sugar?'

'Dark brown and one lump.'

She poured the tea, which made no attempt to be dark brown. As she handed it to him she saw from his hastily concealed expression that he was used to a richer brew than she was offering. 'I'm sorry, it isn't very strong—'

'It's fine, thank you, it's fine. So this is where you work.'

'Yes, the office side of the work. A lot of the job is caring for the paintings. I was in the store-room when you rang.'

He stirred his tea thoughtfully. 'Last night, with your little badge on, I took you for one of the staff. But Townley explained that you were a "colleague".'

'Yes, I was just helping out last night.'

'As I was leaving I asked one of the shop-girls—' He broke off to follow another thought. 'They were all hopping about the place, putting up little pictures on the walls, some of them quite like the things Ma used to buy?' There was a question implied in the last few words.

'Yes, that's the Townley Christmas Event – it's quite traditional, one of the earlier owners initiated it as a way to bring art to the less well-off part of the population.'

'I see. Well, this girl told me who you really were, that you're in charge of this place and quite well known as an expert on Impressionists.'

'That was probably Geraldine. And I don't think she'd like to be called a shop-girl,' Erica added with a laugh. 'She wants to be a specialist in eighteenth-century English portraits.'

'Really? And Townley sells those too – Old Master sort of stuff?'

'He would if he could get it,' she replied, still half laughing. 'But these days very few Gainsboroughs or Lawrences come on to the market and if they do, they generally go to auction. Willard sells what he can get, but it's generally drawings or sketches by masters – lesser works – or else he gets what's called "school of" – you know, by a pupil of one of the masters – that sort of thing.'

'So finding this painting is a really big thing for him.'

'Absolutely. It's the kind of thing every art dealer dreams of.' She offered a plate of biscuits; he shook his head.

'I thought last night,' he began, 'that he didn't take to me. I was a bit annoyed with myself, felt I'd handled it wrong. I was really pleased when he rang to say he was interested.'

She didn't know how to respond to that. It was true, she recalled, that Willard hadn't been too friendly last night.

47

'I asked around,' Zan went on, watching her. 'I gather Townley's a bit pressed for money.'

'Who told you that?' she asked, startled.

'Oh, it's not difficult to get information if you know where to ask. But it's OK, I know what it's like to have cash-flow problems, it's happened in our family in the past. Anyhow, when he came back on the phone this morning making friendly noises I thought probably he'd be interested in making a deal and in the end we did – though of course I had to up my offer, but then I always thought I would.'

Erica sighed. 'So how much did you settle for?'

'Two and three-quarter million.' He didn't tell her that he would have gone to three. He could see she was having enough difficulty coming to terms with the sale as it was. 'You didn't want me to get the painting,' he accused.

'Well . . . no.'

'Why not?'

'Well, what are you going to do with it?' she flared. 'It's by the greatest of the Impressionists. It should be available to everybody to see, to enjoy, to study.'

'Oh, so that's it. It's not because you think I'm an ignoramus.'

She coloured up. He grinned. 'Gotcha,' he said.

When she got her breath back she said, 'I'm sorry. I know people in the art world tend to be a bit snooty to those who don't share their expertise. But' – and she allowed herself a smile – 'that happens in the world of wine, doesn't it? Haven't I heard of wine snobs?'

'Too true. And don't I suffer from them! There are people in the world who really believe that only French vineyards can produce good wine. If you take them through a blind tasting and they discover they've given good marks to a wine from Australia or New Zealand, they nearly die of mortification.'

'But you were saying last night that you'd got some big agreement to put your wine on the market here . . .?'

'It's called McNaughton's Hill. Let me tell you, it's good stuff. I'll arrange for you to have a case of our

'94 chardonnay – you couldn't ask for a better drink on a summer day.'

'Oh, I wouldn't think of accepting—'

'Nonsense, you'll like it. But of course this is all a lure to get you to do what I want.'

'Which is what, exactly?'

He was more hesitant in his next words. He very much wanted her to accept. He'd felt last night during their short conversation that they shared something – that they both felt a special sympathy for the artist who had thrown his work on the bonfire. 'You know last night I was saying I'd ask someone who knew about these things to advise me?'

'Yes?'

'I wondered if you'd take the job on?'

Erica blinked. 'Me?'

'Yes. That girl in the shop – Geraldine – said you were an acknowledged expert on Impressionism and I don't have to tell you that I know nothing about it, so as I'd already met you I thought you were the best person to ask.'

'Well . . .'

'And besides, you have a special interest in that painting.'

'What makes you say so?'

'I could tell, by the way you spoke about it.'

'Well, it's true.' She saw in her mind that moment when she had first looked at the Monet on its stand in the cottage living-room. 'I was with Willard when he brought it from Istanbul. I was the first person he asked for an opinion.'

'Oh yes, all about the finding of it – he gave me the documents – it's a marvellous thing, isn't it, to think it survived all that – being burned by its creator and an invasion by the Nazis and then an invasion by the Communists – it's a real adventure story.'

'Yes it is. You're right. I do have a special interest because I handled it when it was first discovered.'

'By your friend Willard.' He paused. 'Are you and he an item?'

'That's a very personal question,' she returned, offended.

'Oh, so you are, then. OK, perhaps I shouldn't have asked,

but I like things out in the open, and he's peeved enough with me as it is, though I don't know why.'

'Peeved?' she echoed. Really, this man was very hard to keep up with. Peeved? Was Willard the kind of person who got peeved?

'Maybe that's the wrong word. He was pleased to be making a lot of money on the sale, but . . . I don't know . . . he seemed in a funny mood. Thing is, if I get you to help me will that make him more peeved? And if it does, does it matter? Not to me, naturally – but you, I don't know how much it might matter to you.'

'Willard and I understand each other perfectly,' she said with confidence. 'We're both professional people with careers to think about. Willard would be quite happy if I took on the job of adviser over the Monet.'

'He would, would he. So does that mean you're going to do it?'

'I *would* like to be connected with its well-being for a while longer,' she acknowledged. 'There's quite a lot that still needs to be done before it can take its place in the annals of Claude Monet's work.'

'So I gathered – I asked a guy at New Zealand House to talk to an expert this morning before I went to Townley's and it seems there's a mass of stuff that needs to be done – spectroscopy and ultraviolet and all that. But when I asked Townley about verification he said he'd let me have letters, whatever that may mean.'

Erica sighed inwardly. It certainly did seem that Willard was being difficult. 'He was referring to expert opinion,' she explained. 'The first thing he did when he got the painting back to London was to ask experts what they thought of it.' She smiled. 'He'd already asked me what I thought, of course. And I thought it was probably a Monet, and I think he's had five other opinions.'

'All in favour?'

'Well, you'll see for yourself when Will sends you the letters. I think only Halliday Garland "demurred" – that's a word experts use when they're not sure. But if I remember rightly he went on to say that there was nothing *against* its being a Monet. And of course you can call in other experts for their opinion.'

'And what about the spectroscopy and so forth?'

'It's spectrography, actually – examining the spectrum using a spectrograph so as to separate out the colours. Certain painters never used certain colours, you know . . . well, never mind, it gets complicated and it's better to pay someone to find it all out for you.'

He concealed his faint amusement at her explanation. Although she truly believed she wasn't patronising him, she was taking it for granted that as a country bumpkin he wouldn't understand scientific terms. It seemed not to occur to her that modern wine making involved a lot of technology that would equally be a mystery to her.

'You know the someone to ask, of course,' he said.

'It's quite a few someones. You need an analysis of the paint used, not that it will be very helpful because Monet lived in an era when artists no longer ground and mixed their own colours – he just bought paints in tubes from the sundries shop, just as we do today. All the same if, God forbid, they found any acrylics, that would mean it's a fake.'

Zan shuddered at the word. He'd just signed a promise to deliver a certified cheque for two and three-quarter million. 'You don't think it's a fake, do you?'

'No, but then we all make mistakes.' As she saw him grimace at the thought, she smiled in encouragement. 'That's what all the testing's for – to be as certain as humanly possible. And you have to remember that the painting fits into what we know about Monet's life – he did tell friends he'd burned some of the work he'd done while his cataracts were bad and we know the Japanese bridge was a subject he painted often during those years. So, no, I don't think it's a fake, and I don't think Will would have bought it in the first place if he'd thought it was a fake.'

'Well, that's a relief.'

'And there's always the safety net, you know. If in the future a serious challenge was made against its authenticity, you get your money back. Art dealers have to be as careful as the buyers of paintings because if anything is proved unsound, they lose the purchase money, their reputation suffers, and they don't sell anything else for big money for years!'

'Yes, well, good, I wasn't really thinking there was anything dicey about it. And with you to advise me I'm sure I'll get the best experts in the business. So can we shake hands on that?'

'Of course.' They performed a solemn hand-clasp, and she couldn't help thinking how it would amuse Willard, who was accustomed to handling such matters with a nod of the head. She explained that they now had to come to terms over a fee, at which he shrugged and said he'd agree to anything she thought right.

So it was arranged. Zan McNaughton took his leave feeling satisfied he was in good hands. The stand-offish Mr Townley had made him feel somewhat at a loss, but then that had been his intention. 'You know nothing about it so when I say it's worth more, you have to believe me' – that had been the message. Zan grinned to himself as he walked to the station for the train back to London. What would the stand-offish Mr Townley say when he learned that his girlfriend had agreed to act as adviser?

What, indeed. Erica was nervous when she picked up the phone to pass on the news. But to her surprise, Willard seemed rather pleased.

'He needs someone to hold his hand,' he said, 'and it might as well be you because you know the Monet from the inside.'

'I'm glad you see it that way. Mr McNaughton really is an innocent in this kind of thing. It wouldn't be fair to let him flounder.'

'Quite right. So you'll be his guardian angel, and the verification and so forth will go without a hitch. You'll keep me informed?'

'Of course.' They went on to speak of more run-of-the-mill matters – she told him she'd finished selecting paintings for her Christmas show and he said he was almost finished putting up the low-cost art in the Townley Gallery. 'What about Christmas?' she queried. She was hoping to invite him to a Christmas lunch, which she would cook personally for him. And afterwards a long, leisurely walk in the countryside around Gratesford which, though not exactly rural, had pleasant National Trust woodlands.

'Oh . . . er . . . I'm going to New Orleans.'

'Good heavens!' This was totally unexpected. 'What's in New Orleans?'

'Somebody's got a first edition of Berenson's *Italian Painters* for sale. I thought I'd take a look.'

'You're buying it for yourself? Or to sell on?'

'Sell on? What am I, a bookseller? No, it's my Christmas present to myself, a little reward for finding the Monet.'

She waited for him to say, 'Come with me,' but he went on to talk about how he'd always found Berenson the best art historian and how he would treasure the first edition if he was able to buy it. She didn't suggest he should do it through an American agent and stay over Christmas with her. Willard always knew his own mind and trying to influence him was a waste of time. And on second thoughts she decided she'd better spend Christmas in Cornwall with her mother, for she owed her a visit.

The time flew by. She set experts to work on the Monet, which was sent direct from Townley & Co's security room to the laboratory. Asked if he'd like to watch some of the processes, Zan McNaughton gave an eager assent. The firm doing the investigation had premises in Andover, so she drove him there for his first visit.

On the drive, he got tired of being addressed as Mr McNaughton and asked her to call him Zan.

'That's a strange name! Is it Greek?'

He laughed. 'In a way. It's short for Alexander, who was a Greek, if I remember rightly. No, it's just that when I was a kid I got fed up with trying to say Alexander and shortened it to Zan, that's all. Scottish families have a tradition of giving their sons classical names – I was lucky not to get called Hercules. I've got a brother called Hector but of course he answers to Heck.'

'It sounds like quite a clan.'

'Yes, there are five of us working on the vineyard – two

brothers and me and two cousins. I've left them in charge while I swan about in Britain. We ring each other practically every day.'

To Erica, an only child, it sounded wonderful. Lisbet comprised her whole family – her father had disappeared early in her childhood, unhappy at being overshadowed by his talented wife. There had been an amicable divorce and as far as Erica knew, he was now managing a hotel chain in Hawaii. As for her grandparents, John and Phyllis Pencarreth had sold their farm and retired to the Costa del Sol years ago, and were visited rarely because, as Lisbet would mutter, the Costa was a very boring place and the elder Pencarreths talked about nothing except bridge.

Although he had a lot on his mind that day, at the laboratory Zan was fascinated by the investigative processes. He watched as the ultraviolet lamp travelled over the surface of the paint in the careful hand of Maurice Leppard.

'Nothing wrong with it,' Leppard said, taking off his glasses and rubbing his eyes. Zan could see the special lenses in the frames and guessed they made the eyes feel strange. 'It's an ordinary toile, quite in keeping with the time the picture would have been painted. The unblemished surface has of course some "haze" on it, due to smoke drifting across it, no doubt, and then dust and so forth from being stored. There's a scratch or two, from inexperienced handling, but nothing serious. As to the burn – well, that will take a good while to analyse.' He glanced at Zan. 'We'll have to take samples of the burnt paint for microscopy and chemical investigation – you understand that means removing a sample from that corner?'

'I suppose so.'

'Don't worry, it will make no material difference, the samples are minute. And when you have it restored, of course even that intervention will be remedied.'

'I'm not having it restored.'

'Really?' said Leppard, surprised. 'Why is that?'

Zan ignored the question. 'I understand you took a big set of photographs?'

'Oh, yes, Kodachrome transparencies and prints to check

54

for tonal accuracy. Would you like to see them? This way.'

They went into the studio, where the big box file with the photographic material was stored. Leppard set up a viewer for the transparencies. They showed the Monet canvas in sections and in full, lit from different angles by lamps and in daylight. Leppard lectured a little about colour values and possible damage from heat.

'Can I see the prints?'

'Of course.' These were housed in a special album in transparent sleeves. He took them out with tweezers, offering the tweezers to Zan so that if he wanted to pick them up he could do so without leaving fingerprints.

'It's like handling my stamp collection when I was ten,' the New Zealander remarked with wry amusement on his narrow face as he picked the prints up.

'I expect the pictures are better than on any of the stamps you had when you were ten,' Leppard replied, nodding.

'Yes, looks good to me.' Zan appeared to hesitate. 'Could I have a couple of those?'

'No problem. We made several sets so that we could all have them for reference wherever we are working. Help yourself.'

Zan picked up two of the prints showing the whole canvas as it might be seen by a viewer standing directly in front of it, one in daylight and the other by studio lamp. He slipped them into their sleeves, put them in the inside pocket of his jacket, and patted it. 'Nice to have them,' he remarked. 'You know, today is only the third time I've seen the actual painting?'

'It's a shame,' Erica agreed. 'But it's very valuable – it has to be kept in secure premises until you actually take possession. I mean, where would you and Willard be if it was stolen before the authentication?'

'Don't even talk about it,' Zan said, with a look of horror at the thought.

On the way back to London Erica suggested a stop for a meal at a restaurant, but he seemed anxious to get on so instead they went to a very old country pub for a snack. Zan was intrigued by the Tudor building. 'We've got one or two places at home that try to be like this,' he said, 'but they never feel right. Nothing older than a hundred and fifty years, you see. And to tell the truth pubs were disapproved of at one time – dens of iniquity to our Calvinist Scottish ancestors. Most of them were pulled down.'

'So what would your ancestors say to your being a wine maker?'

'Probably whirling in their graves.'

'I don't think they sell much wine in a place like this, but I expect they'd let us look at the cellars, if you're interested?'

He glanced at his watch. 'No time,' he said. 'I have to be in St John's Wood by three.'

'Oh, that's no problem. I can drive you straight there.'

'No, thanks, I have to go to the hotel first.'

'Well, I can drop you and pick you up again—'

'No, don't bother. I can get a taxi.'

'It's no bother—'

'I can manage, thanks,' he said shortly.

Erica was silenced. He seemed anxious to get away from her.

What had she said to annoy him?

Five

Every Christmas Lisbet Pencarreth made a set of figures for the nativity scene in the entrance to the village church. They were never the same – sometimes she used straw, sometimes she used clay, sometimes she used metal.

This year she had produced figures about a foot high in terracotta painted with acrylics, and the Three Wise Men had a distinct resemblance to local farmers. In the new year they would be auctioned in aid of the Church Organ Fund and would fetch high prices, which seemed bizarre to Lisbet because, as she always pointed out, she was a painter, not a sculptor.

She and her daughter paused to examine them on their way out after the midnight service. 'That's David Prout,' Erica said, laughing.

'Yes, and the idiot's so pleased with it he's put in a bid already.' They set off for the outskirts of the village where Lisbet's house stood. The night was mild and clear, not at all Christmaslike.

Erica had arrived late in the evening after closing down the Corie Gallery for the holidays – only two days, Christmas Day and Boxing Day. Her 'Let It Snow' exhibition had drawn good crowds and the Christmas cards using reproductions of the paintings had sold well. But it had been hectic. She was glad to be away from it for a few days.

Her mother slipped her arm through hers as they walked. 'So how's everything?' she inquired.

'Pretty good.'

'And where's Willard?'

'In New Orleans.'

'Really? Is he a jazz fan?'

'He's there to buy a book – a first edition.'

Erica heard her mother's little grunt of derision. She said nothing. Lisbet didn't like Willard – but that was just because he was an art dealer. Had he been a solicitor or a . . . a wine maker, there would have been no objection.

She turned the subject to the next exhibition she was going to mount at the Corie. There were problems – some of the paintings she'd been promised from other galleries had been refused exit permits from their governments, and one private collector who'd promised a Cézanne was now in the throes of a divorce so that his property couldn't be dispersed.

'You'll solve it. You always do. Now, in the morning, when the light's decent, I'll show you what I've been doing. It's that set of views of the tin mines, remember?'

So they chatted as they made their way home, for hot chocolate and the giving of presents. Erica had brought a silk dressing-gown for her mother, Lisbet had bought a quilted jacket from a local craftswoman for Erica. They were too tired to linger.

Erica slept late. When she wandered into the kitchen at ten, Lisbet was already up and dressed, eating toast as she fetched food out of the refrigerator.

Lisbet Pencarreth had never learned to cook. Everything for the Christmas season was delivered to her door by the best hotel in St Ives. Erica helped to set out the dishes in the dining-room, where a sort of brunch would be available until late afternoon, at which point it would turn into a sort of high tea.

Christmas at the Pencarreth house was always a lively affair. Friends began dropping in almost at once. Although some were from the local farming community, most were artists of some kind or another. A few were people Erica had known all her life but many were newcomers, for the artistic fraternity was constantly changing.

They had the freedom of the house, and most of them gravitated to the studio. Lisbet's current work was on an easel covered by a cloth, which no one disturbed – they all understood the need for privacy while the painting was under creation. But they joined mother and daughter in examining the set of angular sketches of the mines. Comments were freely offered: Erica often thought it would be impossible to have a swelled head in this environment.

An elderly man called Daff (because he did flower paintings, mostly spring scenes with daffodils) broached the subject of the newly discovered Monet. 'Quite a commotion, eh?' he remarked. 'It even got into the tabloids.'

'Yes, the press were very interested.'

'But it's quietened down now. Haven't seen a word for weeks.'

'Well, you see, the lab is busy on the chemical analysis and so forth.'

'Can't see how that's going to help much,' Daff remarked, sipping his beer. 'Anybody could get hold of the same equipment that old Claude used.'

'What did he use, actually?' enquired a local potter, with a glance at Erica for an expert opinion.

'Well, he painted on French linen, sealed with a local glue – made from rabbit skin, if I remember rightly.'

'And that's what your experts have found,' Daff said in a sceptical tone.

'Yes, the proper glue, and the buff-coloured primer he used. That's as far as they've got up to now.'

'Well, *I* could get hold of all that if I really wanted to.'

'You mean if you wanted to produce a fake?' asked the potter.

'Oh, come on, Daffy,' said Mary Abbott, a respected graphic artist. 'What are you saying?'

'The whole point of an investigation into a newly discovered Master is to make sure it's not a fake – am I right?'

'Well, of course.'

'I was just saying, Mary, that it would be easy to get the materials to fake a Monet.'

'The materials – yes – but the actual technique, Daff—'

'Ha-ha.'

'Don't be absurd – it would be extremely difficult to fake the technique.'

'It's signed, of course,' the potter put in. 'The painting's got Monet's signature?'

'Of course,' said Erica, laughing. 'There it is, in his neat little handwriting, but difficult to see because, you know, he often signed with whatever he had on his brush when he thought he'd finished. In this case, the signature is in a mixture of ochre and madder.'

'And it's definitely his?'

'Oh, see here, anybody could forge a signature!'

The argument was picked up by the rest of the group in the studio. Lisbet finally said, 'This isn't very kind to poor Erica. She's given it as her expert opinion that it's a Monet.'

'Well, I'm sorry,' Daff insisted with a stubbornness brought on by rather too much beer, 'but I find it hard to believe.'

'But why?'

'Suddenly turns up from nowhere – old Claude was a mean old blighter, I bet he kept a ledger of all his works.'

'But you read in the papers – he threw it on a bonfire because it was a thing he produced while his eyes were bad—'

'Oh yeah?' said Daff. 'Hang that for a tale!'

'But he burned quite a few of his paintings, Daffy.'

'It's a lovely yarn, oh yes,' he agreed, wagging his head. 'Just like a public relations hand-out. The kind of thing every newspaper reporter would love. But' – he pointed an accusing finger at Erica – 'is it true?'

'Well, there's a full documentation.'

'But anybody could forge documents.'

'Oh, shut up, Daff,' exclaimed someone from the back-ground. 'You've had too much to drink.'

Daff protested that he was perfectly sober, Lisbet proposed they go back to the dining-room for tea or coffee, and the conversation turned elsewhere. When at length the guests had gone on to make other visits, Erica and Lisbet spent some time tidying and doing the washing-up.

'Were you upset by what old Daff was saying?' Lisbet inquired, looking earnestly at the plate she was scrubbing.

'Oh, I didn't take it seriously.'

'You *are* sure it's a genuine Monet?'

'Of course I am, Mamma. What a funny thing to ask.'

'Only, you know . . . you tend to take everything that Willard says as gospel.'

'But everybody agrees it's genuine, Mamma.'

'Everybody? Who? The list I saw . . . they were all pals of Willard's.'

'But they wouldn't authenticate it if they didn't believe in it.'

'Well, let's say they do believe in it. But anybody can be wrong. Including Willard.'

'Oh, he isn't easily taken in.'

'But if he was keen to believe it was genuine?' Lisbet persisted. 'It's such a big thing for a dealer to find something like that. And then there's the money.'

'Of course the money is important, I'm not denying that—'

'You know he's dropped Grant Simmells?'

Grant Simmells was one of Willard's protégés. It wasn't unusual for a dealer or an agent to give financial support to an artist in whose work they had faith. Willard had had two or three in the past who had gone on to do well and, as far as Erica knew, he was now supporting a former mercenary soldier who lived in near penury painting angry war scenes.

She said after a moment, 'Is that definite or just gossip?'

'Oh, it's gossip, but I think it's true because there was supposed to have been a one-man show in Bruges or Delft or somewhere this summer and it was cancelled. I wondered if it was because Willard's been a bit hard up.'

Erica gave a little shrug and went on with putting the plates away.

'Even Willard can make a mistake, you know, Erica,' said Lisbet.

Her daughter wheeled on her. 'You've never liked him!'

'I'm not exactly gone on him, that's true. But—'

'Just because some old drunk puts up a silly objection—'

'It's not entirely silly. When I first read the story about the background to the discovery – rescue from a bonfire, papers proving it was sold to a Nazi officer – I couldn't help thinking, How lovely! It's got an almost fairy-tale element about it.'

'But you haven't even *seen* the painting!'

'You have, of course. How often have you seen it, Erica?'

Erica thought about it. 'Four times. No, five.'

'And the first time, so you told me, was on that island hideaway with a lot of romantic trimmings.'

'Oh, for Pete's sake, Mamma, I'm not a fourteen-year-old. I looked at it and I saw a Monet.'

'Have you studied it? Have you really sat down with it and studied it?'

'No, because it's been in Willard's strong-room and now it's at the lab—'

'I understand that. But I'd think you'd want to . . . you know . . . sort of sink yourself into it. Perhaps I'm being silly. It's just that I don't believe Willard is infallible. He could be taken in, just like anybody else. And I don't want your reputation to be damaged if any doubts come up later on.'

They stood together in the quiet domestic setting, knowing that here was the beginning of yet another argument about Erica's love life. Lisbet didn't care for Willard, never had – even before she met him. There were very few art dealers or agents of whom Lisbet had a good opinion. She regarded most of them as parasites or poseurs. And Willard, though respectful of Lisbet's talent, hadn't taken to her.

Sometimes Erica wondered if it was because he'd expected her mother to entrust her work to him for sale. It would have been financially advantageous to him, of that there wasn't a doubt. Erica had mentioned the idea to Lisbet, but Lisbet had said curtly, 'If I must entrust my paintings to someone else, I prefer it to be a friend I've known for thirty years.'

The subject had never been mentioned again. But it was a silent undertone to all the opinions that Lisbet voiced about Willard.

With a great effort Erica forced herself not to leap to Willard's defence. They went on with their task in silence for a few minutes, then she wondered aloud what they should watch on television. They spent the last part of the evening with a happy musical.

Erica found it hard to get to sleep. Lisbet's words kept echoing in her ears. *Have you studied it? Have you really sat down and studied it?*

The answer to that was difficult. She had taken the painting out several times on Parigos, but that had been such a magical episode – the brilliance of the sea, the white *choma* reflecting hard light into the air, the headiness of being alone with Willard for two whole weeks of joy . . .

Had she really looked at the Monet with any serious criticism? Or had it been part of the dream time, part of a wonderland she had not dared to spoil by too much reality?

Next day Erica and her mother had an engagement at a Boxing Day fair. They went there in Lisbet's trusty Land Rover. On the way back through the green countryside glistening under a late winter sun, Lisbet said, 'I'm sorry about what I said last night, Erica. I think that, like Daff, I'd had a bit too much to drink.'

'That's all right.' Erica allowed herself a smile in which there was reflection and recollection. 'We often seem to get on the wrong foot about Willard. I wish you'd just accept, Mamma, that the faults you see in him don't matter to me.'

'I promise not to be such an interfering old grouch. But I do worry about you, maidie.' She took one hand off the wheel to squeeze her daughter's.

'No need. Everything's going fine.'

'Is it? You're sure?' She sighed. 'I made such a bad choice myself – I don't want to see you doing the same thing.'

'There's no chance of that. You always said my father didn't know a Rembrandt from a rocking-horse. Whereas, you know, Willard and I share so many interests, we fit so well together . . .'

'Yes,' agreed Lisbet. If there was still a lack of enthusiasm in her tone, Erica decided to ignore it. It just had to be accepted: her mother was biased against Willard.

Erica had to set out for London by six so as to get a night's sleep before reopening the Corie. As she followed her headlights along the motorway she tried to listen to a talk-radio programme but her own thoughts kept intervening.

The opinions of her mother's friends were troublesome. Not their views about the actual painting, but the rather cruel things they'd said about the provenance. *A lovely yarn. A publicity hand-out.*

Everyone Erica knew in London had read the story and approved it. But that was London. There was a coterie in London who unconsciously set themselves up as the arbiters of everything artistic. They felt they saw everything, knew everything, gave the final verdict on everything.

Elsewhere – outside the metropolitan clique, the chattering classes – were people perhaps less convinced?

Well, that was because they hadn't seen the actual evidence. Notarised statements, the letter preserved with the picture, the handwriting of the former gardener's boy and his manner of expressing himself – it was all there and it was only their unconscious envy of big city life that made them sceptical.

Back and forth went the mental argument.

When she reached home after a long spell in a tailback on the outskirts of London, she was so weary she practically fell into bed. Her last thought was, I must talk to Willard about all this.

But of course, Willard was in New Orleans and intended to stay there for the New Year celebrations. He rang next day from his hotel to give her the news. 'You should see this place, Erica! It's absolutely fantastic! It's a continual party – people break into a dance in the streets at the least provocation – so spontaneous, quite unlike us stuffy Anglo-Saxons.'

'And the book? Did you get the book?'

'No, it went for too high a price.' He didn't seem the least bit downcast. 'Doesn't matter, I'm not a book collector really. Of course there are galleries here, I've had a look, nothing I fancy but it's not art you think about when you're here, it's having a good time. Oh, and speaking of that, how were things in Cornwall?'

'Quiet. Some of Mamma's friends were talking about the Monet and—'

'Even in the farthest reaches of the kingdom, eh? We did well in the newspapers, there's no denying that. It made quite a story even here – one or two people in the galleries recognised my name and I met a biggie at a party who said he wouldn't mind if I looked around for him. But he wants German Romantics. I'd think most of them have been mopped up by now, wouldn't you?' There was a pause, during which she thought she heard him speak to someone else. 'I'm in the hotel lobby, Erica, someone's waiting for me. Got to go!'

'When will you be back, Will?'

'Early Jan, I think, ducky. I'll bring you back a pressie. *Auf wiedersehen* for now, kiss-kiss.'

So even in America the story of the Monet had had exposure and been accepted.

She was worrying about nothing.

All the same, she couldn't quite escape memories of what her mother had said. *Have you studied it? Really sat down and studied it?*

On the fourth of January, a dreary cold day, she took time off from the Corie Gallery to drive out to the laboratory in Andover. There was a small private parking area behind the building. As she got out of her car, whom should she see but Zan McNaughton walking towards her.

She hadn't seen him since the last time she was here. He had parted from her without much ceremony and her calls to his hotel on subsequent occasions had been met with the news that Mr McNaughton was out. She had left her name and number, and though he never returned her calls, a case of wine from McNaughton's Hill had been delivered at the gallery. With it came a card bearing a message: 'Sorry if I seemed a bit grumpy last time we met but I've got a lot on my mind at the moment. Merry Christmas, Zan McN.'

She'd been rather put out. In fact, disappointed. Here was a man who was buying a masterpiece but had something on his mind – the selling of wine to a supermarket.

To find him here was a surprise. Presumably he'd been to check on the progress of the authentication. So perhaps after all he wasn't such a philistine.

'Good morning, Erica,' he called as soon as he was within hailing distance. 'Sorry I haven't been around much lately.' He sounded genuinely pleased to see her.

'Happy New Year,' she returned. 'And thank you for the wine.'

'Tried it yet?'

'Of course! We had a pre-Christmas party in the gallery – everybody enjoyed it very much.'

'I'm glad. I meant what I said on the card – I'm afraid I was a bit preoccupied when we were here last.' He stood at her side as she locked up her car.

'Business problems?'

'What?'

'Something going wrong with the deal about the wine?'

'Oh, that – no, no problem there – that was all done and dusted before I left home, most of it by fax, of course.'

'So what was troubling you, then?'

He hesitated, then said with a shrug, 'A family matter.' Then as if to close that subject he enquired, 'Are you here for anything special?'

'Not really. I just felt that in my "advisory capacity" I should come and take a look.'

'A few more results,' he reported. 'They've identified five layers of paint, which seems to please them a lot – they tell me that was Monet's painting method.'

'Oh, of course – four or five layers, put on to give a textured effect. Anything else?'

'There was something they *didn't* find – no varnish. I thought painters always varnished their finished work? In fact, someone told me that was another name for a first showing – the varnishing.'

She was shaking her head. 'Claude Monet didn't approve

66

of varnish. He didn't want his colours to look shiny on the surface, what he was after was . . . well . . . a sort of inner glow that came from the paint. But all the same, some big galleries put on a thin coat of varnish as a protection.'

'So the fact that there isn't any on my picture says – what?'

'That it's never been in a national collection – that for instance it wasn't stolen from Trafalgar Square.'

'Well, that's a relief,' he acknowledged with an ironic smile. He glanced about at the dreary surroundings and the grey skies. Erica in her bright quilted jacket was the one bright spot. 'Are you in a hurry to get inside and see how far they've got? Or would you like a cup of coffee?'

'That would be nice.' She was pleased by the invitation. She felt she needed to know him better, to find out what lay beneath the quiet businessman's exterior.

'Do you know somewhere? Don't forget I'm a colonial, I don't know my whereabouts.'

'Come with me,' she said, and led him out of the car park and into the side road in which the laboratory was situated. 'Just five minutes' walk away,' she informed him in a conspiratorial whisper, 'is the best-kept secret in the south of England – a bakery where they make old-fashioned wholemeal bread and sultana scones.'

The baker's shop was small, with only a few plastic-topped tables. But it smelt of good things in the oven and when the coffee came, Zan found it was excellent. The scones were still warm from the baking tray, the butter melted as it was spread. It reminded him of the kitchen back home, where Cookie would set out fresh rolls when they came in from their early-morning stint among the vines. Outside was a grey day, inside was a little nest of familiar pleasures, comforting among the troubles that beset him.

'What brought you to the lab today?' he asked Erica.

'Ah . . .' She certainly wasn't going to tell him that her mother had prompted the visit. 'Christmas, you know – it makes a big gap and then you have to try to pick up where you left off.' A thought occurred. 'How did you spend Christmas? Were there festivities in the hotel?'

'Oh, sure, an eight-course Christmas dinner and a tree in the foyer that almost poked through the twenty-foot ceiling. But I wasn't there much.'

'Did you do something nice? Theatre? Sightseeing?'

'I did a short hop up to Scotland and back, just to see the place my folks came from. I generally do that when I'm in the UK. Of course, it's not like it was when they emigrated – ski lifts and things now.'

So was that the 'family matter'? she wondered. 'Do you have snow in New Zealand?' she asked, and immediately realised how inane it sounded. 'Of course you do – you have great big mountains with snow on their peaks.'

He forgave her the blunder with his brief smile. 'A lot of people like to go there for Christmas. There's this folk legend, you see, prompted mostly by Charles Dickens – that it always snows at Christmas and you roast chestnuts on an open fire. It was interesting to see what happens in the land where the legend started – and as far as I could see people mostly went shopping.' He paused a moment. 'What about you? I suppose you and Townley . . .?'

'Oh, Will's abroad.'

'So you've come back on your own?'

'No, actually, I spent the holiday in Cornwall with my mother. Lisbet Pencarreth – you may have heard of her?'

She looked expectant, and he felt foolish at having to shake his head. 'Sorry. She's well known, obviously.'

'Yes, she paints – landscapes mostly.'

'Oh, well, you already know I'm a dunce about painting.' He was apologetic but she had a sudden urge to clear up the point once and for all.

'Please tell me,' she said. 'Why *are* you buying the Monet? Are you thinking of donating it to one of the New Zealand galleries?'

Zan met her earnest gaze. She had pretty blue eyes, and

when she was serious as she was now, they had a lustre like that of a dark sapphire.

'No,' he said carefully, 'I'm not into that sort of thing.'

'Then what sort of thing are you "into"?'

'Why should it matter to you?'

'Because . . .' Her voice faltered and died. She might have said, 'Because my mother urges me to make sure it's a genuine Monet and if you're just going to keep it on a wall at home, perhaps I shouldn't bother. Because, despite what she says, I think it's genuine and I don't want it lost from sight. Because . . . because . . .'

In the end she said, 'I can only tell you that it does matter to me. It'll bother me for the rest of my life if you take it off to the other side of the world and I never hear of it again.'

'Really?'

'Of course.'

He could tell she meant it. Perhaps he was being too cautious about the whole thing. He gained a moment by sipping some coffee then set his cup down squarely in its saucer. 'It's a present,' he announced.

Erica drew in a sharp breath. Some present! Two and three-quarter million pounds' worth.

'Don't you want to know who it's for?' he asked, with a faint surprise at her silence.

She had decided it was for a woman – girlfriend, wife, partner. Men didn't give presents like that except perhaps to relatives, and from what he said, all of the brothers and cousins were outdoor types like himself. His father, perhaps? But she'd got the impression his parents were dead.

She simply sat there, looking at him.

'It's for my kid sister,' he said.

'Your sister!'

'Nyree's mad keen on art. Inherits it from Ma, I suppose. She took down all the pictures Ma had bought from the local talent and had them all tidied up and properly framed a couple of years ago.' There was something touching in his voice, a fond tolerance that Erica found very attractive. 'She used to fly up to Auckland any chance she got,' he went on, 'to roam round the galleries and buy postcards of the paintings she liked best.'

'And you're giving her the Monet?'

He nodded.

'She's . . . she's interested in Impressionists?'

'Certainly is, and especially Monet. She's a real fan.'

A real fan. Good Lord. Erica didn't know what to think. 'Er . . . How old is Nyree?'

'She's twenty.'

Twenty, and about to become the owner of a master work. 'Was that why you wanted the photographs – to let her see what it looked like?'

'That's it.'

'But wouldn't she prefer to have it restored?'

'No – she wants to have it as close as possible to how it was when he finished painting – almost as if it came from his own hands – personally, if you know what I mean. I'm not explaining this very well,' he apologised. 'I can't share that kind of feeling, I suppose. But it's the way she wants it and that's how it's going to be.'

While he was speaking it occurred to her that as Nyree was now twenty, the painting was probably for her twenty-first birthday. In a way that seemed better, but not much. She really couldn't reconcile herself to the notion that a young girl, simply because her family had money, was going to own that painting.

So she was interested in art, and loved the Impressionists. But from the way Zan spoke, it was almost as if she'd been smitten by one of those infatuations that cause fans to collect autographed pin-ups.

She summoned a smile. 'So that's the mystery solved,' she said. 'I really would never have been happy, wondering what was going to happen.'

'Well, it'll be looked after, I can assure you of that. Nyree will treasure it.'

'Yes, of course.' And perhaps would grow out of her obsession with Monet and offer the painting for sale before very long, thought Erica. She rose. 'I must get back to the lab; I've got to be in the gallery this afternoon.'

They retraced their steps. Their conversation seemed to have come to an end. Zan was regretting his admission and Erica was still trying to come to terms with it. Nothing occurred to either of them except remarks about the weather. At the car park they parted, Zan getting into his rented car, Erica hurrying inside to busy herself and avoid thinking about Nyree's present.

Leppard had been expecting her and greeted her with the news of Zan's visit. 'Yes, I met him outside, he's told me of the new results,' she explained. She studied the typed reports for a few minutes and held a discussion with the expert, but in the end confessed that she'd really come just to see the canvas.

'You're not working on it at the moment?' she queried.

'No, we're doing some work with a paint sample. Please, feel free to stay as long as you like.' He unlocked the room in which the painting was standing on an easel, and left her.

Erica raised the venetian blind for better light, but it was a dull day. She switched on one of the studio lamps, and the painting seemed to leap into life.

A rectangle filled with fiery paint. The upper left-hand corner blackened and burnt. Growing out of that, dark reds and browns, what seemed like a jumble of leaves in autumnal tints. An arc across the canvas at about two-thirds of the height, a dark rainbow of ambers and tans and raw sienna. Below it, an imperfect reflection of the arc in the dark waters, roiling with an energy that suggested a high wind whipping the surface. In the foreground on the right, a tall upright, perhaps a tree trunk, closing the pool into itself in all its angry strength.

Everything about it spoke of Monet in the early twenties, when his sight was betraying his colour sense. It was like others she had seen in galleries throughout Europe, like examples in the great Monet exhibition at the Royal Academy.

She switched off the light she'd chosen, switched on another. The surface of the painting altered a little from the new angle of illumination. She leaned forward, eyeing it closely.

It was a Monet. The texture was just what he always ensured by reworking it while the paint was still malleable. The colours were the colours he had seen while his sight was damaged. It was a Monet.

She brought a chair, placed it, and sat in front of the easel at a distance of about four feet. She gazed at the painting. She tried to fill her whole heart and soul with it, to read its message with every fibre of her being.

Burned by its creator, rescued by a gardener's boy, sold for a few Occupation francs, stolen by a Russian invader, brought across the Black Sea for sale in a curio shop . . .

'Tell me,' she whispered. 'Tell me.'

About an hour later, Leppard tapped to ask if she would like to share the sandwich lunch of the lab technicians.

'No, thank you, Maurice, I'm expected back at the gallery.'

He saw her out to the entrance. 'Is anything wrong, Erica?'

'No, nothing, thank you.'

She waved a goodbye and hurried out to her car. She would go back to the Corie Gallery where she would find rich, vibrant paintings to soothe the unease that was creeping into her mind.

Six

The present Willard brought back from New Orleans proved to be a long narrow package wrapped in gold paper. Mystified, Erica unwrapped it, to greet with a cry of delight a parasol such as a Southern belle might have carried in the 1890s – pale blue silk edged with lots of net and lace.

'Oh, it's lovely, Will!' She opened it, to pose in front of the mirror over the mantelpiece in her living-room. 'Looks a bit comic with a sweater and jeans, though.'

'I'm sure we'll find something more appropriate to wear with it before the day is out,' he said with a wink and a smile.

He had rung on reaching his Hampstead flat, to say that he needed a day to get over jet lag but was longing to see her.

'Shall I come on Sunday, then?' she suggested, her heart thudding at the thought.

'No, for a change I'll come to you, love. We'll have an early long lunch and then we'll go for a strenuous walk in your local woods – I need a lot of exercise after the food in New Orleans, I think I've gained ten pounds!'

Which of course was nonsense, for he must have known he looked the same as ever – tallish, impressive in his black silk turtleneck and gabardine slacks, with new alligator shoes on his feet and his black hair slicked back in the style created by a New Orleans barber.

'It *is* so nice to have you back,' Erica cried, kissing him enthusiastically on both cheeks as a thank-you for the parasol. 'Tell me all about it – you said you hadn't seen anything interesting in the galleries—'

'Not interesting to me, but if I ever thought of going in

for Americana there's some stuff worth looking into. Well, perhaps next year.'

He threw himself into an armchair, stretched out, and put his heels on a coffee table in an attitude of total relaxation. Erica smiled upon him. 'Do you want to eat? Everything's ready.'

'Why not? Something simple, I hope – that Cajun food is terribly rich.'

Erica's flat in Gratesford was too small to boast a dining-room so they ate in the kitchen, a pleasant room with a view out over the January back garden. She poured a glass of white wine to go with the chicken and grape salad, and smothered a smile when Willard made appreciative noises – for it was the last bottle of the case of McNaughton's Hill provided by Zan.

For a while they talked about New Orleans. Willard wanted to tell her about some important people he'd met during his stay. After a while he said, 'So how about you? You went down to your mum's for Christmas and did what for New Year?'

'Oh, I took the gallery staff out for a New Year's Eve party and then on New Year's Day itself I drove out to spend the day with some art college friends – they run a framing business in Birmingham now.'

'Sounds delightful,' said Willard with his mouth full. He knew she kept up with all sorts of people. 'Maurice told me you were at the lab a couple of days ago?'

'Oh yes – since I'm being paid a fee to "advise", I thought I'd better see how things were going.'

'As far as I could gather, Maurice is very satisfied with the results.'

'Yes.'

She knew she ought to take this opening. She had some-thing she must say to Willard. But not yet, not now when she had just seen him again after what seemed a lifetime's part-ing. She chose, like a coward, to side-step. 'The insurance transfer has been agreed,' she said. 'The certificate came through yesterday. I told the agent to send it direct to Zan McNaughton.'

'Yes, that's best. Wouldn't do for him to lose a fortune if it got lost like so much luggage when you travel by air.' He sipped some wine. 'When's he going back to the farm?'

She looked down to hide a frown at his words. Somehow it seemed wrong to speak of Zan as if he were a mere bumpkin. 'I've no idea. No date has ever been mentioned. He did say he had some family business to see to.'

'You'd think he'd want to get back to the grapes – surely they need spraying or pruning or something. Let's see, it's January here so it's the equivalent of July down there – harvest time soon, wouldn't you say? He'll need to be home for that.'

'Perhaps not. He told me he had brothers and cousins who help with the vineyard.'

'Oh, Lord, an entire clan of them! Just imagine what they'll say, Erica, when he shows them the Monet! "That's a funny souvenir of London, cobber" – or do they only use "cobber" in Australia?' He laughed at the imaginary scene.

'I think they know all about it,' she demurred. 'There is such a thing as the telephone, Will. He says they talk almost every day.'

He raised dark eyebrows at her. 'My word! I hope you're not taking this consultancy too seriously? You sounded quite protective just then.'

'Well . . . I don't think you should look down on him so much, just because he doesn't know about paintings.'

Willard laid down his fork and knife. He leaned back in his chair to study Erica. She seemed to have got on quite cosy terms with McNaughton while he was away. That, of course, was no bad thing. She would lead this unexpected buyer quietly through the rigmarole of authentication and then the money, held as a promissory bond at the bank, would be made over at last. If she'd decided to befriend the man, it was no bad thing.

'You're quite right. I apologise to Mr McNaughton.' Laughing, he held up his wine glass as if in a toast. 'Here's to Mr McNaughton and his winery and all who drink in her. But come on, Erica, where does he intend to hang his Monet? In the wine-tasting room, perhaps, to give it a touch of class?'

'It's a birthday present for his sister,' Erica blurted out.

'What?' Well, that was unexpected. 'For a *sister*?'

'I think it's a twenty-first birthday.'

'And where's *she* going to hang it?' he enquired, amused again. 'Over her make-up mirror?' Then, seeing that Erica wasn't inclined to share the joke, he went on, 'I'm amazed you got him to tell you. Why didn't he say all this at the outset instead of making a mystery of it?'

'I think he's the sort of man who doesn't . . . well, he's not talkative about himself or his private affairs. And you know, Will, when you look back – there was a lot of fanfare about the Monet. I imagine he just didn't want his family involved in all that.'

'Perhaps. Well, there you are – quite a simple explanation when you get to it.' He pushed away his plate. 'Let's go out for this walk, eh? It's clouding over.'

They put on coats and scarves, Willard flourishing the fine cashmere scarf she'd given him for Christmas – black, of course, with only the faintest edging of white. They drove in Erica's sturdy little Mitsubishi to the edge of the National Trust woods then set off at quite a brisk pace on the upland walk. There was a keen wind bringing cloud across the edge of the North Downs, and the trees were leafless now except for a few tawny scraps still clinging to the birches.

'Quite Rowland Hilderish,' Willard observed. 'What's your mother painting these days?'

'She's dabbing about with a coastal study, but she's just finished a series on the tin mines. I think she just shipped them off to her agent – four canvases. I gather he's got people lining up for them, someone even in New York is champing at the bit to see them.'

'New York,' he said with a sigh. 'That's where the money is.'

'Oh, I don't know, Will. You didn't do so badly last year.'

'Towards the end . . . yes . . . Thank heaven for that little curio shop in Istanbul.'

They walked for a while in silence. This was her opening, and she hesitated yet again, but braced herself. The question must be asked.

'Will? Have you ever had any doubts?'

'About what?'

'About the Monet.'

He stopped short so abruptly that she was half a step ahead of him and had to turn back. There was a look of absolute astonishment on his narrow face.

'Doubts? Never,' he said after an indrawn breath.

They stood on the path through the leafless trees, staring at one another. He frowned. 'What brought this on?'

'Well . . . you know, at home with Mamma . . . a bunch of her friends came in on Christmas Day and they got talking. One of them said . . . he argued for quite a while . . . he said the provenance sounded a bit too . . . I don't know . . . like something a publicity man might dream up.'

'And who was this expert on the history of Impressionism, pray?'

'Well . . . I don't suppose he's much of an expert, really . . . It was Daff – I think you met him once while we were down there.'

'What, the flower painter?'

'Yes, but others said—'

'So, because some rustic wannabe starts arguing you get bothered?'

'It wasn't just that. Mamma—'

'Oh, I might have known Mamma came into this somewhere!' Willard cried. 'Your mother never loses an opportunity to take a jab at me!'

'But it wasn't quite like that, Will.'

'So what was it "quite like"? She spent an hour or two telling you how highly she valued me and was delighted I'd found a master work?'

'Will, please don't be angry. She said something that was perfectly justified. She asked me if I'd sat down and studied the canvas – and you know what? I realised I never had.'

'Oh, for God's sake, Erica! You had it out of that cupboard in the cottage half a dozen times.'

'But I don't think I was *studying* it, Will. I was just enjoying it, enjoying the fact that you were so thrilled with it. I don't think there was any critical aspect to it.' She leaned towards him, willing him to understand the difference she was trying to describe. 'I think I let myself be carried away by the romance of it all.'

'But the others – Sir John, Dewey Davis, Professor Gothe . . . ? They're not romantic!'

'No, but . . . but . . .'

'Now this is absurd, Erica! Four other critics, you yourself, and me – after all, chicken, I'm not exactly a fool, now am I?'

'You're a very able judge, Will, and I feel awful about saying this, but . . . do you think you might have been wrong?'

'*No!*' He had coloured up with anger. 'How dare you? I knew that was a Monet as soon as I saw it. And all the evidence – the chain of ownership, the letter from the gardener—'

'Will, someone who can forge a painting can easily forge a letter.'

She saw the anger mount to something like rage. 'Are you saying I was made a fool of?'

'No – I didn't mean – I'm sorry, Will, I didn't mean to upset you—'

'Upset me? What the devil did you think you would do, coming up with this load of nonsense? All of a sudden you have suspicions that the painting's a fraud – well, where's your evidence?'

She flinched under the lash of his tongue. 'I don't have any.'

'No, by God you don't! Maurice has been examining that canvas since December and everything he comes up with justifies my judgement that it's a Monet.'

'That's true – scientifically it all hangs together – but don't you see, Will,' she urged, clasping her hands together as if in supplication, 'it's easy to get French linen of that period, it's around everywhere in cupboards in Parisian studios. And Claude Monet used the same kind of paints we use today, except that he soaked out the linseed oil. And—'

'That's enough! Stop and think what you're saying, Erica. All this work and for what? To get fifteen hundred pounds from a tourist in Istanbul? Because that's all I paid. You saw the bill of sale yourself.'

'Will, fifteen hundred pounds is maybe an awful lot of money to a shopkeeper in an Istanbul back street.' She longed not to have to keep on arguing but she felt she must put all the points that had been nagging at her since her visit to Cornwall. 'Besides – perhaps it's not the only "Monet" that shopkeeper has sold.'

'*What?*'

'Think about it. Tourists poke about in the little shops looking for finds that they can show off to their friends when they get home. The shopkeeper draws their attention to the painting that might be a Monet. You know, some of them might pay a lot more than fifteen hundred pounds for a thing like that.'

Willard gave a wrathful smile. 'You're saying there are half a dozen "Monets" kicking round Europe that were bought in that shop?'

'It's possible.'

'So where are they? Why have they never turned up?'

She hesitated. 'Perhaps when the purchasers tried to get authentication, the experts said no.'

'Ha!' It was a cry of triumph. 'So why didn't any of them come forward when there was all the publicity about *my* Monet?'

That silenced her. All at once the foolishness of her suspicions came like a wave to overwhelm her. She stood with a hand up to her face as if to hide the shame she felt.

'I'm sorry,' she faltered. 'It was silly of me . . .'

'Silly? It's downright treacherous! How dare you build up a smear like this against me?' He swerved away from her and began to walk back the way they'd come.

'Will – wait—'

'I've nothing more to say to you,' he said over his shoulder, walking even faster as if to get rid of her.

She hurried in his wake. As they stepped out of the shelter of the wood the first drops of the threatening rain began to fall. When they reached the Mitsubishi Willard was a little ahead of her. He stood by the passenger door staring into

79

space. She released the door catches and as she opened the driver's door he said, over the roof of the vehicle: 'Have you said any of this to anyone else?'

'Of course not!'

'To McNaughton?'

'No, no – I—'

'Thank God for that,' he remarked, and got into the car.

Not another word was spoken on the short drive to her street. He got out of the Mitsubishi, went to his own car, and got in.

She was still in her own car. Fumbling with her seat belt, she began to get out, calling in despair: 'Will!' But before she could set both feet on the ground his engine was running and he was driving away, without a glance in her direction.

She sank back in her seat. For a long time she simply sat there, the driver's door open to allow in the cold wind carrying drops of rain. Her cheeks were wet but whether from the raindrops or from tears, she couldn't have told.

She was roused by another resident of her block of flats, who drove up to the kerb behind her. 'Miss Pencarreth? Is something wrong?'

'What? Oh, no – nothing – thank you.' She put the car in motion, drove it round the back to its garage, and locked it in. She entered by the back door, slowly climbed the stairs, and went into her flat. Without taking off the bright jacket, she sank on to a chair.

What had she done?

For some foolish notion of her mother's she had thrown away the most important thing in her life.

Darkness fell. Still she sat unmoving. The heating clicked on, and after a while she was uncomfortable in her padded jacket. She rose to her feet, hung the jacket in the hall, went into the living-room and switched on the light.

The parasol leaped into view, its frills and lace a shrill comment on the collapse of the day. She picked it up and threw it across the room. It hit a table lamp, bringing it crashing down in a clatter of broken glass as the bulb smashed.

She walked on into the kitchen, where the remains of lunch waited to be cleared up. She put the crockery and silver in the dishwasher, threw the uneaten food in the waste bin, put away the salt shaker and the pepper grinder.

Then she came upon the empty wine bottle on the worktop. She picked it up. McNaughton's Hill, she saw on the label, with an engraving of a four-square house built into the side of a hill clad with a few trees. She felt a surge of fierce anger. It was because of *him* that she had quarrelled with Will. If he'd never come into their lives, they would never have disagreed.

But as quickly as it came, the anger went. Zan McNaughton was innocent – innocent in every sense. He knew nothing about painting, and had turned to her for expert advice. He knew nothing about the silly doubts she'd suddenly experienced and would never hear of them. It was she herself who was to blame: she was an imbecile, a tactless bungler, and arrogant in imagining she knew better than Will and his fellow experts.

Very carefully she put the empty wine bottle in the waste bin. She went into the living-room and sat in an armchair. 'Oh, you fool,' she groaned, and began to cry in earnest.

Eventually she fell asleep, worn out by emotion. The bell of the local church tolling evensong roused her. She dragged herself to her feet, astonished that she had managed to doze, went into the bathroom and looked at herself in the mirror. Red-rimmed eyes, puffy face, hair pushed up into a tangle by the back of the armchair. She dashed water on her face, combed her hair, and went to the telephone.

Willard wouldn't speak to her, she knew that. But she must try.

She got his answering machine. She didn't dare ask him to pick up if he was there. She said, 'I'm sorry, Will. I don't know why I said all those stupid things this afternoon. I must have been out of my mind. Say you forgive me – please, please, say you forgive me.'

Late into the night she went on hoping for a response from him but it didn't come. It wasn't until midday next day in her office that she heard his voice on the phone. 'We've got to talk,' he said without introduction.

'Yes, of course.'

'Let's meet somewhere neutral. The wine bar in Edgware, eight o'clock tonight.'

This was a place they used as a halfway house when they wanted to meet for just a drink and a chat. 'Yes, I'll be there.'

'Right.' And that was all.

She went through the rest of the day in a daze. After work she looked through her wardrobe trying to make up her mind what to wear, half ashamed of herself for thinking it mattered. She had a foolish idea that she ought to look penitent and of course black was suitable for penitents but she never wore black when she was with Willard. In the end she put on a grey suit and dark red jersey – and thought she looked mousy, and miserable, and too pale, but what did it matter?

Willard was already there when she got to the wine bar. She took the place beside him and when the waiter came ordered mineral water. Willard waited until it was brought.

'Now,' he said, 'let's get this straight. Who else knows about these daft ideas of yours?'

'No one.'

'Your mother?'

'No.'

'I thought you said she had doubts about the painting.'

'No, she just asked me if I'd really studied it, and so after a bit I did.'

He nodded. 'Maurice Leppard told me you'd shut yourself up with it for over an hour the other day. Is that when you got carried away by your theories?'

'I just felt . . . I just felt, then, that it wasn't "right".'

He sighed in exasperation, leaning back in the booth. The last thing an art dealer ever wants to hear about a master work is that it isn't 'right'. That means trouble. That means it has been tampered with, inexpertly restored, retouched by a Victorian censor because it was originally too erotic, is wrongly attributed, belongs to 'the school of', was finished by a lesser painter when the master grew tired of it, or is an out-and-out fake.

'How can you say that?' he demanded. 'The rest of us approve it, you're one against five. And you yourself were convinced it was a Monet from the moment you first saw it.'

'I know, I know – and I can't explain it. I see now I was an idiot.'

'It looks like a Monet, the subject and the technique belong in the right place in his career, all the scientific tests bear out that it belongs to the right period and uses the right materials, so what wasn't "right" about it?'

'I don't know . . . Something . . . It was the rhythm of the brushwork.'

'But the brushwork is typically Monet.'

'Yes, I realise I was wrong. I just thought for a bit – while I was sitting there with it in front of me, "speaking" to me – I'm sorry, Will, I got carried away.'

'You got carried straight off – to the loony bin,' he said.

'I know,' she said, contrite.

'So you admit you were wrong.'

'Yes.'

For the first time since she had sat down beside him, the expression on his face seemed to relent a little.

'It's this chap McNaughton,' he said. 'You've got quite involved with him.'

'No, not particularly—'

'Oh yes, the helpless amateur – he played that card with you right from the beginning. And you, of course – soft-hearted and always ready to help a lame duck – you fell for it.'

'How can you say that, Will? I've only ever met him three or four times.'

'He was there at the lab that day – Maurice said he was. Had he asked you to come, because he had some doubts . . . ?'

'Not at all, it was pure chance. He was coming out as I arrived and we went for coffee, that was all. It was over coffee that he told me the painting was for his sister.'

'Some horsy little nobody from the New Zealand bush.'

'Oh, Will, you don't know what she's like so how can you—' She broke off, not wishing to annoy him. But justice forced her to say, 'I gather she's quite artistic. He says she goes to galleries a lot. He talked about her in a very nice way, called her his kid sister.'

'Oh, I can practically hear the violins!' Will exclaimed. 'Twenty-one years old and gets to own a Monet! Do you really imagine she's going to know a Monet from a Morisot? Don't make difficulties where none exist – that girl would be convinced without any official authentication that my painting is a two-and-three-quarter-million Impressionist.'

'No, you don't understand – she's particularly interested in Monet, longs to own something that he himself has handled.' She felt she had to add that the girl did seem a bit of a romantic. 'Zan said she was a "fan" – perhaps it's not a very fastidious word to use but you can understand her feelings.'

'So you felt you had to tell him that the painting hadn't been handled by Monet, is that it – that it was a fake?'

'No, no, of course not, Will – it wasn't as strong a feeling as that, I wouldn't ever have said anything to anybody until I'd talked it through with you.'

'So now you've done that, haven't you. And you see how wrong you were.'

'Yes.'

'And you'll stop being sentimental and silly about this hayseed McNaughton.'

'Yes.'

'Good.'

'I'm truly sorry, Will.'

'You're forgiven,' he said, and put an arm round her, so as to bring her close and drop a kiss of pardon on her hair. 'Let's get out of here.'

So the evening ended with reconciliation and love-making and all was well again.

Except that two days later she began to feel she'd been overpowered, almost blitzkrieged. Her chief impulse to question the painting had come from a feeling that there was something about the brushwork – but Willard had almost ignored that aspect of her doubt. He had concentrated on the scientific evidence, the practical points, whereas her uncertainty had been caused by a matter of instinct, of inner judgement. True, she was still in a minority of one among the experts. All the same . . .

She went back to the laboratory to look again at the painting, forced by the inner voice that insisted, You're not sure. There was *something* – perhaps she was imagining it, since the others seemed not to see it, but her heart still misgave her as she turned away from the easel.

What should she do? Should she do anything? After all, as Will said, this girl probably wouldn't know the difference. If all the evidence supported the story that this was a genuine Monet, who was Erica to make a fuss? Offend the other experts, quarrel with Willard, cause him a tremendous loss of prestige and money . . .

February was coming, and she was immersed in preparations for a small special exhibit for the week of St Valentine's. One of the contributors made an appointment to hand over some drawings by Renoir and chose as a meeting place the Mayfair Rialto. Erica tried to avoid it, because that was where Zan McNaughton was staying, but the contributor insisted, 'Oh, I really want to go there, I hear they've got a marvellous new chef.' At this broad hint Erica had to offer lunch, which lasted longer than she would have wished, and as she was crossing the foyer on leaving, Zan McNaughton walked in.

'Why, hello!' he exclaimed on seeing her. 'What are you doing here?'

'Escaping from a tiresome patron of the arts,' she said.

'Oh, that's a let-down! I was hoping you'd come to see me.'

Standing there in the hotel foyer, face to face, his smile open on seeing her, and yet with a certain air of weariness assuaged by meeting a friend . . . She felt a stab of remorse. She was his 'consultant', the expert he was paying to guide him through the intricacies of owning a master work. It was downright dishonest not to give him some idea of her misgivings. He might laugh it off, tell her not to bother.

'Are you busy?' she inquired.

'Well . . . no, as a matter of fact.'

'Could you give me a few minutes? There's something I'd like to talk about.'

He glanced at his watch. 'Come and have afternoon tea.'

'Oh, I've just finished lunch—'

'Come and watch *me* have afternoon tea, then,' he said. 'I love it here. They bring on a silver teapot and a little strainer for the tea-leaves, and eensy-weensy sandwiches with no crusts.'

He went to the porter's desk to leave a valise he was carrying, so she too left the carrier containing the Renoir drawings. They went into the lounge, where the waiter on duty greeted him with a smile of recognition. They were shown to a favoured spot by the window, although the view was only of a paved courtyard with potted shrubs under a cold winter sky.

Zan sat down in the armchair with a sigh. It hadn't been a good day. But in fact few of the days since he came to London had been good. To see Erica Pencarreth was a boon. There was something about her that made him feel better.

'What have you been doing today?' she asked, making conversation. 'Something interesting?'

He shrugged, not wanting to remember.

'Not enjoyable,' she said, looking at him with sudden attention. 'Is something wrong?'

'Well, I've just – Oh, never mind, why should I burden you with it?'

Because you've nobody else on this side of the world to talk to, she said to herself, with an understanding that came instinctively. 'Tell me,' she urged. 'You've had bad news?'

'The worst.'

'About business?'

'Oh, business – if only it were as easy as that.'

'About your family back home?'

'No, my kid sister. She's here, you know. In London.'

Erica was totally astonished. 'But you never said . . . Is she here at the hotel with you?'

'She's in hospital,' he said. And at saying the words out loud, there was the sensation that some of the burden was lifted from his back.

Erica put out her hand across the little table as if to take his. She drew it back, but he felt as if they had touched.

'They've been doing tests,' he explained. 'She goes in for a few days and then comes out, and then I take her around and we try to make out everything's fine, but today they told me . . . My little sister has something they're not sure they can cure.'

Seven

Nyree had seemed easily tired over Christmas of last year. The usual family parties hadn't appealed to her so much, she'd gone to bed quite early while the music was still playing downstairs. Hogmanay, as always, she'd stayed up to see the new year in but hadn't wanted to go first-footing next day.

Cookie, the McNaughtons' housekeeper and cook, gave the old-fashioned opinion that she was 'outgrowing her strength'. But when she didn't improve Cookie took her to the local GP. Anaemia, he said, and prescribed iron tablets: a six-week supply and then-come-back-and-see-me. Quite an improvement, but then she seemed to go back to what their brother Jason called her 'droopy mode'.

Back to the doc. More iron tablets, different variety. This time, no great improvement, and it was mid-summer by now. The doc sent her to the hospital in Christchurch, who sent her on to a specialist in Auckland, who pondered and hugged his chin and said he thought she should see a colleague of his in London.

'She knew it was something serious,' Zan said. 'She's no fool, my kid sister. She didn't want to make such a big trip all on her own, and anyhow I had this deal coming off with the supermarkets and all that, so we decided to make a real junket of it. We decided on a sort of Slow-Boat-to-Europe sort of thing – she's never liked flying, even just to Wellington or Auckland. And the doctors said the sea voyage might do her good. So we went the long haul and took cruise ships with stops at cities where we could go ashore and spend a few days. She went to galleries in Sydney and Nice and Paris and snooped around the fashion stores while I went to vineyards

to sample the opposition. We got here at the end of October.'
He nodded at the remains of afternoon tea between them.
'The travel agent recommended this hotel. All the comforts
of home. A bit fancy but it's not bad.'

'Was the sea trip any help at all?'

He shrugged. 'Who knows? Some of the time, she was all
enthused at being in these great places – I tell you no lie, we
probably would never have gone to most of them if it hadn't
been this special sort of journey. Almost as soon as we got to
London, the news broke about the Monet. There were colour
photographs in the Sunday supplements and this marvellous
account of how the artist wouldn't give up painting even
though he could hardly see.' He smiled in recollection.
'Nyree said, "He's *my* kind of painter," and I thought, why
shouldn't she have it? I mean . . . you know . . .' His voice
died away into silence.

Erica understood all too well. It might perhaps be the last
present he would ever give her – this special twenty-first
birthday present at the end of this special journey.

'I talked about it with the folks at home,' he resumed. 'Of
course it's a lot of money, the price we're going to pay, but –
this is a business view, you understand – if I bought it without
having the restoration done, it was a lot less than the sort of
money it might fetch when it was tidied up. And Jayce and
Heck and Cookie and everybody thought we should do it
because we're not short of a bob or two. These last six years
or so have really been good for us. And when I told Nyree
I'd put in a bid for it . . . well, if you could have seen her
face . . .'

'I can just imagine,' Erica murmured.

'She says she has what she calls an affinity with Monet,'
he explained, looking apologetic. 'I know that sounds high-
flown but she's always been a funny kid, our Nyree. She says
it's because he was a fighter. And it's true, *she's* fighting too.
So we wanted her to have the painting and I only hope it's
not going to take too long to do all these tests and things
because, you know, I may have to call a halt to that if things
get hairy.'

'I'll tell Maurice Leppard to hurry things along.'

'I'd be obliged if you would.'

'If you'd said at the outset that there was some urgency—'

'Oh, Lord, I wasn't going to let on about Nyree – there was a sort of three-ring circus going on and can you just imagine how the press would have loved it? "Monet for Poor Sick Sister" – and Nyree gets newspapers in the hospital, you know, she'd have thrown her bedside cabinet at me if I'd let that happen.' He glanced at his watch. 'I'm sorry, I have to move on. I've things to do' – he jerked his head towards the opening to the foyer – 'that bag I came in with, that's Nyree's laundry, they do it for her here at the hotel. I have to go back this evening with some things she wants.'

'Is there anything I can do?'

'No, thanks.' He broke off. 'Well, perhaps there might be – I'm no good at some of the things she asks. Lipstick, for instance – a couple of days ago she said her lipstick didn't go with her pale complexion – I ask you! But I found another one among some stuff she'd bought in Paris.'

'I'd be only too glad – any time.'

'Well, thanks, that's good of you.' They rose, making for the exit. He paused in recollection. 'You said you wanted to speak to me?'

'Oh, some other time, it isn't anything really.' Now was not the moment to start casting doubt on the authenticity of the Monet. He'd had enough bad news for one day and by comparison what she had to say was unimportant. Instead she suggested, 'I have some books on art . . . Would you like to have them for Nyree?'

'Oh, I couldn't—'

'It's all right, I have shelves full of them. I'll drop them here at the desk, shall I?'

'Well, that's really kind. Thanks a lot.'

'And look – you have my telephone number at the gallery but just a minute—' She got her diary out of her handbag, scribbled her mobile phone number on a blank page, tore it out and gave it to him. 'Any time you need help buying anything girlish – just give me a call.'

He took the piece of paper. He felt at a loss for words, especially after a day like this, when the long conversation

90

with the specialist had been so full of dread. 'You're a gem,' he said.

'Bye for now.' She nodded farewell then moved off to the exit. He for his part went to wait for a lift. He turned to watch her go through the revolving doors. Yes, you're a gem, he thought.

Erica scarcely noticed the discomfort of the commuter crowd on the train to Gratesford. She was deep in thought about Zan McNaughton and his sister.

'Some horsy little nobody' – that had been Willard's phrase for Nyree. He couldn't have been more wrong. She was a brave, stalwart spirit, fighting against an insidious disease, far from home, with only one person to turn to, a brother who loved her but confessed himself out of his depth.

Erica felt shame that she had ever allowed Willard to say such things. Well, she had in fact protested, but not very loudly. She ought to have challenged his views: she ought to do that more often because, as she thought about it, she began to feel she sometimes allowed herself to be dominated.

Willard was a wonderful man – very clever, brought up from childhood to understand and love art, and therefore very experienced in that respect. He had charisma, he had good looks, he had charm, and as a lover he moved her to the very depths of her physical being.

In fact, if you thought about it, he seemed to have everything. So why was it that he was sometimes so sharp to people with fewer gifts? Why did he speak of the artistic community in Cornwall as a bunch of 'wannabes'? Why had he been so dismissive of Zan and his sister from the outset?

She shook her head to herself. If Willard had a fault, it was perhaps that he was ungenerous. She felt somehow that it was up to her to compensate for the lack of consideration he'd shown to the McNaughtons. And that might be difficult, because the circumstances were so poignant. Should she offer to befriend Nyree? As she'd gathered from Zan, the girl was in and out of hospital at the moment, undergoing tests. When she was at liberty to go about London, might Erica offer to take her to galleries? Show her some interesting shopping places – Camden Passage, perhaps, or Covent Garden?

And she ought to do something for Zan himself. How solitary, how desolate, alone in a hotel which, however well run, must be impersonal. She could invite him out for a meal at the sort of restaurant he might enjoy. With a pang, she remembered Christmas – it had never even occurred to her but she could have invited him down to Cornwall.

Unhappy with herself, she dropped by the Corie Gallery to lock away the Renoir drawings, then walked home. There were messages on her answering machine, one from Willard to say he was 'hopping over to Paris' for a day or two, and one from her mother. She returned that call.

'I thought I'd let you know that the first daffodils are out here,' Lisbet said when they'd exchanged greetings.

'Already? And it's so chilly and dull here!'

'Come down for the weekend, maidie. It's sunny and relatively mild in my neck of the woods.'

'I'd love to, Mamma, but I can't do that for a bit. I've got this St Valentine's exhibit to do—'

'But that's only one room, it can't take up much time.'

'Well, I'd rather be in London for a bit, if you really want to know. There's this man who's buying the Monet.'

'The man from New Zealand? What about him?'

'I happened on him this afternoon, we had a long talk. Mamma, it turns out he's in the UK to be with his sister, who's desperately ill.'

'Really? I thought you told me it was a business trip.'

'That too, but it's not the important thing. And the Monet – all the guesses that Willard and I made about why he wants it were all wrong. It's Nyree, his sister, who wants it – and he's buying it for her because . . . well, because . . .'

'You don't have to spell it out, Erica, I understand.' Lisbet was silent for a moment. 'What a terrible thing. Poor child. Have you met her?'

Erica poured out what she'd learned that afternoon about Nyree and Zan. 'And the thing is, Mamma, I feel such a worm for the way he's been treated—'

'Not by you, baby. You may have a lot of faults but you've always had good manners.' She gave a little laugh. 'I expect to get shot down for saying so, but if anyone's treated him badly it's been Willard.'

'We-ell . . .'

'You don't mean to tell me you're actually agreeing?'

Erica hesitated a long moment and then decided to ask her mother's opinion. After all, who else could she turn to?

'Will and I had a big row at the weekend,' she began. 'It was about the painting.'

'The famous Monet? Why was that?'

'I did what you suggested. I went and really studied it. And . . . Mamma . . . I don't think it's "right".'

Lisbet gave a gasp. 'Oh, help,' she muttered.

'You said it. Oh help. I just had this sort of prickle at the back of my neck when I'd looked at it a bit. I'm in a minority of one, of course, but I feel something isn't "right" about the brushwork. There's a big section where the bridge is reflected in the water and somehow . . . I don't know . . . just there, it's too . . . too slack, it hasn't got his rhythm.'

'Ah,' sighed Lisbet, 'water can be the very devil to paint! So you said that to Willard and he bit your head off.'

'Yes.' Erica sighed in her turn.

'Well, you can't expect a man – and especially an art dealer – to be pleased when you're snatching several millions from under his nose.'

'You don't understand,' protested Erica, living that scene again. 'While we were arguing, it was almost as if he didn't care whether it was a genuine Monet or not. He said things about Nyree that were a sort of justification for selling her what might turn out not to be "right".'

'His reputation is on the line, of course. It doesn't do an art dealer any good to be sold a pup. He's *got* to believe it's genuine. Dealers are like that, they hype a thing up so they believe in a dicey provenance and convince everybody else. I take it Willard tried to convince *you* to hold your tongue.'

'It wasn't quite like that. I was so upset at how things went that I apologised and retracted – and now I feel so guilty because that poor girl is longing to hold a real Monet in her hands and this one . . . I don't know . . .'

They both fell silent for a moment. Then Lisbet said,

'What exactly are you saying, Erica? That it's a painting from around the same period as Monet, perhaps by an admirer or a friend – or that it's an intentional forgery?'

'I don't know. And to tell the truth, for a few days after I first had this feeling, I didn't *want* to know. But now that I've heard the reason why Zan McNaughton is buying it . . . things are different.'

'I can see that. What are you going to do?'

'I thought I ought to tell him. I was all set to tell him this afternoon but we got sidetracked into the tale of Nyree's illness. What do you think?'

'He has a right to know, my love.'

So, thought Erica to herself as she set about getting her evening meal, she ought to take the first opportunity. She would take the art books to his hotel tomorrow evening – she'd include a note saying she had to talk to him. She had to do it face to face: it wasn't the kind of thing you could do on the telephone.

About nine o'clock her mobile rang. Thinking it might be Willard from Paris, she darted to her handbag to find it. When the caller spoke, it turned out to be Zan.

'I hope this isn't too late to be calling,' he began.

'Not at all, glad to hear you. Is anything wrong?' she added for after all it was late-ish and he had been to the hospital for evening visiting.

'No, it's just that I wanted to take you up on that book offer. I told Nyree about it and she was absolutely thrilled. You know, I got her some magazines from a posh bookshop and she liked those, but they were mostly about recent exhibitions and auctions. Background stuff, that's what she wants, she says she wants to learn as much as she can about the how and the who.'

Erica smiled to herself. There spoke a true enthusiast. 'I've got a thick book about Monet I could lend her, and a very good paperback about the Impressionists in general.'

'Yes, that sounds just right. So she was going on about when would she get them and I let myself be trapped into saying I'd bring them tomorrow.'

'That's do-able. I can bring them to the hotel in time for you to take them in the evening.'

'I was wondering . . . could I come to the Corie Gallery tomorrow morning and collect them? That way I could take them in to her in the afternoon.' He gave a wry laugh. 'She has to hang about a lot for tests and scans – they put her into a wheelchair and sit her outside the room with the equipment and an hour can go by, and she gets so bored . . . She has a low boredom threshold, my kid sister.'

'That would be fine,' Erica said. 'What time would you be coming?'

'I usually pay a short visit in the morning so I could some straight on to Gratesford from St John's Wood . . . How about elevenish?'

'Come a bit later and I'll take you to lunch in one of those English pubs you found so interesting. Cottage pie and a pint of bitter.'

'Sounds great.'

He arrived bearing a bouquet from the hotel florist – a bunch of daffodils beautifully arranged with hazel twigs and a yellow bow. She accepted them with a pleasure tinged perhaps with some apprehension. This wasn't going to be an entirely happy occasion.

She took him on a tour of the gallery. He was an attentive listener as she recounted the selection of the paintings from the Corie bequest, the reasons for her choices, the problem of lighting them, a little about the technical side of the storage in the cellars of the old house, now installed with perfect air-conditioning.

'So it's more than just keeping them on the walls and keeping the burglars out,' he remarked. He was impressed: she was no head-in-the-air, that was clear. And a lot less grandiose than her chum Townley.

'Nyree would love this,' he remarked. 'There was a gallery in Paris full of stuff like this, I could hardly get her away from it but she got so tired she could hardly walk.'

'You'll have to bring her here next time she's in circulation.'

The invitation brought him to the present with a bump. 'I

don't know,' he replied, 'they seem to think they've at last identified the version of the disease – something obscure and difficult, trust Nyree not to be ordinary! They're saying she ought to start treatment soon.'

She could tell he dreaded the thought. 'But that's good,' she ventured. 'The sooner the treatment begins, the sooner she's going to get better.'

'Maybe.' He gave a final glance at the glowing colours on the gallery walls. 'She has to see this. It's just her kind of thing.'

Erica got her coat, asked the senior member of the gallery staff to see to things in her absence, briefed Suzi over taking messages, and led the way out by a back door. They were almost immediately in the car park. 'It's just a short walk,' she said and continued out by a postern gate into a side lane.

The Bull was a simple place with a simple menu but the food was home-cooked and there was always an open fire in the dining-room except in July and August. Zan looked about him with amazement. The accounts he'd had from grandparents – which he'd always though were somewhat idealised – seemed after all to be true. He let his hostess choose the food and drink, watching the few other lunch guests tuck into enormous platefuls of food. 'Seems to be tasty stuff,' he observed.

'I hope you like it. We could have gone to one of the restaurants more in the centre of the town but this is a quiet place.' And I have something to say to you that needs a quiet place, she added mentally.

When the dessert menu was presented and they both opted for coffee, it seemed time to begin. 'You remember there was something I was going to tell you yesterday?' she said.

'What? Oh yes – but I was yakking so much I never let you get round to it.'

'I'm going to tell you now. And before I start I want to warn you that this is only an opinion – *my* opinion, and I may be wrong.'

'About what?' He sat up straight in his chair, studying her. This was serious, he could tell.

'There may be something wrong with the Monet.'

'Wrong?'

'"Not right" – that's a term we use when we get worried about a painting.'

'Meaning that it may be gash gear?'

She gave a half smile. 'I think that's it. I'm worried in case your Monet isn't genuine.'

'But . . . but . . .' She let him flounder on for a while but he pulled himself together to say in the end, 'All the tests and things – they rate it as OK, don't they?'

'Yes, they do. And so do the other people that Willard asked for an evaluation.'

'So it's you, then, is it? Just you that says there's something wrong?'

'Just me.'

'Townley doesn't agree?'

'On the contrary, Will is quite certain it's authentic.'

He sat shaking his head. It was too much to take in all at once. 'What brought this on?' he inquired.

She took him through the process of her own doubt, starting with Daff at her mother's Christmas gathering and her own personal view of the canvas. She insisted again that she was alone in her opinion.

'But all those other bigwigs – they approve of the picture?'

'Ye-es . . . But they're all friends of Will's, you see. They're unconsciously biased in his favour. And the fact that I was the first to claim it as a discovery – you see, Impressionists are my daily bread, so if I declare it's "right", that puts everybody else at a disadvantage if they think of disagreeing.'

'Hm . . .' Mighty lucky for Townley that one of the foremost experts on Impressionism was not only his friend but his lover. But he put that aside as spiteful. 'So now you've changed your mind.'

'Not completely. I'm worried, that's all.'

'Because a bit of the brushwork doesn't come up to scratch.'

She laughed. 'Neatly put.'

'Well, you know I'm not up to all the jargon,' he apologised. Their coffee came. They were silent until the waitress had left them. 'If it isn't a real Monet,' he said rather grimly, 'Nyree's being taken for a ride.'

'Yes.' She felt herself colour up at the words. She knew she wasn't blameless in that regard. 'She wants to feel some contact with the painter – what did you say, she has an affinity?'

'Something like that.'

'If this isn't a Monet there's no affinity. Quite the opposite, there's what amounts to an insult.'

This is costing her something, Zan told himself. Her own reputation is going to suffer if she's right, and as to Townley . . .

'What would you do if you were in my place?' he asked.

'I'd look for new advisers on authenticity – for experts who aren't friends of Will's.'

He smiled. 'You're all right, Erica Pencarreth! You don't slither out from under like some people might have done. So . . . will you find me a couple of experts?'

She nodded acceptance. She was greatly relieved. He had taken it very well, and instead of reproaching her had offered her a compliment. 'If I could ask,' she ventured, 'let's keep this quiet.'

'You mean not tell Townley,' he guessed aloud.

'Not unless and until it's bad news.'

That was reasonable enough. He guessed she'd already had a considerable dust-up with Mr Clever-Clogs, so it would be wrong to make things worse. Moreover, he had his own reason for wanting it low-key. 'We won't tell Nyree,' he suggested.

'Not unless and until. She's got enough to contend with.'

'Right . . . If in the end it turns out to be bad news, it's not going to do either you or Townley much good, is it?' he suggested. 'The newspapers would love that.'

She could envisage the headlines. 'MONET A MISTAKE!'

Since she made no response, he went on: 'How're you going to feel about that?'

'Unhappy,' she confessed.

Eight

Z an had requested 'a couple of experts'. Erica knew just
whom to ask.

The first was a former teacher from college days who was
now Reader in Modern Art at an African university. The
other was the man who was lending the Renoir drawings
for the St Valentine's exhibition.

Neither of these would ever have been called in for a
consultation by Willard Townley. Dr Broxbourne was too
insignificant and Rob Patterson was too poor. But Erica had
faith in both.

Patterson barely scraped a living by finding and trading in
drawings from the early years of painters who later became
famous. Because he had to ensure he wasn't wasting his
money, he scrutinised each drawing with the most minute care before he bought. Although he could only afford
drawings and sketches, he haunted the galleries learning all
he could about the later works of the artists, because this
helped him to judge the line-drawings and cartoons on which
he hazarded his money.

As for Isla Broxbourne, she hadn't gone to teach in
Uganda because she could get nothing better, as Willard
might have thought. She'd chosen to go, wanting to help
Africans understand European culture through the visual
arts. And Erica happened to know she was in England to
receive an honorary degree from her *alma mater*.

First Erica had to have the Monet available for them to
examine. She didn't want to take her experts to Maurice
Leppard because that way Willard would be almost sure to
hear of it.

It was perfectly reasonable to ask to have the Monet

consigned to her. The scientific tests had been completed with nothing found that could cause alarm. Now Mr McNaughton wished to have the painting, and Erica would be the means by which it was carried to him.

But instead of taking it to his hotel, she took it to the Corie Gallery. Invited there, Dr Broxbourne spent most of a February morning with it, examining it closely both with the naked eye and with a lens. She then sat down to read all the scientific reports, and the documents that had come with the canvas.

Taken out to lunch in one of Gratesford's better eating houses, she delivered her judgement. 'I see nothing against its being a Monet, Erica. I can understand why you might have niggling doubts, and there is a little area where I could have an argument. But after all, the painter wasn't at his best during that time and the provenance is perfect. In view of the fact that the others have given it their blessing, I do likewise.'

Erica made no objection. She wasn't allowed to argue with the experts. She was paying them for their opinion and must accept it.

But Isla Broxbourne had some curiosity. 'Why did you want another opinion, really?'

'The purchaser asked for it.'

'Oh, I see.' People who had money to spend on master works were entitled to their little foibles. That ended the matter as far as Dr Broxbourne was concerned.

Rob Patterson was a different kettle of fish. Delighted to be asked to 'consult', to be offered a substantial fee, and to be brought to the Corie Gallery – all expenses paid and a first-class lunch thrown in – he roamed round Erica's office, taking squinting glances at the canvas from every angle.

'Nice, very nice,' he muttered. 'Tremendous energy. Colours typical but why has he put that raw sienna in there? Well, he's allowed to if he wants. Tree trunk's thick – was he closer to the tree this time?' And so on, a string of comments of the kind that often alarmed the attendants in the Tate or the National.

He too read all the documentation. Because he was a dealer

in works generally using ink or pencil on paper, he spent a long time on the letter written by the gardener's boy.

Over his lunch, with which he demanded an Orvieto Classico and, to end with, a fine cognac, he gave his verdict.

'I hope it's not going to shock you, Erica, but I'm not convinced.'

'Meaning what?'

'It could be a Monet. It has all the . . . the appurtenances. Tremendous energy, rich texture, colours right for the period although I'm surprised by that raw sienna because even if his colour sense was damaged, he could still read the labels on the tubes.' He sipped his brandy. 'But . . .'

'But what?'

'There's a funny patch under the bridge – the reflection has a "catch" in it, as if he'd lost his rhythm.'

Erica felt her heart give a little lurch. This was the point where she herself had seen something that troubled her, and although Dr Broxbourne had waved it away, Erica felt sure she too had sensed it.

'Anything else?' she inquired.

'Maybe it's nothing. I'm just not too keen on the letter.'

'The letter?' Once again that little throb of the heart, that start of recognition. Hadn't Daff said, 'Anyone can forge a letter'? 'What's wrong with it?'

'Nothing. It's on a piece of good writing paper that you wouldn't have thought a gardener's boy could have, but then you could suppose it was pinched from Monet's study. The ink's "right" – but you can find bottles still sealed with wax in many a flea market. The handwriting . . . of course you can't tell age from handwriting, and it is in the French style . . . I dunno, Erica. Something about it bothers me. I don't say it's a fake, because the analysis from Leppard's technicians vouches for the paper and the ink and everything else. But I wouldn't buy it if I found it on offer somewhere.'

'You wouldn't.'

'No.'

'And that affects your view of the painting.'

'Well, see, dearie, it's two things taken together. I might

101

not worry too much about that patch under the bridge – though it bothers me. And I might not worry about the letter if I'd just been shown it on its own. But something about the letter is . . . is bothersome, and the same goes for the technique on that little patch.'

'So are you saying you can't accept the painting?'

He swallowed the remains of the brandy, put down the glass, and shrugged. 'I wouldn't dare to go against all those scholars that Willard Townley called in. Who am I, after all? But if I had the money to buy it and was offered the painting, I'd call in six other scholars before I was totally convinced to write a cheque.'

She gave a rueful smile and summoned the waiter to pay the bill. 'Thank you for being so honest with me, Rob.'

'Think nothing of it.'

They sat waiting for the credit-card routine to be accomplished. Patterson said suddenly, 'You're not convinced either, are you?'

She eluded the question, accepting her receipt and her card. They made their way out of the restaurant. On the pavement he took it up again. 'What made you uncertain?'

'Who said I was uncertain?'

He gave her a derisive grin. 'Please yourself,' he said. They got into her car and she drove him to the station. He talked appreciatively about the paintings in her gallery. Before he left to find his train he said, 'Thanks for the lunch and everything. But if you think your friend McNaughton is going to get his money back on *my* judgement of the painting, forget it. And since it's not a bad painting in itself, you'd better just let him enjoy it, Monet or not.'

But she knew she couldn't do that.

She rang Zan that evening to say she had two opinions to pass on. 'What did they think?' he inquired.

'It's rather a long story. I have to come to town tomorrow on business – if I drop in at your hotel, would that be convenient?'

'That would be great. What time did you have in mind?'

'Sixish?'

'Great. We'll have a drink in the bar – it's quiet in there. OK?'

'See you there.'

She was there first, and had time to take out her own handwritten notes and the letter Dr Broxbourne had sent. This briefly repeated her view that she found no reason to dissent from the general verdict. As for Rob Patterson, it would never have occurred to him to put anything in writing.

Zan came in looking somewhat different from the business type she'd seen on their first meeting. He was clad in jeans and an Arran sweater. 'I've been out for a day in the country,' he explained. 'Or in other words, I went to visit a winery in Sussex. Not a bad product.' He gave his brief smile. 'Not as good as McNaughton's Hill, of course – but then, what is?'

She asked after his sister, and was told the doctors were discussing when to begin treatment. 'They talk to me about using this drug and that drug, but the names are so long and to me, meaningless. But I gather it won't be much fun for Nyree. Today they were going to put her on a blood transfusion so I only saw her for ten minutes or so.'

'And how is she in herself?'

'Oh . . . taking it all on the chin, as usual. She told me to say thank you for the books – they're first rate, she says.'

They ordered drinks and took them to a quiet corner. The atmosphere was rather like that of a gentlemen's club – leather settees, oak wainscot – with few other patrons to disturb its calm.

Erica reported Dr Broxbourne's opinion, to which Zan suggested, 'She's sitting on the fence?'

'I think that's a bit harsh. She doesn't have any real doubts but she did mention that there was one spot on the canvas that worried her – and it was exactly the same area that worries me.'

'Did you tell her that?'

'No, I didn't want to bias her decision. But I think we could say that it's a fairly neutral one. But Rob Patterson, on the other hand . . .' She went on to give a full account of her conversation with him.

'So he thinks it's dicey but he doesn't count for much.'

'I'm afraid that's the size of it.'

'Why did you call him in, then? If he's a nobody?'

'Just because he has no letters after his name doesn't mean he's a know-nothing,' she explained. 'Rob Patterson is one of the keenest students of technique that I know. He's self-taught, yes, but he's one of those mad enthusiasts who practically lives inside the galleries, living and breathing the atmosphere, trying to *will* himself into the mind of the painter.' She paused. 'His opinion may count for nothing among the elite, but I have confidence in him.'

'So . . . There really may be something wrong with my painting?'

With a sigh, she nodded.

'But you haven't any real evidence, only a feeling?'

'That's it.'

'So what do we do now?'

'I don't know,' she confessed. 'That's why I thought we ought to meet, to see if we can sort out what to do.'

Zan sipped the glass of Chablis he had ordered for comparison with his own product. She could see he was giving the matter deep thought. There was a silence for a time. Then he said, 'Your pal Patterson had a "feeling" – about the letter by the gardener's boy.'

'Aristide – yes.'

'If the painting isn't "right", it might follow that the supporting evidence isn't "right" either.'

'That's true. The same holds good for the letter as for the painting. It isn't hard to get hold of paper and ink of that period – you can buy old correspondence in many a junk shop and often there's a blank page. You know, people used to write letters on paper folded in octavo but they only used the front fold, so the second fold might be blank and yet they wouldn't tear it off – because that would seem miserly. So pieces of paper made about 1920 – or 1900 or any other era – aren't hard to come by, and bottles of ink and steel pens are the same – look around in flea markets and you'll find them.'

'Ye-es,' he agreed, and there was a frown on the narrow face. 'That's not unheard of back home, you know. Memorabilia about the days of the early settlers can fetch quite a price, and I gather questions have been raised about some of the stuff.'

'So you see,' she took it up again, 'the letter may not be genuine and it could have been used to trick the shop owner in Istanbul – or anybody else back down the chain of ownership.'

'*Was* there a boy called Aristide Whatever living in the Giverny area at that time?'

'Aristide Curacie. Well, we don't know. But we could find out.'

'How would we go about it?'

'I've got contacts in Paris. I'll send an e-mail tomorrow from the office computer.'

'If he existed,' Zan said, 'could he still be alive? He was – what – fifteen in the 1920s. No, he'd be a very old man now.'

'But the Curacie family may be traceable. Anything we could find out would be a help.'

They agreed on that. Zan hesitated then said, 'Perhaps you'd like to stay for dinner?'

'I'd love to,' she said, 'but I've got neighbours coming in this evening for supper.'

'Oh, of course.'

She could see he was disappointed though he hid it at once. He's lonely, she thought. 'Some other evening, perhaps?'

'I'll hold you to that.'

Next morning first thing she sent her e-mail, the same message to two acquaintances from her student years. Could they please ascertain if anyone called Aristide Curacie had lived in the neighbourhood of the Giverny home of Claude Monet in the 1920s and if so, what was known of him?

The reply came late next day from the more practical-minded of her friends. Research on French Internet sites showed the Curacie family as having lived in Rue du Portier in the village of Epte-Rouet from 1882 until 1936. At that time the youngest son of the existing family, named Henri, had been called up for the army, and on his discharge after World War II was awarded a pension for a disability. The pension had been paid to him at an address in Paris until his death in 1971. According to the Paris telephone directory, there was still someone called Curacie living at the same address: Albert Curacie, perhaps a son or grandson of Henri.

'I'm sorry it's a bit patchy,' the message said on her screen, 'but a lot of official records got lost in World War II.'

Erica thought it an amazing result in so short a time. She sent a reply thanking Lucien for his quick work.

She rang Zan but he wasn't in his room at the hotel. She left a message to say that she'd had a result from her enquiries. Just before she was about to leave her office, he called back.

'Can you come to town?' he suggested. 'We ought to have a council of war, and you did say you'd come to dinner.'

'So I did. Well, all right, but I must scurry off home again afterwards because I have to finalise the hanging of the exhibition before we open the gallery tomorrow.'

'Would it be easier if I came to you?'

'Well, it would really. But wouldn't that be difficult? Don't you generally visit Nyree in the evening?'

'I was there this morning; they only let me look in on her for a second and said she ought to be left very quiet for a day or two. So I shan't be going this evening.'

They arranged he would arrive about eight. She scurried home, shopping at the supermarket *en route* for substantial foods because Antipodean men in her experience had hearty appetites. But Zan had scant desire for the large salmon steaks she provided. His attention was all on what she was telling him about the Curacie family.

'So what now?' he queried.

'I thought I'd go over Saturday evening. I've got some holiday time due, as it happens, although it may be that the whole question will be settled by a chat with the Curacies.'

'You're thinking they may remember a family story about how Grandpa – or Great-Uncle, or whatever he was – how he had an awful old burnt painting in the cellar?'

'Something like that.'

'I'll come with you,' he said.

The announcement caused several strange reactions within Erica. First there was a flash of pleasure at the thought of having him as her companion. Then there was the thought, What would Will say? Next she found herself thinking, You'd be more of a hindrance than a help. And lastly she was ashamed of most of those feelings.

Zan watched her struggling to find her way out of that morass. Maybe it was a bit unexpected but he was determined to go with her. This whole thing about the painting was simply a business problem that needed solving. 'I'll get the hotel to set it all up, no problem. What time do you want to travel? You'd have to arrange for someone to look after the gallery and all that?' He knew from experience that if you took the initiative, others generally followed.

'I could get Suzi to see to locking up and setting the security, she's done it before, but—' She felt for some obscure reason that she oughtn't to let this happen.

'Right, then, how about going by Eurostar? Nyree and I found it quite handy, and I think there's one goes about seven in the evening.'

'Yes, but—'

'That's settled then. OK?'

'But it means you'd be out of London for a couple of days.'

At last she had an objection that needed an answer. He drew in a weary breath, and as he spoke she realised he was confiding in her more than ever before. 'They're starting chemotherapy on Saturday,' he said. 'It means Nyree will be hooked up to all kinds of tubes and stuff. They said that for the first couple of days, she'd be very tired and perhaps there would be a temporary reaction while they adjust the dosage – so it would be best not to be around. They're letting me spend tomorrow and Friday with her more or less on a drop-in basis and then after that . . . Well, they told me to stay away until probably Tuesday.

107

Of course I can phone – and I can do that just as well from Paris.'

'I see.' No wonder he wanted to go with her. Anything to fill in the time until he knew how the little sister was faring under the treatment. 'In that case,' she said, 'will you let me know as soon as it's fixed up? I need to make arrangements at the gallery. We can meet at the station Friday evening.'

'Right.' He felt a need to justify all this dashing about. 'I suppose it's silly to be bothering about this stupid painting when the important thing is to get Nyree better . . .'

'Not at all. One day soon she's going to be looking at it and you want to be able to say, "We made sure it was the real thing."'

He heard the kindness behind the mundane words, and understood her intention. He felt suddenly very close to her – but what was the point, when she was so involved with Townley? He ended the moment with a joke. 'And besides, we don't want to be swindled out of close on three million pounds.'

'That too,' agreed Erica.

Before he left, he wandered around her living-room inspecting her bookshelves and studying the one painting on her walls. 'I'd have thought you'd have a whole collection of paintings,' he remarked.

'No-o. I like to have one that I really pay attention to, and then after a month or so I take it down and put up something else. Otherwise, you see, it becomes like the wallpaper – you scarcely notice it.'

'This is an interesting one.' It was a rather stark study of rocks seen under a dawn sky. After frowning at it for a moment he snapped his fingers. 'It's by your mother, isn't it?'

Erica laughed in surprise. 'How did you know that? Was it a guess?'

'Oh . . . Well, as a matter of fact . . . I asked in a shop and they showed me a book with a lot of reproductions of her work.'

She was amazed, and somehow complimented. He, who kept saying he knew nothing about art, had actually taken the trouble to seek out some of Lisbet's work. 'Did you buy the book?' she challenged.

'Well . . . yes . . .' He was laughing too. 'But only because Nyree was interested when I told her about your ma, and said she'd like to see the kind of thing she painted.'

She shook her head at him as she ushered him to the door. 'Between us, perhaps your sister and I can get you to take a real interest one day.'

He found that he had taken her hand in his. 'You've really been great over this thing,' he said. 'I can't thank you enough.' And then, because she'd said she had to have an early night, he hurried away.

As she tidied up and put the dishes in the dishwasher, Erica was pleased in some inexplicable way. She was beginning to think of Zan McNaughton as a friend, not a business acquaintance.

But next morning the pleasure was dashed away by a phone call from Willard. 'Just touching base with you,' he began in a breezy tone. 'We seem to have been out of contact for a long time – it must be ten days or more.'

'I suppose it is. Not since you "popped off" to Paris. It so happens—' She was about to tell him that she too was going to Paris, but she hesitated. That might mean explanations, and she'd agreed with Zan not to say anything until they had some definite conclusion over the Monet.

But in any case Willard didn't wait for what she was going to say. 'I thought it would be nice if you came to my place this evening,' he suggested. 'We could have drinks and then there's this late show at the Curzon. They've got that weird Hollywood film about Michelangelo, I thought it might be fun.'

'I'm afraid I can't, Will, I'm installing my new exhibition and in any case—'

'But that St Valentine thing is only a one-room affair. Good heavens, it's not going to take you all day and all evening.'

'But I've got other things to think about.'

'Well, if you must know, so have I!' he broke in, rather sharply. 'I particularly wanted to talk to you because Maurice Leppard tells me you've collected the Monet.'

'Yes, a week ago.'

'You didn't tell me.'

'You were away.'

'And of course you couldn't possibly leave a message or anything. Really, it's so inefficient—'

'I can't see how it matters all that much, Will. The painting is at the Corie under lock and key.'

'But what's it doing there? When I heard it had been taken from the lab, I thought it meant McNaughton was flying off home.'

'No, he's . . . he's got matters to attend to.'

'Well, look here, is he to be regarded as having taken possession of the painting? Because if so, that cheque that's sitting in the bank can be cleared into my account.'

'Ah . . . now . . . I don't think the painting can be regarded as accepted by the buyer. Not yet.'

'Not yet? Why not?' His tone became even sharper. 'It's been authenticated by experts, it's been authenticated in the laboratory – what's holding things up?'

There was no help for it. She would have to let him know something of what was going on. With great reluctance she began, 'Mr McNaughton would like to have some enquiries made about the letter.'

'What letter?' Willard demanded, but she could tell by his voice that he knew very well.

'The letter by the gardener's boy. Mr McNaughton wondered if we could find out anything about Aristide Curacie.'

'For God's sake!' he cried. 'What on earth brought that on?'

She ought to have said, I did. But she was too much of a coward to tell Willard that she herself had started doubts in the mind of Zan McNaughton.

Instead she said, 'It just seemed to him that we ought to look into the letter. In New Zealand, he told me, there's quite a lot of stuff gets sold – put on the market as being genuine, from the time when the country was settled—'

'Will you explain to me how memorabilia in the Antipodes have got anything to do with Monet?' Willard burst in.

'It's just that he knows letters can be produced that look authentic—'

'*Look* authentic? What's he insinuating?'

'It's nothing personal, Will, he just wants to find out if the letter is in the handwriting of Aristide Curacie.'

'And how is he going to find that out, pray tell?'

'Well, I ran down what still exists of the family at an address in Paris—'

'*You* ran them down?' Now there was more than exasperation in his voice. 'Why didn't you tell me what you were doing?'

All at once Erica had had enough. 'Why should I tell you what I'm doing?' she riposted. 'Zan is paying me a consultancy fee – you yourself said you were glad I'd taken it on. If he decides to look into the authenticity of *any* of the evidence concerning the Monet, it's my duty to help him. Isn't that so?' She paused, but he made no response. 'There was never any suggestion that I was going to report back to you and, if you want to get querulous about it, it's quite unethical for the seller to be questioning any verification by the buyer.'

There was a shocked silence on the other end of the line. At last he said in a changed tone, 'I'm sorry, Erica. I didn't mean to criticise—'

'Yes you did, and it's becoming very disagreeable, Will. You cavil and bicker every time Zan McNaughton is mentioned.'

'Bicker? I never do anything so small-minded.'

'You should listen to yourself sometimes. You take up an attitude that's very haughty—'

'Oh, now, Erica!'

He sounded very hurt. She was stricken. What had she been saying? And all because she wasn't being straight with him about Zan's investigation into the letter. Yet she didn't feel it right to tell him everything – she'd agreed with Zan to keep things quiet. And besides, Will would be *really* upset if he knew she had continued to have her doubts about the Monet.

She tried to think of something to say, and while she was still searching for words Willard said, 'I think perhaps I've been insensitive to your feelings recently, love. I apologise. I've had a lot on my mind, and I admit I don't take to your friend McNaughton, but of course he's entitled to do whatever he wants to, as far as the painting is concerned. But do remember this, Erica. I spent a lot of money on promoting the work and I have heavy expenses – it would be a great help to me if that cheque could be cleared.'

'Of course. I understand that.' She was contrite. What was she thinking of, getting angry with Will when she was going behind his back – carrying out investigations of the Monet that, if proved correct, would make him look foolish? 'It will all be settled quite tidily by the weekend. I'm going over to Paris to see if I can talk to the Curacies.'

'You're actually going yourself?'

'Yes.'

'I'll come with you.'

'No, thank you, Will.' That idea had to be scotched at once.

'Oh, come on, precious. We could make it a fun weekend, once we'd done the interview.'

'No, really, Will.' Two prospective companions for a weekend in the most romantic city in the world, one after the other, within two days. She'd never been so much in demand, she told herself. But of course it was by no means amusing. She simply couldn't let Willard Townley know that she already had a travelling companion. 'This is business,' she said. 'I prefer to treat it as business.'

'Oh. Well.' A long, baffled pause. 'If you get to talk to the Curacies, will you ring and let me know how it goes?'

'No-o, Will, I'd rather not feel you're at my elbow in this.' She added cheerfully, 'You know it's all likely to come to nothing. How many families can provide information about a great-uncle who's probably been dead for twenty years or more?'

'If they can't tell you anything, does that mean McNaughton will let the thing drop?'

'Ah. As to that . . . I'm not sure.'

'The man's a bore,' Willard said under his breath.

'I heard that,' she rebuked. But she wasn't angry with him any more. He was as he was, bright and talented and impatient with less fortunate souls. 'I have to go, Will. I've got a lot of work to do.'

'Yes, OK. When will you be back?'

'Monday midday, I think.'

'So can we meet Monday night?'

'We'll see, shall we?'

'But you'll ring me, yes?'

'Yes, yes, of course.'

'Bye, sweetheart. Kiss-kiss.'

'Goodbye, Will.'

For the first time in her life, she was glad to end a phone conversation with Willard Townley.

Nine

At the Gare du Nord there was a young man in a travel agency blazer. He came up at Zan's nod. 'Mr McNaughton?' He took their overnight bags, and ushered them to an assigned parking space. A limousine awaited. He put their luggage in the boot, stood back sketching a salute, and they rolled away without any need to instruct the chauffeur.

A swift drive through a brightly lit and busy Paris night brought them to the 8th Arrondissement. They drew up before a haughty pillared entrance. A uniformed doorman leapt to open the car door and gesture at a bellboy to fetch their bags and they went into the Hôtel Romain, where marble and busts of emperors emphasised its name. At Reception a middle-aged man in a frock coat beamed at them. 'Mr McNaughton, welcome again to the Romain. Your rooms are ready.'

A lordly wave, and they were escorted into the lift by an underling who took them up to the second floor and opened the doors of two rooms, side by side. Erica hesitated, uncertain which one to enter. The bellboy settled the matter by taking her bag into the first. Zan came after, glanced about, uttered a satisfied, 'OK,' and tipped the bellboy.

'Everything is satisfactory?' twittered the assistant manager.

'Perhaps something to eat?' Zan suggested with a glance at Erica.

'No, thank you.' They'd had dinner on Eurostar, Erica had done a full day's work, and it was now getting on for midnight. All she longed for was a bath and bed.

'Right, see you in the morning.'

'Yes.' Yawning and nodding, she closed her door and opened the valise for her night things. In fifteen minutes she was in bed and asleep.

She didn't wake until late Sunday morning. At first she couldn't think where on earth she was, but the little statuette of Venus on the bedside table reminded her. What a splendiferous place, she thought, sitting up and stretching. Zan's London hotel had certainly made a great job of getting them accommodation.

She showered in what she now noticed was a very luxurious bathroom with gold taps and a marble floor. Everything she could possibly want in the way of toiletries was there – buttermilk soap, a huge sponge, a bath towel big enough for a Roman toga, a gilt box with little bottles of expensive scent . . .

Amused, she tried one of the scents – L'Air du Temps – and got dressed. In view of the splendour of her surroundings she didn't put on the jeans and sweater she normally wore for Sunday breakfast, but instead chose a dark red flannel skirt and a shirt of silk scattered with little roses.

Although it was after ten, there were many guests still in the dining-room reading the newspapers over their croissants and coffee. She was ushered to a table, served immediately, and offered both French and English Sunday papers.

She was still there when Zan walked in. She smiled a greeting. 'Are you very late or were you very early?' she inquired.

'I went out for a run,' he said. 'I'm a country boy, you know – town life doesn't really agree with me, I need to get physical from time to time.' He sat down beside her and immediately a waiter was at his elbow. 'No, just coffee,' he said, waving him off.

'You never went running in that suit,' she challenged, laughing.

'I would have if I'd wanted to,' he riposted. 'No, I showered and changed when I got back. And in view of the fact that we want to make a favourable impression on the Curacies, I thought I ought to look a bit blue-blooded.'

'Well thought of,' she agreed. 'How about me? Will I do?'

115

'You look . . .' He hesitated. 'Very nice.'

'Oh, thanks a lot. This is my best silk shirt!'

'All right, then, I'll say what I was going to say at first – you look good enough to eat. And smell nice, too.'

To her own surprise, she felt herself blushing. She'd fished for the compliment and got it – why couldn't she accept it without feeling all flustered?

Zan's coffee came. As it was poured for him he said, 'So what's the plan of campaign?'

'Well, I don't think we ought to telephone in advance. I think we should just drop in on them unannounced.'

'If you think that's best.'

'And I don't think we ought to go to the Rue Sarabande now. It's mid-morning and they may be at church.'

'Possible. And they'll be having lunch afterwards, and if they go to a café for that, they may not get home until somewhere around four.'

'That's only too true.'

'So we ought to aim at reaching Rue Sarabande at about four-thirty, right?' When she nodded he said, 'So what are we going to do until then?'

'What would you like to do?'

His answer was prompt. 'When Nyree and I were here last year we either kept dashing in and out of boutiques or mooching round galleries. The Bois de Boulogne isn't far, is it? I'd like to take a look at it.'

'Nothing easier. Straight along the Champs-Elysées and Grande Armée, and we're there.'

'Walkable?'

'It's a big place, the Bois, if you want to see much of it. Better to take a taxi there and then walk.'

'Oh, we'll hire a car.' They finished their coffee, rose together, and in the foyer approached the porter's desk. Erica primed herself to start the negotiations for a car but was startled when Zan immediately plunged in in very good French. When the porter picked up the telephone to order the car, Zan studied her face a moment then laughed outright.

'It's all right to be surprised but you shouldn't let it show so much,' he told her.

'But I . . . but I—' She stopped, pulling it all together. The travel arrangements, the splendid hotel, the quiet assurance with which he handled himself. She'd been allowing Willard's estimate of him to colour her judgement. 'You come on as if you're a hayseed, but . . . you're not, are you?'

'Oh yes I am. Check my ear, there's a straw behind it.' He was still amused, but seeing she was embarrassed he took pity. 'I'm a country man,' he insisted. 'I live in the country and I prefer it. But selling wine, you have to get out and about a lot, and then, you know, we bought ourselves into the local supermarket chains so I travel a bit on the Pacific rim. But the French thing comes from an old bloke we had as *chef de cave* for a couple of years. A cantankerous old coot, he refused to speak English so the only way to communicate was to learn French. But I think you'll find,' he added apologetically, 'that I speak it with a pronounced Bordeaux accent.'

Erica, released from her mortification, gave him a grateful smile. '*You* can do the talking when we get to the Curacies',' she decided.

They drove out along the great avenues to the Bois, left the car in a parking area near the Pavillon d'Armenonville, and began their walk. At the Lower Lake they found the usual crowd of mamas and papas helping their children to feed the ducks, the children wrapped up like little Eskimos against the February chill. Erica found herself recounting little incidents from her student days in Paris.

'So you've really been wrapped up in this art how-d'ye-do all your life?'

'Except for a couple of years in New York.'

'What did you do in New York, then?'

'Made a fool of myself.'

He paused in his walk. 'How d'you mean?'

'Oh, the kind of daft things a seventeen-year-old kid can get up to – ganging up with the wrong kind of people, railing against the powers that be, blaming everybody but myself for the stupid things I was doing.' She shook her head at the memory, and marvelled that she was telling him about it. 'I

117

remind myself of it now and again, just so I don't waste any more precious time being an idiot.'

'You surprise me,' he confessed. 'I'd have thought you'd always been a perfect little lady.' But he was teasing her. He went on, 'I know how easily you can do daft things when the world goes wrong, though, believe you me. I went out quite a lot and painted what we laughingly think of as "the town" . . . That was when the sheep-rearing business began to go down the drain. But you know, you have to come to terms with things in the end, don't you? And we were lucky, we had good vine-growing soil and some long southern slopes for the vines. So in the end I gave my attention to growing grapes and learning how to turn the juice into something worth drinking – we all did, my family are all involved in it.'

He told her about his brothers and cousins at home, as they walked and talked in perfect amity. In the early afternoon they settled at one of the cafés, ordering tea and sighing over what they were brought. 'How can people who make such good wine make such insipid tea?' groaned Zan, dangling the tea-bag from its string.

By and by they set off for the northern arrondissement where the Curacies lived. It was quite a long way, at first through crowded streets where well-dressed Parisians were coming out for their evening's entertainment. But after a while the street lamps showed a more working-class neighbourhood. Erica had the map, folded so that she could see Rue Sarabande clearly. Once there, they had the usual difficulty looking for a parking space. They found one near a Métro then walked back.

The Curacies had an apartment on the first floor. They climbed an old stone staircase littered with cigarette ends. A faint trace of cooked food lingered from Sunday's lunch. In the rather dim light they found the name card inserted in the holder. They rang the bell at the door, and waited.

After a few minutes they heard footsteps. A man of about thirty, in his shirt-sleeves and holding a magazine in his hand, opened the door. 'Yes?' he said.

'M'sieur Curacie?' asked Erica, since Zan seemed to want to stay in the background.

'Yes?'

'M'sieur Albert Curacie?'

'No, that's my father. Who's asking?'

'My name is Erica Pencarreth and this is Mr McNaughton. Is your father here? If so, we'd like to speak to him. We've come from London to do so.'

The thick eyebrows rose towards the untidy black hair. He retreated into the flat and called from the passageway, 'Papa! Two foreigners here to talk to you!'

'What?' cried a muffled voice.

'Two English types.'

'Good God,' said Papa, and appeared in a doorway putting on wire-rimmed glasses. He approached, peered at them, then said in bewilderment, 'You want to talk to me?'

'If you could spare us some time.'

'What's it about?' Very suspicious, as if he thought they wanted to sell him insurance.

'It's about Aristide Curacie. Who used to live near Giverny.'

'Uncle Ari?' If possible, he looked even more bewildered. 'What about him?'

'We wanted to ask you about a letter he may have written when he was a boy.'

'Eh?'

'May we come in?' suggested Zan, moving slightly as if to enter the flat.

The two men in the passageway shuffled for a moment, then Albert Curacie led the way into a shabby but comfortable sitting-room. A television set with the sound turned off dominated one corner. It showed a racing scene from the weekend's sports programme. Beer bottles and two half-empty glasses stood on the table. The Sunday papers were spread carelessly about. The son made a pass at clearing some of them away so as to make places available.

'Take a seat,' he said, with rather reluctant hospitality. 'I'm Laurent Curacie. How do you do.' They shook hands all round, reintroducing themselves before settling to talk.

'What's this about Uncle Ari?' asked the father. He had the same broad face as his son but his hair was thinning noticeably. His gold-rimmed glasses gave him a studious look.

Erica produced the photocopies of the documents that had accompanied the Monet painting. She selected the letter written by Aristide Curacie in 1943 and offered it to his nephew Albert. 'We would very much like to know if this is the handwriting of your Uncle Aristide,' she said.

Albert took it, without attempting to read it, and stared at her. 'Is this a joke?' he inquired, somewhat annoyed.

'I assure you, not at all,' said Zan. 'We've come to Paris on purpose to ask you.'

Albert Curacie studied the visitors for a moment. They were both very well dressed, and Mademoiselle had a look of sincerity that calmed his distrust. He adjusted his glasses and read the letter.

'A painting?' he said. 'Uncle Ari had a painting?'

'You didn't hear him mention it?'

'Well, no. But then this was years ago, wasn't it?' he remarked, gesturing with the letter. He handed it to his son, Laurent, who took it but without bothering to read it. Instead he looked longingly at the beer on the table.

'Would you like a drink?' he asked.

'Thank you, that would be nice,' Zan said, knowing Laurent couldn't have his drink if no one else did.

'Beer?'

'Not for me, thanks,' Erica put in.

'Soft drink? Cola?'

'No, thanks, we had tea a little while ago.'

'Ah, tea,' said Laurent, with a grimace. He fetched a bottle of Belgian beer from a credenza, opened it, and offered it with a glass to Zan. Zan poured it carefully so as to settle the head. Erica understood he was trying to create a convivial atmosphere.

Albert, as host, did his best to make conversation. 'Uncle Ari was a bit of an odd character,' he said apologetically. 'We didn't see all that much of him.' He gave a little flourish of the letter. '1943 – as far as I could gather, he had a more or less cushy life in the country during the war. He was in some sort of reserved occupation to do with food – market gardening? – but as to a painting, I never heard anything like that.'

'You actually knew him?' prompted Zan.

'Oh yes, he visited now and again and we went out there to his place when we were kids – down by the Epte, you know, it's nice down there. He'd come to Paris now and again for the racing at Longchamps, or for a football match.'

'Was he interested in art?' Erica asked.

'Art?' Albert echoed, with a puzzled glance at the photocopy.

'Yes; did he work for Monet, the painter?'

'Never heard him mention it if he did.'

'Did he speak about life during the war?' Zan suggested.

'The war?' Their host shook his head. 'Hardly ever. Hard times then, you know? All the old folk wanted to forget it.'

'The Occupation? Life under the Nazis?'

The answer was a very Gallic shrug and a nod toward a framed photograph hanging on the wall of the sitting-room, showing a family group of about the late 1950s. 'Uncle Ari didn't look back much except at the bloodline of racehorses. He was a sports fan. Liked football and the ponies, liked a bet on them, and so do I, as a matter of fact. In the picture, he's the one in the back row with the peaked cap. That's my papa at the other end of the row, holding a kid in his arms. The kid is me, though I had more hair then.' He stroked his balding head to point up the joke.

Erica rose to study the photograph. It was a family photograph in black and white, the women in 'trapeze' or A-line dresses and their hair gamin style, the men in narrow-trousered suits and very wide ties. One of the women held a baby draped in a white gown.

'That was for my daughter's baptism,' Albert said. 'My wife Mireille likes to keep it in view, our daughter's married and off in Canada now, you see.'

Erica made complimentary remarks about the family and chatted about how fashions had changed. Meantime Zan was trying to engage the uncommunicative son in conversation.

'I suppose you don't have anything in your great-uncle's writing we could compare this letter to?'

'No, I don't think we keep much—'

Albert caught the exchange. 'But your maman, Laurent – she has a photo album and some stuff – on the shelf in her wardrobe, I think.' He paused. 'My wife's visiting her sister in Faubourg St Jacques this evening.' Zan smiled at him in encouragement. 'Should I get it?'

'If it wouldn't be a trouble,' Erica said with eagerness.

'Not at all, Mademoiselle. Just a moment.'

He went out of the room. His son's attention had gone back to the television, where a race was about to start. From somewhere in the inner regions of the flat came the sound of furniture being moved and muffled curses. In due course Albert returned with a fat album and a cardboard box. His hair was ruffled and there was dust on his fingers. 'Had to get a chair to reach it,' he explained. 'Here you are.'

He seemed to expect them to go through the photograph album but Erica's attention was drawn at once to the box. It proved to contain marriage, birth and death certificates with other official documents, together with some birthday cards and notes in stamped envelopes. One of the notes was dated 1962 and signed, 'Your affectionate uncle, Ari'.

'Here we are, Zan!' She smoothed out the note, offering it to him.

He read aloud: 'Dear Mireille, I won a packet on the Tour de France leader yesterday so send you a little gift for your birthday. I know you and Albert want a car so this should help towards the cost.'

'Ah yes, our first car!' sighed Albert. 'That's why she kept it. A dear old *deux-chevaux* – they don't make them like that any more.'

They laid out the old letter and the photocopy side by side. To the untutored eye it was definitely the same handwriting.

'Well, that's that,' said Zan. 'Thanks a lot, M'sieur Curacie.'

'Wait, there's another letter,' Albert said, caught up now in the desire to be useful. 'It was for Lucie's first communion – he sent us the money for her dress.' He flicked through the contents of the box. 'No? Must have given it to Lucie, I suppose, when she was packing up to go overseas with Victor.' He appealed to his son. 'Did she give Lucie that note about her communion frock?'

'Don't know,' murmured Laurent, his eyes on the television screen. 'Lucie took some stuff – family pictures and so forth.'

'Sorry,' his father said to the visitors. 'But you've seen what you wanted, eh?'

They said thank you and made their farewells. Erica left a card with the address of the Corie Gallery, suggesting that they might get in touch if they recalled anything about their relative Aristide and a painting. Zan lingered a few minutes and Erica heard a murmured exchange: 'To buy a drink or two . . .'

'Well, if you insist . . .'

On the way downstairs she said, 'Not much help.'

'Could you tell if the gardener's boy's letter was the same writing as the note about the Tour de France?'

'It looked the same . . .'

They walked back to the Métro for the car. After they got in Zan took a moment before starting the motor. 'He never said anything to his family about working for Monet,' he remarked.

'Well, if he wasn't interested in art . . . ?'

'If he wasn't interested in art, why did he save the painting from the bonfire in the first place?'

'Because it was by Monet, who was already a famous artist.'

He nodded and turned the key. They slid forward past the station and turned south for St Honoré.

As they waited for traffic lights in the Rue Fontaine Zan said, 'He worked for one of the most famous painters in France – in the world – and never boasted about it to his family?'

Erica said nothing while she considered that. 'Well, if they were all sports fans . . .'

'According to nephew Albert, *his* main interests were sports and betting too.'

'But maybe he was more of a romantic when he was young.'

'Maybe. Or maybe he took it thinking he'd sell it, but of course he couldn't do that while Claude Monet was alive.'

'That could be the reason – he took it hoping to make money.'

'So why didn't he sell it as soon as Monet died? There must have been a lot about that in the papers.'

'Oh, a tremendous lot. That was in the twenties – long tributes, the legacy of the water-lilies, Clemenceau and all sorts of politicians arguing over where to display the paintings—'

'So why didn't he try to make a bob or two with the burnt canvas?'

'Perhaps he'd forgotten about it.'

'And yet he remembered it twenty years later to sell it to a German officer?'

'Times were very hard during the Occupation—'

'And they weren't in the twenties? If I remember what I read in my economics books, there was a tremendous depression after World War I.'

'I don't know . . .' She fell silent. She'd played devil's advocate as long as she could.

They were nearing the Hôtel Romain before she spoke again. 'I still have a funny feeling about it,' she murmured. 'What do you think?'

'I think if I were a wine buyer and somebody offered me a bargain vintage with such a fuzzy history, I'd be mighty dubious.' He shook his head. 'And yet it looked like his handwriting.'

Eric said slowly, 'Anyone can forge a letter.'

'What?'

'That's what Daff said – one of my mother's friends.'

'But how would the forger get a sight of his handwriting? The Curacies knew nothing, they'd have mentioned if anyone had been enquiring about Uncle Ari.'

'There are other ways to get a look at his handwriting, I suppose.'

'Such as what?'

'Official documents? Army papers?'

They drew up at the hotel. The doorman leapt to open the car door, summoning a henchman to take the car to the underground car park. In the hotel foyer they turned towards the sitting area. Metal chairs in the style of the Augustan Era, but padded with huge cushions, were set around a delicate marble fountain. They sat down.

'We could try getting a look at his army papers tomorrow,' Erica suggested.

Zan blew out a breath. 'Take decades,' he said. 'You know what bureaucracy is like.' He beckoned a waiter. 'Would you like an aperitif?'

The waiter who approached was bearing the dinner menu although it was only six o'clock as yet. 'Are you eating in the hotel, sir? Have you a table reserved?'

Zan glanced at Erica. 'What shall we do? Would you like to eat here or shall we go out somewhere?'

She didn't want to think about that for the moment. Her head was full of speculation about Aristide Curacie and his letter. Zan waved the waiter away. Then he said, 'The next step is really the German officer.'

'What?'

'Thingummy – Loebletz. It might be easier to track down the Loebletz family than to tackle French bureaucrats.'

'We-ell . . . I suppose we could start on that tomorrow . . .'

'Why wait? The hotel has fax and computer and secretarial facilities. Are you on for it?' Scarcely waiting for her response, he got up, heading for the reception desk. 'I'll get them to find me a German-speaking secretary. Shan't be a minute.'

Erica followed him, scarcely knowing whether she agreed. Zan had a quick conversation with the desk clerk, who picked up a telephone and began giving instructions. After a short wait a young woman appeared from behind the partition that formed the wall behind the reception desk.

'You wish to use a private office, sir?'

'Yes, please, and with Internet connection.'

'This way.' She led them along a passage off the main hall, into a room with marbled walls in the Roman fashion but with a great deal of modern communications equipment as its main furniture.

They sat at a small table, clearly intended for a mini-conference. 'What we want to do is to find the family of a German officer whose name was—' He glanced at Erica who, still trying to catch up, produced from her capacious handbag the envelope with the photocopied documents.

She found the statement by Yamin Emin, the Turkish shopkeeper, and pointed out the name: 'Hauptmann Andreas Loebletz.'

The secretary waited. Clearly there was more information available.

'This was during World War II,' said Zan. 'A captain probably stationed in the Paris area during 1943 – that's right, Erica? He wouldn't have been visiting Giverny if it was a long way off, would he? So let's make a guess that he was stationed hereabouts.' To the secretary he said, 'Can you call up the regiments that were stationed in and around Paris in 1943? Then see if you can get the roll call. Look for Andreas Loebletz.'

'Do you know the name of his regiment?' the girl inquired.

'Sorry, no. Is it too difficult?'

'Perhaps we should try looking for the name in German directories,' suggested the secretary. 'Particularly if he lived in East Germany. Their records were tremendously thorough and still are.'

'No, sorry, he seems to have lived in Hamburg.'

'Well, even so . . .'

'Whatever you think best,' said Zan. 'We'll leave you to it. Ring my room if and when you get it. Come on,' he added to Erica.

'Where are we going?' she asked as they went out into the corridor.

'To pack.'

'To pack? What for?'

'Well, if that lass gets an address, we want to be on our way there as soon as possible.'

'*This evening?*'

'Why not? Trains and planes leave for Germany at all hours of the day and night.'

'Well . . .'

'Are you in or not?'

She certainly wasn't going to be left out. Besides, what did he know about checking on a painting? That was her job. 'I'm in,' she said, and hurried at his side to the lift.

It was extraordinary to be putting her belongings back into her travel bag so soon after taking them out. After the leisurely morning and the stroll around the Bois, to be dashing off to Germany seemed too much of a contrast. But as she zipped the last of her things away, there was a tap on her door.

It was Zan. 'Münster,' he said.

'Excuse me?'

'There's a family called Loebletz have a farm in the plains around Münster, which is in Westphalia. Come on, there's a car waiting.'

'We're not driving to Münster?' she gasped in astonishment

'Don't be daft. We're going to the airport – flight to Essen in fifty-five minutes – arrival time eight-thirty. From there to Münster by helicopter in the morning . . . Let's go.'

Speechless, she snatched up her bag and coat and followed him. A Mercedes with a driver was purring at the kerb. They were whisked away to a chorus of farewells from the hotel staff.

After a few minutes Erica got her breath back. 'Zan, is it really worth all this hurry and flurry?'

'Don't you want to find out if the Loebletz family ever owned a Monet?'

'Of course I do, but what's the rush?'

'No sense in wasting three hours eating a big French meal and starting out again in the morning, is there? We can be in Essen in time for dinner. Do you know Essen?'

She shook her head.

'Don't believe all you hear about the Ruhr – it's not a complete industrial wasteland, Essen's even got some Gauguins and Van Goghs in its art gallery—'

'Well, I know *that*.'

'And they like good wine – I've tried to sell McNaughton's Hill to them but they don't seem keen as yet.'

It was clear he was enjoying himself enormously. Despite her bewilderment Erica found herself smiling. This weekend, rushing about at top speed with everything first class, was totally different from the life she usually led. She couldn't help the thought that perhaps Zan was showing off a little, and it pleased her to think he was doing it so as to impress her.

'How did your secretary girl come up with this so quickly?' she inquired.

'Oh, that – luckily she paid no heed to what we were saying about army HQ and so forth. When she read the Turkish shopkeeper's statement she latched on to the fact that the painting was "taken" – we might say looted – from a house in Hamburg in 1945, looked up the electoral rolls, and came up with the fact that the Loebletz family sold their property to the town council during the rebuilding operations after Word War II. The payment for the property was made to Andreas Loebletz of Dehlheim, near Münster. The telephone directory for the area shows they're still there.'

'Andreas Loebletz?'

'No, that was too much to expect. The phone's in the name of Bernhardt Loebletz.'

'So you think that's a son or nephew or something.'

'Yes, like the Curacies.'

Once again there was a travel agent in a blazer to hand over their plane tickets and conduct them to the right departure gate at the airport. It seemed to be a weekend commuter service for business people, nearly full of passengers with briefcases and organisers. Excellent coffee and snacks were served. They swooped through the night sky, seeing lights from towns sparkle far below them as they crossed northern France and Belgium.

At Essen a limousine was waiting to waft them to their hotel, which couldn't have been more unlike the Romain in Paris. Called the Werdenhaus, it aimed at being a bijou residence of the late nineteenth century with much

128

mahogany furniture, dark panelling, everlasting flowers tastefully arranged in black iron urns, and heavy looped curtains at the windows. Clearly, since it was on the edge of the business centre, it prospered.

Zan's name was recognised at once. 'Ah yes, Mr McNaughton, welcome to the Werdenhaus – your instructions were faxed through to us. Unfortunately we could not provide two separate rooms for you and your colleague but we have put you in a suite – this will be suitable?'

Zan gave Erica a glance of apology. She frowned and half nodded, meaning they should wait and see.

The suite consisted of three rooms, an en suite double bedroom at each side of a small sitting-room furnished in the Biedermeier style. Erica's first thought was, This must be costing the earth! But Zan, after watching to see if she approved, nodded at the manager, who had shown them up.

'You approve? I am very glad, Mr McNaughton. As you requested, I reserved a table for dinner but perhaps may I ask – no great delay in coming to the dining-room because unfortunately last orders are at ten thirty on Sunday. The menu is here.' He pointed to it on a side table. 'If you could find a moment to choose at least the entrée and telephone the *maître* . . . ?'

He withdrew as the bellboy brought their luggage. Zan waited for Erica to choose where hers should go. With a shrug she gestured at the right-hand room, which proved to have a Turkey carpet, a canopied double bed clad with an old-fashioned duck-feather quilt, a vast wardrobe of whorled walnut wood, and a dressing-table with a triple gold-framed mirror.

She came out to rejoin Zan in the sitting-room. 'My room's absolutely gorgeous, like a museum piece!' she cried. 'How's yours?'

'Two single beds with carved oak headboards and a view of the Minster. Not a bad choice but I suppose this one and the Romain are part of the same management group. We'd better decide what we're going to eat in case the kitchens shut down while we're unpacking.'

They decided on something from the fish menu described as *'ortlich'* which Zan thought meant 'local'. He telephoned the order and asked for a bottle of Sancerre to be chilled. Erica gave a rueful glance at her crumpled appearance. These were the same clothes she'd put on at ten that morning.

'I've nothing smart to change into,' she mourned.

'You look fine.'

She shook her head as she went into her room to do what she could towards improving her appearance. A quick shower, a thorough hair-brush and a touch of lipstick and eye shadow made a difference, and on second thoughts she decided to put on the clothes she'd travelled in on Saturday – a lightweight dress of caramel-coloured wool and a Christian Dior scarf.

Zan looked approving when she joined him. He had changed into gaberdine slacks and a dark blue shirt worn open at the neck. 'This is the weekend look,' he explained.

The dining-room had a high, ornately plastered ceiling, and there were huge wall mirrors reflecting back the diners. Chandeliers of Bohemian glass tinkled in the faint movement of air. Most of the people at the tables were in semi-evening dress although there were one or two young diners in more casual clothes.

The meal was excellent, the simple wine just crisp enough to underline the flavour of the large and beautifully cooked fish. There were half a dozen vegetables to go with it and, hungry when she began, Erica soon began to feel sleepy from the effects of the food and wine. The crowd in the dining-room thinned out, and it was clearly time for all good citizens of Essen to call it a day.

'I'm dead on my feet, Zan,' she confessed.

'No dessert?'

'I couldn't eat another thing, thank you.'

'Coffee?' he suggested with a grin. 'Or would that keep you awake?'

'Nothing could keep me awake.' She gathered up her handbag and got to her feet.

'I'll hang on for coffee,' he said. 'Goodnight, and ask them for an early call tomorrow morning. The helicopter is booked for seven thirty.'

'*What?*'

'We don't want to hang about. We've got to get to Münster, make certain the Loebletzes still live at Dehlheim, and find our way there.'

'Oh dear,' she said from the depth of her weariness, and trudged out of the dining-room.

But a good night's sleep improved her outlook, so much so that even the buzzing of her telephone at six thirty and the darkness outside couldn't dampen her spirits.

She put on the jeans and thick sweater she'd packed against the possibility of harsh winter weather. In the dining-room there was a delicious smell of fresh rolls and coffee. Zan was already there, with a copy of the *Essener Zeitung*. 'Good morning,' she greeted him. 'What's the news?'

'Hanged if I know. I only speak enough German to get by in a *Weinhändler*. How about you?'

'Same here. I'm all right in an art gallery, but I don't go much farther than that.'

'Should we hire an interpreter?'

She thought about it. 'Let's leave it for the moment,' she suggested. 'How are you going to find out if the Loebletzes are really at this place called Dehlheim? Phone them?'

'I thought so. By the time we get to Münster it'll be mid-morning – not too early to ring them.'

'So if you find they speak English, we might not need an interpreter.'

'Well thought of.'

A car was waiting to take them to the heliport. It was Erica's first ride in a helicopter so she found the noise greater than she expected. There were two other passengers but conversation *en route* was somewhat limited. When they grounded at a small clublike airport outside Münster, she was glad to alight. There were taxis waiting as the helicopter landed and one of them took Erica and Zan to the centre of Münster in quick time.

Erica had scarcely heard of the place, but it turned out

to be quite an imposing city with a rebuilt town centre faithfully reproducing the atmosphere of its past. Zan asked to be set down at the town hall, a fourteenth-century building of Gothic pinnacles and gables and yet with an efficient rank of pay phones in its entrance hall.

He consulted the notes given him by the secretary at the Hotel Romain, dialled a number, and inserted some coins. Erica, sitting on a bench nearby, watched his progress. She could make out that he said, 'Hello? The Loebletz house?' then what followed became indecipherable. She'd told him the German word for 'painting' and that 'Impressionist' was the same in both English and German. But she couldn't make out whether he used them. After about five minutes he hung up the receiver.

'That was Frau Loebletz. She thinks I'm nuts. But she speaks some English and told me the farm's called Fernerdehl, says her husband should be in for coffee soon, so she'll tell him we're coming. She says he'll probably be able to understand what I'm talking about.'

'That implies that he speaks good English?'

'I hope so. Now let's go hire a car and get there – out on Route 219 past the *Aasee*, I think she said, then after fourteen kilometres turn right on the Merfelder road. We'll get a map.'

Though Münster was a handsome city, the weather was dismal. They stopped for a heartening cup of coffee at the Rathaus café then walked round the main square in a chilly drizzle, glancing in side streets until they found a car hire firm. Zan chose a recently registered BMW, signed the papers, accepted a map with instructions from the desk clerk, then followed him out to the yard where the car was waiting. Erica was glad to get out of the cold into the welcoming interior, and the heating system soon began to have a cheering effect.

Getting on to Route 219 wasn't exactly easy in the morning traffic. At length they were bowling along in a convoy of vehicles past the *Aasee*, which proved to be a lake with a zoo and other amenities, quickly glimpsed and quickly gone. Erica was map reading but the road signs were clear so they had turned off for Merfeld and then for Dehlheim by ten thirty.

The wooded plain through which they'd travelled looked prosperous and well tended. The village of Dehlheim had a main street with signposts alerting the passer-by to the '*Historische Allee*' and other sights worth visiting. Shop windows offered local pottery and brasswork. They crept through it and out into open country again. The Loebletz farm was said to be on their left with a sign, though Zan felt he might have got this wrong, showing a pig.

But it was so. A wrought iron sign swung from a post. It depicted a round-bodied pig with pricked ears and a very curly tail. 'FERNERDEHL. *Zuchtschweine Loebletz*' read an engraved name plate on the farm gate.

'It's a pig farm!' Zan exclaimed with amusement.

'Do you think so?' Erica said, winding down the window on the passenger side. 'Aren't pig farms usually smelly places?'

'That's true,' agreed Zan. 'Maybe a *Zuchtschwein* isn't a pig after all.' He got out, opened the gate, then got back in and edged gently through the entrance. Erica sprang out to close the gate behind them.

The road underfoot was well made though unpaved. They drove along it for a couple of hundred yards until they came into view of the farmhouse, a big building of old grey stone with a tiled roof but with much white paint to relieve any dullness.

As they drew up, the house door opened. A burly man with sparse grey hair stood on the threshold. 'Herr McNaughton? Welcome to Fernerdehl, the home of the pedigree *Westfalener!*'

Erica and Zan got out of the car. Bernhardt Loebletz shook hands with Zan in a hearty manner. He ushered him into the house, past a small lobby into a spacious living-room with a parquet floor and very fine old elm furniture. There Frau Loebletz was waiting to greet them, with coffee and cake on a tray in front of a bright wood fire. On a low table between two settees were some coloured brochures.

Frau Loebletz seemed to have less English than her

husband, but he made up for any hesitancy on her part. 'Let me take your coats! Poor weather today, I'm sorry you won't see them at their best, but never mind, it may clear. Sit down, sit down. Gertrud, our guests are thirsty, I'm sure. Coffee? Something stronger?'

They settled for coffee and some of Frau Loebletz's excellent *Pfefferkuchen*. Bernhardt hustled on with his remarks. 'I don't know whether you've been interested in it as a hobby, Herr McNaughton, or are you in business?'

'Business – er, yes – I grow grapes.'

'Grapes?' echoed Bernhardt, looking surprised. 'In England?'

'New Zealand.'

'*Ach nun* . . . The import rules are very strict there, I understand. Have you got import licences?'

'For what?' Zan asked, baffled.

'For the animals, of course,' Bernhardt replied, frowning a little.

'What animals?'

Erica had picked up one of the brochures on the low table. It was in English, and across a picture of a very healthy-looking pig it bore the words: 'Westphalia Pedigree Pigs, bred by Bernhardt Loebletz, Best in Europe'. She handed it to Zan, who stared at it in disbelief then shook his head at their host.

'Herr Loebletz, I'm afraid there's been a dreadful mistake. We're not here to buy pedigree pigs.'

'No?' said Bernhardt, taken aback. 'But my wife said—'

'You said you wished to speak with my husband on a family matter,' said Gertrud Loebletz carefully. 'The family matter of the Loebletz family is *Westfalener*.'

'No, I'm sorry – I didn't mean that,' Zan said, and Erica could see he was trying hard not to laugh. 'My colleague and I – Miss Pencarreth – we're here to ask about something quite different.'

'But something about the Loebletz family?' asked Bernhardt, still trying to catch up. 'Something about Wilhelm? Or Dorothea?'

'I'm afraid I don't know . . . ?'

'You don't know them? My son and daughter. It's not about them?'

'No, it's about Andreas Loebletz.'

There was a bewildered silence. 'My father?' asked Bernhardt at last.

'Yes. He was in the army during World War II?'

'The *Westfalenartillerie* – yes – why do you ask?'

'Did you ever hear him speak of a painting he bought then? While he was serving in the Paris area in 1943?'

'A painting?'

'*Ein Bild,*' supplied Erica. 'By Claude Monet, the Impressionist.'

Bernhardt said something under his breath in which she caught the word '*verrückt*', which Erica knew meant 'crazy'.

'No, we're quite serious,' she said in a very gentle tone. 'We're trying to track down a painting by Claude Monet—'

'*Ach, das ist unglaublich!*' cried Gertrud Loebletz, and went into a torrent of emotional German, far too fast and far too colloquial for either Zan or Erica to understand.

'What's wrong?' Erica muttered to Zan. 'What did I say?'

'No idea.'

Bernhardt had gone to his wife and was patting her and murmuring soothing words. She crumpled into a chair with her handkerchief to her eyes. Bernhardt turned back to his visitor. His manner had changed completely. 'I must ask you to leave. It is very upsetting to us to have these . . . these accusation. Years now, the war is over, a long time ago it is over, and yet people say these wild things about how we took their treasures. My father was an honourable man, a professional soldier, I can show medals—'

'No, no,' Zan broke in, 'believe me, Herr Loebletz, we're not accusing your father of anything—'

'Why then do you come? This allegation about a painting – we have no paintings, Vati was not such a man as to collect paintings – look and see if we have paintings on our walls!'

Indeed, the living-room walls had only plates and tiles of

blue Delft for decoration. Zan tried again. 'We're here to ask about a painting your father bought, Herr Loebletz. He didn't loot it or steal it, he bought it from a peasant who lived near the home of Claude Monet.'

'Ah, so now it is the peasant who stole it! I suppose now you say my father paid him to do this? *Wie können Sie sich unterstehen?* I will not have it said! He worked hard all his life, he made this farm by his own hands, he never did a dirty deal in his life!'

Frau Loebletz, hearing the resentment in her husband's voice, cried all the more. Bernhardt raised a fist in anger. 'Please leave. You should not come to us with this bad manners.'

Erica and Zan exchanged a glance. It was clear they were doing no good here. 'I'm sorry,' Erica said. 'We didn't mean to upset you. We only wanted to know if your father had ever mentioned a painting by Monet.'

'Never!' shouted Bernhardt. 'Never! Get out, get out!'

The car started at a touch and they drove in silence out to the road. Erica opened and closed the gate. As she got in again Zan made no move for a moment. 'Not one of our better efforts,' he remarked.

'Started in farce and ended in near-tragedy.'

'Frau Loebletz certainly went over the top about it. What's that Shakespeare bit – the lady doth protest too much? Something in the war record of *her* family she doesn't want to discuss.'

'If there is,' said Erica, 'it's none of our business. Besides, she could only have been a baby during the war, if she was even born then. She's not to blame.'

'Right.' He turned the car back in the direction of Münster. The well-tended fields sped by, some of them showing the faint green of young barley.

Erica said: 'I didn't leave a card. I didn't think they'd ever get in touch if they remembered anything about a painting.'

'Too right. And to tell the truth, Erica, I don't think they knew anything about that.'

'No.'

'After all, if Andreas Loebletz did buy the painting, he only owned it for a couple of years. Bought it in 1943 . . . what then, took it home next time he had leave?'

'I suppose so.'

'Left it there when he went back on duty. Then perhaps he gets posted somewhere further off – the Russian front, maybe, who knows? He survived the war, though, because the town council paid the money to him for his wrecked property. Hmm . . .'

'It's all so sad, Zan.'

'Not too comical, that's true. He comes back to find his house bombed and everything gone due to the attentions of the invading Russians.' A pause. 'Erica . . . ?'

'What?'

'If you were looting a house, would you enquire who owned it?'

'I'm sorry?' she countered.

'You're a Russian soldier in 1945, you've just rolled up to this house – let's say in a residential quarter of Hamburg. Perhaps it's already been damaged by bombing. You go in, you order the occupants out, you ransack the place and take what you fancy . . . At what point to do you say, "Excuse me, who owns this house?"'

At last he had wrenched her attention from the tears of Frau Loebletz.

'Well,' she said slowly, 'that does seem odd.' She opened her handbag to take out the papers she'd so hastily stowed away on their departure from the farm. She spread them out, and reread Yamin Emin's statement. Aloud she repeated: 'The house was probably the home of Hauptmann Andreas Loebletz . . .'

'How did he know that?' Zan inquired. 'Did the Russian family – what was the officer's name?'

'Sergei Piotrovitch,' she supplied.

'Did Sergei Whatsit's family tell him the German's name? And if they did, how come they knew it?'

'That is odd,' she said.

'You know what?' he exclaimed, feeling annoyance at his own stupidity. 'We've gone about this all wrong. We went to

Paris and we came here, because it was near at hand – we let geography dictate to us. But who are the last people to have actually handled the painting? The Turkish shopkeeper and the Russian family in Yalta.'

'Yes, that's what the statement says – some time last year Emin bought the box of things from the Piotrovitch family.'

'Istanbul . . .' muttered Zan. 'Yalta . . . They're a heck of a long way away.'

'Not far by air,' she objected, but without much enthusiasm. She saw again Frau Loebletz's tear-stained face. The mere suggestion that someone in their family might have taken something illegally had reduced her to misery. The idea of doing the same thing all over again with a Russian family wasn't enticing.

'Well, too far for the present expedition, at any rate. I have to be back tomorrow to find out how Nyree's getting on.'

'Yes, of course. Have you telephoned – I should have asked!'

'I rang from the hotel last night. The nurse said she was doing as well as could be expected – means nothing, of course. I left a message, saying I'd see her Tuesday afternoon.'

'You must buy her something to take back as a souvenir.'

'A book on German art? What's German art like?'

The conversation for the rest of the drive back to Münster was about the possibilities of shopping for a present. Zan used a public phone to check whether there were places available on the helicopter service. It proved they had until three o'clock. It was still raining off and on, the sky still leaden grey. They sought a comfortable restaurant for lunch then browsed the stalls in the Prinzipalmarkt. Since it was a Monday, there were fewer stalls than normal and nothing there appealed.

'We'll get something in Essen,' Erica suggested.

The return trip was dull because of low cloud and approaching darkness. But the centre of Essen was bustling with activity, shops spilling brightness out on to the pavements, neon signs opposing the winter darkness.

At Erica's suggestion they visited a shopping mall in which there was a boutique selling *Trachten*, variations of what had once been national costume. Zan stood back while Erica looked through the clothes on the rails. When she picked out an embroidered blouse in white silk muslin for his approval, he gave an embarrassed nod. He felt a fool in a woman's dress shop – but there was a charm in watching Erica as she studied the clothes, head on one side, a faint frown of concentration on her forehead.

The present problem solved, they walked back to the hotel. Shops were closing, home-going crowds thronged the pavements.

'Time to head for a bath, a drink, and dinner?' Zan suggested.

'I vote for that,' she agreed, feeling physical weariness begin to drag at her limbs.

In their suite, fresh flowers had been arranged and the curtains had been drawn against the dark. Erica had left her silk blouse and flannel skirt to be cleaned and pressed so after a refreshing shower she donned these. No little bottles of perfume were offered among the toiletries at the Werdenhaus so she used some of her own, an Italian fragrance with a background of almond blossom. This was all in an effort to cheer herself up, for the interview with Frau Loebletz had depressed her. She felt responsible in some way, because it was almost as soon as she mentioned the word 'painting' that Frau Loebletz had become distressed.

Sighing to herself, she came out of her room. Zan was in the sitting-room, speaking on the telephone. Erica at once began to draw back into her doorway but he held up a finger that meant 'Wait'.

'Yes, thank you. Yes, I'm glad to hear it. Tell her I'll be there tomorrow afternoon. Tell her I've bought her a present. Yes . . . Yes . . .'

Erica pointed to herself. 'Give a message from me,' she said. 'Good wishes – something like that.'

'Would you tell my sister, Erica Pencarreth sends good wishes – Pencarreth . . .' He began to spell it out but amended it to, 'Oh, never mind, just tell her "Erica", she'll know. Thank you. Goodbye.'

'What's the news?'

'Not bad. She's coming through the first stages rather well.' He made a little grimace. 'I hope she's not still hitched up to all those tubes and things when I get there tomorrow. I know it's stupid, but I find it sort of . . . scary . . .'

'I don't think it's stupid,' Erica responded. 'All that specialist treatment is foreign territory to most of us. But I'm glad she's doing well.'

He nodded, then put the subject aside. Here was this attractive girl, probably tired and hungry after a long day, and he was maundering on about his own affairs. He'd have to get a hold on himself, he was probably becoming a bore about Nyree.

'Let's go and see what the chef is offering us this evening,' he said, and led the way to the lift.

They went into the bar for a pre-dinner drink. There was a pianist in a corner playing softly, performing music from popular shows but adding his own variations. Erica asked for something light and at Zan's suggestion they ordered glasses of a rose Rulander softened with plenty of soda water. The waiter brought the menu for their appraisal.

'Now here's something with *Westfalenisch* attached to it,' Zan cried, laughing. 'I think we owe it to ourselves to have it, whatever it is.'

The waiter was prepared to give them a long explanation but Erica didn't really mind what they ate. She let Zan make the choices, especially concerning the wine. She heard him discussing vintages – 'No, no, the Niersteiner Pettenthal '89 . . .'

'Let me recommend *Feine Auslese*, sir . . .'

The dining-room was just as busy as the previous night. The hum of conversation was comforting to Erica, who didn't feel much like talking. She asked a few questions about the wine, which enabled Zan to share some of his knowledge: 'German wines are mostly at their best when you drink them near where they're produced – they don't seem to travel very well. But I like their lightness and back home we're trying to produce something like that for local consumption – something to please a growing market for table wines.'

After a bit he said, 'What's the matter?'

She was startled and then ashamed. Had she been such a dull companion? 'Nothing, really.'

'You're over-tired, perhaps—'

'No, no, nothing like that . . .' She sighed. 'I can't get Frau Loebletz out of my mind.'

'That wasn't your fault.'

'Whose was it, then?'

'You mustn't blame yourself. I was there too, remember – I'm as much to blame as you, if there *is* any blame.' He reached out and took her hand across the little table. 'Come on now, forget about it.'

The warmth of his fingers clasping hers seemed to offer a remedy for her dejection. She twined her own in his. 'You're so tolerant,' she said, smiling. 'I didn't mean to be a bore.'

'You're never that, Erica.'

He raised her hand to his lips and imprinted a kiss on it, soft as thistledown, thrilling as a spark of electricity. She gave a little gasp, trying to withdraw. But he refused to let go and after a moment she leaned forward slightly, taking their clasped hands to her cheek.

They said very little after that. Zan summoned the waiter and signed the check for the meal. The lift seemed to take forever to climb to their floor. He opened the door of the suite, closed it behind them.

The next moment they were in her bedroom and in each other's arms.

Ten

U nwilling to awake from the glorious dream, Erica stretched in the downy bed. Her eyelids still closed, she could sense that light was filtering into the room from around the curtains. She stretched languorously, one hand touching the pillow alongside her head.

She awoke more fully, pulling herself up on an elbow. He was gone. The pillow held the impression of his head and the faint scent of sandalwood. An early riser, a country man . . .

She focused her glance on the bedside clock. Well past eight in the morning. She should get up.

But instead she pulled his pillow to her and hugged it against her breast. She breathed in his scent, holding the memory. Last night his head had rested here, his lips kissing her skin, his hands caressing her body, and pleasure had suffused her entire being.

Faint sounds reached her through the mists of recollection. In the streets outside, traffic was going by. Within the hotel there was movement, doors opened and closed.

She should get up.

Reluctantly she swung her legs out from under the eiderdown. She rose and stretched, breathing in deeply, for she knew that all too soon everything in the room would be aired and swept and tidied – and the afterglow of that sojourn in paradise would be gone for ever.

She padded into the bathroom. Its mirror reflected her body, naked, still flushed with the warmth of love-making. She smiled, and seeing her reflection smile back at her, she paused. She stared at herself.

What had she done?

In the glass, the face staring back at her coloured up with

shame and remorse. Tears welled in her eyes, her mouth twisted in an unspoken cry of pain.

She had been unfaithful to Willard.

The thought stunned her. How could she have let it happen?

Because she was depressed, because he had been sympathetic and seemed to want to comfort her, because the night had loomed black and drear with the memory of the German woman in tears . . .

But none of that was an excuse.

'Oh, no,' she moaned, head bent, arms coming about herself defensively. 'Oh, no, how could I?'

For a long time she stood, huddled into herself, trying to get a grip on the beginnings of the day. The night was gone – gone with its physical joy, its sense of wonder, its promise of an eternal bond. An illusion, brought on by weakness, cowardice, the need for someone to hold her and tell her she was kind, pleasing, a loving and a good person.

He had said all those things to her, had said she was wonderful. And she had believed him because it was what she needed, so that in gratitude she had opened herself to him, rewarded him with what he asked –

No, that was untrue, she was making excuses for her own weakness. The truth was, she had wanted him as much as he had wanted her.

But that was last night. This was the chill light of morning. Now she was awake and in full control of her thoughts, and she knew she had been unfaithful, treacherous. What would Will say if he knew? The thought filled her with anguish. Tears began to stream down her face.

When at last she roused herself to start the day, the shower washed away the tears. But the remorse she felt was heavy within her breast, heavy as a stone.

At last she set about the hard task of facing the outside world. She made up her face, brushed her hair, and put on her dress. Her throat dry with the aftermath of her tears, she longed for the simple comfort of a cup of coffee, though she dreaded the thought of the busy breakfast-room.

But when she opened her bedroom door, there was Zan, sitting at a table laid with a white cloth and all the accoutrements of breakfast. He was watching the television, on which there was a German news programme with the sound turned very low.

He switched it off as she came into the sitting-room, jumped up, took one hand, kissed her lightly on the lips, and drew her to a chair. 'I thought this would be nicer than being in with the mob,' he explained. 'Coffee's fresh, I ordered it when I heard you moving about.'

When she sank down on her chair, she saw that there were three yellow roses in a slender silver vase at her place. She felt herself flush. She couldn't find a voice to speak with.

'We don't need to hurry,' Zan was saying. 'There's a feeder flight to Cologne at ten forty-five. From there we can fly direct to Heathrow.' He was pouring coffee, offering her the cup, perhaps a little too busy to study her.

The thought of sharing the seat next to him on a plane for the length of the journey was horrifying to her. She forced herself into speech. 'I thought of staying on a day or two,' she blurted.

At her words, at her tone, he looked up at her. He stared. 'Staying . . . ?'

'Yes.'

'What for?'

'I . . . I thought I'd visit the Folkwang, take a look at the Gauguins and Van Goghs.'

He shook his head in perplexity. 'But I have to travel today, Erica.' There was the beginning of reproach in his voice.

'Of course, yes, I know that.'

There was something wrong. She looked . . . unhappy. He studied her with more alertness. 'What's the matter?' he asked, his heart sinking.

She had automatically taken the coffee he had offered. She was stirring it now, although she'd put in no sugar, and was watching the whirlpool she caused in the dark brown liquid.

'About last night,' she began, face averted. 'I've got to say something.'

'Yes?'

144

'I don't think we should take it too seriously.'

He heard the words, couldn't take in the sense. 'Why not?'

'It was a . . . a mistake. It should never have happened.'

'That's your opinion,' he rejoined, knowing it was a sharp and foolish response.

'It has to be your opinion too. It can't mean anything.'

'No, wait – I can't believe this – it seemed to mean something last night, when we were together in the dark—'

'No, that was illusion,' she broke in, grasping for the words to convey her meaning. 'And it only happened because I was feeling sad . . . weepy . . . I couldn't get Frau Loebletz out of my mind and—'

'Let's leave Frau Loebletz out of this,' he said in a tone that was beginning to have an edge. 'This is between you and me.'

Now she faced up to him. 'But that's just it – there *is* no you-and-me.'

'It all just vanishes – into thin air?' Disbelief was in every syllable. 'If you think I'll accept that—'

'But you have to, because you see there's no true link between us. How could there be?' she rushed on, trying to prevent him from contesting her view. 'You know – you must know – that I'm deeply involved with someone else.'

'Townley, you mean.' He could hardly bring himself to utter the name.

'Yes – Will – he and I have been tied up together for a long time.'

'That didn't seem to bother you last night!' As soon as he'd said it, he wanted to snatch back the accusation. Berating her, telling her she'd been in the wrong – that was no way to win this fight. But it was too late, and she began self-censure at once.

'No, I know I was wrong. I apologise. I was weak – silly—'

'Willing?' he suggested, anger getting the better of him. 'Co-operative?' He couldn't control the resentment he was feeling at this rejection.

She bowed her head. How could she challenge those

words? After a moment she said, 'I can't deny it. I admit I was totally in the wrong. I can only ask you to forgive me if I've hurt you badly.'

He wasn't going to admit that she had hurt him. He rose from the table, walked to the window, and stood looking out. A little silence fell.

At last he commented, 'Now I understand why the Van Goghs in the museum seem so alluring. We'd hardly make good travelling companions.'

He heard a sound that was half a sob, half assent.

'I have to get back to London. You know that,' he continued.

'Yes.'

'Perhaps it's just as well.'

'Yes.'

Another silence. Erica could feel her breath catching in her breast as she stifled her tears.

'So this seems to be goodbye.'

'Yes.'

He swung round. He decided to treat it all as simply a business matter. 'Of course it makes no difference to your involvement with the painting. You'll carry on enquiring into the background of the Monet.'

'Oh, no!'

'Why not?'

'It would be . . . Wouldn't it be embarrassing?'

'We don't have to see each other,' he said. 'You can finish up in your own time and let me have a report.'

'But wouldn't you rather hire someone else?'

'Who, for instance? A complete stranger that I'd have to explain everything to? Makes no sense.' That put her in her place. What was she, after all? Simply a hireling.

He was so terse and cool that she found she couldn't argue. She said, trying to keep the quaver out of the words, 'You really want me to go on with it?'

'Certainly. But of course I'd like the painting transferred to my keeping. There's a perfectly good safe at the Mayfair Rialto.'

'Of course. I'll see to it.'

146

Somehow this wounded her almost more than anything else he had said. It implied that because she'd given in to physical temptation, she wasn't to be trusted in any other way. But she couldn't make any protest – what right had she to do that?

'Is there anything else we ought to discuss before I leave?'

'No, but can I just say . . . I want you to know how deeply I—'

'I'll alter the travel arrangements on my way out,' he cut in, 'and arrange for your stay-over. Do you have enough Deutschmarks?'

'Yes, thank you,' she said, although in fact she had none.

'That seems to be all, then. Goodbye, Erica,' he said, walking towards the door to the corridor. 'I'd say it's been nice knowing you but it wouldn't be true.'

Next moment he was gone.

The closing of the door behind him was like a signal of release. Tears flooded down her cheeks, she leaned over the table and hid her face in her arms. In doing so she upset her coffee cup and capsized the vase with the yellow roses. At the cascade of liquid over her hands she grabbed at a napkin and began stupidly dabbing at the mess.

Then she threw down the cloth and ran into the bedroom, where she fell on the bed and sobbed as if her heart was broken.

After a few minutes she got control of herself. She thought she heard a sound in the sitting-room. Smoothing the tears from her cheeks, she ran out in hopes of finding Zan there.

But it was a bellboy, going into the other bedroom to collect Zan's bag and coat. It dawned on her that Zan was going – leaving the hotel now, this minute, never to be met with again if he could help it. She caught the boy's arm as he made for the door.

'Wait!'

'Fräulein?'

'Tell Mr McNaughton – please say that—'

'*Bitte?*'

Her hand fell away. There was no message she could send. 'Nothing,' she said. 'Go ahead.'

And then the bag and coat were gone, and the room was empty, and she stood looking at the roses scattered over the table. She had an impulse to gather them up, rescue and keep them – but for what? What would be the point?

Half an hour later she had washed her face, put on some lipstick, picked up her bag and coat, and left the hotel. She went, as she'd said she would, to the Folkwang Museum.

For an hour she wandered round it. The Renoirs, the Gauguins . . . She saw them but they meant nothing to her. Usually, in times of trouble, paintings had been her refuge. But today they offered no respite from the misery of her thoughts.

Midday saw her in Haraldstrasse, thinking she ought to eat because she felt light-headed. She would need to buy some Deutschmarks because she only wanted something simple, something she could hardly pay for with her credit card. The currency bought, she had coffee and a sort of savoury pastry at a kiosk, then faced the fact that she ought to ring Willard.

She'd given him the impression she'd be home by now. If he was ringing her flat, he'd be getting her answering machine and wondering what had happened to her.

The easiest place to make the call was the hotel suite. So she walked back, the chill air bracing her and making her a little less distressed. She mustn't let Will know she was upset. She mustn't give him any clue to what had happened. She could never tell him. He would never forgive her.

Settled in a comfortable chair with the phone in her lap, she dialled the Townley Gallery. She guessed Will wouldn't yet have gone out to lunch. If he had a lunch engagement it would be for one thirty, in the late-lunching Mayfair fashion.

He picked up on the third ring. His cheerful announcement, 'Townley Gallery,' made her heart lurch. Just to hear his voice seemed an accusation in itself.

'Will darling, it's Erica.'

'Ah, so there you are! When did you get back? I've been ringing—'

'I'm not at home, Will, I'm in Essen.'

'*Essen*? In *Germany*?' When she didn't disagree he asked, 'What on earth are you doing there?'

148

'Finding the Loebletz family.'

'In Essen?' She could tell he was struggling to catch up with what, to her, was a continuous stream of action. 'But . . . Loebletz . . . don't I remember they were connected with Hamburg?'

'It turned out they'd moved to a farm near Münster.'

'Münster? I thought you said Essen?'

'Oh, it's just travel routes, that's all, just a way to get to the farm.'

He took a minute to assimilate that. 'So what did the Loebletzes have to say about the Monet?'

'They'd never heard of it.'

'Oh dear,' said Willard. 'And after all that hopping about to get to them. But I suppose it was a long time ago that – what was his name? – Andreas? – owned the picture.'

'Yes and when it came to mentioning it, Frau Loebletz – she's the daughter-in-law of Andreas – got very upset, thought it was an accusation of some sort, so that was perhaps why they didn't want to talk about it. But it was the same with the Curacies in Paris. They'd never heard anything about a painting.'

'So it's all been a dead loss?' he said in a sympathetic tone.

The interview with the Curacies came back to her. It seemed to have happened in another world. 'No-o,' she countered, 'it wasn't entirely a waste. They had a note in the handwriting of Aristide, and, what do you think, Will – it matched the gardener's boy's handwriting.'

'Now that's good!' cried Will. 'That's really great! Oh, I *am* glad. So that settles that. What with the handwriting, and Frau Loebletz being a bit cranky about what her pa-in-law might have got up to during the war, which implies there *was* something . . .'

She was going to protest that the scene hadn't been quite like that, but held her tongue. She didn't really want to talk about it; it still grieved her to have hurt the farmer's wife.

'So now that's all settled, eh? When will you be back?'

She ought to say, 'This very day.' But something prevented her. Some echo of this conversation came back to her so that she realised she'd never once mentioned Zan. She hadn't intentionally avoided his name, yet all the same she'd given Will the impression she'd been alone on her trip.

So now she was to go home and actually face Will – and what would she do then? Keep up the lie – for it was a lie – that she'd had no companion? Tell Will that she'd forgotten to speak of Zan when she phoned? And account for it – how?

She found she couldn't face it. She was still too confused and distressed by what had happened. She couldn't return to ordinary life as if she hadn't gone through a traumatic experience – not yet. She needed time to convalesce.

'No, I shan't be back just yet,' she said. 'I have a few more days' leave due to me.'

'But what on earth are you going to do?' Will demanded. 'You're not going to hang around in Essen, surely?'

'No, I—'

'And if you're thinking of going back to Paris, leave that for now, Erica, and you and I can go together at Easter and have a lovely time – how about that?'

'No, I'm not going to Paris,' she said. 'I'm going to Yalta.'

She'd had no idea she was going to say it, and once said, it seemed outlandish. But on the heels of that thought came another – why not? She had the time, and she had credit cards, and the hotel had a travel department, and it might not be too difficult to get to Yalta and find the address of Sergei Piotrovitch, who had owned the Monet before it reached the curio shop.

And it was something useful to do, something that might take her mind off the disaster she had caused.

Willard was still making no response at all on the other end of the line.

'I thought I'd go on to Yalta,' she resumed, as if it had been a long-held plan. 'Speak to the family of the Russian officer.'

'Erica!' he exclaimed. 'That's a crazy idea!'

'What's crazy about it?'

She heard him draw in an exasperated breath. 'Well, in the first place, do you speak any Russian?'

'No, but I don't speak much German and it went all right.'

'Russia's different—'

'In what way? They have a travel service – what's it called – Intourist – I can get in touch with them.'

'They always sound like the absolute end,' Willard protested, 'and besides, Russia's freezing cold in winter.'

'But this is Yalta – it's a health resort sort of place, isn't it? – on the Black Sea. The climate's probably a bit like Turkey.'

'But why do you want to do this, in any case? You've just said the handwriting in the letter is OK, that's verification enough surely—'

'No, I think I'll go, Will.'

'Erica, it's too dangerous! I forbid you!'

To her own surprise she felt a stab of annoyance pierce through the depression that had been engrossing her. 'What's dangerous about going to a health resort?' she countered. 'It's probably like Bournemouth or Torquay.'

'No it isn't. You'll be alone in a country where everything is going to the dogs and you don't even speak the language.'

'Oh, don't be silly, Will! I'll hire an interpreter, a courier – it'll be no problem.'

'Erica, you're not to do it!'

'Will, stop giving me orders,' she said, irritated.

There was a startled halt on Willard's part. Then he said, 'But you're being foolish!'

'Well, I have a perfect right to be foolish if I want to.'

'Even if I tell you not to do it?'

'Even then, my precious.' She heard the sarcasm in her tone and was astonished at herself.

'Erica, you're making me very cross. Stop talking nonsense and get on the next plane home.'

She took a moment before she spoke. 'I'm going to Yalta, Will. I'll send you a postcard.'

He was saying, 'You'll do no such thing,' when she said, 'Bye, Will,' and put the phone down.

It took Willard two or three seconds to recover from his astonishment. Then he hung up and was just about to press the buttons for return-call when his phone rang. It was his lunch guest ringing to say he'd be a little late at the restaurant. So after that, the return-call buttons were no use. He sat silent, thinking hard. Somehow he must stop her from carrying out this wild plan. That was imperative.

While Willard was thinking what to do, Erica had contacted Reception and asked to be put through to the travel service. 'Someone who speaks English, please,' she requested.

'Madam,' said the girl on the switchboard, 'everyone at the Werdenhaus speaks English.'

So it proved. She heard the click of the connection then a polite male voice asking, 'How may I help you, Ms Pencarreth?'

'I'd like to make arrangements to travel to Yalta,' she replied.

There was just the merest trace of a hesitation. 'Yalta in the Crimea, Fräulein?'

'In Russia, yes.'

'It's the Ukraine now, I believe.' Very efficient, very well informed. 'Since the break-up of the Soviet Union. When would you wish to travel?'

'As soon as possible.'

'By air or rail?'

'Oh, by air, of course – the train must take for ever.'

'I believe it is a lengthy rail journey, Fräulein. By air . . . I believe the airline is . . .' There were faint sounds of clicking as he looked it up on his computer. 'Ah, naturally, Ukraine International. Now, you are able to fly from either Berlin or Frankfurt. If you will tell me which you prefer I will inquire for tickets.'

'I suppose . . . Frankfurt . . . that's nearer, isn't it?'

'Oh yes, and also on your way eastwards,' said the travel agent, with something in his voice that told her he didn't think much of her geography.

'Very well, then, from Frankfurt, as soon as possible.'

'I'm making the enquiry now . . . I see no problem about getting a seat, Ms Pencarreth. You could travel tomorrow.'

'Tomorrow. What time – because I have to get to Frankfurt first, don't I?'

'You could be in Frankfurt in time for lunch. The Ukraine flight leaves at fifteen hundred hours – no problem. Except that . . . ah . . . I believe . . . you need a visa for the Ukraine.'

Erica's hopes suffered a blow. A visa. It could take weeks to get a visa. She'd once wanted to attend an art exhibition in St Petersburg but the visa hadn't arrived until after the exhibition finished. 'Where do I apply?' she asked.

'Wait . . . a moment . . .' There was a short pause during which she heard conversation in German going on in the travel office. 'Ms Pencarreth, if you could give us an hour or so . . . one of my colleagues is a Georgian by birth – by this I mean he is from the part of Russia that was once the Georgian Soviet Republic. He says he could probably help in this matter.'

'Well . . . that's very kind of him. Thank you.'

'Is there any other requirement, Fräulein?'

She was trying to think ahead to the next day or two. 'I don't speak any Russian. I'll need an interpreter. Could you contact Intourist and see about that? To meet me when I land.'

'Do you also wish accommodation?'

'I don't know. How long is all this going to take?'

'That remains to ascertain. Let me make investigations and when you come to speak to Tulya, we will perhaps have an itinerary.'

'That sounds good.' She glanced at the little ornate clock on the wall of the suite. 'I've another phone call to make and after that I'll have some tea in the lounge and then come to the travel office.'

'Very good, Fräulein.'

She rang her mother in Cornwall. The call went through without difficulty but she got her mother's answering machine. No doubt Lisbet was out on the moors with an easel in front of her. She left a cheery message: 'Here I am in Germany on the track of the Monet, setting off again tomorrow, ring you from the next stop.'

It was now well after two and the lunchtime crowd at the hotel had more or less dispersed. The hotel kitchens,

153

accustomed to catering for business people from all over Europe, knew how to present afternoon tea. It was brought on a silver tray with matching pot, creamer and sugar basin, together with a plate of tiny sandwiches, and a little two-tiered rack offering cakes covered with fondant icing. Erica found she was hungry enough to eat a sandwich or two but it was the tea she really enjoyed. She found herself remembering Zan's dismay at the tea-bag in the café in the Bois. But she immediately made herself think of something else.

Yet his image was persistent. She found herself saying inwardly, I'll teach him to think I'm silly and weak! I'll prove it by sorting out this problem about the Monet and I'll write a businesslike report and present my bill and that will be that!

It was a version of 'I'll show him!' and when she recognised the fact, she was both ashamed and amused. What did it matter what he thought of her now? They could never be anything but cool business acquaintances. But she wanted to prove she had integrity. That was what was impelling her to make the trip to see the Russian family in Yalta.

She passed some time with an English-language magazine. At three thirty it was time to test the efficiency of the travel service. She signed the check for afternoon tea then made her way across the foyer to the door marked *Reiseburo*. Inside she found a pleasant sitting area with plantation chairs and potted palms, to conjure up the idea of holidays in balmy countries. At one side there was a desk with computer screens. She glanced towards it, and immediately a man with a shock of black hair and piercing black eyes came to greet her.

'Ms Pencarreth? I am Tulya.' He touched the name badge on his lapel. He was holding a folder of dark blue plastic with the name of the hotel on it. 'May we sit down? I have here beginnings of your travel arrangements.' His English wasn't as good as that of the other hotel staff but after all he was a Russian making his living in Germany and having to communicate in yet another language.

They sat. He opened the folder. 'First, you are booked

on fifteen hundred hours flight tomorrow from Frankfurt to Odessa—'

'Odessa?' She was startled. She didn't even know where Odessa was.

'Yes, there is no flight to Yalta. It is popular holiday resort but it is not on international airlines. But however, no problem! Odessa is large port on the Black Sea. From there, by boat to Yalta, easy trip. On hydrofoil – you know hydrofoil?'

She shook her head.

'Very fast, very modern – much used in Russia for travel on big rivers and inland water. I myself have never been on Black Sea hydrofoil but is surely pleasant, passengers mostly tourist, with money to spend, you see?'

'Yes, I understand. So I fly to Odessa – arriving when?'

'Late evening, in time for supper and overnight in hotel. Shall we book hotel? Many good hotels in Odessa, you pay on departure, no problem.'

'Yes, you'd better do that. Will they speak English at the hotel?'

'You ask for interpreter, no?'

'Well, yes, I did. Have you been in touch with Intourist?'

'Intourist, huh.' The impressive black eyes flashed contempt. 'If you are pleased, I arrange something better. Now there is *perestroika*, it is possible to have small private firm – there is co-operative tourist agency, some graduate students, speaking languages, you understand. I contacted now through friends, there is office of agency in Odessa but only one courier because now of course is winter, few tourists. But I have arranged English-speaking guide, will meet you at Odessa airport, conduct you to hotel, accompany on hydrofoil to Yalta and there, arrange whatever you need. Is this satisfactory?'

'It sounds marvellous,' said Erica with gratitude. 'How will I know him at Odessa?'

'Will hold up sign with initials of agency – Friendly Tourist Agency.'

'But won't it be in Russian letters?'

'Of course not,' exclaimed Tulya, almost offended. 'Vasyli

155

understands it must be English. Look for FTA – and Vasyli, I understand, is about fifty, ex-teacher, from Kiev which is capital of Ukraine.'

'Excellent. Thank you, I appreciate this very much. Now, you were to tell me how to get a visa?'

'No problem!' he cried with delight. 'Vasyli tells me on telephone, arrive at Odessa, he conducts you to state office there, you pay fifty dollars and visa is handed over at once.'

'As easy as that?'

'I say, no problem. Things are a little bit different now in former Soviets, not all, but some.'

'So I pay the equivalent of fifty dollars – in Deutschmarks?'

Tulya looked doubtful. 'Deutschmarks . . . ye-es . . . but better dollars. Dollars are more welcomed everywhere. You have dollars?'

'Not at the moment—'

'Shall I arrange some currency? It is better to have small value notes – one dollar, ten dollar, not hundred dollar. I will see to it.'

'Do I take it that credit cards are no good, then?'

'Oh, credit cards . . . yes, no problem in hotels, et cetera, but for small buying – newspaper, taxi, so forth – buy Ukraine coupons with dollars, pay in Ukrainian. But Vasyli will see to such, no problem.'

It began to seem as if the journey might have its difficulties, yet Tulya seemed able to foresee them all. He pointed to the sheets of paper clipped into the folder. 'This is beginning of travel instructions. Now you have agreed to Friendly Tourist Agency, I finalise everything with Vasyli, I have it organised by the computer, I give you print-out by this evening or first thing in morning. You will want taxi to airport, no?'

'Yes, please.'

'Very good. If anything else occurs you wish to do, ring one-four-nine, here is twenty-four-hour service. When all is complete, we add it to your hotel bill, no?'

'If you would, please. Thank you.'

They shook hands. As she was going out, she turned back. 'Will it be cold in the Ukraine?'

Tulya gave her a mischievous smile. 'You think Stalin

goes on holiday to cold place? No, nice climate, not very cold winter but perhaps sea breeze, eh? A good coat, what you call Burberry?'

'Thank you.'

She already had a good coat. But perhaps she needed a few things because she'd expected to be away only three days at most. She went out into the main shopping street of Essen where her trusty credit card was all she needed. She bought a supply of underwear, a couple of cotton shirts, an extra sweater, a warm scarf, a Russian phrase book and two paperbacks to see her through the inevitable boredom of air travel.

Next morning she was roused by the wake-up call she had arranged. She showered and dressed, finished her packing, and went down to breakfast. No yellow roses this morning, no elegant table in the privacy of the sitting-room. She could have ordered that, but it would have reminded her of the painful explanation to Zan. The memory caused her a pang as she hurried through the room to the outer door.

As she came out of the lift in the foyer, the head porter approached. 'Your taxi will be here in one hour, Ms Pencarreth.'

After the buffet breakfast she went to the desk with her credit card to pay the bill. She knew it would be a big one but her standing at the bank was good, there would be no problem, as Tulya liked to say.

But there was a problem – of a very unexpected kind.

'But Fräulein, there is nothing to pay,' said the desk clerk.

'I beg your pardon?'

'Everything is taken care of.'

'Taken care of? What do you mean?'

'Your bill is pre-paid.'

'But how—' Yet even as she said it, she knew how.

'Mr McNaughton gave instructions before he left – everything on your bill was to be added to his – so you see, there is no bill for you.'

'But I can't permit that.'

'*Bitte?*' responded the desk clerk, startled into German. '*Was wollen Sie sagen?*'

157

'I can't allow Mr McNaughton to pay my bill!' Erica cried in horror. 'It's out of the question!'

'But, Ms. Pencarreth—'

'Let me see the total. Here is my card.'

'But Fräulein, it isn't necessary—'

'Yes it is, it's very necessary – I insist.'

The desk clerk, a young man with a fresh early-morning shine, became very perturbed. '*Moment, bitte,*' he requested, and went to the door in the partition behind him. He put his head in, there was a murmured conversation, then the duty manager appeared, frowning a little.

'There is some difficulty, Ms Pencarreth?'

'Not the slightest. I just want to pay my bill.'

'But my colleague has explained, the bill is paid.'

'I understand it is to be added to the bill of Mr McNaughton. Well, I don't wish that to happen. I'll pay what I owe.'

There was a stifled sigh from the manager. 'Fräulein, the total bill was put through the computer this morning as soon as you sat down to breakfast. There is nothing we can do now, I fear.'

'It's been paid?'

'The transaction was instantaneous, as you would expect.'

'It can't be undone?'

'Not without instructions from Mr McNaughton.'

Erica felt hot with embarrassment. She'd spent an enormous amount of money – return air fare to Odessa, currency, hire of a courier, travel agency fees, to say nothing of the bill she'd run up here in the hotel.

But what could she do? There was a taxi just about to arrive at the hotel, and a plane to be caught at Essen airport. She gave a shrug and a nod, then waved at the hall porter to take her travel bag, which had just been brought down from her suite.

She consoled herself by handing him a very large tip before she stepped into the taxi.

Eleven

Naturally there were delays. The flight from Odessa didn't come in on time and therefore was late going out again. A problem arose with a weather front over the Carpathians.

So when Erica disembarked it was the early hours of the next morning. The airport seemed to be empty except for the arrivals from her flight. Since she was carrying her overnight bag slung over her shoulder, she didn't have to wait at the baggage carousel. She made her way to Passport Control wondering how she was going to explain the lack of a visa to a crotchety official at this hour in the morning. Her courier, she supposed, had long ago given up and gone home.

But no. Hard by Passport Control a small middle-aged man in a dark blue suit was wagging a placard on the end of a little stick. She read, with fervent gratitude, the letters 'FTA'. As the short queue diminished and she reached the window, he squirmed into place beside her, flourishing a piece of paper. A short colloquy ensued. The official produced a small wooden case from which he took a stamping device.

'Sign, please,' whispered the courier, pushing the piece of paper towards her. She obeyed, the official thumped an indecipherable design in purple ink on a page of her passport, and she was waved on.

No problem, as Tulya would have said.

The courier put his placard in a canvas satchel slung across his shoulder. He made a formal inclination of the head. 'Vasyli Galyatavenko,' he announced. 'Welcome to the Ukraine, Miss Pencarreth.' She knew she had not the slightest chance of ever remembering a name like that but he solved it by saying, 'You must of course call me Vasyli.'

'Thank you. I'm so glad to see you – I thought you would have gone home by now!'

'No, no, waiting is part of the occupation, you know. I found a quiet corner in the bar and had a nap. This way to the taxi rank.'

His English was impeccable, with only the faintest accent and none of the tendency to miss out 'the' and 'a' heard in most Russians. At the taxi rank there was a bargaining session after he helped her in, then he too took a seat beside her and they were off.

'First let me tell you the next arrangement. I have booked you in at the Stralava, a quiet hotel. Odessa, you understand, is a seaman's town so one must choose with care. Unfortunately, the hotel restaurant will be closed but we could either stop at a café *en route* – which I don't recommend – or you could buy the late-night tray at the hotel. This provides biscuits, a savoury spread, and a slice of honey cake. Drinks you can get from a machine on the landing.'

'Thank you. I'm not very hungry, food was available on the plane.'

'Understood. Now, as to the hydrofoil. The first departure is at six—'

'Oh no,' she groaned, with a glance at her watch. 'I don't think I could make it.' She was longing for a shower and a bed on which to stretch out – leg room on the plane had been very limited and she'd been locked in by a large lady encumbered with a baby.

'Very well, the next one at eight?'

She nodded. 'How long is the journey to Yalta?'

'Approximately six hours, sometimes longer if there is much to load or unload at intervening ports. We could, if you like, stop for lunch at Sevastopol – there are some interesting ruins, a few miles outside, of a Greek settlement—'

'No, no,' she interrupted. 'This isn't a sightseeing trip. I might take a look on my return journey but before anything else, I must try to contact the Piotrovitch family.'

'Concerning that,' said Vasyli, producing a notebook, 'as requested I made some enquiries. Piotrovitch is not an entirely uncommon name, and by the way in the Ukraine it is usually transliterated not with 'i-t' but with a 'y' – but no matter. I found several in the telephone directory for Yalta. To narrow it down, I consulted the Office of Public Records in Kiev – that is my home town, you understand, our capital city – and I found that a Colonel Sergei Piotrovych had been in the 4th Ukraine Tank Regiment during World War II. His children were or are Danila and Tanya. Now, of course, daughters usually marry and they then take their husband's name. Danila married Teofan Sakovych, and I am happy to tell you that Sakovych is listed as dwelling in staff quarters at the Sanatorium Bonne Santé on Ulitsa Markeyan.'

'In a sanatorium?' she cried. 'He's a doctor?'

Vasyli gave a cynical laugh. 'Ah, Miss Pencarreth, you don't understand the system under which we used to live. Officials and heads of departments and factory directors were entitled to treatment for their health, free of charge and of course in the very best establishments. So Yalta is full of so-called clinics, but these are really mostly hotels – as in a spa, you know?'

Erica understood. 'So Sakovych may be a member of the hotel staff?'

'Or, perhaps, he simply lives there. These places have had to adapt – we are all, dear lady, very adaptable these days. The former staff quarters of the clinic are probably just rented out – but we shall see.'

'You speak awfully good English,' she commented. 'Did you study in the UK?'

'Alas, no – that was very difficult to achieve when I was a young man. But I went to Kiev University and the tuition was excellent, though I am told by others for whom I've acted as interpreter that I am very pedantic. My favourite English author is Sir Walter Scott, you see. I am told he is very much out of favour in his homeland these days.'

Erica laughed. 'I'm afraid that's true.'

'I taught for many years at an Intermediate Academy. But you know money is not available these days so the Academy was closed. I take private pupils now but they want American phrases I find it hard to keep up with. So I also act as courier and guide. I find it interesting to meet new people.'

They were coming into the city now, through streets that seemed broad and were tree-lined but not very well lit. 'I will see you into the hotel and translate for you at the desk. They will ask to keep your passport but don't worry, I will retrieve it in the morning.'

'And what about the morning? Do we need to book tickets or anything?'

'Not at this time of year. I will come at seven thirty, and it is a short walk to the jetty. Don't worry about breakfast, you can have it on the hydrofoil.'

They drew up at a hotel entrance. The place seemed to be in darkness except for some subdued lighting in the porch. Vasyli paid the taxi driver, took her bag, and led her in through stiff swing doors. A young man was fast asleep in a chair behind the desk, a book open on his chest.

'Levko! Levko!' called Vasyli. Levko leapt up, the book falling to the floor.

Apologies and acceptance of apologies followed. Erica was asked to register in a big, thick ledger. Her passport was asked for, as Vasyli had said, and looked at with much interest by Levko. 'Mu-se-um cu-ra-tor,' he read out syllable by syllable. He beamed. 'Ver-ry good.'

He handed over a key – an old-fashioned key with a wooden tag, not a smart card. Vasyli examined it. 'Third floor, to the right when you leave the lift. And by the way, when you leave the lift, tap the light switch on the right-hand wall, this will give you a light that stays on long enough to find your room.' He put his hand in his pocket and brought out some coins. 'In case you want to use the drinks machine.'

'Drinks machine,' echoed Levko proudly. 'On every landing. Tea, coffee, chocolate and Pepsi.' He and Vasyli then had a short conversation in what Erica supposed was Russian.

'I will say goodnight now – or rather good morning,' said Vasyli, turning to her.

'Wait – what about you – have you a room here?'

'Oh, Miss Pencarreth, I have a friend who – do you say "puts me up"? – when I am in Odessa. I could not afford the rates here. I shall be back at seven thirty. I have arranged for the chambermaid to knock on your door at seven.'

162

They shook hands formally at parting. Levko carried her bag to the lift and put it in. The lift initially seemed to have no light but it came on when she pulled the grating shut. It trundled slowly up to the third floor.

She stepped out into darkness, felt wildly along the wall for the switch, and sighed in gratitude when a dim bulb came on. With rapid steps she went along the corridor. The light went out as she passed room number four but by counting in the dark she reached eight without mishap. At the far end of the corridor the drinks machine glowed in a miscellany of orange, red and blue. It gave light enough for her to put in her key, open the door, feel for a light switch, and find herself in a decent enough bedroom with warmth flowing from an old-fashioned radiator.

She decided to forgo the shower. All she wanted was to lie down and sleep. She locked the door, pulled off her clothes, and fell into bed.

Ten minutes later, or so it seemed, the maid was tapping on her door. 'Lady, lady!' and then something in Russian. Unwillingly Erica raised her wrist and looked at her watch. She'd reset it by the airport clock last night. Alas, it was seven o'clock and time to get up.

'Thank you!' she called. And then, remembering her phrase book, '*Spasibo!*'

Now for the shower she had not had last night. The bathroom proved to be only a cubicle with a folding glass door. The shower had very little power and the hot water shut itself off unexpectedly but she felt refreshed. She pulled on her travelling clothes: jeans and cotton shirt, though the dressing-table had no light by which to put on her make-up, so she had to do it by the help of the single lamp hanging from the ceiling. But that was unimportant: she merely applied lipstick, brushed her hair hard, and put all her things back in her travel bag.

When she got downstairs Vasyli was waiting for her. He was in the dark blue suit again and carried the canvas satchel, but under the jacket he now wore a grey sweatshirt. She took this to be sea-going attire.

They shook hands. 'Did you sleep well?'

'Like a log. How about you?'

'Like a top,' he said, with a smile that invited admiration of his grasp of English.

He had her passport and helped her with the rather lengthy process of paying her bill by credit card. That done, they went out into a mild, drizzly morning. It was fairly light and the street was broad with traffic already moving on it, and shops opening for business. On the pavement next to the hotel a man sprang forward, brandishing what appeared to be slips of paper.

'Ukraine currency,' explained Vasyli. 'I hope it is in order, but I have already bought some on your behalf.' As they walked he produced an envelope with notes and some coins in it. 'If you would be so good, this is twenty dollars' worth. And also for the tickets on the hydrofoil, which I have already purchased, another twenty-four dollars.'

She supplied him with the money. He tucked it away in the canvas satchel.

The quay for the hydrofoil was only a short walk away. There was a wooden office at which Vasyli showed the tickets, then a rough cobbled lane with a few people queuing between wooden barriers. The hydrofoil, a modern-looking boat with glassed-in decks, swayed gently at anchor against a background of the harbour. There were many very large vessels, cargo ships, and some naval frigates. A workaday scene, behind which glinted the slate-blue waters of the Black Sea under a blue-grey sky.

The queue shuffled forward. Some of the passengers were carrying luggage, or large shopping bags bulging with food, or children in hand cradles. Vasyli led the way to a forward section beyond which there was a little counter selling refreshments.

Erica now became aware that she was extremely hungry. The food on offer consisted of soft rolls, sausages reminiscent of hot dogs, which had to be fished out of a pot of hot water, tomatoes, fresh cucumbers and sliced beetroot, hard-boiled eggs, tea without milk and instant coffee. She bought a pair of sausages and two rolls in which to put them, and decided on tea with lemon. Vasyli supplied himself with several hard-boiled eggs and tea with plenty of honey.

As they were settling down on a banquette with the food, the hydrofoil moved away from the jetty with much calling of instructions and waving of goodbyes. It turned very slowly, and seemed to inch its way past the other shipping for a long time. This is going to take for ever, thought Erica.

But once past the harbour bar, the engine note changed, the boat raised itself up on the water, then the scenery began to skim past at an unexpected speed.

'Hydrofoil *Minerva*,' said Vasyli proudly. 'This is the newest of the fleet. Perhaps when we return we will travel on *Poseidon*, which is also very fine. Today we stop at Yevpetoriya and Sevastopol only, arriving at Yalta about fourteen thirty.' He cracked the shell of a boiled egg before adding, 'Lunch will be brought on board at Sevastopol, it is usually a chicken dish with vegetables.'

'Fine by me,' said Erica, tucking in to her hot dogs, which proved to be exceptionally good.

For a time she watched the coastline gliding by in the distance but after a while it faded, to be replaced by a vast expanse of dark blue water. Vasyli told her this was the bay that led to the narrow isthmus joining the Crimea to the Ukraine. Erica had never even known that the Crimea was in any way separated from the mainland, and remembered the hotel travel agent who had thought so little of her geography.

That brought her to thoughts of having had the bill for her travels paid for by Zan McNaughton. During her flight last night she had rationalised this to herself. Travel in search of information about the Monet was a valid expense, which she would have added to her bill when she at last presented it. Zan was paying for her journey now, instead of being asked to pay for it in the future. There was, therefore, no logical reason to be upset because the bill had been provided for in advance.

No logical reason. No, just some silly emotional hang-up.

It seemed strange that in the midst of his justifiable anger, he had still thought to take care of her. It was very considerate, very good-hearted. He was . . . he was really a very nice man, and she regretted with all her heart that she had lost his friendship.

Perhaps somehow she could make amends. Not soon, because it would take time for the memory of that disastrous night to die away.

If it ever did . . .

The view from the hydrofoil was monotonous, and her eyelids began to close. She needed rest. She laid her head back on the plush velvet upholstery and fell asleep.

At about ten o'clock the arrival at the first port roused her. It was a short stay – mail was delivered and accepted, a few passengers boarded or left, and then they were off again. Now the view of the coastline returned, and there was more to see – little colonies of white buildings here and there in a narrow strip on which there was much greenery, then behind that mountains with pine trees on their shoulders and occasional castles or forts.

'Those are from the olden days,' Vasyli commented. 'My country has seen many wars.'

'So it has,' Erica agreed. After all, the Crimean War . . . Florence Nightingale . . . And before that, hadn't there been wars with Turkey, just across the Black Sea? She sighed. How sad that a place of so much beauty should have been ravaged by war.

Sevastopol at just after noon wasn't so very beautiful as seen from the hydrofoil. A very large harbour was crowded with naval vessels, their grim shapes a decided drawback to the scene. The city cladding the slopes had a fresh, pleasant appearance. Vasyli told her it had been largely rebuilt after the Crimean War.

The lunch menu was brought aboard in large steel containers and passengers at once began to queue. Vasyli told Erica to stay in her place while he fetched their meal. When it came it proved to be chicken Kiev, which Erica greeted at first with surprise and then with a grin. It dawned on her that, of course, chicken Kiev had come first of all from the capital of the Ukraine.

The food was good, as good as she might have got in many a London restaurant though perhaps not as hot as it should have

166

been. Dessert was *baklava*, folded pastry dripping with honey which she found uneatable.

Soon after, the resort of Yalta began to be seen on the port bow. The sky had cleared. White buildings gleamed in sunshine even from a distance. The music over the boat's public address system changed from national tunes to more sophisticated rhythms, so that when at last they edged along-side the handsome jetty they disembarked to the theme from *Phantom of the Opera.*

Vasyli led the way on to the main quay, where little carts were offering drinks – alcohol, wine and tea, iced or hot. Cafés had tables out on the promenade, with canvas barriers to keep off the sea breeze. Taxis sped about, gift shops exhibited their wares on tables, spun toffee on sticks was for sale to the children of casually clad parents – it was all very like the Mediterranean except that the buildings were more ornate, houses boasting fretwork at the windows and gilt tiles on the cupolas of churches.

'What would you prefer to do now?' Vasyli inquired. 'Would you like to have some little refreshment before we go on?' He indicated a café table. 'The local vineyards make a very pleasant wine. Have you had Massandra wine?'

She'd been about to say yes to a cup of real coffee, but the mention of vineyards brought Zan immediately before her. All at once she was filled with an urge to get on, to be busy, to show that she was dutiful in this search.

'Let's go to the sanatorium first,' she said, slinging her travel bag over her shoulder. Though Vasyli seemed disap-pointed he hailed a taxi and asked for Ulitsa Markeyan.

It seemed to Erica that the taxi driver demurred. She was about to ask why when the production of some currency settled the matter. She and Vasyli got in, they were off. It wasn't far to Ulitsa Markeyan and on entering the street she failed to understand why the driver had seemed unwilling. If it had been a tough district, yes . . . Some parts of London or Paris weren't in favour with taxi-men. But Ulitsa Markeyan looked quite clean and neat.

The driver hesitated at a gate where an avenue led uphill between palm trees and oleanders. A large building painted a creamy yellow dominated the crest of the hill. This presumably was Sanatorium Bonne Santé. It was quiet, except for two men in fawn windcheaters and slacks, strolling about on the forecourt. These two stopped to watch as, at Vasyli's insistence, the taxi made its way round to the back of the building, where a cobbled back alley led to the staff quarters.

Erica and Vasyli got out. Vasyli paid the driver, who sped off towards the back exit in a rush of petrol fumes.

'What's wrong with *him*?' demanded Erica.

'I don't know, Miss Pencarreth. Very odd.'

They approached the door of the staff building, which was under an iron staircase leading to the upper storey. A small foyer with a desk, an in-and-out indicator now damaged and out of use, and a door leading to the interior – this was what they found on going in. No one seemed to be about.

They looked at each other in perplexity. 'Hello?' called Erica. Vasyli contributed something in Russian which might have been, 'Is anybody here?'

A voice answered from the entrance. Startled, Erica turned. It was one of the burly men from the forecourt.

Vasyli hurried into speech. The burly man shook his head and pointed silently to the exit. Vasyli adopted an apologetic tone and Erica heard the name 'Sakovych'. The burly man growled, taking Vasyli by the lapel and hoisting him towards the exit.

'Don't!' cried Erica in alarm, and put out a hand to stop him.

Her arm was grasped from behind. The second burly man had appeared.

He seized her travel bag, unzipped it, and began to rummage about among its contents. Impulsively she tried to stop him. He dropped the bag and grabbed her hair, saying something in a soft, menacing tone as he hustled her out into the daylight.

Shoes clattered on the outside staircase. Another man came storming down from an open doorway above. He was wearing a shoulder holster in which Erica could see the butt of a gun.

An angry dialogue began between the two men – who had proved to be some kind of guard – and the man with the gun. They were apparently trying to explain how these interlopers had got past their security. Vasily looked helplessly from one to the other, and it seemed to Erica that he was at a total loss. His captor shook him and threw him aside. He collided with Erica.

'Please, Miss Pencarreth,' pleaded Vasyli, clutching her, 'I am an intellectual, I am not equipped to deal with this!'

'What's it all about?' Erica cried, aghast.

'I don't know. I think they're from Rostov, they speak a dialect that I don't understand.'

The man with the gun snarled something at him, which clearly wasn't complimentary. Some instinct told Erica they were being accused of being spies or enemies of some kind.

Just then another car came rushing round the narrow alley from the front of the sanatorium. It pulled up in a squeal of tyres.

And out stepped – Willard.

Erica was so shocked that, for the first time in her life, she almost fainted. If Vasyli hadn't been hanging on to her for dear life, she might have fallen.

'Will!' she screamed.

He gave her an anxious glance then turned back to the car. Another man leapt out – as burly as the guards, but taller, and wearing a white polo-neck sweater under a black leather waist-coat. He stepped to the startled group of antagonists, making smoothing motions with his hands. He spoke in a coaxing tone.

The tension among the other men relaxed. Vasyli's grasp on her arm loosened. The tall man kept murmuring, the others growled half-angry responses.

Erica had got her wits back. 'Will! What are you doing here?'

'Looking for you, angel!' He put his arms around her. 'And finding you just in time, I think.' She huddled against him, drinking in the comforting scent of his aftershave. He hugged her close. 'You idiot,' he said into her ear, 'didn't you know this was a hang-out of the Russian Mafia?'

She clung to him in apprehension. Vasyli, for safety, came as close to them as possible. The tall man was gently urging the inhabitants of the staff quarters into the building. They all went in at the ground floor, the door closed behind them.

'How did you know I was here?' Erica gasped.

Willard gave a little laugh and kissed the top of her head. 'Well, you said you were going to Intourist, so I did the same – and they'd never heard of you. Panic stations! But they have connections all over the town so they knew the minute you got off the hydrofoil. We were just too late to stop you getting into the taxi and rushing off.'

Vasyli said in formal tones, 'I thank you very much, sir. We were in great difficulty.'

'Will, this is Vasyli, my interpreter. Vasyli, this is Mr Townley, from London.'

'Delighted,' said Vasyli, determined to be good-mannered despite the fact that he was still trembling with reaction.

'But how did you *get* here, darling?' Erica demanded, looking up at him with wonder.

'Let's get in the car – we'll all probably feel a lot safer.' Will urged her into the back seat, where he joined her. Vasyli got in the front passenger seat. 'After that scary phone call from you, I caught the next flight to Bucharest,' he explained. 'From there I travelled by train to Constanta and then eastwards to Yalta, courtesy of the Black Sea Navigation Company. I got here yesterday. The Intourist people here had never heard of you but, as I say, they soon had you spotted – it's a bit like Big Brother, they keep an eye on things.'

'Oh, Will!' She was overcome with gratitude and love. Nothing could have been a greater proof of his feelings for her than this instant dash to her rescue. It was so unlike his usual blasé style that she knew he must have been very deeply worried. 'I'm sorry if I scared you,' she said. 'I didn't expect anything like this.' She nodded towards the site of the confrontation.

'No, well, of course neither did I, but I do know there's a funny attitude in Russia – or the Ukraine, as this is – towards people making enquiries about art.' He held up an admonishing finger. 'You don't seem to have thought of it, Erica, but they always leap to the conclusion you're going to buy religious icons illegally. I was going to warn you about that when you put the phone down.'

'Oh, Will,' she groaned again, and hid her face in his shoulder.

She was divided between ecstatic happiness and shame at her own blundering. She couldn't find a word to say. But in a moment their rescuer had come to the car, and in handing her travel bag to her released her from the grip of her emotions.

'This is Igor Prokopon,' Willard introduced as the man got into the driving seat. 'This is the lady I've been so worried about, of course – Erica, my partner.'

Igor put a massive hand over the back of the driving seat and they shook. 'Welcome to Yalta,' he said with irony. 'I'm sorry you had this trouble. The locals send their apologies; they thought you were up to no good.' He spoke good English with a strong American intonation. He gave Vasyli a nod. 'You're one of the independents?'

'That is so,' said Vasyli, with a polite bow.

'You ought to keep up to date with what goes on, friend. You sure made a mistake coming to the Bonne Santé. Well, let's get out of here.'

He set off, continuing on towards the rear exit, which took them out to a narrow lane and, by twists and turns, back to the main street. 'Where are we going?' asked Erica.

'To my hotel, darling. I imagine you could do with a good stiff drink, after all that.'

Igor drove them to a handsome establishment all trimmed with white fretted woodwork and polished brass. The sign over its door was unreadable to Erica. They all went in together. Erica and Vasyli were conducted to a sitting area with a sea view fringed by a row of potted palms. Willard went with Igor to the foyer, where they could be seen talking earnestly. Erica thought that money changed hands. After a few minutes Willard came back. 'I have a room here, sweetheart, so we can stay as long as you care to. As for your friend here' – Vasyli rose and bowed as Willard turned his glance on him – 'what do you plan to do?'

'I should go back to Odessa,' said Vasyli. 'I have to be in Kiev at the weekend, I'm taking a class in English.'

'How are you for travelling money and so forth?'

'I have a return ticket to Odessa, thank you. And as for the rest, my services were paid for in advance.'

'Oh, but I must compensate you for all this distress,' Erica cried. She got her wallet from her bag and, taking out all the Ukrainian currency Vasyli had bought for her in Odessa, she handed it to him.

'Oh, Miss Pencarreth! I could not take this—'

'Yes, yes, please, I insist!'

'Yes, you take it, old man,' urged Willard. 'And when you get home, have a drink to remember us by.'

'Thank you. Most kind. I really did not expect . . .' But he was taking the notes, and unfastening the studs of his canvas satchel to stow them away. He offered his hand to Erica, who rose to take it and go with him to the entrance to say goodbye. As he was about to push the swing door he paused. 'That man from Intourist,' he ventured.

'Yes?'

'He didn't seem . . .' He faltered into silence.

'Didn't seem what?'

'Oh, nothing, nothing!' Whatever he'd been about to say about the man from the rival agency, he'd thought the better of it. 'Goodbye, Miss Pencarreth. Safe journey home.'

'Goodbye, Vasyli, and thank you for all your help.'

He gave a nervous smile and was gone.

Willard was ordering drinks when she rejoined him. 'What'll you have, sweetheart?'

'A brandy,' she said, 'for my nerves!' The white-jacketed waiter smiled politely at the joke as he withdrew. In this town, people drank brandy or vodka at all hours of the day or night – after all, why not? It was a holiday resort.

Later, upstairs in Willard's room, she showered in a rather luxurious bathroom with hot water that seemed plentiful. She let the spray beat down on her, washing away the travel-weariness of the morning and the fright of the afternoon. She wrapped herself in a big towel and, drying her hair with a smaller one, came into the bedroom.

Willard was lying on one of the beds, hands behind his head and shoes off. He sat up as she came in and smiled a smile she knew well.

'You look very nice in that outfit,' he said, and swung his feet to the floor. Coming to her, he undid the towel from around her. 'But you look even better without it.'

172

Twelve

B efore they dressed for dinner, Erica telephoned home to her mother. It was three hours earlier in the UK but the light was probably too poor by now for Lisbet to be out painting. So it proved.

'Well, hello stranger, I played back the message you left. Have you got home again?'

'No, and you'll never guess where I am now!' After Lisbet had made some mock guesses, such as Japan and New York, Erica explained that she was in Yalta with Willard. 'He came rushing after me, Mamma, because he was afraid they'd mistake me for an icon smuggler.'

'We-ell,' said her mother. 'You surprise me.'

'It amazed *me*,' said Erica, 'but I was so glad to see him, I can't tell you. Anyhow, the trail of the Monet owner has gone dead here, so Will and I have decided to leave tomorrow for Istanbul.'

'Istanbul! My word, you are getting around, aren't you! Remind me what's in Istanbul.'

'It's where the shop is,' Erica explained, 'where Will found the painting in the first place.'

'Oh yes, I remember.'

'The shopkeeper got it from someone in Yalta, but we don't fancy pursuing that line – it's rather a rough crowd at the address I unearthed so Will and I decided it would be better to talk to the man in the shop.'

'In Istanbul.'

'Yes, romantic, isn't it?'

'Ecstatically so,' Lisbet said dryly. 'Are you sure you're concentrating on the business side?'

'Well, perhaps I'm not,' confessed her daughter. 'But if

you knew what I've been through in the last couple of days, you'd agree I deserve a little romance.'

'Maidie, you deserve everything that's good and rewarding,' said Lisbet. 'Goodbye for now, love, I've got to go, I've got something on the Aga for my evening meal.'

The idea to go to Istanbul had been Willard's. He'd said at first that he couldn't get over the idea that the Mafia would have their eye on them if they stayed in Yalta – 'And after all, what's the point?' But when Erica asked how they would travel home – whether back to Bucharest and then by air, or back to Odessa by hydrofoil and by air from there – he'd suggested Istanbul.

'By sea,' he explained. 'I think I can hire one of the local boat people to take us – while I was on the watch for you yesterday I had time to take a good look at the yachts and cabin cruisers in the harbour, and I bet it would be easy to find someone to ferry us over to the Turkish side.'

'But how long would that take, darling?'

'Oh, a couple of days? We're not in a hurry, are we?'

'I suppose not,' she said in a tone of doubt. The phrase 'local boat people' made her think of fisher folk in sailing boats.

'Think of it, sweetheart! Sailing through the Bosporus into the Sea of Marmara! I've always wanted to do that but when I've been in Istanbul I've always approached from the Aegean.'

'Would it be all right? It would be safe and everything?'

'Good Lord, what are you imagining?' he cried, laughing. 'I'm not going to hire a dinghy! It'll be a comfortable cabin cruiser – probably a lot posher than my dear old *Connoisseur*! In fact I've made a few enquiries already because I thought of making this trip one day, if not now . . .'

'But wouldn't it mean you'd spend an awful lot of time at the wheel, Will?'

'No, no, we'll hire the boat and its owner – I shouldn't care to sail the thing, I don't know enough about the weather in this region. No, it would be pretty well idyllic, precious – plenty of time for you and me to catch up on things while we head for the most romantic spot in the world – Istanbul, city of legend!' Seeing she still hesitated he went on, 'We could find that little shop where I bought the Monet and talk to the chappie. Now, that would be a good thing, wouldn't it? It would wrap up all this investigation nonsense that McNaughton insisted on. Come on, Erica, what do you say? Two days to ourselves on the way there, then at least one Arabian Night in the city of the Golden Horn before we have to fly home to dreary old London?'

Put like that, it sounded wonderful.

The cabin cruiser was a handsome boat, very new-looking, very well kept. The man who was to skipper for them wasn't the owner; he seemed to be a hired crew member and perhaps was making a few hundred roubles on the side. When Erica whispered something of the sort to Willard, however, he said, 'Shh,' and shook his head as if it were better not to enquire too closely.

They were examining it under the harbour lights after a leisurely dinner. The evening was calm and chill, with a few gauzy clouds drifting past the moon.

'Ideal weather,' said Willard. 'A nice smooth passage.'

So next morning they boarded, and off they went with apparently no formalities. The skipper, Joaniki, told Erica in halting English that the journey was six hundred kilometres, which meant nothing to her until Will translated it as four hundred miles. It was clear to her that the boat couldn't match the speed of the hydrofoil but, as Willard said, they weren't in a hurry.

It was an uneventful voyage from the point of view of covering the sea miles. But in Erica's estimation it was a time of magic. Willard was at her side almost all the time, never called away by business as so often happened back home, never made anxious by some new turn of the art world, always attentive, always carefree. He even stayed with her when she prepared their meals in the galley, an astonishment in itself because he always said domesticity of any kind was a bore. 'You look rather sweet,' he told her as she stirred gently at scrambled eggs for breakfast clad in a nightdress and an apron.

Late on the second day they could see the long southern

shore with the passage of the Bosporus cleaving it in two. Far off on the starboard side was the town of Sile, while on their port bow lay Kilyos, on the same side of the long channel as the city of Istanbul. It was dark as the cruiser gentled its way between the lighted markers that signalled the route for pleasure crafts that kept them out of the way of merchant shipping.

When they tied up in the harbour of Istanbul, it was fully dark. Joaniki put their luggage ashore, accepted a handsome tip from Willard, shook Erica by the hand with a *'Do svidanya, khoroshenskiya dama'* and returned on board without a backward glance.

'What will he do now, go back to Yalta?' Erica asked Willard.

'I shouldn't think so, darling. He's probably gone below to put on his best suit and set out in search of a good time.' He tucked her arm in his. 'Which is what we're going to do, and the first thing is to find a taxi and head for a hotel.'

They settled in the same hotel which he had used on his last visit, the Laamba. It was an old building, cleverly modernised so that although it offered everything the Western traveller could wish, it had an atmosphere that summoned up something of the Orient.

They bathed and changed then went down to dinner. The menu was international, the wine was French. They lingered over their meal before going for a walk in the city. Although it was growing late, there were crowds of people enjoying the calm, springlike evening. They wandered about, their arms around each other, until a lingering fragrance of spices told them they were near the *suk*.

'Somewhere hereabouts is the shop of Yamin Emin,' Willard remarked.

'It's too late to go there now.'

'Oh yes, and besides, I don't think I could find it in the dark. But we'll go in the morning.'

'And that will be the last of the enquiries.'

'Yes, thank the Lord. I don't want you putting yourself in danger ever again!'

176

'I won't, I promise. I won't ever do anything without asking your advice,' she said, half laughing.

'That would suit me down to the ground, sweetie. It's really too hair-raising, having you miles away and doing something risky. And if it hadn't been for that idiot McNaughton, you'd never have started on this caper in the first place.'

Now was the opening to tell him that she had been with Zan in Paris. That much at least, she could tell him. She sought for words, and while she was still hesitating Willard went on, 'I've no idea where we are. We'd better find a taxi to get back to the hotel.'

And since he took her in his arms in the taxi and began to kiss her, all thoughts of even mentioning another man went out of her head.

In the morning they rose late and breakfasted in a sheltered courtyard at the back of the hotel. A finchlike bird chirped in the fig tree. The sun was shining, the air was much warmer than in England. Erica stretched and smiled. Everything was absolutely perfect: here she was in this charming place with the man she loved who, in the most unexpected way, was proving that he adored her.

They set out on foot for the curio shop, hoping to retrace their steps of last night. But somehow they seemed to miss the right turnings, so in the end they had to hail a taxi to be delivered at the narrow doorway.

There was a window, somewhat in need of a clean, and beyond it on an artistically draped stand was a silver jug. A few ornamented daggers lay on a shawl. Strings of beads – ivory, amber – hung from a gilt candelabrum. Two or three paintings were propped at the back, two of them depicting Arab dhows on the waters of the harbour, the third a darker European scene with a rowboat and a jetty.

As Willard was about to turn the door handle, the door flew open. A plump middle-aged man was bowing in the entrance. '*Effendi, hani, merhaba, merhaba!*' They were ushered in with a flow of effusive welcome. There was a cushioned bench, where he urged them to sit. He clapped his hands twice. A young boy appeared, was given an order, and vanished.

The interior of the shop was lit only by the daylight that filtered past the objects in the window. The walls were hung with prayer rugs, paintings, engravings, and carvings. Shawls and scarves were draped on a screen painted with a scene showing a Persian garden. A table at one side held trays of rings, brooches, necklaces and bracelets.

'Mr Emin, do you remember me?' Willard asked. 'Willard Townley?'

'Ah, English! I should have known, the clothes so quiet and good. Let me see, let me see.' The shop owner peered at Willard with lustrous brown eyes. 'I seem to think . . . Did I sell you something at one time, dear sir?'

'A painting,' Willard rejoined. 'With some documents that implied it was by Claude Monet.'

'Aha!' He clasped his hands together in recognition. 'Some time ago. Last year, was it not, dear sir?' And then in alarm, 'I make no refunds if you are now displeased, sir – that was quite understood when you made the purchase, I am sure, because that is how I carry on business, dear sir—'

'No, no, I'm not here to ask for my money back,' Willard broke in with a smile in which there was some disdain. 'Miss Pencarreth and I just want to ask you a few questions.'

There was a sigh of relief from Mr Emin. The youth appeared with a tray of Turkish coffee, which he set on a low table. At a sign from his employer he poured from the little brass pot into tiny cups, and handed one to Willard and then to Erica. Mr Emin took a seat on a padded stool drawn close to the table, poured coffee for himself, and prepared to spend the rest of the morning with these two visitors, perhaps in hopes of eventually selling something.

Erica sipped her coffee. It was extremely strong and sweet. She tried not to grimace at it and took up the conversation. 'I'm interested in how you came to be handling the painting, Mr Emin.'

'Ah . . . but naturally, you see . . . it was offered to me.'

'But why to you? Modern European paintings don't seem to be your field.' She glanced about at their surroundings.

'No, how true, you are very perceptive, dear madam. No, I don't deal in such things as a rule – I prefer to

178

handle Victorian and Edwardian paintings of the Middle East, because you understand that is what my customers prefer – something to take home, to remind them of the real, the old Istanbul.'

'Yes,' said Erica, and waited.

'Ah yes, the Impressionist painting you are asking about . . . It came to me from a Russian family, in Yalta – this was on the papers I gave you, dear sir, surely?'

'The family of Sergei Piotrovitch,' prompted Erica.

'Ah, of course. Now I remember.'

'The Piotrovitch family came to you with the painting?'

'No, it came through a friend of mine . . . you know how it is . . . so much is through recommendation and contacts . . .'

'So a friend of yours negotiated between you and this family in Yalta?'

'Exactly.'

'And may I know the name of this friend?'

Mr Emin looked at Erica in surprise. 'The name?'

'Yes, the name of your friend.'

'We-ell . . . dear madam . . . I have my principles . . . I don't think it would be right to pass on the name of someone without first consulting him.'

'That's fair enough,' Willard put in. 'Can you telephone him and ask for his permission?'

'Telephone . . . I hardly think . . . My friend is not often available on the telephone.' The shopkeeper was embarrassed He clapped his hands twice to summon his servant and, without waiting for him to appear, jumped up saying, 'You have no sweetmeats to take with your coffee, where is that boy!' With this he disappeared behind a curtain leading to a dark passage at the back of the shop.

'What did I say?' wondered Erica aloud.

'You put him in a dilemma,' said Willard, laughing. 'I bet the man he bought the painting from was a smuggler! I can just imagine how much stuff comes across the Black Sea – things filched from Ukrainian churches, furs stolen from Yalta holiday-makers, jewellery, and of course paintings and other things from families who are feeling the pinch.'

'Smuggled?' echoed Erica tonelessly.

'Of course! And all sorts of stuff goes back the other way – cigarettes, computers, CDs – all the things the Russians want and can't get.'

Erica nodded. Now the embarrassment of their host was understandable. 'But I want him to tell me,' she insisted. 'I don't care what he gets up to with questionable characters – I just want to know about that painting.'

'We aren't going to get it out of him by asking him direct questions in his shop.'

'You think not?'

Willard shook his head. 'He's rattled. He needs time to recover. Leave it to me, sweetheart.'

The boy appeared from behind the curtain bearing a glass plate on which there was an array of little sticky cakes. Behind him came his employer, smiling again. 'Please, eat, eat,' he begged. 'These are made by the finest confectioner in the district.'

'Thank you very much,' said Erica, at a nod from Willard. He for his part avoided the cakes but offered a cigarette from a silver case to the shopkeeper.

'Ah . . . American – how nice . . . Thank you, dear sir.' The boy leapt forward to supply a light for the cigarette. Yamin Emin drew on it deeply.

'Mr Emin, it's not very civilised of us to try to deal with this matter in your place of business – you might have clients coming in at any moment.'

'That is very true, dear sir.' He looked hopefully at Willard.

'Miss Pencarreth and I would be honoured if you would have dinner with us, if you are free this evening.'

A look of relief flickered in the luminous brown eyes. 'This evening,' he mused, apparently making up his mind whether he would risk it.

'I suggest this because Miss Pencarreth and I are only here for a short stay. If not dinner, perhaps a drink—'

'Oh, dinner would be very excellent, and although I have an engagement I can put it off, my dear sir, it is nothing compared to the honour of your company.'

'Then may we take that as settled? And perhaps you would like to choose the restaurant, since Miss Pencarreth and I don't know the city.'

'How hospitable! I of course know all the best places. Yes, yes – do you like Turkish food, Miss Pencarreth?'

'I've only had it in Turkish restaurants in London, Mr Emin. But I'd love to get to know more about it.'

'Ah, it will be my honour to show you the good food of my country, dear lady. Shall we say, Mr Townley, the *Gece Yarisi*, at nine tonight? I will book a table, shall I? That will be easier.'

'And how shall we find it, Mr Emin?' Erica enquired.

'Oh, ask any taxi driver, it is very well known, famous, you understand?'

'Then we shall see you this evening, Mr Emin.' Willard shook hands, Emin bowed Erica out of the door, and next moment they were out in the narrow street.

'Well!' cried Erica. 'There's a diplomat, if ever I met one!'

'One of the most charming, you have to admit.' Willard was grinning to himself. 'Still, I think we held up our end pretty well.'

'Oh, you were great, Will! That idea about taking him out to dinner – that was what prevented the whole thing from dying on the spot. *Gece Yarisi* – I wonder what it means? Will, if it's a famous restaurant, I have to buy a dress! I can't go to a famous restaurant in jeans and a shirt, and the only other things I've got are office clothes.'

He laughed and hugged her at this outburst. 'Right you are, we'll do the tourist bit for the rest of the day. Topkapi, the markets, the shops; we'll forget about the Monet and enjoy ourselves.'

The dress she bought was a strappy soft muslin sprinkled with little emblems of the signs of the zodiac. It was cheap by the standards of British boutiques and, she told herself very sensibly, it would do as a sundress afterwards. Because she'd packed only walking shoes, she also bought herself a pair of high-heeled sandals, tottery things she'd never have looked at if she'd been in her right mind. But this was Istanbul, and she was with Willard, and she was on the verge of finding out something that would wrap up any doubts about the Monet, and all in all she felt light-headed with pleasure.

Gece Yarisi meant 'midnight', they'd learned – and it looked like living up to its name when they arrived there, for at a little after nine o'clock it was sparsely patronised. But Yamin Emin was already at the table to which they were shown, resplendent in a cream linen suit and a stiff shirt. He leapt up, beaming and bowing. 'Dear lady! Dear sir! Welcome to this evening's enjoyment! First we eat of our good Turkish dishes, and then there is entertainment – typical Turkish performers, very good, very appreciated by those who judge talent. Please, sit, sit!'

The table was in a curve of the wall, not exactly a booth but with looped-back gauze curtains so as to give a feeling of privacy. The table was spread with a large soft raffia mat on which already stood shallow bowls of water for rinsing the fingers, a large jug of iced fruit juice, and tumblers banded with gold.

'Please, what will you drink? I because of my religion may not drink wine, but you please must have whatever attracts . . . Sali, Sali, the wine list – I believe, dear Mr Townley, there is some very good Greek wine on the list but Sali will advise.'

Amidst much fuss and furore wine was chosen, little dishes full of cubes and curls of vegetables were brought, a first course of courgettes in yoghurt was served, and all the while Emin chattered about the menu, the restaurant's fame, the day's news on television and stock market prices.

At last what appeared to be the main item was brought. A stand with a deep tray containing hot charcoal was rolled to their table's side. On a grill over it lay six skewers with kebabs. 'This is chicken,' Emin informed them. 'Next we will have lamb and then kid.'

'Kid?' breathed Erica, looking at Willard.

He mouthed the world 'goat'. She gave a tiny shudder and a shake of the head. He shrugged and allowed the waiter to put the kebab of chicken on his plate, together with heaps of rice and roasted peppers.

The meal seemed to go on for ever. The restaurant filled up. Musicians appeared, sitting cross-legged on a low platform. They began to tune their instruments: a kind of clarinet, stringed guitarlike things, and a set of hand drums.

'The performance is about to begin?' asked Erica, who as yet had had no chance to ask about the painting.

'Oh, not for a while,' Emin said, leaning back and patting his little embonpoint. 'You will have the kid kebab now, dear lady?'

'No, thank you. I couldn't eat any more.'

'You, Mr Townley? Please, don't disappoint me – I want you to try all our best dishes—'

'No, no, really, Mr Emin! The food is marvellous but I'm not used to big meals.'

'Dessert? We have very delicious ice-creams – many flavours – Sali, Sali! Bring the dessert menu!'

When they at last persuaded him they would prefer to have coffee and nothing more, he seemed to sense that it was time for serious talk. He looked at Willard, who took up the questioning.

'We would like to know how you came into possession of the painting I bought from you, Mr Emin.'

Emin sighed in surrender. 'Of course, I see it is important, so I will tell. But this is confidential, dear sir, dear lady. Have I your word you will not speak of this?'

Willard said, 'Certainly.'

Erica hesitated. 'I have to make a report—'

'A report?' echoed Emin with every appearance of horror. 'No, no—'

'Only to a client,' Willard hastened to explain. 'Erica is making this enquiry on behalf of the man who in the end bought the painting – whatever you tell us will go to him, and no further, Mr Emin.'

Emin made rather a show of calming down from his scare. Erica got the impression that he was perfectly ready with his story but wanted to be persuaded. She and Willard spent a few more minutes assuring him of their good intentions and when the coffee had been brought and poured he settled down to tell his tale.

'You must understand, dear lady Erica and dear sir, that the painting I called *Bridge after the style of Monet* was brought to me with other things in a large cardboard carton. One of the other things was the painting still on show in my shop window – perhaps you were so good as to notice it, a dark painting with a little boat. But no one will buy that, it is not "typical" enough for my customers . . .' He sighed. 'This box of things was brought to me from Yalta by a good friend of mine who makes the trip across the sea very often. He has his own boat, you know, and he deals in goods that might make him money.'

'What's his name?' Erica asked.

'His name . . . Well, I will tell you but please do not let it go further – do you promise?'

'I promise.'

'His name is Dergu. He is . . . quite well known among the sailors of the Golden Horn. I have bought from him often. Sometimes he does not bring artworks and then I am not interested but these days, you know, even the people who come on holiday to the Crimea from other parts of Russia – and they are usually rich people, of course – even these people can run short of money.'

'I understand. Go on.'

'And then they barter. So sometimes Dergu brings a wrist-watch made by Cartier, and then I am not interested. But sometimes he brings items that are better for me, household treasures – paintings, silver, ivory, Sèvres china . . . And last year there were these things from the family Piotrovitch, and I gave him a fair price, and sold the silver and the medals and a little clock almost at once. I gave one painting as a present to a friend because it was of a harbour he knew, I think in northern France. The other I still have.'

'Did your friend Dergu actually get the items from the Piotrovitch family?'

'Yes.'

'In Yalta?'

184

'Well, dear lady Erica, in Yalta or somewhere near – Dergu visits many ports along the Crimean coast.'

'But he specifically told you he had got these things from the Piotrovitch family?'

'Specifically?' Emin repeated, puzzled by the word.

'He actually mentioned the name Piotrovitch?'

'Ah, now. This is much to ask . . . It was months ago, yes? But how else do I know the name if he did not tell it to me?'

'That's true,' commented Willard.

'Could I speak to Dergu?' Erica enquired.

Their host uttered an exclamation which might perhaps have been a Turkish swear word. 'My dear, dear lady!' he cried. 'What are you saying? Dergu would cut my throat if I tried to bring him to speak to you! Perhaps he would cut my throat if he even knew I told you this I have spoken of tonight. No, no, out of the question to speak to Dergu!'

Erica was taken aback by his outburst. She thought he was overstating the facts by quite a large margin. After all, this Dergu seemed to be nothing but a petty smuggler – talk of cutting throats seemed a bit over the top. But Willard was nudging her.

'Be reasonable, Erica,' he murmured. 'Maybe he'd lose a supply line if he was too talkative.'

Of course. Supply lines had to be maintained. Erica smiled her gratitude to Emin for his information, Willard ordered a liqueur, Emin ate some sticky sweetmeats and drank more coffee, and the entertainment began.

Belly dancing seems to have been invented to entertain a male audience. After watching two or three girls in succession shivering their sequinned girdles and clicking their little finger cymbals, Erica had had enough 'entertainment'. She gave herself up to thoughts about the Monet. It seemed certain now – the smuggler Dergu was just the sort of man who might have been given some old unwanted belongings by a member of a Mafia gang.

So once she was home she could write her report, saying that she had 'explored every avenue and left no stone unturned', and that the only concrete evidence – the letter

185

written by the gardener's boy Aristide in 1923 – was genuine, as comparison with a sample of his writing proved.

She'd say nothing about her encounter with the Crimean Mafia. She'd say very little about Yamin Emin and his less than legitimate friend Dergu. She didn't want to make her report sound as if she'd been associating with criminals nor raise the idea that she'd been in danger. It would all be very businesslike and cool. She'd set out the accounts in the usual way, only noting by the expenses for Essen 'Already paid'.

Yes, that was the way to handle it.

It was impossible to leave the restaurant until their guest showed he'd had enough of the entertainment. He kept ordering fresh coffee until Erica thought he must be a caffeine junkie, but she supposed that perhaps he wanted to stay fully awake to appreciate the finer points of a performance that was more or less wasted on her.

Well past midnight he at last seemed to notice that she wasn't enjoying the dancers very much, and turned his beaming smile upon her.

'Dear lady Erica, I hope this little glimpse of Turkish life has pleased you! And soon you return to your home-land, yes?'

'Tomorrow,' agreed Erica.

'Ah then, I wish to offer a little memento of Istanbul which will look most beautiful when you wear it. Look, I brought this with me, in hopes you will accept.' From the breast pocket of his cream linen jacket he drew a chequered silk handkerchief, spread it out on the table, and lifted from it a stunning gold chain on which several little coins were suspended. He touched one of the coins with a fingertip. 'Very old,' he said. 'Not uncommon, many of these are found in excavations and they are of little value each by each. But these were formed into this necklace by some goldsmith during the reign of the Turkish Empire. So dear lady, I hope you will allow me to put it about your beautiful neck.'

Erica drew back. 'No, no – I couldn't possibly accept—'

'Please, it is a tribute from me to you. You are so brave, lady Erica, to pursue this investigation across Europe and to

186

our wonderful old city. I admire you and it is my humble wish that you will take this to your cool homeland and sometimes, when you put it on, you will think of your true friend and devotee Yamin Emin.'

Getting to his feet, he came behind her to clasp the necklace. Erica looked in embarrassment at Willard, who gave the faintest of nods. Perhaps it would offend if she refused . . . She let the necklace encircle her throat and felt Emin's fingers fasten it.

'There!' he cried. 'Is it not beautiful where it now lies, dear Mr Townley?'

'Very beautiful,' agreed Willard.

And later, when she was about to take it off before going to bed, it was Willard who unfastened it and covered the back of her neck with kisses.

Thirteen

S pring hadn't arrived in England when Erica got back. The flimsy muslin dress bought in the Istanbul boutique would have to stay at the back of her wardrobe for many a day.

February had ended. When she went to work she found the St Valentine's mini-exhibition at the gallery was being dismantled. One or two telephone conversations to her office while abroad had assured her that everything was going along as usual – which was just as well because for the first few days after her return, she felt totally disorientated.

By the end of a week she'd caught up with almost all the messages and correspondence. The next mini-exhibition at the gallery was 'Impressions of Trees', for which pictures had already arrived from elsewhere or been selected from store. Arrangements were well in hand for the main summer exhibition, which would open at the beginning of June. She could allow herself some breathing space.

Of the telephone messages not yet dealt with, two were from Zan McNaughton. Her secretary, Suzi, reported that when she had first told him Miss Pencarreth was extending her stay abroad, Mr McNaughton had merely said that he was expecting a report from her. A week later, when she told him that Miss Pencarreth had headed for Odessa and points east, he had seemed not only surprised but somewhat anxious.

Despite herself, Erica couldn't help feeling a little spark of pleasure at that news. No matter what had happened between them, he still had some concern for her. On the Thursday after her return, she nerved herself to ring him at the hotel.

Of course, he was out. Probably at the hospital. She left

a message: 'Miss Pencarreth called to report on a business matter and to enquire after Miss McNaughton.'

She expected – or hoped – that he would return the call that day. But Thursday passed, and so did Friday, and there was no response. She told herself that the mere fact of her phone call would let him know she was safely back in action, and as to enquiries after Nyree – well, he might feel no wish to share any family news with her.

As the gallery was closing on Saturday afternoon, the office phone rang. 'I got your message,' said the cool voice on the other end.

'Oh! Zan? Is that you?'

'How did things go?'

'I . . . er . . . went to Yalta—'

'I heard you were headed in that direction.'

'I felt it was worth the trip to see if I could contact the Piotrovitches.'

'And did you?'

'Well, no . . . But in Istanbul I paid a visit to the shop where the Monet was discovered—'

'You've covered some ground.'

'That was because I wanted . . . I wanted to show you that I'm . . . I'm dependable.'

'That was never in doubt,' he returned calmly. 'Where business is concerned, I have absolute faith in you.'

She didn't know whether to say thank you to that; it seemed a rather double-edged remark. But who was she to complain if he was less than enthusiastic about her private life?

'The man who owns the shop – Mr Emin – he gave us chapter and verse about how he acquired the Monet.'

'And you're satisfied?'

'I think so.'

'You got this through an interpreter?'

'No, no, Mr Emin speaks very good English.'

A pause. 'So who was "us"?'

Erica could feel her face glowing crimson red at the question. She couldn't find the words with which to answer.

'OK,' said Zan, very businesslike, 'put it all in writing and send it to my lawyer for notarising, will you?'

Now all at once she was so hurt by the curtness of his manner that she burst into speech. 'Oh, please, Zan, can't we at least be friends?'

She heard him sigh. 'I'm not interested in being just a friend.'

'But . . . but . . .'

'So my solicitor will hear from you?'

'Yes, within the week.' It seemed there was no use in trying to remedy what had gone by.

'Thank you.' And the phone was put down.

She'd hoped to see Willard over the weekend. He was to have come for lunch on Sunday. When she told him she thought of beginning her report to Zan McNaughton, he offered to help her with it. She couldn't tell whether he was joking or serious. 'It's something I have to do by myself, Will.'

'I thought I could help you remember what happened.'

'I took good notes, thanks all the same.'

'So what are you saying? You don't want me around tomorrow?'

'No, I'm not saying that at all. I can get quite a bit written in the morning before you arrive.'

'Humph . . . Sounds like a fun day!'

'What's the matter, Will? You know you never arrive before about noon – that should give me plenty of time to get a start on it.'

'So long as you're not going to moon over it for the rest of the day. You know what you're like when you've got something on your mind.'

'I'm sorry,' she said, quite upset. 'I didn't know I was a bore.'

'Oh, come on, don't get in a huff! It's just that I can think of better ways to spend Sunday than driving in the rain to spend an afternoon with a girl who isn't paying attention.'

He meant that if they made love he wanted to have her entirely to himself, mind and body. Somehow it hurt her, to think that perhaps in the past he'd found something wanting in those times that to her had always been magical.

'Perhaps you'd rather not bother, then,' she suggested.

190

'Oh, now look here, Erica—'

'The weather forecast is for more rain, and I'd really like to get on with this report. After all, you said yourself you wanted me to write it and get shot of Zan McNaughton.'

'Well, that's true, but—'

'I'm really quite tired, Will. Getting back into harness after that hotchpotch of a trip has really been quite hard.'

'But you've been back for a week.'

'And tomorrow will be the first Sunday I've had to get my breath back.'

'We could get our breath back together, precious. Wouldn't that be fun?'

But she decided to ignore this olive branch. 'Let's just call it off for tomorrow,' she said. 'I just . . . sort of don't feel in the mood.'

'Oh, then far be it from me to force myself on you. Let's leave it for the time being, shall we? When you feel in a better frame of mind, give me a buzz.'

She could hardly believe it. She'd managed to quarrel with Willard, and all because she'd been depressed by her earlier conversation with Zan.

Well, she *would* spend the weekend on the report, and send it off, and hope never to hear another word from him as long as she lived.

She kept to the first part of the plan. She organised her notes on Sunday morning, spent the afternoon typing up a first draft, but by the evening had had enough. It wasn't easy to phrase things, and when she came to the episode in Yalta she couldn't make up her mind to confess that Willard had joined her there – nor how to account for the fact.

It was strange that although she'd been looking forward to seeing Willard, his absence today didn't trouble her at all. On the contrary – she had a strange sense of . . . independence? Liberty? She couldn't understand her own feelings.

Those few days after he had appeared like her guardian angel and then swept her off to the romance of Istanbul now seemed like something out of a fairy-tale. Illusory, unreal. Yet they had happened and she had felt wonderful

191

while they lasted. Why now did they seem like a rainbow that was fading and changing before her eyes?

She loved Willard. For the last three years he'd been the most important strand in the cords that bound her to her life. And yet today, when he wasn't with her, she felt as if she could breathe more deeply, think more thoroughly, feel herself to exist within her own boundaries with more certainty and vigour.

Because it was true, in a way. Willard liked to be in control. She looked back and realised that they almost always did what Willard wanted to do. She almost always gave in to any proposal of his. And though she'd sometimes felt that he was more important in her life than she was in his, she'd accepted that.

Out of gratitude.

And why not, she chided herself. She owed so much to darling Will . . . It was thanks to him that she was where she was now in her career – established, well regarded, the curator of a small yet important collection. Even more important, perhaps – it was Will who had taught her the joys of physical love.

His *savoir-faire*, his sophistication had led her into the upper echelons of the art world. At his side she'd met people who would never have come within her orbit otherwise. He had brought clients to her for her expert opinion, extending both her bank balance and her reputation.

And if he asked for recompense for all he had done for her, why not? If he wanted her attention and her compliance she should give it. Even if she wasn't the most important part of his life, she should be glad to have some share.

Well, she was. She was glad, she was grateful.

But there was no denying that today, on her own, she was rather relieved not to be in his company. She couldn't account for it but it was so.

At about six o'clock she gave up on both work and self-analysis. She telephoned a woman friend who lived across the town, and ended up by going with her for a comforting pasta dinner and a glass or two of Italian wine.

On Monday, a very odd letter appeared among her mail

at the gallery. Suzi had opened it, along with the rest of the correspondence, so it lay among a little pile of official things. But the letter was a blue airmail form, and the printing, other than the usual French '*Par avion*', was in Cyrillic lettering – except for a little circle stamped on the outside which held the letters 'FTA'.

It was from Vasyli, the Ukrainian courier.

Dear Miss Pencarreth,

I write to you in the old-fashioned way because I am not very expert with e-mail. Also I think a written letter can convey so much more and be looked at more deeply.

This is to apologise for my shortcomings as courier and interpreter. Please believe that I regret what happened and if you come to the Ukraine in the future, FTA will not fall short again.

You will be interested to hear that I have been rereading a novel in English by my great favourite, Sir Walter Scott. The novel is *Ivanhoe*. It is very remarkable, don't you agree, that in the days when knights were the main contestants in the struggle between right and wrong, it was often very difficult to know which was a friend and which an enemy. With the visor of the helmet closed, a man could claim to be anyone he liked. When on that extraordinary day our rescuer appeared, his clothes led me to assume that he was perhaps an enemy. I was surprised when he proved to be an employee of Intourist, I had never before seen any of that agency wearing clothes that were so 'trendy' – is that slang word still in use with you?

However, I must not take up your valuable time with my wayward thoughts, although I hope you will find something to interest you in my views. With many good wishes and thanks for your financial generosity, Vasyli Galyatavenko.

Erica read the letter with amusement. Poor man! His sense of honour made him feel he must apologise but he could only do it by wrapping it all up in some wordy discussion of *Ivanhoe*. Shaking her head, she put the letter in her handbag

193

so as not to get it mixed up with official correspondence.

She was busy the rest of the day and on Tuesday there was a junior school visit to the gallery, always something of an ordeal for the entire staff because the gallery was small and the pupils usually boisterous.

She and Suzi were in the café at about four o'clock, recovering, when the girl at the cash desk beckoned her. 'Call for you, being put through from your office, Miss Pencarreth.'

Stifling a sigh, she rose with some reluctance. She took the receiver from the cashier. 'This is Erica Pencarreth.'

'Erica? Zan McNaughton here.'

She was so surprised and pleased that she was utterly speechless.

'Hello? Hello? Are you there?'

'Yes, I'm here,' she managed to say. 'I was just . . . taken aback. I didn't expect to hear from you again.'

'Ah.' She heard him mutter something to himself, which sounded almost like 'stupid idiot'. 'That's why I'm ringing. I wanted to apologise.'

Apologise? Why should he be apologising when she was the one at fault? She hurried into protest. 'You have nothing to apologise for.'

'Oh yes I have. I think I was downright rude to you the last time we spoke.'

'No, not at all—'

'Listen, Erica, let me say my piece. I've been feeling rotten about it all. I want to try to put it right.'

'Zan,' she said, half laughing in her relief, 'I'm actually in the gallery's café! The call was put through to me here. Are you at the hotel? Let me get to my office and I'll ring you back.'

'Right.'

She hung up, waved goodbye to Suzi and almost ran to her office. She could hear her telephone bleating its call while she was coming along the corridor. She snatched it up.

'Not a bad sprint,' Zan commented.

'And I'm not even out of breath.'

'Well done.' There was a little hesitation, as if he couldn't find a way to get back to the former conversation.

Because she understood exactly how he felt, Erica decided

to take the lead. 'You were saying you wanted to apologise. But there's absolutely no need—'

'Oh yes there is. I was being judgemental, and I had no right. You were totally honest with me that morning in Essen, Erica, and I was an absolute fool to take it the way I did. And I realise now that I've let it colour my views ever since – which is non-adult, to say the least.'

'Let's just say that it was a difficult thing to deal with,' she said.

'Yes, and matters weren't improved by my anxiety about Nyree.'

'Oh yes, Nyree, I wanted to ask about her—'

'If I'd given you the chance? It's good of you to be concerned, and in fact, Erica, things today are a lot more hopeful than when I spoke to you last week. Perhaps that was one of the reasons I was so bad-tempered . . . Anyway, it looks as if they've found the right mix of drugs to give the poor kid and she's doing well.'

'Oh, you must be so relieved!'

'So much so, that I want to celebrate. And I've no one to celebrate with, Erica – unless you take pity on me.'

She was suffused with delight. He wanted someone to share his good news with, and he turned to her. 'Oh, of course – how lovely – it would be great—'

'Champagne and caviar – how about it?'

'When?'

'Tonight? Tomorrow night?'

She would have said she'd see him that very night but she was so physically tired that she felt she would be poor company. 'I'm beat, Zan,' she confessed. 'Forty schoolchildren have been firing questions at me all afternoon. Can we make it tomorrow?'

'Tomorrow it is. Let's go to this marvellous restaurant in the new Docks area – the Houseboat, I read in a magazine that it's great.'

'Wherever you like.'

'What time? Will you be driving?'

'No, if I do that I can't drive home afterwards, not after

drinking champers. I'll come into town by train and take the Tube.'

'You'll do no such thing! I'll send a car for you – I'd come myself but I want to drop in on Nyree before we have dinner.'

'No, really, I can manage perfectly well by public transport, I do it all the time.'

'I wouldn't hear of it—'

'Now listen, I've just come back from a trans-European jaunt by train, plane, helicopter, hydrofoil and cabin cruiser – do you really think I can't deal with the rail service?'

He laughed. 'Oh, sorry, Miss Marco Polo. Right, what time shall I book the table?'

'Eight thirty?'

'You're on. See you at the Houseboat.'

Although she was very tired, Erica found she couldn't get to sleep that night. Before she went to bed she inspected her wardrobe and for a moment was tempted to take out the muslin dress. But no, that breathed the perfumes of Istanbul and was irrevocably linked with Willard – somehow it didn't seem appropriate for a date with Zan. She settled on a halter-neck dress of dark blue silk jersey, short-skirted and to be worn with a matching little silk-taffeta bolero that accentuated her slender waist.

She woke in the middle of the night with the realisation that she must somehow juggle her working day so that she could get to the hairdresser. She hadn't had time for a visit since getting back from abroad, and her short hairstyle was developing a shagginess that certainly wouldn't go with the slinky dress.

And shoes – should she wear the fragile sandals she'd bought in Istanbul? No, no, they wouldn't be good for dealing with escalators at stations. Yet the dress demanded something more than a pair of black courts.

And so on, until about dawn she fell into a sleep that made her almost late for the start of her day.

In the evening she took a taxi to the station, travelled by train to King's Cross, from there by tube to Whitechapel, and finally by taxi – because she didn't know its exact whereabouts – to the Houseboat. It proved to be a floating restaurant not far from the old Limehouse Hole Stairs. Zan was hovering in the vestibule.

There was a moment of awkwardness. Neither knew just how to greet the other after what had passed between them. Erica solved the dilemma by rising on tiptoe to give him a welcome-kiss on the cheek.

A waiter hurried up to take her coat, then they were ushered to their table by a window through which they could see the bright lights of the new buildings near Pageant Stairs and, across the room through the opposite window, Canary Wharf and West India Quay. The Thames, glamorised by darkness, gleamed like black satin around them.

The place was full. Clearly it was a rendezvous for the young and rich from the City. The first few minutes after they were seated were taken up with remarking on the crowd, and the decor, and then Erica pointed out the landmarks for Zan, and then they were ordering pre-dinner drinks and the first few unhandy moments were past.

'You look very nice,' Zan said. 'Not at all worn down by all the trans-European safari.'

'I can't say the same for you,' she replied, having studied him from behind her menu. It was true. He was thinner in the face and she thought she could discern some lines around the eyes that hadn't been there before. 'Have you been very anxious about Nyree?'

'It wasn't any fun . . . But who am I to complain? Nyree was the one they had fixed up with loops of tubing and drips and things. You can call me a coward, but it took me a couple of minutes outside the door of her room to get myself together before I could go in. Not that she felt much like talking.'

'But you said she was better?'

'Oh yes, in the last couple of days – noticeably better – you could tell when she began to make fun of me in the rig they made me wear – "barrier nursing", I think it's called. On Sunday evening, you know, she said I looked as if I was got up to rob a bank.' He gave his brief, glinting smile, and he was restored to the Zan she had first met, a milder, easier

197

man than the one she had faced in that last dreadful moment in the Werdenhaus Hotel.

'Is the treatment still going on?'

'No, they unhooked her yesterday. I think it's called "remission", which may mean they'll have to do it all again by and by, but for now she's good. She'll be able to leave hospital fairly soon, and then they say she has to rest, so I've found a place near Bath, a sort of clinic where she can have lots of care but won't be ordered about so much by the nurses . . .' He paused. 'I'm sorry. You shouldn't let me maunder on. I'm as bad as the man who insists on showing off snapshots of his kids.'

'Don't be silly. I wanted to hear how she was getting on.' To change the subject just a little she asked, 'Did she like the blouse we picked out for her in the *Trachten* boutique?'

'Oh, she loves it. She's dying to be allowed up so she can try it on. She wants me to tell you . . . She thinks you're awfully kind.'

'Oh, nonsense—'

'And she says she'd like to meet you but not until she looks less like a scarecrow. Not that she *does*, but the treatment's taken it out of her and she needs a couple of weeks to fatten up a bit and look less wan.'

'I'd love to meet her. Tell her she's only got to give the word and I'll be along to see her.'

'But not until she's fit enough to come back to the hotel.'

'No, really, Bath is no distance and besides it's lovely – I'd be quite happy to have an excuse to wander around it. It's full of Georgian houses, you know.'

They chatted about the architecture of Bath and the countryside around it, and the television versions of Jane Austen's novels which he'd seen though he'd never read the books, and then on to the countryside around McNaughton's Hill, and then on to his wine, and that led to a conversation with the wine waiter who earned Zan's whole-hearted approval by saying that he not only knew of the winery but liked the wine.

It wasn't until the dessert that they got to the subject of

the Monet. 'Oh, let's not go into that now,' Erica said. 'You said to send the report—'

'So I did. I'm sorry about the way that sounded. I was just . . . a bit woebegone at that moment.'

'It's nothing, forget it,' she replied.

'And of course when you finish the report, I want you to send it to me, not to that old stick of a lawyer. OK?'

'Yes, and it oughtn't to be too long.'

'What's your opinion about it? When you got out to the Crimea, did everything check out?'

'Well, there was nothing to contradict what we were given as background, but I just got a peculiar letter from Vasyli – that was the man who acted as my interpreter.'

'How d'you mean, peculiar?'

'I don't know. He seems to be trying to tell me something but I can't make it out.' She shrugged. 'It's probably nothing.'

'I don't quite get it. "Trying to tell you something" – you mean his English isn't good enough?'

'Oh no, his English is perfect. But he goes on about Sir Walter Scott and knights in armour—'

'Sounds daft.'

'No, no, Vasyli is by no means daft. If he writes to me about Ivanhoe and mistaken identity, it's for a reason – only problem is, I don't know what the reason is.'

Zan was laughing. 'Maybe it's in code!'

'Well, you know . . . That did cross my mind,' she mused. 'The people he and I came across in Yalta were a weird bunch – quite unsavoury characters, and we were rather glad to back away from them. This chap from the rival tourist agency came along and sorted things out for us. Igor something . . . I sort of wondered if Vasyli was trying to convey some sort of message about him but didn't want to lay himself open to . . .' She wandered into silence and then asked, a little embarrassed, 'They don't censor people's letters in Russia these days, do they?'

'Who knows? And anyhow, old habits die hard – if you've grown up being very careful about what you put in writing, perhaps you keep on being careful. What sort of message did you think you were getting?'

'That's the mystery.'

'If he thought it was worth sending, perhaps it's important?'

'But important to whom? It seems in a way to be saying that this Igor wasn't an employee of Intourist, the big official agency – but so what? Is it just hurt pride on Vasyli's part, because this man arrived and helped us when Vasyli was at a loss? Well, never mind, when I've worked it all out I'll finish the report and give it to you. The conclusion seems to be that the painting is genuine.'

'I'll drink to that,' said Zan, raising his glass. 'Here's to Nyree's Impressionist.'

'Here's to it!'

They drank, and were easy with one another in a way that seemed to Erica more than just agreeable. There was a current between them, an understanding that needed no words but was strong and full of warmth.

By and by it was time to go. Zan summoned the bill and while waiting for it looked at her with what seemed to be some discomfort.

'Now I hope you're not going to be cross about this,' he said, 'but I've ordered a car to come for us' – Erica felt her heart give a little lurch – 'and it'll drop me off at a taxi rank so I can get back to Mayfair, and then it'll take you home to your door in Gratesford.'

She was covered with confusion. What had she thought he was going to say? That the car would take them both to his Mayfair hotel? Had she *wanted* him to say that?

Stunned at the thought, she fell into silence. She smiled and thanked the head waiter for the meal, accepted her coat, and allowed herself to be ushered out of the restaurant to the quay where, sure enough, a limousine was purring.

Zan handed her in then followed. The driver, Bert Allgood, had become a regular part of the McNaughton set-up since first bringing the boss from Southampton to London. He set off without further instruction.

Erica felt she must break out of the tongue-tied net she'd

fallen into. 'Thank you for a lovely evening,' she said – and knew she'd never sounded so trite in her life.

'I enjoyed it too.'

The short drive to the taxi rank was soon over. Zan got out. 'Safe home,' he said.

'Yes. Thank you. I'll be in touch.'

'Look forward,' he said as he stepped back and waved goodnight while the limousine slid away.

She sat back on the leather seat and closed her eyes. The car sped through the empty streets taking her north towards her home.

I wanted to go with him, she said within herself. I still want to. If I had the courage I'd tell the driver to turn around and take me to the Mayfair Rialto. *I want to be with him.*

For a long time that was as far as she would let her thoughts take her. She was shaking her head as if in an argument, half-formed words coming to her lips but dying away. What am I thinking, what am I *imagining*! – the protest made a barrier against a realisation she couldn't accept.

At length the car drew up outside her block of flats in Gratesford and Bert Allgood hopped out to open her door for her. She got out, opened her handbag to tip him. He shook his head. 'That's all taken care of, miss. And I'm to wait until I see you safe inside.'

'Thank you,' she said.

'No problem.' Nice lady, thought Bert. Just the sort that Mr McNaughton would choose. He faithfully stayed on guard until she'd gone into the entrance of the block and the door had swung closed.

Erica dragged herself up the stairs to her flat. At last, with her door shut behind her, she sank into a chair.

'I'm in love with him,' she said aloud. And then again, 'I must be mad but . . . I'm in love with him.'

Fourteen

Erica rose next morning with the determination to be sensible. There was no use getting tearful about the way things had turned out. She herself had told Zan – in no uncertain terms – that Willard was the important man in her life. She could hardly walk up now to Zan and say, 'That was all wrong, I was under a misapprehension.' He'd think her either a fool or a floozie.

In a way it was almost funny. Somewhere in the back of her mind she could hear a voice from that comedy duo, Laurel and Hardy: 'Another fine mess you've landed us in, Stanley.' But she had no one to blame but herself. She wanted to laugh, to cry, to hit something, to run and run until she was out of breath but had left the dilemma behind her.

She tried to keep busy all day, but from time to time she found herself going back over lost ground. She had first met Zan when he wanted to buy the Monet. She had felt she had to befriend him to some extent because he was such a stranger to the art world. So she'd helped him find experts to do the verification. And then she herself had begun to have doubts.

She began to think again about the painting itself. For the last three or four weeks that visual contact had almost vanished from her mind. She tried to recall what she had seen, what she had felt when she began to doubt. It was unclear to her now, but it had been enough to make her call up experts of her own. One had said there was no reason to doubt previous approval. The other had said there was something not 'right' about it.

A thought struck her now. She had called up her own experts, she hadn't returned to those who had first authenticated the Monet. Was that because . . . could it possibly be because . . . they were friends of Willard's and she didn't trust them to be impartial?

No, of course not. It was because they were important people and she didn't want to offend them. She made herself stop thinking about it all and went home to a quiet evening in her flat. But her mind wouldn't let the thing alone. While she was whisking eggs for an omelette, her mind wandered away to her problem.

Putting aside the matter of expert opinion: there were the descendants of the previous owners to consider. The Curacies had never heard their uncle Aristide mention a painting or the fact that he'd worked for Monet. Wasn't that just a little bit odd? On the many occasions when Claude Monet's name appeared in the papers, or was mentioned in the news, Aristide had never once said, 'I used to work for him?'

It was possible, of course. But then the Loebletzes – not the slightest word of ever having owned a Monet. True, that was less significant because the captain had only owned it for a couple of years during World War II. So she should discount that.

Next came the married daughter of Sergei Piotrovitch. She got out her notes and looked her up. Her name was Danila. Danila had married Teofan Sakovych (Sakovych with a 'y', as Vasyli had insisted). But their efforts to speak to her or her husband had ended in a mini-disaster, from which they had been rescued by Igor Prokopon.

Igor Prokopon . . . Of Intourist . . . About whom Vasyli had taken the trouble to write a letter, or so it seemed.

She got out the file of notes and picked out the letter. 'Very remarkable . . . very difficult to know which was a friend and which an enemy . . . his clothes led me to assume that he was perhaps an enemy.' The mental picture of Igor Prokopon arose before her. A great hulk of a man, the kind who might formerly have been a Soviet weightlifter or a boxing champion. Dressed in slacks, a white roll-neck sweater, and a black leather waistcoat. Except for his clothes, very like the two burly guards who had attacked Erica and Vasyli.

In fact, if she hadn't had to feel grateful to him, she'd have written him off as a thug.

She went back to the letter. 'I was surprised when he proved to be an employee of Intourist.'

Well, now that she came to think about it, so was she. Did Intourist usually employ rather scary-looking men who dressed in what Vasyli called 'trendy' clothes? Weren't couriers on the whole inclined to wear rather conventional gear, so as not to frighten off conventional clients?

Igor Prokopon. She had had almost no conversation with him. All she could say about him with certainty was that he wasn't the kind of man she'd have approached to ask the way to her hotel, and that he had an American accent when he spoke English.

It was seven thirty now. Too late to telephone the Werdenhaus Hotel in Essen and ask to speak to the travel department. But no – she remembered Tulya saying, 'Twenty-four-hour service!'

When she got through, someone told her in very good English that Tulya wasn't on duty this evening. 'Ah . . . could you give me his home telephone number?'

'Oh, no, madam, I'm afraid that is not our policy.'

'I understand. Then could I ask you, as a great favour, to ring Tulya at home and ask him to ring me. Tell him to reverse the charges and that it is rather urgent.'

'Ah . . . well . . . I see nothing against that. Give me your number, madam.'

That done, Erica went back to making the omelette. Just as she was sitting down to eat it, her phone rang.

'Hello? Miss Pencarreth? Here is Tulya.'

'Tulya! How kind of you to answer so quickly.'

'But of course quickly! It is so interesting, to be asked by English lady to telephone her in England.'

'So you do remember me?'

'Remember? Of course I remember! Only English lady I ever arranged to travel to Yalta in winter. What is problem?'

'Tulya, would you do something for me tomorrow when you go back to work? Could you, through the travel department's computer, find out if Intourist has an employee at Yalta called Igor Prokopon?'

'Contact Intourist? Why should you want this? Was Friendly Tourist Agency no good? I am sad if that is so.'

'No, Tulya, Vasyli was great. It's because of a letter he's written me that I want to enquire about Prokopon.'

'Prokopon,' repeated Tulya, with a slightly different pronunciation so that it sounded entirely foreign. 'Ukrainian name. What is first name again?'

'Igor.'

'And you want – what? To find out if Intourist employs?'

'If that's possible.'

'What reason do I give to ask?'

'Could you say . . . he did a great favour for one of your clients and she would like to get in touch to say thank you?'

'Is this truth or lie?'

'It's sort of true.'

He made a hissing sound between his teeth. 'Why should I help member of stupid state tourist agency get nice letter from English lady, huh? Stupid bunch of puppets.'

There was so much animosity in the words that she almost decided to give up. But she did very much want to check up on Prokopon if she possibly could. 'I'm not really going to write to him, Tulya. I don't want be in touch with him really.'

'Huh?' A pause. 'Very strange.'

'If it's too much trouble, then I apologise—'

'No, no, Miss Pencarreth. Is small thing you are asking, I don't know why I make problem. Sure, I will call up Intourist tomorrow and ask about Prokopon. May take some time. You know, they are not what we call whizz kids.'

'I understand. And of course I'll pay the travel department the costs of getting this information for me.'

'No problem,' said Tulya cheerily, and after checking her home number and writing down her office number, he hung up.

Erica put Vasyli's letter back into the file. She took the file with her into the kitchen, where she sat down and began to eat the cold omelette. She turned over the notes she'd made. The most recent were about Yamin Emin in

205

his shop and at dinner with herself and Willard in the restaurant.

Really, they knew nothing about Emin. Willard had happened on his shop in the first place, and since then he had had two contacts with him, one at the shop and one at dinner. Willard had accepted the story about how the Monet came into his possession and so had she.

Emin had read the letters originally glued to the back of the painting. The letter claimed that the work had been rescued from a fire in Claude Monet's garden. Now, for all his undoubted charm, Emin had struck her as being quite shrewd. Why then hadn't he consulted an art expert about the authenticity of the painting? Surely there were art experts in a cosmopolitan city like Istanbul, and if there were no experts on the Impressionists, it would have been easy enough to get a recommendation to one elsewhere.

A newly discovered Monet was sure to be worth a lot of money. Millions, in fact. Yet Emin had put it on display in his window and accepted fifteen hundred pounds for it.

Really? Why would he do such a thing?

Perhaps because he knew the painting was stolen. That crowd at the sanatorium in Yalta – they were presumably gangsters. The smuggler Dergu might very well have contacts with gangsters and Emin might be a receiver of stolen goods.

She mulled it over. She could see that the tracks of the painting seemed to be broken off at Yalta. She hadn't been able to speak to Piotrovitch's daughter. Danila lived in that block of former staff quarters; it was quite possible for perfectly innocent people to live in the same neighbourhood as thugs. Perhaps the picture had been stolen from her? And passed on to Dergu for disposal?

But why wouldn't the leader of the local Mafia call in an expert if he thought he had a Monet? Well, because the letter about Monet was in French, and perhaps no one in the gang spoke French . . .

Oh, come on, she said to herself, this is all flim-flam. It's just one speculation on another.

What she needed was some factual information. Factual

information about criminal activity. And, strange to say, she had an acquaintance who might give her that.

In the course of a career in art, she had seen and helped to uncover some minor forgeries, particularly in the area of the early drawings supposedly by master painters. From time to time these investigations had led to prosecution. The Art and Antique Squad of Scotland Yard had been involved, so that she'd come to know Sergeant Groume, now approaching retirement and with a long career in the hunt for art swindlers.

It was too late to get in touch with him at the Yard but he was usually at his desk by nine. She'd ring him tomorrow and ask for help.

As she ate the rest of the dreadful cold omelette she browsed through the rest of the notes. By now she was too tired to see her way any further. But one thing kept recurring to her. She hadn't seen the Monet in several weeks. She felt a need to look at it again and, seeing as she would with fresh eyes, find out whether she still thought something in the brushwork seemed 'not right'.

The painting was now in the safe at the Mayfair Rialto. She'd had it delivered there at Zan's request. To see it she needed his permission. She'd have to ring him.

She told herself she wasn't ringing him just to be in touch with him. She really needed to see the painting and she really needed his permission.

The desk at the hotel told her that Mr McNaughton was not in the building. Of course. He was at the hospital.

'Please give him a message,' she said. 'Tell him Miss Pencarreth rang and would like a word.'

'Certainly, Miss Pencarreth.'

He would ring tomorrow, before he set out on whatever matters he still had to deal with in London or before he went back to the hospital, she told herself. And felt a little glow at the thought.

About ten, when she had given up on the film on television and was thinking about bed, her phone rang.

'Erica? Is this too late to be ringing you?'

'Oh, Zan – no, not at all—'

'You wanted to speak to me?'

'Yes, I – it's about – well, first of all, thank you for a lovely meal last night.'

'I should thank you for giving me your company. Bert told me you got home all right.'

'Bert?'

'The driver of the car. He's part of my extended family now,' he said with something that seemed like a smile in his voice.

'Yes, he saw me safely indoors. Zan, there's something else. Could I have another look at the Monet?'

'The Monet?' he echoed. 'Sure – it's in the hotel's safe. Should I send it to you?'

'Send it here? Oh, you mean to the gallery – no, we're in the middle of setting up an exhibition, a lot of things are being moved about there – it could just happen that your painting might get knocked or damaged or even misplaced.'

'So what do you want to do?'

'I could come to the hotel – if that would be possible.'

'Of course. They've got little conference rooms where you could put it on a stand or something – I'll arrange it. I'd have to be there, though. The hotel won't open the safe unless I'm there. When do you want to do it?'

'Tomorrow?'

He sighed. 'Sorry, no can do. Tomorrow I'm taking Nyree down to Bath, to this convalescent place. I won't come back for a day or two, I want to see her well settled in.' He thought it over. 'Let's say Sunday. Or no – wait, that's your day off—'

'That's all right.' No problem, as Tulya would say.

'Well listen, if you're coming into town on Sunday for a viewing, let me give you lunch – how about that?'

'I'd like that.'

'OK, it's a deal. What time can you make it?'

'About eleven?'

'Right, I'll set it up about the painting for eleven and we'll go somewhere – you say where, Erica, you know the terrain a lot better than I do.'

'Let me think about it,' she said.

'Fair enough. See you Sunday, then.'

'Yes, Sunday. And all the best to Nyree.'

'Thanks, Erica.'

So she went about getting ready for bed in a very happy frame of mind, and slept like a top.

She was at her office as usual by nine next morning, and while the usual preparations for opening went on around her she telephoned Sergeant Groume.

She had to introduce herself, for it was some time since they'd met, but he soon placed her in his catalogue of past cases. 'Oh, yeah, you're the expert who helped me nail Sam Rickerby. Of course, how are you, Miss Pencarreth?'

'Very well, thank you. How are you?'

'Busy. But you didn't ring me to ask after my health. Can I do something for you?'

'Well, I *am* in a bit of a quandary and I wondered if you might help me out.'

'Is this official business?' he asked dryly, his voice letting her know that *he* knew she was about to ask a favour.

'It may all be my imagination so I don't want to start a fuss. But I would very much like to have a word. Could we meet for a drink?'

'I don't see why not so long as you're paying! When and where?'

'This evening? Are you otherwise engaged this evening?'

'Well, in fact, I've got something on, but not until lateish. Could you make it about six, six thirty?'

'That would be fine. How about that little pub round the back of the Bluecoat building?'

'You're on, then. See you there.'

In spare moments during the rest of the day she made notes on what she must ask the sergeant. When five o'clock came, she hurried through the formalities of closing the Corie Gallery – security checks, temperature checks, lighting checks, and then out of the building, to catch a passing bus to the station. By six she was at King's Cross and by six thirty was threading her way between the little tables in the Regimental Drum.

Sergeant Groume was already there, a pint tankard in his hand. He waved her to the quiet corner he was safeguarding and they shook hands. He was a rather skinny type, grey-haired, clerical-looking. No one would have picked him out as a detective.

'So there you are. How've you been doing since last I saw you? You'd just landed that job at the Corie.'

'Yes, it's been great, lots of chances to do something different by way of putting paintings before the public. And you, have you caught a lot of criminals?'

'Not as many as I'd like,' he growled. 'So, what'll you have to drink?'

She asked for a glass of white wine, he went to fetch it. While he was gone she got out the notes she'd made for herself.

'I wonder if I could ask you to help me with something abroad,' she began when he returned.

'Abroad – why not? I needn't tell you that art swindling is an international business these days. And highly profitable.'

'But this is someone in Istanbul.'

'Oh yes, well, Istanbul is abroad,' he agreed, unperturbed.

'You've got contacts there?'

'My spies are everywhere,' said he, grinning. 'I wouldn't say that there's a lot I know about oriental art, but I can always ask a friend of a friend. Who do you want looked at in Istanbul?'

'There's this man who owns a shop in Kazneri Sokak, a little curio shop—'

'Ah,' breathed Groume, 'a little curio shop. Lots of odd things come out of places like that.'

She told him the history of the Monet, starting with the letter originally found glued to the back of the canvas and skipping from there to what Emin had said about the smuggler during the dinner at the restaurant. Groume produced an envelope from his pocket and began making notes on it. 'Yamin Emin,' he murmured, 'Dergu . . . frequent sailings Black Sea . . . deals in dodgy goods . . .' He put the envelope back in his pocket. 'Leave it with me a day or two,' he said.

'From what you say, it looks like a regular set-up. The locals will probably know all about it, if I'm any judge – I'll see if I can get a pal to ask them for a few pointers.'

Erica tried to pay for the drinks but the sergeant waved her money away. 'No, no, glad to do something for you in return for your help in the past, Miss Pencarreth. I'll be in touch.'

Erica spent an hour at a bookstore before heading for home. As she came in, she saw the light blinking on her answering machine. She picked up and listened. 'Miss Pencarreth, here is Tulya. Please ring me back for information.' He gave his number and hung up.

Still in her outdoor things, Erica rang back.

'Miss Pencarreth, how quick to ring back. Here is Tulya with answer to question. You wish to hear?'

'I certainly do, Tulya.'

'Igor Prokopon is not employee of Intourist. Stupid officials there know very little but they know who is employed by them and Prokopon is not.'

'Oh dear,' said Erica.

'Also, Prokopon is not in Yalta phone book. This means not much, because he may have ex-directory number. This is very chic at present in Russia and other former Soviets – means importance, you know? "I am too important to be telephoned by ordinary person."'

'I wonder if that's what it means in the case of Igor Prokopon.'

'How does he come to be important to you, Miss Pencarreth?'

'Vasyli and I got . . . well, we were in a situation with some rough characters and this man arrived and persuaded them to behave.'

Tulya seemed to consider this. 'Ahem . . . he might have been policeman.'

'What?'

'You say, "persuaded" – this means what? Persuading with threats? Shove them about? How?'

'He talked to them. I think he called at least one of them by name – Kasivan, Kasilan, something like that.'

'Kasiyan,' corrected Tulya. 'Favourite Ukrainian name, a

211

hero of the past to them, I think. Oh, if he called them by name, probably a policeman.'

'You think so?'

'Could be. These days, there are many "rough characters". The police, they don't drive around in armoured car or wear uniforms with peaked caps any more. *Some* police are . . . wait a moment, I think of word – cahoots? Is this what I am thinking?'

'Ah,' said Erica. 'Yes, in cahoots – I could imagine that to be the case.'

'But anyhow, he is not Intourist, for sure. So this is what you needed to know?'

'It's very helpful, Tulya. Now, let me send you a present as a thank-you for your efficiency.'

'No, indeed, you owe nothing—'

'But I'd like to, Tulya. Please. Is there anything you need?'

'Well,' said Tulya, 'I don't really need – but could you perhaps send CD of John Coltrane? Difficult to get, in Essen.'

Laughing, Erica promised to put a selection of CDs in the post to him at the Werdenhaus Hotel.

She took off her jacket, hung it up, and went to make herself a much-needed cup of coffee. Tulya's words echoed in her mind. 'Prokopon is not employee of Intourist.'

No. Vasyli had been telling her that same thing. And Prokopon wasn't in the phone book. That might mean nothing, he perhaps didn't even live in the town of Yalta – but he had behaved as if he was someone of local importance. So he was perhaps a local cop, one of the new breed who co-operated with the local Mafia.

It looked as if Willard had applied for help, not to Intourist, but to the police station. Was that how it had happened? It was logical enough, although a bit extreme – if you were looking for someone on a business trip with a courier, your first move was surely not to ask for help from the police. And if you did, why should the police pay any attention? They had more important things to do. It wasn't as if she'd been missing for a month or anything scary like that, she thought to herself. She was simply on a business trip to the Crimea.

But Tulya was suggesting that the police these days were . . . well, not perhaps corrupt, but out for themselves. Willard, like Erica herself, spoke hardly a word of Russian. Just suppose he'd gone into the police station for information and perhaps Igor, speaking good English, had seen a chance to earn a few roubles or, better still, dollars. She seemed to remember that money had changed hands at the departure of Igor Prokopon.

Erica was beginning to worry about Willard. The finding of the Monet had been such a triumph for him, but all her efforts to track it back seemed to make the whole thing more rather than less blurred. The only actual fact to emerge from her investigation was that the letter attached to the back of the canvas was really and truly in the handwriting of Aristide Curacie – she and Zan had seen that with their own eyes.

Some day she'd have to tell Willard that she had finished the report on the painting. She would have to say that she – she, Zan's consultant – had had doubts about its attribution and that now the only thing that seemed to remain valid was the letter. Everything else was say-so.

It remained to be seen what Sgt Groume could find out about Dergu. If he could get his whereabouts, Erica would hire someone in Istanbul to question him. She knew that she herself could never succeed there – Dergu probably spoke no English and wouldn't want to talk to anyone about his clandestine activities, least of all to a woman and a foreigner. But she would hire someone to ask him if he had got the painting – legally or illegally – from Danila, daughter of Sergei Piotrovitch. She would ask for a signed statement about that – perhaps offer him a 'reward'? But could that be seen as a bribe where someone like Dergu was concerned?

She wanted to get it all straightened out for Willard's sake. She wanted to prove the Monet authentic. Although she wasn't in love with Willard any more, and perhaps had been growing out of love with him for some time, she still wished him well. She owed him a lot, and he in his own way loved her – was fond of her – well, at least had enjoyed the physical side of their relationship. She would let him know one day soon that it was over between them. But before then she wanted to do him this one last favour – to ascertain that he'd been right when he claimed the painting as a Monet.

Because anything else would be such a blow! If he'd made a mistake, if somehow the painting was a fraud and he'd been taken in . . . It didn't bear thinking of.

She longed to talk to someone – ideally, she would have liked to talk to Zan. But Zan was at the convalescent clinic in Somerset. So she rang her mother.

'Are you coming down for the weekend?' Lisbet at once asked. 'Things hereabouts are looking very springlike.'

'I can't come this weekend, Mamma, I have a date on Sunday.'

'With Willard, I presume. I won't say, give him my love, because you know I can never love an art dealer.'

'Oh, *Mamma*! That's such an old joke. Anyhow, my date isn't with Will, it's with Mr McNaughton, the man who's buying the Monet.'

'Oh yes, him – how are things going on that score? Have you proved it's a Monet?'

'No-o. No, Mamma, I haven't. But I haven't proved it isn't.'

'Pardon?' said Lisbet. 'I didn't understand that.'

'It's still as much a Monet as it was when Zan bought it.'

'Zan? That's Mr McNaughton, isn't it?'

'Yes, it's short for Alexander.'

'I rather like that. So he's Zan now, is he?'

'Well, yes. You can hardly be involved in all this huha about authentication without getting to know someone quite well.'

'All right, all right, I didn't say you oughtn't to call him Zan. What's he like?'

'He's—' She broke off. She didn't want to talk to her mother about Zan. Lisbet was far too keen-sighted where her daughter was concerned. 'Never mind about that. Are you working?'

'Like mad. I've been doing sketches for a study of a little

wood – you know that copse on the slope just before the rocks jut out at Shilly Top? You know, Erica, trees can be eerie . . . I was looking at them and they seemed to be – sort of resisting the rocks, making their roots hold on to the thin soil – well, never mind. All I can say is, it's very hard to get the feeling into a charcoal sketch.'

Erica made sympathetic noises and encouraged her mother to talk about her work. But it never lasted for long; Lisbet was always secretive about what she was doing. She turned back to the matter of Erica's investigation. 'Are you anywhere near writing the report yet?'

'I've begun it, but I find I need a bit more information.'

'This Zan McNaughton is getting a lot for his money, by the sound of it.'

'It's nothing to do with money!' Erica flashed.

'Oh-ho,' said her mother. 'That was a strong denial.'

'Well, it isn't.'

'No. I can tell it's maybe nothing to do with money.'

'Now, Mamma, don't start getting silly—'

'Me? Silly? Never. All I can say is, if Mr McNaughton has taken your mind off Willard, he has my support.'

'Oh, for goodness' sake . . . !'

'Goodnight, maidie. Sleep well and pleasant dreams.'

Half laughing, half sighing, Erica disconnected. And if she had pleasant dreams, in the morning she couldn't remember them.

On Saturday, Willard rang. He had told her that she must make the first move, that she must ring when she felt like being sensible. She had never expected *him* to make the first move. 'What about tomorrow?' he asked as if there had never been a disagreement.

'No, I can't, Will, I'm doing something else.'

'What, for instance?'

There was no reason why she shouldn't tell him. 'I'm going to look at the Monet.'

'The Monet. You're not still on about that? McNaughton has it now, hasn't he?'

'Yes, that's right. In the safe at his hotel.'

'You're going to town just to look at it?'

215

'That's the main reason.' She didn't feel like adding that she was going to lunch with Zan. It would only cause trouble, and she didn't feel like another telephone quarrel with Willard.

Willard seemed to be thinking it over. She knew he understood quite well why she wanted to see the painting again. If you were assessing the bona fides of a work of art, you had to keep it in your mind's eye. Good photographs helped, but in this case there were no photographs of the work except those taken in November by the laboratory. In many cases it was possible to compare a painting that had been lost and rediscovered with photographs taken in the past, and published in learned books discussing the painter's technique. But this Monet had no prior history, so there were no photographs taken in the past, no discussion and speculation by other experts. This photographs had no history except the story provided by Yamin Emin.

'What time are you at the hotel?' Willard inquired.

'Mid-morning.'

'Oh, then we could meet in town afterwards.'

'Er . . . no, Will, that won't work.'

'Why not?'

'Because I have a lunch engagement.'

He didn't ask with whom. She knew that he knew. After a faint intake of breath he said, 'This is a bit much, Erica.'

'Could you just explain that?'

'Two weeks have gone by without my seeing you.'

She'd thought he was going to complain about Zan. A little taken aback she said, 'But we've often gone two or three weeks without seeing each other.'

'But things are different now.'

'In what way?'

'Well . . . after Istanbul . . . I felt those few days made a world of difference. They did to me, anyhow. I felt we'd committed to each other.'

Erica could think of nothing to say.

'Didn't you feel like that too?' he went on. 'I was sure you did. And you know, darling, if we look forward, there's

216

a whole life for us to share, and it can be like that, like those wonderful nights in Istanbul.'

'I didn't realise you felt like that.'

'I can't believe that. You're so quick to catch every nuance between us, I just know you understood that Istanbul was the beginning of something more, something special.'

'No, I hadn't understood that.'

'Sweetheart, we've got to see each other, talk this through. Cancel whatever it is you were going to do tomorrow and come to my place, we'll have lots of time together, we'll think about the future and make plans.'

She felt as if she were being battered with a cudgel. In a way she thought she understood. Will was feeling – for the first time – that he had a rival. He was reinforcing his claims on her.

She was meant to fall apart at the appeal in his words. But instead she felt only something like embarrassment. It was so unlike Willard to *plead*.

She made herself speak calmly. 'I can't alter my plans for tomorrow. I can't get in touch to cancel the arrangements.'

'You could leave a message at the hotel, surely.'

'But I don't want to, Will.'

There was a long, long pause. 'I don't understand this,' said Willard in a stifled voice. 'What's got into you?'

'It's a long story,' she said, 'too long to go into on the phone.'

'Then let's meet' – quickly urged – 'Monday evening – I'll come to your flat—'

'No, let's not meet, Will. Not for the time being.' She was searching wildly for some form of words to use as a shield against his insistence. 'There's a lot on my mind at the moment,' she said lamely, 'so I'd rather have some space.'

'Some space?'

'I know, it's jargon, but it means what it says. I'll be in touch, Will. Bye for now.' And she quickly disconnected.

She sat for a few minutes, feeling quite exhausted. She had actually begun the process of saying goodbye to Willard.

She'd never actually let herself think about it. Since she understood what she was feeling for Zan, she'd known at the back of her mind that she'd have to loosen the ties with Will. It had always seemed a hard thing to do but now that he was beginning to talk about committing to each other for the future, it began to seem horrendous. He'd always been possessive, and sometimes she'd felt just the tiniest bit offended by that. Now he sounded as if he were in love – and that was somehow very touching. And it filled her with remorse.

Her intercom buzzed. She was half afraid to answer, thinking it might be Willard, somehow getting in touch by indirect means. Suzi said, 'There's a Sergeant Groume asking for you.'

'What, here?'

'Yes, in the foyer.'

'Tell him I'll be right there.'

She hurried out of her office, and found the sergeant surveying one of the Renoirs in the first display. 'Ve-ery nice,' he remarked. 'Amazing when you think nobody approved of it at first.'

'It's nice to see you,' she said. 'But you'd no need to come all the way out here to see me.'

'Oh, it made a nice little trip, a chance to see your collection again. Can we move along while we talk? You've got a Degas I'm fond of.'

They moved like visitors through the rooms. He said, 'I asked a chum to check up for you.'

'Yes?'

'First of all, your friend Yamin Emin is well known to the Istanbul force.'

'Oh dear.'

'Nothing serious, I gather. Nobody takes him seriously.'

'Ah.' She was relieved. 'You mean he's not a criminal.'

'Well, he's not Snow White either. He does a little of this and that, nothing too heavy. His story about the painting may be true. On the other hand, he may have made it all up.'

'Sergeant Groume, you're not being helpful,' she sighed.

'Well, the next bit may be more of a help. It's about Dergu.'

'Tell me.'

'He doesn't exist.'

'What?'

'There is no such man smuggling goods between the Crimea and Istanbul or any other port along the Turkish coast. The customs officers in Istanbul are in the know about every aspect of smuggling in their area. They know every man and every carrier of drugs and every boat that crosses the Black Sea – all they lack for a conviction are witnesses. Dergu doesn't own a boat, he doesn't serve as crew on one, he doesn't have an address and nobody on the waterfronts has ever heard of him. He doesn't exist.'

'Sergeant!' Erica gasped.

The detective looked at her in a friendly, almost fatherly way. He took one of her hands and patted it. 'Don't take it to heart. Dergu is just another one of Mr Emin's little lies.'

'But he told us Dergu got the painting from the Piotrovitch family.'

'That probably isn't true either.'

'What, you mean the family doesn't exist? But we got an address for the daughter – in Yalta.'

'Oh, the family may exist. But it's just a name. Perhaps he selected it out of a phone book or something. Did you meet the daughter?'

'No-o – a couple of toughs prevented us from going into the building.'

'Really? Well, I don't know enough to give an opinion, but I'm passing on what I got from Istanbul. Don't believe a word you heard from Mr Emin. You can trust him about as far as you can throw St Paul's.'

It so happened that Erica was wearing the necklace given to her in token of friendship by Yamin Emin. She held the chain out from her neck and said, 'Mr Emin gave me this, Sergeant.'

Groume bent his head to examine it. 'It's nice,' he said.

'He said it was made up of some of the gold coins they find in ancient ruins.'

Groume shrugged. 'I'm no expert,' he replied.

After the detective had left, Erica told her secretary she was slipping out for a short while. She hurried to the main shopping street of Gratesford, where there was a jeweller that specialised in antiques as well as modern work. She asked to have a valuation of her necklace. The manager attended to her personally, recognising her as the curator of the local art gallery.

He examined the coins with a loupe, then with her permission took the necklace into the back of the shop. After about fifteen minutes he returned.

'Did you buy this, Miss Pencarreth?'

'No, it was a present.'

'Ah. Er . . . did the person who gave it to you buy it as genuine?'

'I was told it was genuine, yes.'

He shook his head in regret. 'The chain is gold but is modern, not made in Europe – perhaps Thailand, somewhere like that. The coins are reproductions of Greek currency – I'm not expert enough to say what era they're supposed to belong to but they're not gold, they're some sort of alloy.' He laid the necklace on the velvet pad on the counter. 'I'm sorry, Miss Pencarreth.'

'Thank you very much for your opinion.' She scooped the necklace up and put it in her handbag.

'You could always consult someone with more knowledge than I have, of course.'

'No, I'm sure what you told me was right.'

She went out, drawing deep breaths to get her feelings under control.

The necklace was a sham, Yamin Emin was a liar, and she'd been played for a fool.

Fifteen

Sgt Groume had given Erica his mobile number at parting. She rang it now. He answered at once, from his car. 'Groume.'

'Sergeant, this is Erica Pencarreth.'

'Oh? Hello again.'

'Sergeant, I went straight out after you left, to have that necklace valued. It's a fake.'

'Aha,' said Groume.

'You expected that.'

'I thought it likely. So, Miss Pencarreth, why are you ringing?'

'I'm hoping for another favour. Could you ask Kevin Cheffield to look at the painting?'

Cheffield was an expert, often asked to testify on behalf of the prosecution in causes of art fraud. His reputation was such that practically no one dared to challenge any of his decisions. His laboratory in Hereford handled work from all over the world, so he was a busy man. Erica knew that without pulling strings, she might have to wait as long as a year for him to examine the Monet.

'Well now . . . You know he's no infallible judge when it comes to *technique*—'

'It's not technique that worries me. I could go on asking connoisseurs of painting for opinions until kingdom come, and I'd keep getting different answers. But if Mr Cheffield would do an analysis of the materials . . .'

'You've had that done already.'

'Yes, but I'm at the stage now where perhaps a second opinion would help.'

'I see,' said the sergeant. 'Well, let me ask Kevin how

he's fixed at the moment. I know he's got some work for the Yard, but that's paper analysis for yet another so-called "Picasso drawing" – and of course he has private work too, he's doing X-rays on a possible Piazetta—'

'But you could ask him?'

'No harm in asking. OK, leave it with me, I'll get back to you with an answer one way or the other.'

'Thanks a million, Sergeant.'

The transition from anger over the necklace to stronger doubts about the painting had occurred as she was hurrying back to the Corie Gallery. Emin simply wasn't to be trusted, not in anything. If the necklace was a fake, the painting too was suspect. And although analytical work had given it a clean bill of health, she was suddenly beset with doubts over that verdict. She had been taken in, so had Willard – there was no doubt the plot had been quite clever. Yet Yamin Emin had probably never envisaged the painting causing so much interest. He'd probably thought he was selling it to a gullible tourist.

Yet it was so strange – everything used in making the painting was exactly what Monet himself would have used. Was Emin really capable of producing a result like that? He must have a backroom boy somewhere, a man who knew all about how to reproduce a Monet. Who could tell? Perhaps all the paintings sold in that shop were fakes – even that dark little painting of the boat at the jetty, the one that looked as if it were by some German of the Victorian era. Produced by some clever hack, glad to earn a few hundred pounds a painting, which were then sold by Emin at fifteen hundred apiece – not a bad profit.

No, no. It was too far-fetched. Emin was a petty receiver of stolen goods, that was all. And the painting was by Claude Monet. She must stop imagining massive conspiracies. It was making her paranoid, she told herself.

All the same, if Sgt Groume could get Kevin Cheffield to examine the painting, she would jump at the chance. She needed all the help she could get.

The painting itself was produced from the safe of the Mayfair Rialto next morning with some ceremony. It was now in a proper carrier of the kind that illustrators use when they are taking originals to magazine offices, a rectangular flat case of good quality plastic, zipped all around and with a secure handle. A porter carried it for them to a small conference room on the first floor of the hotel.

There an easel had been set up, of the kind used at lectures, with a white-board and an array of coloured pens. It faced a conference table capable of accommodating eight. Erica asked for the easel to be turned so that it faced the window. The porter set down the carrier, took the board off the easel, turned it, and was about to set the board back on the ledge when Zan made a move to stop him.

'No,' said Erica, 'let's have the board there, as a background to the painting. The white surface will reflect light around it.'

The porter completed the set-up and left. Erica unzipped the case, took out the Monet in its wrapping of blue paper, shook it free, and set it on the easel against the white-board.

Once again, at that first glimpse, she felt the impulse of certainty. It *must* be by Claude Monet. Everything there proclaimed him – the fervent need to catch the moment, the surge of movement as the wind rustled leaves and turned them so that their colour varied, the vigour, the intensity . . . The old man desperate to make his statement – 'I *see*, I *see*!'

She drew in a breath, turning to Zan. She found that he was standing by, arms folded, watching her, not the painting. He was looking businesslike, as if all that interested him was her opinion of the Monet.

'So you think it's the real McCoy,' he observed.

He saw her hesitate. She made no reply. She bent her head and he could imagine that she was trying to look within herself, to find an observer who wouldn't let her emotions run away with her. Then she took a step towards the painting and began to study it minutely.

She took her time. She gazed at the canvas as a whole, she let her eye examine it inch by inch, she took out a lens and studied the surface, and then she went to a chair as far from it as the room would allow, and sat there, challenging the painting to tell her the truth.

223

Zan meanwhile sat on the edge of the table, giving her the privilege of silence. In any case, it was a pleasure just to watch her, to see how her thoughts were mirrored on her features.

After a while she picked up a square of dark green silk which she'd worn as a scarf. She spread it over the white-board to change the value of the surrounding light. She stayed beside the easel, looking with an intense scrutiny at the brushwork. She gave a very deep sigh, audible in the stillness of the room.

'I don't know,' she confessed. 'Something about that area under the bridge doesn't seem "right" – the play of the water seems . . . I don't know . . .' She sighed again. 'If it's a forgery, it's by a master forger. I don't think that any of the experts on technique would be able to write it off with certainty. We could go on getting second opinions for the next two years and it would come out fifty-fifty or perhaps even seventy to thirty.'

'But you're still worried.'

She nodded. 'And that's why I'm trying to get the leading expert in forensics to have a go at it.'

'You mean, laboratory tests?' He was surprised. He'd thought they were finished with that element of the investigation.

'Yes, if he can find time to take it. His firm is always very busy.' She explained about Kevin Cheffield. 'You'd agree to having it looked at again?'

'Sure. I don't want to be gypped,' he told her, although he felt it made him sound a tightwad. 'I want Nyree to have a real Impressionist, not a phoney,' he amended.

'If Cheffield takes the job, can you arrange for the painting to be handed over to the courier? It'll be someone from a bonded firm who'll show identification.'

'I'll have to put it in writing for the manager – apparently a signature will suffice, my presence isn't strictly necessary – but that's OK, I'll do it whenever you want.' He picked up the carrier. 'Let's put it back in its hidey-hole again and go out for that lunch I promised you.'

The safe bestowing of the painting took some time. The

assistant manager had to be summoned, a receipt had to be signed, Mr McNaughton had to go into the office to witness the painting being put back in the safe. Zan was kicking himself for wasting the time. Why hadn't he left it where it was, in the safe keeping of Erica at her gallery? Fathead, he told himself.

She took him to a pub on the Thames near Hammersmith. It was a bright, cold day of early spring, with daffodils beginning to break into flower in the beds provided by the town council, and rowing eights out on the water practising for the Head of the River races. Although it was really too cold to sit outdoors, they found a sheltered spot behind a wall of old red brick, where they settled with thick sandwiches and glasses of dark ale.

Zan was delighted, because he knew she was remembering his words from a previous conversation, that really old pubs were hard to find in New Zealand. 'Now this is the kind of place we always think of as "typical",' he remarked. 'Mind you, seems to me the people aren't as "typical" as I'd imagined – I thought I'd see blokes with cloth caps and maybe a Pearly Queen or two.'

'You shouldn't take *Me and My Girl* as gospel truth,' she chided. 'Though I will admit this area has changed a lot. But everything changes,' she added with a sigh.

He studied her in sympathy. 'Something's happened to upset you,' he guessed, and waited for her to say she'd rather not talk about it – because it was probably something about that idiot Townley.

'I feel such a fool . . .' Slowly, she told him something quite unexpected – the story of Yamin Emin and the necklace. She brought out from her capacious handbag the file containing photocopies of Emin's statement. 'It's probably all a lie,' she said, pointing to the words about how he came to have the Monet.

'You're saying the local cop-shop have never heard of Dergu?'

'They say he doesn't exist. Everything Emin told us was a complete lie.'

'That doesn't quite follow, Erica,' he said, in an effort to comfort her. 'There could well be a smuggler who brought that painting from Yalta, but his name may be something different. Emin might not want to give his right name.'

'Oh! I hadn't thought of that.'

'And as to the necklace . . .' He frowned. Mr Emin, another stupid idiot. What a thing to do to Erica . . . 'Well, that's a cheap shot at getting you to like him. But it doesn't necessarily mean any more than that.'

'Why should he bother to make me like him? I felt – I still feel – that he was trying to disarm me, to get me to feel kindly towards him so that I'd accept that painting.'

'The painting. Let's go back to that.' That was safe ground, that was fact, not feeling. 'You didn't find out whether Danila Thingamabob had owned it and given it to somebody to sell in Istanbul.'

'No, because this pair of hard men stopped us—'

'So that's a dead end. Go back another step. We were pretty convinced that the Loebletzes had never heard of the painting.'

She nodded agreement. She found herself unwilling to talk about the Loebletzes and what a fool she'd made of herself over that.

'The Curacies in Paris had never hard of the painting either.'

'Nor ever heard their uncle speak of being employed by Monet.'

'Another step back – three experts who were originally consulted say it's genuine.'

'Yes, and me too – I thought it was, then.'

'Since then, one other has said it's OK, one says not.' He was keeping track of points by counting on his fingers.

'Yes. And me too again, I now say not. At least, I'm very doubtful now. It's not just the feeling I get when I look at the painting dispassionately. It's all this haziness about the provenance. When I first looked at those documents that came with the painting they seemed to guarantee a line of authenticity but, Zan, *it never checks out.*'

He thought about it, treating it just like a business proposition. Would he trust someone whose background seemed so full of evasions? But there was one certainty. 'The handwriting checks out,' he pointed out. 'We compared the letter from the gardener's boy with the letter about the win on the Tour de France, which we *know* was written by Aristide Curacie.'

'But, Zan – remember what Daff said. Anyone can forge a letter.'

That was a scary thought, and only too true. He himself had had an employee who'd forged signatures on the company cheques. 'But we come back to the question then,' he countered. 'How can you forge a letter in the handwriting of Aristide Curacie without having a sample to work from?'

'We talked about that. Someone might have looked up official papers – his signature on his ID, for instance. French citizens have IDs.'

Zan sipped from his tankard and considered it. 'Could you do that?' he wondered. 'You go into some office and ask to look at old documents like passports or army discharge papers . . . But you can't take them away. Could you really forge a signature from such a casual look?'

'You could photocopy the documents,' she countered.

'So you could. There might be a record of that. But you'd have to guess which office was involved. That's a big undertaking. And look here, Erica – this painting gets sold in Istanbul for fifteen hundred pounds – isn't all that a lot of work to do just to earn fifteen hundred?'

'Oh, don't,' she groaned. She'd been over that ground in her head a hundred times.

He set aside the tankard. 'I don't really care for this stuff,' he had to admit. 'I guess I'm a wine lover at heart. I'm going to inspect the wine list. Can I get you something?'

She laughed. 'Weakling!' she scolded. 'You're supposed to think it's all part of the great tradition – like roast beef or the Pearly Queens. Well, to tell the truth, I'd like something hot – my nose is froze. Could I have a cup of coffee?'

'Let's give up this whole Thames-side bit – there's a devil of a chill coming off that water. Let's find a nice warm Starbucks or Coffee Republic,' he suggested.

They got up. He couldn't resist the impulse to fold her

coat more closely around her neck, then took her arm, and off they went.

Erica let herself lean as close to him as she could, for the pleasure of feeling the long, strong body in motion. They took some stairs up to street level, making their way towards Hammersmith's busy centre.

Zan made himself ask the important question: 'What does your friend Townley think of all this?' He'd never willingly spoken of him before and could tell from something about the rigidity of her arm in his that it surprised her.

'Well, you know we agreed not to give him chapter and verse until we'd come to a definite conclusion.'

'But he turned up somewhere along your journey. I gathered he was with you.' He hesitated. He wanted to make sure it came out easily. 'In Istanbul.'

'Yes. Well, you see, I telephoned him because I'd said at first I'd only be gone for a couple of days, but then I decided to go on to Yalta.' She was walking along at his side, looking straight ahead. 'So I let him know my plans. And he was very worried because the Russian authorities tend to think foreign art experts are after their icons—'

'Icons? Church paintings?'

'Yes, they're worth a fortune in the West, and let me tell you the former Soviets seem to have a lot of people willing to rob a church and sell the proceeds to the highest bidder.'

He wasn't really concerned about the trade in icons. 'So Townley turned up to make sure you didn't get arrested, is that it?' he asked jokingly.

'Yes, and a good thing he did.' Erica felt she must do justice to Willard. 'My interpreter and I were having a very unpleasant encounter with some toughs, when Will arrived on the scene with a . . . a man who was able to sort it all out for us.'

'That was very lucky,' Zan said.

There was something in his tone that made her lean forward as they walked, trying to read his expression.

'Well, it was,' she insisted. 'He'd arrived before me because it turned out I'd chosen a rather roundabout way to get there. So he knew the situation wasn't straightforward.

It just happened that he was a few minutes too late in spotting me, and so he followed when Vasyli and I set off to this sanatorium—'

'Sanatorium!'

'Oh, it's just another name for a hotel. It's a hold-over from their Soviet past. Anyhow, it turned out this sanatorium was a sort of headquarters for the local Mafia—'

Horror made him stop short. 'Erica!' He wheeled her round to face him, and glared at her. 'Were you out of your mind? I never meant you to put yourself in that kind of danger!'

'No, well . . .' She smiled, half in reassurance and half in embarrassment. 'My guide didn't realise the set-up until too late. Anyhow, up drove Will with this henchman, and it all died away to nothing. But of course we didn't feel like pursuing the enquiry any further.'

'Thank God for that!' Getting possession of this problematical work of art wasn't worth endangering so much as her little finger. But she clearly wanted to play it down so he said, 'You went on to Istanbul.'

'Yes,' she said. She continued their walk. She didn't want to be face to face with him, as she remembered those last passionate nights with Willard on the cabin cruiser and in Istanbul. Gone now, part of history, like the Dizzy Days of revolt in New York. Part of the learning process that never seemed to stop.

Zan seemed to have decided not to ask any more questions. For her part, Erica felt it was best to go on.

'Will was perfectly satisfied with the explanation we got from Yamin Emin.'

'He was?' There was something in the way she'd said it. Some change in attitude, some difference in her tone of voice. He spent a moment or two trying to read what it meant. Perhaps she was embarrassed in speaking of her precious Will, so to bring it all down to mere reportage he asked: 'What did he say about the way the trail seems to falter after Paris?'

'I don't know that we've actually discussed it.'

There it was again, that something in her voice. It was

almost a disclaimer. 'It's not important to tell him every-thing' – was that what she was saying?

No, come on, he told himself. Of course he's important. She emphatically told you so, didn't she? Don't get carried away because you've managed to get back on a friendly footing with her.

Erica went on: 'Of course I did tell him about seeing Uncle Aristide's letter about winning a bet on the Tour de France. And he felt that was pretty conclusive. So as far as Will is concerned, the trail doesn't falter – he thought that was good enough proof that the provenance was reliable. And what he heard from Mr Emin simply reinforced that view.'

'But he doesn't know that Emin is regarded as a prac-tised liar by the locals, and that the smuggler Dergu is a fabrication?'

'No, I haven't been in touch to tell him that. Because it'll be such an awful shock . . .'

'To find that he's been had?' To his own shame, Zan found that he rather enjoyed that notion.

'Yes.' She wanted to add something about sparing Will's feelings, just for old times' sake, but she didn't know how to phrase it.

They came to a coffee house and hurried into its friendly warmth. It was the kind of place Vasyli would have called 'trendy', aluminium chairs against tables with reflective black surfaces and, behind the serving counter, shining machines producing coffee in about twenty different versions.

They ordered their drinks then found a table near the windows so they could look out at the passers-by. The counter-man brought the coffee. Erica buried her nose in the fragrant warm steam. They sat in reflective silence for a few moments.

'We did agree not to say anything to anyone about our conclusions "unless and until", didn't we?' Zan said.

'Yes. Unless and until we're certain.'

'Seems to me,' he said, 'that the only "certainty" is that letter in Aristide's handwriting. We can't go round all the bureaucratic centres of Paris looking for something with his signature, it would need all kinds of diplomatic permissions and it would take for ever. I vote we go back to the Curacies in the Rue Sarabande and ask to borrow their letter. You could find an expert to compare the two – our letter with Uncle Aristide's letter?'

'I could ask Sgt Groume. He'd know a handwriting expert.'

'Are you on for another trip to Paris?' he asked hopefully.

'I couldn't take any more time off, Zan, not at the moment.' There seemed to be real regret in her voice. 'I've been away quite a bit recently, and we're in the middle of preparations for the Easter show.'

'We could do it in a day,' he coaxed. 'In fact, I'd prefer that. I don't want to be away from Nyree too long at the moment . . .'

'No, I don't think I can take even a day. It's unfair on the others. I don't even have an assistant, officially – Suzi is only my secretary although of course I chose her because she's knowledgeable about art. But you see, I haven't got anyone I can really keep delegating to.' She saw he looked frustrated and she added, 'But *you* go. You don't need me there.'

'Oh . . .' It was true. But the idea of going without her wasn't nearly so attractive.

'Yes, do. Your French is more chatty than mine, and you're better at offering a little encouragement in the way of money.'

'You really can't come?' he asked. 'What about next Sunday?'

'Well, I was going down to Cornwall to see Mamma, and I *could* put it off—'

'But you'd rather not.' He was the last person in the world to deny the importance of family ties.

'I haven't been down since Christmas. I ought to go.'

He shrugged and nodded. 'OK, I'll go on my own. I'll go this evening and come back tomorrow.'

'That's fast!' She kept forgetting that he was a businessman, used to quick decisions and quick action.

'Well, why not?' He could have said that he had nothing

231

important to hold him in London at the moment, but that was self-pity – and the truth was, he knew he couldn't keep her here for the rest of the day, she had a life of her own, for heaven's sake. So the evening loomed ahead of him, empty and cheerless. Far better to be doing something useful.

They parted at mid-afternoon. Erica gave him the photocopy of the gardener's boy's letter from the file she'd brought with her. She also reminded him to give instructions so that the painting could be collected from the hotel by the courier if Kevin Cheffield agreed to take it on. He put her in a taxi for King's Cross, wondering if he should hazard a kiss of farewell, but the taxi driver was worried about impeding traffic and she was gone before he could lean in and kiss her.

He caught the six o'clock Eurostar, reached the Hôtel Romain soon after eleven. After a leisurely *café complet* next morning he looked up the Curacies in the phone book and put a call through. He wanted, if possible, to make sure of seeing Madame Curacie this time. He thought it likely she would remember more about family history than her menfolk.

It turned out that the son was at work at the Renault factory. Papa Curacie had just gone out to collect a repaired video recorder. However, Mme Curacie would be delighted to see him; her husband had told her about the visit of the English monsieur and mademoiselle, and she had a lively curiosity.

Zan bought a handsome bunch of tulips from the hotel florist then took a taxi to the Rue Sarabande. Mme Curacie, a dark, plump, blue-eyed woman with the look of Brittany about her, must have been waiting practically behind the door. She welcomed him in and was utterly delighted by the gift of flowers.

'Albert told me about your visit of last month, Monsieur. I was so sorry to have missed it.'

'It's very kind of you to spare me your time, madame.'

'Please, sit down. I have coffee ready. Would you like some?'

'Thank you, that would be nice.' He sat. The room looked

232

better than it had when he and Erica had come. There were no untidy newspapers, no beer glasses, a lace cloth over a dark blue one covered the table, and all the cushions had been plumped up.

Mme Curacie came back almost at once with the cafetière and all the other necessities. A handsome apricot tart was on the tray with a silver server and crockery that looked like her best china. This was a big occasion for Mireille Curacie.

'I understood from Albert that you were inquiring after Uncle Ari?' she said, pouring the coffee.

'Yes, my colleague and I – Miss Pencarreth – are interested in his early life. We believe he worked for Claude Monet, the painter.'

'Ah,' she said, offering sugar, 'my husband told me something like that but I couldn't quite make it out. Claude Monet, the famous painter, the one who did *The Waterlilies*?'

'Yes.'

She made a little grimace of surprise. 'I never heard of that.'

'You knew him, of course – Uncle Ari.'

'Oh yes, a decent old man, quite interested in the family but his main interest was horse racing and the Tour and things like that.' She looked at Zan for his understanding. 'He was a gambler, you see.'

'Yes,' Zan said, seizing the opening, 'your husband was good enough to let us see a letter your uncle wrote to you, when he sent you money towards the cost of a car.'

'Ah yes, our dear old car . . .' Like Albert, she fell into a reverie for a moment. 'We kept that letter as a memento of one of the great days of our lives. We went out the following Saturday and with the help of that money we put down the first instalment.'

'Would it be possible to see that letter again, Madame?'

'It interests you? Well, I don't see why not. Unfortunately it's in a box on the top of my wardrobe, and I can't reach it without getting on a chair – and you know, monsieur, with my figure' – she made a little laughing nod towards her own plump legs – 'I don't like getting up on chairs.'

'Oh, but you must allow me to do that, Madame,' Zan offered enthusiastically, getting up.

Surprised, but seeing no help for it, Mme Curacie led the way into the master bedroom of the apartment. An old-fashioned oak bedstead dominated the room, and a matching dressing-table with mirrors sent back three reflections as they crossed to the door of the closet. She threw it open. Inside were rails of clothing running round three sides of the cubicle, and above the rails two layers of shelves.

'Up there,' explained Mireille, pointing to the shelves opposite the door. 'On the top shelf.'

He could have reached the box had it been at the front of the shelf, but it was pushed to the back so he had to use a chair. He brought the box down, she took it from him. They went back to the living-room and their coffee.

Madame took a few sips before she opened the box. She took out papers, photographs, murmuring to herself as she did so. 'That's our marriage certificate. Here's part of the veil from Lucie's first communion. Oh, look, there's Laurent's school report the year he came first in mechanics . . .'

Zan gave her time to browse. When he had emptied his coffee cup he began, 'Might I see the letter from your Uncle Ari?'

'Of course, just a moment. Here it is.' She produced it. Zan felt in his breast pocket for the photocopy of the letter that had come with the Monet. But just as he brought it out Mireille said in a fretful tone, 'Where's the letter about Lucie's first communion? It should be with the piece of veil.'

He stopped. 'The letter . . . About paying for her communion frock?' he said, pulling the details out of his memory.

'Yes, it was such a kind letter, he called her his little white rose . . . Now where has it got to?'

'I understood your husband to say your daughter took it with her when she went to Canada, madame.'

'Lucie took it?' She shook her head in denial. 'Who said that?'

'Well, your husband.'

234

'Huh! He never pays attention to family matters, you know? Why are men like that?' Then, apologetic, 'I'm sorry, monsieur, you are probably different. But my Albert, he sits there saying, "Yes, yes" and it goes straight through his head like water through a sieve. No, Lucie took only photographs with her to Quebec. She wasn't interested in taking the letter or the veil. You know, young people these days aren't as interested in religion as people of my generation. So a letter about her communion didn't mean much to her. But where is it, where has it gone?'

She ferreted about in the box. In the end she tilted it so as to empty it then put each item back one by one, examining it as she did so to make sure the letter hadn't got caught up with something else.

She had to admit defeat in the end. 'It's not there,' she said in mystification. 'How could it have gone?'

'Have you had the box open recently, Madame?'

'No, not for ages. Albert told me he got it down for you—'

'The letter was missing then, Mme Curacie.'

'It was?' She shook her head. 'I don't understand it. It's quite upset me.' She cut a piece of apricot tart and comforted herself with an ample bite. 'No one else but me ever bothers with what's in that box. And I certainly wouldn't mislay the letter about Lucie's communion.'

Zan gave her time to arrange her thoughts. Then he asked, 'You said you hadn't opened the box for ages. Can you remember the last time?'

'Well, Albert opened it for you—'

'But that was recently. When you say "ages", what do you mean?'

'Oh, it must be over a year – eighteen months at least. When that man came from the *gouvernement Quebecois*.'

'From Canada?'

'Oh, probably, because he didn't speak ordinary French – I mean it was all right, but he had an accent.'

'Someone came to see you all the way from Canada?'

'Oh, no,' she said, amused, 'he was based here in Paris, at the local office, although of course I suppose he came from Quebec originally. He had one of those pass things, in a plastic holder, as proof of identity.'

'And he asked to see – what – papers concerning your daughter?'

'No, not actually about Lucie, no, it was a general enquiry. They wanted to know how new immigrants felt about their reception in Quebec, what they might have said to their relatives back home. It was so as to improve the reception facilities, you understand.'

'So can you recall his name, Madame?'

She looked abashed. 'I'm afraid not, Monsieur. It's so long ago, you know, and it wasn't important.'

'But you showed this man the family papers in this box?'

'Yes, he was interested.'

'And now that you look, the letter from Uncle Ari about buying Lucie's communion frock is gone.'

She gazed at him with blue eyes filled with dismay. 'You think he took it, Monsieur?'

'I think it's possible.'

'But why?'

To use as a sample for a forgery, he thought to himself, but didn't utter it aloud. 'Can you remember what he looked like?'

'Oh yes!' she replied with animation. 'Such a handsome man! With so much of an air about him, like a Spanish grandee!'

And she went on to give, as only a Frenchwoman can, an accurate description of Willard Townley.

Sixteen

Z an McNaughton came away from Rue Sarabande with a
strong feeling of satisfaction. He'd always thought that
Willard Townley was an arrogant bonehead but now he could
with good reason label him a crook.

Just wait till I tell Erica – that had been his first thought.
But as his taxi sped back towards the centre of Paris, he
began to see that it wouldn't be an enjoyable experience.

It was going to break her heart. She thought the world
of that nincompoop, although why, he couldn't understand.
Sure, the bloke had looks – looks enough to impress Mme
Curacie – and knew a lot about art. But Zan had always felt
there was something disagreeable about him, something that
a sensitive soul like Erica would find hard to bear.

Of course, he told himself, I'm biased. In the first place
he tried to make me look foolish when I wanted to buy
the painting. And then he turned out to be the love-light of
the girl I want. Can't expect me to think well of a fellow
like that.

But now he had evidence. Hard evidence that Townley
had presented himself at the home of Mireille Curacie and
told her he was doing a survey on behalf of the government
of Quebec. Madame couldn't remember the name of 'the
man from Quebec', but the description was undeniable.

Now . . . How had Townley found out that the Curacies
had a daughter who had emigrated? A moment's thought told
Zan that the family probably gave a farewell party attended
by all the neighbours, so that all Townley had to do was hang
around for a day or two, chat up the locals in the nearest café,
and he'd hear all about the daughter in Quebec.

So that gives him the entrée to the apartment. Once

there, he goes into his spiel, Madame gets out the box of family papers, he sends her off for a fresh cup of coffee or something like that, and abstracts the letter about the communion dress.

And hands it to his pal to use as an example when forging the gardener's boy's letter.

'I, Aristide Curacie of Rue Whatever-it-was in Epte-Rouet, accept some sum of money for a painting rescued by me from a bonfire at Giverny.' Or words to that effect. A pack of lies. Young Aristide had lived in Epte-Rouet but as to being employed by Claude Monet and rescuing one of his paintings from the flames – no, he'd never done that. He'd never ever said a word to any of his relatives of having once worked for the great painter. And the reason was that he'd never earned a sou from Claude Monet, nor handled any of his work legally or illegally.

Had Townley thought up that tale? It was the kind of thing he'd be good at, Zan told himself. And then it dawned on him that he was going to have to say this to Erica.

The feeling of triumph died. He saw it now as a task he must accomplish, but he dreaded it. So he put it off by hanging around in Paris, visiting the wine shops to see what was popular with the customers, buying a silly handbag of see-through plastic for his sister, ordering a de luxe meal which he then only picked at. In the end he boarded the train and tried to read a book until Waterloo rolled up to meet him.

Back in the Mayfair Rialto, he at last put through a call to Erica. It was late; luckily she seemed to have gone to bed. He left a message on her machine. 'I'm driving down to Bath tomorrow. I'll make a detour to come to the gallery around mid-morning. You'll hear all about my Paris trip then.' And then, because he couldn't just leave it at that, 'Hope you're having sweet dreams, Erica.'

Erica was annoyed with herself for not staying up a bit later on the previous night. It would have been so nice to have a conversation with Zan. From his voice on the message machine, he seemed rather downcast, as if the

Curacies had refused to let him borrow the letter for the benefit of a handwriting expert. That was understandable, of course.

She told the gallery's café that when she ordered tea later in the morning, it was to be, 'Good strong tea, put in more tea-bags!' She kept taking out her handbag mirror to check that her hair looked good and wondered if she should have worn a dress instead of jeans and a thick blue sweater.

Zan arrived about ten thirty. When he was shown in he looked a little careworn and it occurred to her that perhaps it was nothing to do with the Monet; perhaps his sister had had a setback. 'How are you?' she asked. 'How's Nyree?'

'Oh, fine, fine – we're both fine, thank you.'

So what was troubling him? She picked up the phone, asked the café to send the tea and biscuits. After that diversion, she was able to put her question. 'Is something wrong?'

'Well . . . I'm afraid so, Erica. I've got something to tell you.'

'They wouldn't let you borrow the letter?' Although that hardly seemed enough to justify his reluctance to tell her.

'No, Madame didn't want to part with it since it was the only one left in Uncle Ari's writing. But it's more than that. The letter about the communion dress – the one daughter Lucie was supposed to have taken with her to Quebec?'

'Yes?'

'She didn't take it, Erica. Someone else seems to have filched it.'

She met his eyes. She waited.

'It seems to have been Townley.'

As his lips formed the words, her heart was already sinking. She rubbed her hands against each other as if to warm them but said nothing. Zan waited for a rebuttal, a cry of indignation, but none came.

'You're . . . not surprised?' he ventured.

She shook her head, jumped up and went to the door. Opening it, she looked out. 'Where's that tea?' she asked no one in particular.

He went to her, put an arm around her shoulders, and led

her back to her chair at the desk. 'Don't take it too hard,' he said. 'It might not mean anything.'

She sank into her chair. 'Oh-h-h,' she groaned, and put her head in her hands.

'Don't, Erica! There may be an explanation.' He was hovering over her uselessly. He wanted to hold her, to comfort her, but when she was in the midst of such anguish over her lover, he knew his touch would be utterly unwelcome.

Erica had felt as if a tidal wave of understanding had rushed over her when Zan made his announcement. Something she'd been trying *not* to know for weeks was now undeniable knowledge. Her head was in a spin, her heart was thudding, she couldn't seem to get control of her breathing. She was aware that Zan was bending over her, and she put up a hand to grasp his. His fingers twined themselves in hers, strong and reassuring. After a moment she began to sort herself out. She sat up straighter, released herself from Zan's grasp, took a deep, deep breath.

'Well,' she faltered. 'So that's what's at the back of all this.'

Zan's face was a picture of bewilderment. 'You aren't surprised?'

'I sort of . . . thought something like this might be the story.'

'But you and Townley . . .'

'Yes. That was what made me shy away from it. But my brain was working it all out somehow, without instructions from me. Somewhere in my mind I was asking myself, Who *gains* from this? Of course, Yamin Emin gained, according to that statement of his. And the mythical owners of the painting gained, because they sold it to Emin. But really – we said this to each other, didn't we? – it was such small amounts of money when they seemed to have a great work of art in their hands. So . . . who in the end gains the sort of reward that a genuine Monet would fetch?'

He didn't bother to answer the question. He stood gazing at her, marvelling that she wasn't in a storm of weeping. He looked about for a chair and sat down.

There was a tap on the door; the tea had arrived. The waitress from the café brought it in, placed it on Erica's desk, and went out. Erica stared at the tray for a moment as if it had arrived from outer space. Then with a visible straightening of the shoulders, she began to pour the tea.

Normality. Mid-morning tea and biscuits. No matter that the man she'd once loved and respected above all others was revealed as a common swindler, the world must go on. She handed tea to Zan, who took it mechanically and set it down on his side of the desk.

He didn't dare speak. He didn't know what to say. He was afraid of hurting her feelings yet further. If he could have got his hands on Willard Townley at that moment he would cheerfully have throttled him.

'Let's go back to the beginning,' Erica said, after a gulp of tea had eased her aching throat. 'Let's try to work out how this scheme was hatched. It goes back to Giverny, doesn't it? Somebody – let's call him X – thinks about the story that Claude Monet burned some of his paintings when he realised how wrong the colours were, after his cataract op.'

Oh yes, thought Zan, let's call him X. His name's Willard Townley but she's not ready to admit that yet.

'You could set up a nice chain of phoney evidence from the burning of the paintings,' Erica went on. 'You could pretend that someone "rescues" one from the fire. Who could do that? Someone living near the Monet house.'

'It could be anyone in the neighbourhood, I suppose,' Zan said, going along with her thoughts because clearly she wanted to deal with it dispassionately. 'X ferrets around, looks at the Curacie family who used to live around there, and it happens they have a son who later set up a market garden. So he could have been a gardener's boy at Giverny.'

'Right. So X decides that Aristide is supposed to have stolen a painting, and later sold it to a German officer. The German officer's name was picked out of the list of officers who served in the Paris region in World War II – it was quite easy for my friend to find out about that on the French web. And there were plenty of names to choose from.'

241

'So what you're saying is that Loebletz was just a name picked out at random.'

'Well, that's how it seems, doesn't it? That couple in Westphalia knew nothing about a painting. Although that wasn't so important because we said to each other, didn't we, that Captain Loebletz probably owned the painting for only a couple of years during the war. Only he didn't,' she said. 'I don't believe Loebletz comes into it at all.'

'Then X has to get the painting to somewhere in the world where it can be "discovered",' Zan prompted.

'Yes – Yamin Emin's shop is a good place but how do you get the painting from Captain Loebletz's home in Hamburg to the Black Sea? Easy: the painting is "liberated" at the end of World War II by a Russian soldier who lives in Yalta.'

'Dergu the imaginary smuggler brings it over to Yamin Emin, and X "happens" into the shop and buys it for a song.'

'Then,' Erica said with undisguised bitterness, 'he shows it to this idiot "expert" who has the misfortune to be in love with him and she, poor fool, lets herself be beglamoured into saying, "Yes, yes, it's a Monet."'

Zan shook his head at her. 'You weren't the only one—'

'No, but I was the *first*, the most important. What do you call that sheep that leads the flock where it's supposed to go? That was me, totally taken in and deluded.'

'But only at first, Erica. You began to have suspicions very soon – don't be so hard on yourself.'

'You don't understand,' she objected. 'The moment my mother told me that Will was having money problems—'

'He was?' Zan exclaimed, startled. Townley had given the impression of being rich and aristocratic.

'Still is. He gave up financing his protégé – a painter he was providing with a regular income because as yet his work hasn't found a market. Mamma told me that at Christmas. I knew then – I *knew*! But I wouldn't let myself believe it. He's been such an important part of my life, Zan, these last three or four years, since I first met him over those early drawings by Sargent—' She broke off. 'Those drawings,' she muttered. Her face had gone pale. 'I wonder . . .'

'What?'

'I thought they were "right". They seemed perfect. And I was so flattered to be asked as an expert.' She threw up her hand and clutched at her hair. 'Oh, Zan! Maybe I've been even more of a fool than I thought!'

He had no way of knowing how much of her doubt was well founded. For himself, he was willing to think the worst of Willard Townley. But for her the humiliation of believing she'd been duped all along would be crushing.

'No, no,' he soothed, 'don't let your suspicions run away with you. All we really know is that X went to the Curacies' apartment in Paris to get hold of something in Uncle Ari's handwriting and we think it was so as to forge the gardener's boy's letter. And from the description given by Mme Curacie, X does sound like a ringer for Townley. It's a safe bet X was a prime mover in the entire set-up, but that doesn't mean he's always been – you know – a double dealer as far you were concerned.'

She was shaking her head in determined rejection of his attempt at comfort. 'You don't understand! I was blinkered because I was in love and I was so indebted to him. He got me my job at the Corie Gallery, you see. I looked up to him, he was the leader and I was the follower.' She felt her face colour up with shame. She began to think that from the very first she was being *groomed* to help Will carry off this fraud. The thought was so awful that she couldn't utter it.

'There was no way you could have known—'

'Yes, yes!' she insisted. 'Something's been hinting at it, warning me – but I wouldn't listen because he meant so much to me. What a *fool*! What an absolute *dope*!'

'No, that's not right. You were on to it almost from the first. You just said so yourself. X "discovered" the painting last October and by Christmas you were having doubts.'

'And then I faffed about for months—'

'Oh, stop with the sackcloth and ashes,' he said curtly. He could see he had to shake her out of this trough of self-blame. 'It was a clever scheme but you've poked holes in it. The minute we set out to look at the provenance, it all began to come to pieces.'

'Well—'

'He had to rush to Yalta to prevent you from finding out Danila What's-her-name never had a painting to sell, now didn't he?'

Erica stared at him. 'Yalta . . . and that business at the sanatorium . . . he set it all up!'

'What?'

'Those toughs that got huffy with poor Vasyli and me – and the one who arrived with Will to "rescue" us – they were doing an act. Vasyli was trying to tell me in that letter – Igor Prokopon was no Intourist courier, he was just another thug. And I actually *saw* Will paying him off in the hotel foyer, I saw it with my own eyes but I was too stupid to work it out!'

Zan tried to understand what it must mean to her, to have to say such things about the man she adored. Townley had actually made her play a part in her own deception. He tried to deflect the guilt a little. 'Presumably our friend Yamin Emin provided him with the thugs.'

'Yes, I'd imagine so.' There was a deadness in her tone. 'And provided all the colourful background with all that yarn about the smuggler Dergu and so forth. Dergu really doesn't exist, the police are right about that. All that exists is a cunning little man in a shop in Istanbul who got paid for playing his part in the plot – supplying the false documents, lying his head off to me and probably laughing behind my back all the time.'

'It was quite a scam.' There was no use denying it – Townley had made a good job of handling everybody.

'Think of the reward! The original intention was to get about eight million for that painting.'

'But I wasn't paying anything like that.'

'No, and that's where it all began to come unstuck, you see,' Erica explained. 'I know Will got a friend of his who lives in Nice to contact some of the American museums – so they'd put up the money to pay for the "restoration" – that burnt corner, you know? Then I'm sure he was going to get on the track of some of these new young millionaires from Silicon Valley and sell the painting for about eight or

244

nine million. That would have enabled him to refund the sum spent on the restoration. There would have been a very handsome profit except that you offered a quick sale – and he needed the money so badly, he had to give in.'

She said it with great calm, as if she were getting over the shock of learning that the man she loved was a crook. So Zan let himself see the funny side of it and began to laugh. 'No wonder he took such a dislike to me,' he said.

'Yes, and he goes on disliking you,' she agreed grimly, 'because that cashier's cheque that he needs so badly is still sitting in the bank. Poor man, he can't have it paid into his business account until he gets my report – which of course has to be favourable to complete the transaction.'

'And it won't be, so the deal is off.' He'd stopped laughing. It really wasn't funny. This thing was far from over.

Erica surveyed their teacups. Their tea had grown cold while they talked. 'Let's go out to the baker's shop,' she suggested. 'I need a breath of fresh air to clear my head.' Then, remembering that Zan was *en route* to Bath, she added, 'Unless you're pressed for time?'

'No, I said I'd be at the rest home some time in the afternoon. Come on, let's go.'

He helped her on with her coat, and when his hand lingered a moment to touch her neck she smiled up at him, a faltering smile that made his heart almost hurt with pity. She was having so much misery thrust upon her, poor little lass.

As they went out into the March morning, she put her arm through his. He held it close to him, hoping she'd find comfort in the knowledge that he was there for her. He looked down at her, and once again she smiled, a little more certainly this time. Brave soul, he thought.

She was trembling with reaction from the realisation of what had been happening. She longed for more than just her arm through his. She wanted him to hug her, to hold her close. But who could tell what he thought of her, a poor simpleton who'd let herself be duped into a love affair with a man like Will? Perhaps, in time, she'd be able to prove she had at least some discrimination, that she'd stopped being dazzled by Will some time ago.

They went to the baker's shop where the smell of fresh coffee and baking was irresistible. Erica found that she was dying of thirst, and drank her coffee eagerly. Zan appeared to be thoughtful. Rather nervously she said, 'What are you thinking?'

'I'm wondering what we should do next?'

That hadn't even entered her head. She'd been so taken up with trying to disentangle Willard's scheme that she had never looked ahead.

'We-ell,' she began, trying to face it, 'I could confront Will with the fact that we know he stole a letter from the Curacies.'

'He could deny it.'

'Mme Curacie would identify him, surely?'

'Oh, like a shot. If I offered to bring her to London she'd jump at it, because she was thoroughly put out at the idea that someone could make a fool of her. But, Erica – think about the painting itself. *It's been authenticated by three or four experts.* He could invent some yarn about getting in a muddle over the provenance – I'm sure he could manage to put some different interpretation on what we've worked out. But nothing actually says the painting is a forgery.'

'But we just know it is,' she insisted.

'That's not good enough for a court of law.'

'A court of law?'

The dismay on her face made his heart sink. Didn't she understand that this dream boy of hers had been intending to carry out a fraud?

'If we get hard evidence, that's where it's likely to end up, isn't it?'

'Oh no. No!' The idea of Will in the dock . . . ? It was too horrible, too unimaginable. He'd been doing wrong – of course that was not to be denied. But they'd found out in time, they'd prevented it from becoming a completed crime. 'Surely there's no need to take it that far?' she faltered.

'What else do you suggest?'

'Well, I don't know – I hadn't thought—'

'Were you just going to let it go?' he asked.

'No, of course not. I was going to tell him I can't write

a favourable report, tell him the deal has to be called off because . . . because . . .'

'Because you've found out he's a swindler.'

Her eyes filled with tears at the word. She blinked them away. It was silly and weak to feel protective about him – but she'd admired him so long, it was difficult to adjust to thinking so badly of him.

'But he's not going to sell it now.'

'Can you be sure of that?' He was angry with her. She couldn't still have any sympathy for this crook? 'How about if he keeps it for a couple of years and then tries again? Finds another buyer?'

'But he wouldn't—'

'You're sure of that? If we don't go public with what we know, what's to stop him?'

She made herself think about it. 'We can't go public. We don't have any hard evidence to disqualify the painting – you just said so yourself. I could sort of . . . spread the word among art dealers . . . there's a grapevine, you know . . .' She hesitated. 'I know you'll think I'm silly,' she said, 'but it would mean the end of Will's career.' She was picturing it. She knew he deserved it. But could she really do that to him?

Zan was watching her rather grimly. But he could see that the idea of taking the man to court at this stage was anathema. 'How about this,' he suggested. 'Let's try to find out who painted the fake.'

'How would we do that, Zan?'

'We could make some enquiries about what Townley's been doing over the last year or so – who he's been seeing.'

'I couldn't do that!' she confessed helplessly. 'That would be like spying on him.'

He understood there was a barrier here that she wasn't yet ready to surmount – perhaps never could. Even after all that she'd just been saying to him about how foolish she'd been in the past, she was ready to go on being foolish, still wanted to protect him.

'It would be exactly like spying on him,' he said coldly, 'and maybe you couldn't do it but by heaven I can!'

247

Seventeen

The painting was collected from the Mayfair Rialto while Zan was visiting his sister in the nursing home. Kevin Cheffield admitted to being intrigued by the problem so he made a space for an inspection in his busy schedule.

'It'll be ten days, perhaps a couple of weeks,' he told Erica on the phone from his workshops in Hereford. 'Do you want me to redo all Maurice Leppard's tests? Because that seems a bit of a waste.'

'Yes, please, Mr Cheffield. I have every confidence in Maurice Leppard but . . . well, it's just possible he missed something.'

Cheffield actually chuckled with enjoyment. 'Right you are then, but if I find something he missed, Maurice is never going to forgive me.'

Erica knew they had given evidence on opposite sides of fraud cases. She realised there was a certain rivalry between them and that Cheffield was going to enjoy himself.

But for her part, Erica wasn't enjoying herself. In the first place, she knew Zan McNaughton meant it when he said he would investigate Willard's affairs. And – worse still – she had parted from Zan in an atmosphere of hostility.

She didn't know where he was staying. It was perhaps at the nursing home, which might have accommodation for overnight visitors. Or perhaps he was in some comfortable hotel in Bath or Bristol. She couldn't get in touch directly. So instead she left a message with his London hotel – but there's little you can say in a message you leave with a desk clerk.

Who knew how soon he'd return there? It might be several days, it might even be weeks.

Meanwhile Zan was playing Scrabble with his sister in

the sun-lounge of the rest home and thinking about Willard Townley.

'Oh, do pay attention, Zan!' scolded Nyree. 'That's twice I've beaten you in a quarter of an hour. I know I'm the brainiest member of the McNaughton family but I don't have to keep proving it.'

He laughed at the reproof. She was so much better. The doctors at the hospital had been very wary about the improvement in her health and had murmured something about 'coming to decisions about bone marrow by and by'. But that was OK, there were plenty of siblings back home who'd be only too glad to supply marrow transplants. Anything, so long as it helped the kid sister.

She'd always been bright, always up to tricks. Today she was wearing, for his benefit, a fright wig of bright red curls – this was to hide the fact that her real hair had suffered from the chemotherapy but also to make him laugh. With her pale cheeks and her grey eyes, she looked a bit like something out of a sci-fi comic – a young beauty 'from another civilisation far across the Galaxy', as they had it in *Star Wars*.

'What's bothering you, bro?' she inquired. 'You've got something on your mind.'

'No, no, I'm concentrating, I'm concentrating!'

'Then why have you put down counters that seem to be in Urdu or Tibetan? They're certainly not English.'

'Oh.' He retrieved the counters, thought a moment, and added a weak 'ed' to something else.

'Brilliant. OK, let's have it. Had a row with the girl-friend?'

'She's not my girlfriend.'

'But you want her to be.'

'I never said so.'

'And you were doing quite well last time I enquired.'

'We're friends, Ny. Nothing more.'

'Uh-huh,' she said with undisguised scepticism. 'Well, you're less friendly than you were last time I asked after her.'

'Oh, shut up, minnow. When you start this "woman's intuition" stuff, you're a bore.'

She put down some counters, added up her score, then said, 'I don't want to be a pest, Zan, but you seem really bothered.' She sat waiting for an answer.

He sighed to himself. It was always difficult to pull the wool over her eyes. 'Well, all right, I'll tell you, but don't start getting upset about it.'

'Oh, this anxiety about my state of composure is really the pits. Just because I had something that needed hospital treatment, it doesn't mean I have to be kept in a box lined with cotton wool. What's eating you, bro?'

'I think Erica's boyfriend is a wrong 'un,' he said.

His sister grinned. 'Well, you would say that, wouldn't you?'

'I'm serious, Nyree. I think he's a no-goodnik.'

'What, the art dealer?'

'Yes.'

He'd always edited what he told Nyree about Townley because he didn't want to sound peevish and jealous. And they'd agreed, he and Erica, not to say anything about the authenticity of the Monet 'unless and until'. So he skirted round the facts, merely saying that he couldn't exactly explain but that he'd come to think rather the worst of Willard Townley. 'And you see, Erica's worried and bothered about him, too, and I hate that.'

'Well, do something about it,' his sister commanded.

'I thought I'd maybe make a few inquiries . . . But you see, sis, it could take up a bit of my time.'

'Oho, so that's it. You're using me as an excuse to skirt round it. Listen to me, McNaughton. You know our family motto – "If a thing needs doing, do it."'

'That's not our family motto, you just this minute made it up.'

'Yes, good, isn't it? But seriously, Zan, you're all cut up about something and the sensible thing is to get cracking on it. And if,' she added, holding up an admonishing finger, 'you think I can't get on without you for a few days, think again, maestro. I can go shopping mad in Bristol while your attention is elsewhere.'

In the last day or two his sister had been well enough to

be driven to Bath for a couple of hours' diversion. He knew she'd enjoy longer trips, and if she was always accompanied by an experienced staff member there could be no harm, and even some positive good, in it. And he did very much want to get to work on Willard Townley.

'OK, then. I'll give it a go.'

'All right, get going.' She waved a hand towards the door of the sun-lounge.

'What, now?'

'Why not? You're no good at Scrabble, that's for sure.'

Shaking his head at her, he left her to gather the equipment into its box while he went in search of a telephone. The home's management was glad to supply the use of theirs. After all, any costs would be added to his already substantial bill.

The London law firm he used for business contracts in the UK was willing to provide the telephone number of the detective agency they used. He rang them and was put through to one of the directors. When he explained what he wanted, he was told he needed one of their financial investigators. The call was transferred. A voice said, 'Mr McNaughton? This is Herbert Pleydell.'

'Mr Pleydell, I need a financial check on someone. I'd like to know if he has debts and if so how heavy, I'd like to know whether he's sole owner of the business he runs, what his assets are, and anything else you can find out about him.'

'Quite so, sir. When would you like the information?'

'As soon as possible.'

'I see. Please don't mention any names at the moment. These days newspapers are always on the look-out for items they can use in their gossip columns, and they try all kinds of tricks to listen in if they can. If you'll give me your number there, I'll ring you back in a few minutes.'

Surprised and rather amused, Zan did as he was bid. This was super-security, he thought. True enough, Pleydell rang back within ten minutes.

'Good afternoon, Mr McNaughton. Now I'm in a public phone booth. I'm sorry about the precautions but we have one or two cases going on at the moment that the press would love to know about. So now – if you'd like to provide me with the name and address of the subject?'

Still amused but obedient, Zan gave the name and the address of the Townley Gallery.

'Oh, that should be pretty easy,' promised Herbert Pleydell. 'There'll be quite a lot about him in the back numbers of the newspapers.'

'I thought you were wary of newspapers?'

'Only when they're not being helpful. But when they can provide us with info we need, then I like the newspapers quite a lot.'

'Don't forget I want hard facts about his finances.'

'That's not difficult, sir. Leave it with me. Shall I call you in a day or two at this number?'

'No, I'm coming back to London. Could you let me have what you've unearthed by late tomorrow?'

'Late tomorrow . . .' Pleydell seemed pensive. 'Well, that would only be the preliminary report.'

'I'd like to have that, as a starting point.'

'You're the boss,' said Pleydell. 'Shall I telephone you?'

'Could you bring the stuff around seven tomorrow, to the bar of the Mayfair Rialto?'

'Of course, Mr McNaughton.'

Later Zan had dinner with his sister in the dining-room of the rest home. It was very like a dining-room in a good private hotel. They had a little table to themselves, so she was able to ask him what he'd been up to.

'I've set things going,' he told her. 'It means I have to go back to London tomorrow – is that OK?'

'Ducky, so long as I have my credit cards and a good department store, I shan't miss you at all.'

'So what are you going to buy?'

'I thought I'd start with another wig. How do you fancy me in a green one?'

'You're a nut,' he told her. The fact that she could make silly jokes was reassuring, yet he still felt uncertain about the rightness of leaving her just to pursue his own selfish affairs.

She was packed off to bed by a kindly nurse at nine

o'clock. Zan drove to his hotel in Bath, where he telephoned the family back home with the news that the kid sister seemed to be doing well. He was brought up to date with the state of work on the vines: looking good, harvest could start in about a week, his brother Jayce wanted to know when he might start for home.

'It depends on what the doctors say about Ny,' he replied. 'Might be fairly soon. But you know if we travel again by slow degrees you'll probably have to deal with the crop without me.'

'Oh, I *think* we can manage,' Jayce said with kindly sarcasm. 'You concentrate on looking after the shrimp.' He paused a moment. 'She's really doing OK?'

'Aye, getting cheeky again. Why d'you ask?'

'Dunno. You sound a bit down, that's all.'

'Nothing of the sort,' Zan assured him, and disconnected.

He was in London by mid-morning. At the desk they told him that a bonded courier had collected the Monet and showed him the receipt. It gave him an odd sensation: it meant that Erica was still taking part in this business, starting another set of laboratory tests that might incriminate the man she loved. That was integrity. But did he have the right to demand so much from her?

Feeling worn and dispirited, he went for a swim in the hotel's leisure centre, churning with his unstylish crawl for length after length. Although it did little for his state of mind, he emerged feeling physically fresher and ready for the fray.

After lunch he asked for the use of one of the hotel's computers. He sat in front of it for a couple of hours hunting on the Internet for information about art dealing and art auctions. The kind of money mentioned made his eyebrows rise. He understood now that when he first intervened to buy the painting for Nyree, he'd been making an enormous difference to Townley's plans. The fact that Townley had accepted their eventual settlement of two and three-quarter million showed how desperately he needed money, for if he'd toughed it out he could have made three times that much, and perhaps more.

This was borne out to him when Pleydell arrived with the results of his preliminary investigation. An ex-policeman who'd retired early on health grounds after an accident in pursuit of a car thief, Pleydell now had a permanent limp.

Over a drink in the comfortable bar of the hotel, he spread papers out for Zan's perusal. 'You see here a print-out of my estimates – his debts are heavy, but the word is that he's expecting a big input in his business account which will take care of them. I gather, Mr McNaughton,' with a sharp glance at him, 'that the expected input is the payment for your painting.' His investigation had shown him the facts about the purchase of the Monet, and he waited now for his client to expand on this.

But Zan merely said, 'I think you're right.'

'His credit rating is a bit dicey – nothing major, you understand, they're not thinking of withdrawing his credit cards or anything like that. But if he went to a merchant bank for a major loan, he might have problems.'

Zan cast his eye over the figures. Accustomed to looking at a balance sheet, his feeling was that if McNaughton's Hill Vineyards were in a state like this, he'd be getting very worried.

'Thank you, this is very helpful. Did you learn much about the man himself?'

On Pleydell's bony face, a shade of anxiety appeared. 'Can I ask a question, Mr McNaughton?' Zan shrugged assent so he went ahead. 'You're not a married man, sir?'

'No. Why do you ask?'

'I was just wondering if this was anything to do with . . . ahem . . . divorce proceedings or anything like that? Because that's not my field.'

'Not at all.' But Zan understood the implication. 'Townley is a bit of a ladies' man?'

'Well, he has a bit of a rep. I asked a chum of mine who's a stringer on a newspaper, and he says Townley is a target for photographers – he's got looks, you know, and from time to time he shows up at those big parties that are featured in *Hello* and mags like that.'

In fairness Zan had to admit to himself that if Townley

liked to go to parties, that was none of his business. All the same, he couldn't help being interested in Townley's lady friends. Asked for names, Pleydell produced a notebook and read out a few names.

'At the moment the girl he's seen around with most often in London is a Miss Pencarreth.'

'Yes, go on.'

'Last Christmas he was in New Orleans with a lady called Lottie Siegler—'

'With? How d'you mean "with"?'

'"With" as in sharing a hotel room, sir.' Pleydell hesitated. 'Are you . . . er . . . interested in Miss Siegler?'

'Never heard of her,' Zan said. 'But my understanding is that Miss Pencarreth and Mr Townley are . . . you know . . . a main item.'

Pleydell gave a little shake of the head. 'That's not my impression, Mr McNaughton. This Miss Siegler – she turns up again earlier last year at a party in Nice, with a picture showing the pair of them dancing and a caption . . . wait a minute, it was in French but I got it translated – "Long-time friends Lottie Siegler and Willard Townley lead the samba at the party given for Polly Polmeche's birthday at La Rosaraie on the 11th." The eleventh; that was October. And there was another mention in a Greek magazine—'

'A Greek magazine?'

'Well, yes, sir, another chum of mine does the international jet-set and he gave me this item in an Athens mag. I particularly asked for mentions in Greek papers, you see, because Mr Townley owns a house on a Greek island and a cabin cruiser big enough to take him there when he wants to. I found that out when I was doing the study of his assets.'

Zan had heard mention of a Greek cottage. Erica had said it was while staying there that Townley had first shown her the Monet. 'Staying with him on a romantic Greek island.' He could hear her voice, full of bitterness and regret.

'Mr McNaughton?' Pleydell prompted, seeing that his client had drifted off into his own thoughts.

'Yes, go on.'

'Well, this Greek mention says the pair of them were at

an open-air theatre thing for charity and would be leaving for their hideaway on . . . wait a minute, I've got it written down . . . Parigos, which of course I take to be an island.'

'"A romantic Greek island,"' quoted Zan, half aloud.

'I dare say,' Pleydell agreed. 'There was another young woman bracketed with Mr Townley in New York in March of last year, but I didn't have time to go any further back than that.'

'Anything else about the Greek bit? The cottage?'

'Er . . . em . . . He goes there three or four times a year. Miss Siegler spends some time there too. She's an artist—'

'*What?*'

'An artist, sir. She's quite fashionable, the rich people hire her to do paintings of their bits of sea-shore or their yachts under sail – that kind of thing.'

'Thank you, Pleydell,' said Zan with fervour.

'Was that important, then?'

'You just said the magic word.'

'The bit about Miss Siegler, you mean.'

'Lottie Siegler, you said her name is?'

'That's right. Swiss national, aged about twenty-eight, brown hair, brown eyes – nothing else to tell at the moment because I've only had the one day so far, Mr McNaughton.'

'Fine. Keep at it. I'll be going away for a few days but I'll ring you at your office for any other information you may get.'

'About Miss Siegler or Mr Townley?'

'The pair of them,' Zan said. And rising, shook hands with Pleydell to let him know that was the end of the meeting.

In the hall they parted, Zan going straight to the reception desk. 'I want to fly to Greece as soon as possible,' he said, 'and from whatever airport I arrive at, I want to get on towards an island called Parigos.'

'Parigos?' said the desk clerk politely. 'Yes, sir. Could you tell me which archipelago that belongs to, Mr McNaughton?'

'No idea,' he replied, 'but I want to be there yesterday!'

Travel arrangements made by high-class hotels are usually

faultless. Zan had arrived in Athens by the following morning. But even the Mayfair Rialto couldn't calm an angry sea, and so it was not until the early hours of the morning two days later that he stepped ashore at the old jetty under the rocks of Parigos.

His carrier had been old Giorgiou, whose English was scanty. However, the name Townley had evoked nods and smiles. He helped Zan ashore with the proud announcement: 'Townley!' and an upward gesture towards the steep path.

Zan said, 'Thank you.' And then, with tappings of his wrist-watch, 'Wait!'

'*Neh, neh,*' agreed Giorgiou, nodding. '*Ti ora?*'

Zan took this to mean something like, 'How long?' He tapped his watch again and held up three fingers. The boatman nodded, shrugged, took out a packet of dreadful local cigarettes, and settled down for a smoke.

It was very cool as Zan climbed the path. All the same he was perspiring when he reached the top. This was a cottage where the owner's first consideration was privacy. As he crossed the stony garden, he could smell the delicious aroma of French croissants, so he was expecting someone to come to the door at the sound of his crunching approach. But there was no response.

He tried the cottage door. It opened. 'Hello?' No answer. He stepped inside. 'Hello, anybody here?' Still no answer. He followed the scent of the croissants into the kitchen. On the basis of the idea that no one puts frozen croissants in the microwave to defrost without intending to eat them, he sat down to wait.

No one came. The microwave switched itself off. Zan got up, looked into the living-room. On an easel stood a canvas covered by a piece of old cotton sheet. Another Monet, perhaps? He lifted one corner, revealing about half the work. Not a Monet. Lots of browns and greens and olives, difficult to discern but he thought it was a landscape. I'm too ignorant to know whose style this is, he said to himself with a sigh. I wish Erica was here.

He dropped the cloth back in place and he went into the bedroom. The bed was unmade. Piles of books, large books and small books, lay on the bedside table and on the floor by the bed. He picked up one, looked at the title. *The Life of André Derain*. He put it down, picked up a big paperback with a glossy illustrated cover. *Catalogue of the Chicago Municipal Gallery* – a piece of paper marked a page. He flicked the catalogue open. *Scene in the Ardennes* by André Derain, 1936 – lots of browns and greens and olives.

A glance at some of the other titles told him that the occupant of the cottage was studying the work of Derain. It was an easy guess that the canvas on the easel was – to say the least – after the style of Derain.

Zan went back to the kitchen, and sat down to wait.

About half an hour later, when the sun was beginning to shine quite warmly through the kitchen window, the cottage door opened. A young woman entered. She was clad in a dark blue fleece, leggings, and trainers. Under her arm she carried one of the big sketching blocks. From her shoulder swung a hard-cased satchel which might contain pencils or pastels.

She gave a sound of alarmed surprise. Zan spoke at once in reassurance. 'Hello, sorry to drop in so early. I'd hoped to find Townley here?' The latter piece of information was expressed with a questioning tone.

'Will? He won't be coming until after Easter.'

'You must be Lottie. I've heard Will speak of you.' He made sniffing sounds. 'Your breakfast is waiting, so I won't keep you. I'm looking at a time-share over on the east side – what do you think?'

She relaxed, satisfied that there was nothing to fear. She set aside her sketching things and went into the kitchen. 'You're a friend of Will's? What's your name?'

'Is a microwave a good thing for croissants?' Zan inquired, following her and peering in at them. 'Never tried that.'

'I have to have frozen, they only bake local bread here,' she said, deflected from her enquiry. 'I'm going to make some coffee, would you like a cup?'

'Love it. Will told me the place was pretty civilised but it's better than I expected. Though mind you, they're asking the devil of a lot for a three-month share.'

'Oh, it's worth it,' she assured him, putting ground coffee

into a filter. 'The man who did the original modernisation spared no expense – it was Kurianos, you know, the shipping millionaire.'

Zan shrugged to let her know he was an ignoramus. 'I saw you had artists' stuff. Is that why you come here, to sketch and so on?'

'Will didn't tell you I'm a painter?'

'Not that I recall. But then I'm not interested in all that, if you'll forgive me for saying so.'

'Then how do you come to know Will?'

She spoke English with only the faintest of accents. She was a good-looking girl, perhaps just past her mid-twenties, with luxurious brown hair highlighted with tints of gold and cascading down her back. The tan came from hours out of doors in a sunny climate.

'Oh, my company owns the lease of his shop,' Zan explained.

'His gallery,' she corrected sharply.

'Oh, sorry, gallery.' He put on an apologetic expression. 'That's me, commercial to the core!'

The coffee machine would take a few minutes to accomplish its task, and Zan wandered off to the living-room. 'I see you're working on something now,' he called.

Quickly she came to join him. 'It's nothing,' she said.

'I bet it's jolly good.' He twitched the sheeting aside before she could stop him. 'Ah, it's a landscape! Is that a view from around here?'

Lottie gave him a pitying smile. 'No, of course not. It's northern France.'

'Oh, you're doing it from memory! Now that's really clever!' He moved closer, but she caught his shirt-sleeve.

'It's not quite dry. Please don't touch it.'

'Righto. You know, it's really good. It looks quite like an Old Master or something.'

She gave a little sarcastic laugh. 'Not quite an *old* master. But it's in a quite traditional style. Do you like it?'

'We-ell . . .' He produced a shamefaced grin. 'I suppose it's nice. But there are some nice views and things around here, wouldn't it be better to paint those?'

'Oh, this is just . . . an exercise. It's a copy of a work by Derain.'

'Never heard of him, I'm afraid. Is that what you do? I mean, do you do it for a living or is it just for fun?'

'Fun?' Lottie blew out a breath. 'If you knew how much *work* goes into a thing like that!'

The coffee machine made its final burbling sound. She went back into the kitchen. 'I have no cream or milk,' she called.

'Black is fine.' He came to accept the mug of coffee she was pouring. 'Thank you. So do you live here all year round?' he asked, trying a new angle.

'No, no, I travel quite a bit. In the art world, you have to keep up to date with what's going on. I'll be gone from here before Easter.'

'When Townley takes over. Do you and he share the lease of this place or something?'

She shook her head. 'Will owns it. He lets me use the place when he doesn't want it.'

'My, that's good of him.' Zan sipped coffee. 'Is that what they call . . . what is it . . . are you a protégée?'

She stirred sugar into her drink. 'Something like that.'

'Fascinating. Have you had . . . you know . . . exhibitions?'

'One or two.'

'And will that painting' – he nodded towards the living-room – 'be in the next one?'

'Hardly!' She was highly amused.

'But why not? It's jolly good.'

'Because I only *exhibit* original work. A copy of someone else's wouldn't do.'

'But somebody would be sure to want that if they saw it,' Zan protested.

She made no reply, and instead set about putting her croissants on a plate.

'Could I buy that painting?' Zan inquired.

'But you just said you weren't interested in art.'

'No . . . well . . . I just thought it would be nice, you know, like a souvenir of my first visit to Parigos.'

'You couldn't afford it,' she told him, with an arch smile.

'But you just said it's a copy. Does a copy usually cost a lot?'

'Why not? If it's as good as the original?'

Zan allowed himself to look totally perplexed. 'I don't follow that.'

'If someone can paint as well as, say, Cézanne or Monet, why shouldn't they get the same money? They put in the work, they have the skill – why should they receive a smaller reward?'

Her voice had taken on a sharp note, and the brown eyes had a little glint of resentment. This was something she'd asked herself a hundred times, and he certainly couldn't supply an answer.

'Now there you have me,' he said. 'Well, I'll be pushing off and leave you to your breakfast. Thanks for the coffee. And you think a time-share on the eastern cliff is worth the money?'

'Good views of the sunrise,' she said with a disdainful shrug. 'Perhaps you'll take up painting.'

'No fear. So long, then.'

As he turned to go she asked, 'What was your name again?'

'Marsh,' he told her, 'Ngaio Marsh.' And with the name of New Zealand's famous female detective writer lingering on the air, he made his way back to the waiting boat.

Eighteen

On the day before Good Friday, a letter arrived at the Townley Gallery in Mayfair by special messenger. A junior member of the sales staff signed for it, then took it at once to the boss's office.

Willard was on the telephone, negotiating for some work of Angelica Kauffmann that would sell on sight to the foreign visitors expected once the tourist season began. He eyed the envelope as it lay on his desk, while he chatted money with the owner of the work.

'Special Delivery.' Something urgent? No postmark. Must have come by hand. He turned it over while he continued his conversation. On the flap was the return address: the Mayfair Rialto.

'I have to go, Joss,' he said, interrupting a spiel about the rarity of the watercolours. 'Something's come up.' And, knowing he'd probably lost the Kauffmann, he put down the receiver. But that didn't matter, because this letter would be from McNaughton accepting the Monet.

He tore the envelope open. The letter bore the heading of the hotel and that day's date, and under that, 'From Alexander McNaughton.'

> Dear Willard Townley,
>
> Examination of the painting now named *Bridge at Giverny* and attributed to Claude Monet is now almost complete. I have given instructions for it to be returned to you and you should receive it within a day or two.
>
> A cashier's cheque signed by me to the sum of two and three-quarter million pounds sterling (£2,750,000) is held at your bank, the Mayfair branch of Northern

National. This cheque can only be deposited to your account on the agreement of both parties, such agreement not to be unreasonably withheld.

I have good reason to think the attribution of the painting is incorrect. I have given instructions to the bank that the cashier's cheque is not to be deposited and that in due course I shall retrieve it from them.

Any objections to this procedure or any enquiry should be directed to my solicitors, Messrs Sudham, Cooles & Prior.

Yours faithfully, Alexander McNaughton.

Dictated and signed at the Mayfair Rialto Hotel.

Willard felt his heart give a dreadful lurch, as if it would somehow escape from his chest and fly into the air. His breathing seemed to halt. I'm going to die, he thought.

But the moment passed. Life flowed back in a sudden current. He crushed the paper in his hands. He would diminish it, destroy it!

Then his brain began to function too, so that he smoothed out the letter. The typed words began to appear clearly again.

'I have good reason to think the attribution of the painting is incorrect.' What reason? Everything had gone smoothly. Expert opinion on the style had been unanimous – it was a Monet. Leppard's laboratory work had turned up nothing, nor could it, because all the materials had been bona fide stuff from Monet's era. There was nothing, *nothing* that could hint it was not an authentic Monet.

He got up, went to a cupboard, got out a bottle of whisky, and poured a good three fingers into a glass. He downed it and poured another. Taking the bottle and glass with him, he settled himself again in his chair at the desk. As he swallowed the second drink he began to feel better, his sense of being at a loss began to die away.

Erica. It must be something to do with Erica. But he'd thought all those doubts she muttered about had been satisfied. Just like her to go on ferreting about like a loyal little helper just because someone asked her to. But what could she have done, what could she have achieved?

He was certain nothing could upset the original verdict of the consultants he'd called in. Then, when following up the provenance, she'd found the Curacies in Paris, but the letter she'd seen there had only reinforced the authenticity: compared with the letter from the 'gardener's boy', the handwriting was totally convincing, he'd had it done by an expert. And after that he himself had been with her, had seen how charmed and convinced she was by Yamin Emin.

So what did McNaughton mean, 'I have good reason'? What reason? The man was a know-nothing, incapable of doing any investigation into a work of art.

His reasons must originate with Erica and her doubts. What had she been doing, what had she been saying? How could she be so disloyal?

He was about to pour himself yet another drink when he stopped himself. A clear head. He needed a clear head.

And he needed to find out what Erica had been up to.

He'd been a little bit anxious in the past couple of weeks because he hadn't been able to get her to himself. He looked back now and blamed himself for the quarrel they'd had. He should have patched it up much more thoroughly. He'd rung her, apologised, and offered to take her to a gallery opening a few evenings away. She'd said quietly that she was already engaged with someone else for that evening. And there she was, at the opening, with some draggy female she used to know at college. It had seemed odd to him that she'd turn him down in favour of this nonentity but he'd had a business contact to pursue that evening and so he had let it go.

The next time he'd tried to phone her at home, he'd got her answering machine. She hadn't returned the message he left, and he saw now that he should have followed that up.

In a word, he'd let himself drift away from Erica before it was safe to do so. And now was the time for some damage repair.

He dialled her at her office. He knew she was sure to be there because her 'Impressions of Trees' exhibition was due to go on that weekend.

Her secretary said she was busy. He said, 'Give her

a message, please. Tell her I've had a letter from Mr McNaughton and ask her to ring me back.'

He expected that to have an immediate effect. But nothing happened. What was going on?

He had a business lunch he couldn't cancel now, so out he went to entertain a fellow agent, one of the contacts he'd made in New Orleans at Christmas. He held his end up well enough but it wasn't the enjoyable meeting of minds he'd hoped for. When he got back to the office he redialled Erica's number. Suzi the secretary told him her boss was in the store-room. 'Buzz her on the intercom,' he urged. But she said Miss Pencarreth had left orders that she wasn't to be disturbed.

By now Willard Townley was so angry he was ready to hit someone. It was just after three in the afternoon. Erica would be at her gallery until six. He told his staff he was going out, that they should lock up and see to security without him, and took a taxi to King's Cross. All through the short journey he was fuming. This wasn't the way he expected to be treated and he was going to do something about it.

The doorman at the Corie Gallery made no attempt to stop Willard, who was quite a familiar figure. He threaded his way through the rooms, opened the door marked 'Private', walked down the corridor, and without knocking entered Erica's office.

It was empty. The sound of his arrival brought the secretary to the door. 'Oh, Mr Townley – I didn't realise it was you.'

'Where's Erica?'

'Er . . . I told you on the phone – she's busy in the store-room.'

'Show me the way.'

'But – excuse me – she doesn't want to be disturbed.' Suzi was eyeing him with alarm. Not only was he breathing fire, but also the after-effects of a very bibulous lunch.

Suzi wasn't entirely in her boss's confidence, but she had good instincts. She'd sensed that there was a lack of the former rapport between Erica and Willard. Now here he was demanding to be shown to her workplace, when

Erica had specifically ignored his messages – which meant, as far as Suzi could work it out, that she didn't want to see or speak to him.

'Never mind all that,' said Willard. 'I've got something very important to discuss with her.'

'Well, I could make an appointment for you—'

He stepped towards her so menacingly that her voice died. The man was really in a very, very bad mood. Ashamed of herself, Suzi said weakly, 'I'll tell her you're here.'

She used the intercom to get through to the store-room. One of the porters answered. She said to him, 'Will you tell Miss Pencarreth that Mr Townley is here and insists on seeing her.'

'Will do,' said Tom.

After a moment Erica spoke. 'He's actually here, Suzi?'

'Yes, with me now, and I think it's *important*.'

Something in her voice told its tale. Erica said, 'I'll be there in a minute.'

She was wearing jeans and a shirt, and was hard at work shifting paintings about – one of the items promised on loan had failed to turn up and the gap must be filled. The last thing she needed was Willard in one of his moods. But in the end, she'd known this had to come. She brushed dust off her shoulders, told the porters to carry on, and made her way to her office.

Willard was sitting in her chair behind her desk, clad as always in his perfect black ensemble. Under the sleek black hair, his face was flushed.

He threw the letter on the desk. 'What's the meaning of this?'

'Of what?' Erica asked, making no attempt to approach and pick it up.

'That letter. Did you put him up to it?'

'Who? What are you talking about?'

Willard was forced to take up the letter and come round the desk to thrust it into her hands. It was what she'd wanted: while he was sitting in her place he was enforcing his superiority, but now they were equals. She urged him to the bench that stood by a small table bearing a vase of spring flowers. She sat down, unfolded the paper. After a moment Willard sat down too.

He watched as she read. Unless she was a consummate actress, the contents were a complete surprise to her.

'What have you been doing?' he demanded. 'He talks about "examination" as if it's just being done. We *had* all that, ages ago.'

'No, I told you he'd asked for other opinions.'

'But that meant experts on style, on brushwork—'

'We took it a stage further.'

'But for what reason? You had Leppard's report – the analyses were all favourable. What have you been saying to that man?'

'Very little,' Erica replied with a suppressed sigh. 'I haven't spoken to him in a couple of weeks, he's been away.'

'Well, he's in London now – this came from his hotel by hand this morning.'

'It's news to me, Will.'

He snatched back the letter. 'He says he has "good reason to think the attribution is incorrect",' he said, pointing. 'What reason? What does he mean?'

'I don't know. We haven't been in touch.' She had no intention of saying that when she and Zan parted, he was determined to make enquiries about Willard. It looked as if those enquiries had yielded results – very unfavourable results – but Zan hadn't been in touch. Proof that he was still vexed with her. She felt a sadness at the thought that made Willard and his anger seem unimportant.

'I thought you and he were supposed to be friends?' Willard challenged.

'Yes, we were – I hope we still are – it's just that we've been thinking along different lines recently.'

'Then you don't agree with him about his "good reason"?' Willard cried in relief. 'Thank God for that!'

'I didn't say that, Will. You know very well that I've had doubts.'

'Oh yes, doubts, but you saw the letter at the Curacies – that proved everything was OK.'

267

'You're talking only about the provenance, Will. There were other things—'

'No, that's not true. Everybody agreed about the painting itself, the way it presents itself, the technique—'

'Not everybody. *I* for one don't agree.'

'Oh, you don't!' He couldn't keep the sneer out of his voice. Who did she think she was? 'And who else? What other great expert have you got to support your silly theories? Not one, or you'd be making a lot more noise. Admit it, anybody you've called in has agreed it's an authentic work by Monet.'

'Not everyone.'

'Who, then? Who? Ha, some tinpot professor from your art college days, is that it? Listen, Erica, I've been patient with you but enough is enough. You've got to get in touch with that grocery-shop man and tell him it's all been a mistake. And do it now!'

'I'll do nothing of the sort.'

'You've got to!' He wanted to take hold of her and shake her 'He's sending back the painting!'

She tried pacification. 'You wouldn't be the first dealer who's had to admit a mistake—'

'Oh, you don't understand!' He jumped up, threw up his hands in despair. *'I need that money!'*

She sat for a moment, looking up at him as he stood almost statuelike, glaring at his future as it threatened him. 'That's what it's all been about,' she murmured. 'Just a money-making swindle.'

The word made him come to himself. He couldn't allow her to get anywhere near the truth. He put on a look of astonished indignation. 'Swindle? What do you mean? How dare you!'

She shook her head. 'Give it up, Will. I know all about it.'

'All about what? There's nothing to know. I don't know what's got into you—'

'A great deal of disillusion, that's what's got into me. I advise you to take back the painting from Zan McNaughton and release the money. It's your best way out.'

'Way out? Way out? You must be insane. I sold a perfectly authenticated Monet to McNaughton—'

'You sold him a fake.'

'Don't dare say that to me!' He heard himself say it and knew it was too defensive. He went on the attack. 'You yourself agreed it was a genuine Monet. Your reputation is going to take quite a knock if this kind of nonsense gets out.'

'Your reputation is what we're talking about at the moment, Will. And let's drop all the play-acting. You had a painting forged, invented a story to back it up, and sold it to get money.'

The flat certainty of her manner gave him pause. After a moment he said with less indignation, 'That's slander and you'd never prove any of it.'

'Not even if I bring Mme Curacie to London and get her to identify you as the "official from the Quebec government" who stole her Uncle Ari's letter?'

Willard felt a stab of coldness. It seemed that she'd actually been too smart for him. There was a moment that seemed to stretch to eternity. He felt behind him for the bench then sank down on it.

'How did you find that out?' he mumbled.

Erica was shocked at the collapse of that once-haughty character. She felt almost guilty. *She* had brought this about; her challenge had defeated him. It had been the right thing to do, but to see him brought so low was pitiful.

'I found out by using my head instead of my heart,' she said wearily. 'You had me quite entranced, didn't you? For a long time. But by and by I began to see . . . to think . . . In the end I had to start being honest with myself and it came down to this, Will – you were trying to keep me from giving proper attention to that painting. The lab reports seemed to justify it in every way, but the provenance . . . Well, I'm afraid that's where the cracks began to show.'

'No, no . . .'

'All that rushing to my aid in Istanbul – that was all an act to make me think you were wonderful before introducing me to your star performer. Did you have to pay him a lot for all those lies? Never mind, it worked – for a while . . .'

'I can explain, Erica.' She could sense his mind summoning up a fall-back story. 'The painting is genuine but I knew it had to have a good background. Just coming across it in a junk shop in Istanbul wouldn't have been enough. So I got Emin to help me with a little story—'

'No, don't, Will. Don't try to pretend you ever thought that was a painting by Claude Monet.'

'Then who else is it by?' he challenged, beginning to recover. 'The technique, the materials, the placing of the work in Monet's career—'

'It's a forgery. I don't know who painted it. Whoever it is, he's very clever. Yes, he found all the right materials, yes, he caught the mood, and the technique is practically faultless—'

'It's a genuine Monet. It will stand up to every test you care to put it through.'

She shook her head. 'You've forgotten about the charcoal, Will.'

'Charcoal?' She could see he was truly perplexed. 'Of course there's charcoal on it. It was burned on a bonfire at Giverny. Smoke and scorching, contamination from the twigs and old wood on the bonfire—'

'Stop, stop!' She could see that he really didn't know. 'My friend Sergeant Groume got Kevin Cheffield to take a look.'

'Cheffield?' Willard echoed, and now he felt scared. Cheffield was an expert who often acted for the prosecution in cases where art forgeries were brought to court.

'There's charcoal among the paint, Will. Yes, the painting was burned on a fire with twigs from fruit bushes and rose prunings. There's charcoal in a layer along the burnt edge, and that came from the bonfire. But, Will' – she paused to emphasise the importance of what would come next – 'that couldn't explain how there's charcoal *on the canvas*.'

'What?'

'Yes. You understand what I'm saying, don't you? There's charcoal not on the paint surface, but on the actual canvas surface *beneath* the paint.' She let him take it in. 'We all know, don't we, Will, that Monet never sketched a charcoal outline before he began to paint. He painted directly on to the canvas.'

'There must be some mistake.'

'Yes, on the part of your forger. Clever though he is, he didn't have quite enough confidence to portray the Japanese bridge at Giverny without an outline for a guide. So he sketched it on the canvas – an arc and a horizontal bar, using a charcoal stick. Willow charcoal – we've all used it, haven't we?'

'You're making this up.'

'I've got Cheffield's report at my flat. It arrived yesterday. He gives it as his expert opinion that the painting is a close copy by some modern artist of a work by Claude Monet.'

'That's just his opinion. It's inconclusive. It relies on tradition. You . . . you can't prove that Monet didn't use a charcoal stick on this one occasion.'

She couldn't help a little laugh of disbelief. 'Is that going to be your defence? Who else do you think would stand alongside you as you said that? You *know* Monet never used black – it was part of his painting philosophy, that black and white are not prismatic colours, that what looks black in nature is a series of tones that never really end as black. But now all at once he uses black charcoal to outline a bridge he's painted hundreds of times?'

Willard had almost ceased to listen once she uttered the word 'defence'. He saw himself in a court of law, trying to uphold a theory that no one would take seriously.

He would have to try a new tack.

'You say you haven't been in touch with McNaughton recently? He doesn't know about the report?'

'Not yet, but don't ask me to say nothing about it, Will. He's asked for this investigation, he's paying for the laboratory work, and he must have the results.'

He hesitated. 'What . . . what do you think he'll do?'

It was Erica's turn to stop and think. She picked up the letter, which had fallen to the floor. Rereading it, she saw no threats. 'He's giving you a way out. Take back the painting, agree to the cancellation of the sale and the return of the cashier's cheque.'

'You say that as if it's so easy!'

'It is easy.'

'No it's not. You see . . . I've got commitments . . .'

'Commitments?'

'I . . . well, I was short of funds so I . . . Everybody knew there was this big lump of money waiting to be paid into my account so I . . . I . . . Well, it was as good as cash in hand, really so I . . . used it as guarantee.'

In a flash she understood. 'You borrowed against it?'

'I had to make *some* arrangement, Erica. Running a business isn't all profit, you know! And there was that big cheque – and there was no reason to imagine it wouldn't become available—'

'There was every reason, you fool!' she cried. 'Your scheme fell to pieces!'

'Everything would have been fine if you hadn't started poking about! Why couldn't you let well alone?'

'Because I was asked to verify your "discovery". Because it's not as perfect a forgery as you seem to think. Because once I began to have doubts I had to follow it through.'

'But you've gone far enough, Erica,' he urged. 'I understand, you had to satisfy yourself, you wanted to see if your doubts had a cause and now you've done that but it can end there.'

'End there? What do you mean?'

'Don't show that report to McNaughton! What does he know about painting? He only wants to take it home and show off to his neighbours – he'll be perfectly happy if you tell him it's "right".'

He had taken her breath away. When she recovered she said, 'You mean lie to him.'

'Yes, why not? You don't really want it all coming out, do you? It won't do *your* reputation any good and it would make me a laughing stock—'

'And you need the money.'

'Yes, I do, and if you'll just play along—'

'Will, if you ever had any chance of tricking Zan

McNaughton out of that money, it's gone now. He says in that letter that he has good reason to doubt the painting. Even without hearing what Cheffield's got to say, he's convinced it's a fraud. He's never going to let you bank that cheque.'

'But I *need* the money!'

'Then get it honestly! Sell something – that cabin cruiser, your house on Parigos – change your lifestyle—'

'But you don't understand – how could I explain all that to – it's not just myself—'

Erica studied him. His features seemed to be crumpling, all the pride seemed to be oozing out of him.

'Not just yourself,' she repeated. 'Who else?' Some inner voice was hinting at the answer as she asked.

'It's none of your business!'

'Quite right. The time has long gone by when it would matter. But let me guess – it's a girl, isn't it?'

He gave her a glance of such dislike that she felt herself shiver.

'Oh, you think you're so clever, don't you! So high and mighty, giving me a lecture about honesty and integrity! And what's it got you? A two-bit job as curator of a gallery tucked away in a two-bit town! And let me tell you, I can soon take that away from you – I've got friends in the council's Arts and Leisure Department, I got you the job and I can see to it that your contract isn't renewed. Don't think you're immune – if I go down I can take you with me!'

A shocked silence followed. Then Erica said, 'Who is she, then? Not by any chance the woman who left a linen skirt in the wardrobe on Parigos last spring?'

'Very good. You've really got quite good at this detecting thing.'

'And I believed you when you said it was just someone who had rented the cottage from you.' She sighed. 'What a fool I've been.'

'Try to show some sense now. Treat this purely as a business matter. Keep Cheffield's report to yourself. I can talk McNaughton into keeping the Monet—'

'No you can't,' she flashed. 'Believe me, Will, if you try

any more tricks with him he'll break you in pieces and put you in the nearest dustbin.'

He was indignant at the warning. 'Oh, I can handle him, Erica – he's no great threat if only you'll be sensible. All I need is a little help from you—'

'Well, you're not going to get it! Ten more words from you about carrying on this fraud, and I tell the whole story to Sergeant Groume of the Art and Antique Squad.'

'Erica!'

'And I'd like you to leave now.'

'But – but—'

'And don't ever come here again, or ring me or write to me, or contact me in any way.'

'If this is about Lottie,' he blurted, 'forget about her. She's not really important to me.'

'Lottie. That's the famous "other woman". Do you really think that's what this is about?' She made a dismissive gesture. 'Just go.'

'But you can't *do* this to me!'

'I didn't do it to you, Willard,' she said sadly, 'you did it to yourself.'

Nineteen

So it was over.

Three years of her life, wasted, spent on an affair with a man who had no real feelings for her.

Regrets – yes, she had those in plenty. For all the times she'd fallen in with Willard's opinions, been persuaded to agree when perhaps she'd been in doubt. In her professional life she'd given him a superiority which perhaps he'd never really earned. His ardent belief in himself had made her believe in him.

There had been a strong physical attraction too – no use denying that. Before she met Willard, Erica had never known the joy of being completely at one with another human being. Her little romances at college, the sexual encounters of her time in New York that were best left in limbo, the celibate years of her climb back to self-respect and a life of work – none of these had prepared her for what she'd experienced in Willard's arms.

But as she looked back, she saw that this was his way of keeping her in thrall. Whenever she'd been about to become too independent he'd recaptured her with promises of the rapture of passion, the fire that consumes yet regenerates.

Gratitude, too. He'd given her a career. It had seemed so generous, so altruistic, and she had loved him for it. Now she wondered whether there had always been a long-term plan to make use of her. Long-term, because the preparations for forging the Monet must have begun at least two years ago, and who could tell what other schemes Willard had had in store?

She gave her mind to that thought. The provenance – the letter by the 'gardener's boy' and the trail of names of fictional

275

owners – all that had been researched well in advance. The letter about Lucie Curacie's communion frock had been stolen about eighteen months ago so that the gardener's boy's letter could be forged. Conspirators had been at work for a long time: the painter of the fake Monet, the letter forger – though that might be the same person – Yamin Emin in his folksy little shop in Istanbul, and Willard Townley himself.

He had told her he needed the money, begged her to let the fraud go forward because he was desperate for the money. He'd been certain he could hoodwink her and everyone else, so he'd been spending – wasting – funds for years in expectation of having perhaps eight million pounds to play with.

What astounded her now was the callousness of it all. At the end of this devious game someone was to be a victim, was to pay out a huge sum for a forged painting. In his mind's eye Willard had had some *ingénue* with a recently acquired fortune – a lottery winner, an Internet millionaire. He'd never intended to let it go anywhere near a museum or a state gallery, of that she was now sure. He'd wanted to get hold of a simpleton, and the first simpleton who appeared on the scene – according to Will's reading of it – had been Alexander McNaughton.

Tough luck for you, Will, you didn't know what you were letting yourself in for, she said inwardly. The thought was a mixture of amusement and asperity.

So now Zan had given instructions to the Cheffield laboratory to return the canvas direct to Willard. Willard would accept it – would have to accept it. He would sign the receipt, the receipt would be shown as evidence to the bank, the cashier's cheque would be returned to its issuer and the deal would be over.

And Zan McNaughton would return to his vineyards with his sister, thankful to be rid of the illusions of his stay in Britain – the illusion of a painted scene, the illusion that it was by a master, the illusion of friendship or perhaps even love with a woman who had thrown it all away.

She ought to get in touch with Zan, she told herself. She had the report by Kevin Cheffield, it was his by right and she ought to forward it to him. But she felt she ought to hand it to him in person because there were things in it that needed explanation – at least so she told herself.

He hadn't been at his London hotel the last time she tried to get in touch. But he had been back since then, because the letter to Willard had had the day's date on it. So perhaps he was there now, and if she rang, he would answer.

But she was too weary after the scene with Willard, too spent and dejected to want to do any more. She supervised the last changes in her spring exhibition, closed up the gallery and set the locks, then walked home. A cool spring dusk was falling. Trees still showed the faint green of opening leaf buds, beyond which the first star was glinting in a grey-blue heaven. The stars in Zan's home sky would be different, she thought – was there an evening star there, to tell you that the night was coming, the friendless, endless night?

The message light was blinking on her answering machine. Without taking off her outdoor things she dashed to play back the callers. But none of them was Zan McNaughton. Fool, she told herself. He just gets back from seeing his sister, carries out that stiff piece of business with the man he thinks is your lover, and you expect him to telephone? Shaking her head at herself, she took off her coat.

One of the calls was from her mother. After she'd made herself a cup of herb tea she rang back. 'Ah, there you are, maidie,' said Lisbet. 'You coming down for the Easter break?'

'It wouldn't be worth it, Mamma. The gallery has to be open on the Bank Holiday, you know.'

'Seems a long time since I saw you. Tell you what – I'll come to you.'

'You're coming to London?' Erica exclaimed. Her mother hated London.

'Oh, might as well. One or two things I'd like to see – your little spring exhibition for one, and I'd like to go to the Tate. And my agent is setting up a lunch thing for me, so why shouldn't I take advantage of him, eh?'

'What sort of a lunch thing?'

'You know those people in New York who were waiting to buy my last set? Seems they're flying over and want to meet me. It turns out they're a mining corporation, so they're keen on those studies of our old tin mines. Weird, isn't it? Do I want to become the favourite painter of a mining corporation?'

'Well, do you?'

'It might be fun. But on the other hand, if American buyers began descending on me in Cornwall, I'd hate that.'

'Dear me, the trials and tribulations of being a good painter.'

'I'm sorry, love,' her mother said, at once contrite. 'I know how much you would have liked to do well – but it just wasn't to be. And I oughtn't to complain about imaginary drawbacks that go with my little bit of talent, ought I?'

'You said it, Mamma, I didn't.'

'Erica, are you all right? You sound a bit tetchy.'

'I'm sorry. It hasn't been a good day.'

'What's been happening? Something go wrong with your exhibition?'

'That too.'

'Meaning that's just one of many. Tell me.'

'I don't want to talk about it, Mamma.'

'Oh dear. You sound really doomy. Well, when I get there you can cry on my shoulder.'

Despite herself, Erica found herself chuckling. 'All right, I get the message – I should snap out of it. I'll try, I'll really try.'

'That's the spirit, dear. And if you're really good I'll take you with me to the lunch and you can eat my share of the caviar.'

Somewhat cheered, she got through the evening and, thoroughly exhausted, slept quite well. She was preparing an early breakfast and writing a list of 'must do' items for the day when her phone rang.

'Erica?' said Zan. 'Did I wake you?'

She was too flustered to speak at first.

'I'm sorry,' he went on in apology, 'I know it's early-bird time, but I've got a lot on for the rest of the day and I wanted to get back to you. You've been leaving messages for me.'

'It's all right,' she managed to say. 'I've been up for a while.'

'Really? Oh, well, good. Listen, Erica, I just came back yesterday to sort out a few things but I'm off back to the West Country as soon as I can get started. I had a long confab with the consultant and he says it's OK to bring Nyree back to London.'

'Oh, how marvellous! Oh, Zan, I *am* glad.'

'Yeah, she's done amazingly well. Of course she's got to be looked after – not that she lets me do it – but the doctor said that so long as she gets plenty of rest, she should do fine. So yesterday I arranged things here and today I'm fetching her back, so it's a bit hectic, you know?'

'Of course. You shouldn't have bothered to ring me.'

'No, no, that was a priority. I wanted to get in touch – I mean, just to be on proper terms because I think I was a bit scratchy with you—'

'No, no, not at all.'

'And what I wanted to say now is, are you going away over Easter or something?'

'No, I'm not—'

'Because if you're going to be in London, I'd like you to meet my sister.'

'Oh, that would be lovely!'

'And I've got a lot to tell you.'

'I've got a lot to tell you too.'

'Well, then . . . that's great. Nyree will be thrilled. She's been saying for a long time that she wants to talk to you instead of hearing about you and getting messages.'

'I'm looking forward to it.'

'Can we sort of set a date? It'll take me all of today to bring her here and get her settled, and I think tomorrow she ought to rest up, and of course I suppose you're tied up at the gallery even though it's a holiday weekend for everybody else?'

'Only too true, alas. But I could come in one evening.'

'Well, just for a bit, Nyree's supposed to go to bed at nine. Awful, isn't it? But it means you'd hardly get a chance to say two words before she had to stagger off.'

'I can arrange to take a day off,' Erica offered. 'So long as it's scheduled ahead and my secretary is here to handle any problems, it can be done.'

'What day, then?'

She thought about it. 'My mother's coming to town,' she ventured. 'It's a lunch that her agent's arranging, and she wants me to go too – so after that's over, I could come for afternoon tea. How about that?'

'That sounds good. Which day is it going to be?'

'I don't know yet. But it'll be one day next week. Could I ring you back about it?'

'Absolutely. You'll have to forgive me if I'm not around – Nyree's threatening to go to every gallery in London once she gets here.'

'Good for her. Right, I'll leave a message if you're not there.'

'Great. That's great. I've got to go now – the car's waiting for me.'

'Of course. Tell Nyree I'm looking forward to seeing her.'

'I certainly will. Bye for now, Erica.'

'Goodbye.'

It was noticeable to the staff of the Corie Gallery that the curator was in a much better humour today. Troubles over the paintings that had failed to turn up seemed to vanish, the replacements fitted in perfectly, their somewhat ornate frames were given a final dusting, the window shades were adjusted to give the best daylight levels, and the whole thing was ready for opening.

When she got home in the evening, her mother was there stacking packages in the freezer. 'Oh, hello, buttercup, how're you?' She paused to give her daughter a light kiss on the cheek. 'I did some shopping for you – there's eight different healthy-diet meals there so we'll always have something to eat while I'm here.'

'And you'll never have to get out a saucepan or a baking dish.'

'Well, who wants to waste time on all that cooking non-sense, that's what I always say.' She closed the freezer. 'But I do make coffee, and there's some in the pot if you want it, only about half an hour old.'

Erica poured herself a cup then sat down at her kitchen

table. Her mother sat across from her. 'So, here I am, do you still need my shoulder for a good cry?'

'No, thanks, I got the better of that.'

'So I see. What was it all about, that downcast bit?'

Erica heaved a deep sigh. 'It's a long story, Mamma. I'll tell you the main thing to get it over with. That painting?'

'What painting? Oh, the Monet.'

'Well, it isn't. I got a report from Cheffield that definitely establishes it as a forgery.'

'Oh, my.' Lisbet studied her daughter. 'Have you summoned up the courage to show the report to Willard?'

'I didn't need to. Zan McNaughton had written to him already saying he was sure the Monet was a fake and saying the deal is off.'

Lisbet couldn't help a great grin of pleasure. 'How nice,' she said. 'I wish I'd been there when he read it.'

'Mamma!'

'I'm sorry, dear. No wonder you were upset when you rang. So the estimable Willard Townley, art dealer extraordinaire, got taken in! I can't help being pleased.'

'It's worse than that, Mamma. Willard was behind the forgery.'

'What did you say? Behind the . . . You mean, he knew the painting was a fake?'

'Exactly. In fact, I think he instigated the plot from the very first – and, you know, it couldn't be a spur-of-the-moment thing, it needed long-term planning.'

'Erica,' said her mother, very serious now, 'are you saying Willard is . . . a con man?'

Erica said nothing. By and by her mother said, 'Well, all art dealers are inclined to be double dealers, I've always said so. But this is a bit over the top. Are you sure he knew the Monet wasn't "right"?'

'I'm sure. He as good as admitted it, and asked me to suppress Cheffield's report because he's desperately in debt and needs the money.'

'He tried to get you to go along?'

'Yes.'

Lisbet sprang up, walked to the kitchen door, hit the door

jamb with her fist, uttered a few Cornish oaths under her breath, then came back to the table.

'I *never* liked him,' she exclaimed, 'but that was because I have this thing against art dealers. And he always seemed a bit too pleased with himself to suit me. But *this*—' She broke off. 'Have you told the police?'

'No.'

'Are you going to?'

'I don't know.'

'That poor man who got tricked – is he going to take it further?'

'I don't know. This has all come to a head a bit suddenly, Mamma. We haven't had a chance to talk it through.'

'How do you feel about it?' she asked anxiously, coming to take her daughter's hand.

Erica squeezed her fingers. 'I don't know yet. I'm still in a bit of a muddle over the whole thing. A lot depends on what Willard tries to do. Mr McNaughton sort of offered him a way out – take back the painting, call off the deal, and that's the end of it.'

'Well, of course Willard will take him up on it.'

'I think he will.'

'McNaughton came to the conclusion it was a fake off his own bat, did he?'

'It seems so. He and I had looked into the provenance together, to some extent, and he decided to go on looking. That's all I know so far. I'm meeting him next week so we can bring each other up to date.'

'Next week? You'd think he'd be in a lot more of a hurry over a thing like that.'

'Oh, Mamma, he doesn't really care about the painting himself. He was only buying it for his sister.'

Lisbet laughed. 'One of those lordly millionaires.'

'No he's not! He's a thoroughly decent man and as I've told you before, the painting is for his sister's twenty-first birthday and when he bought it he thought there was a good chance she might not see her twenty-second!'

At this outburst her mother stared at her. She made no response. She got up, picked up the cafetière, shook her head at the dregs that were left, and opened the cupboard for the instant coffee. She switched on the electric kettle.

Erica got up, put an arm round her waist, and gave her a little hug. 'I'm sorry,' she said. 'I didn't mean to bite your head off. But the whole thing is . . . it's serious, it's not just that Willard tried to pull a fast one on a stranger, he made a fool of me, and the people he thought he was tricking don't deserve that kind of treatment.'

'I agree.'

'I'm so angry with Willard I can hardly bear to think about him.'

'I notice you've started to call him Willard. That seems to signal a decided alteration in your feelings.'

'That happened quite a long time ago. I suddenly woke up to the fact that I wasn't in love with him any more.'

'Uh-huh,' said her mother, spooning coffee into her mug. 'Are you sure you mean it?'

'Oh yes.'

'Because he's had you under his thumb for a long time, you know.'

'That's over. The time has gone when Willard can have any influence over me.'

'Delighted to hear it,' said her mother.

Erica believed what she said, but she was proved incorrect to some degree. Next day, Easter Saturday, when the gallery was very busy, who should turn up but Councillor Dulliver.

He was hovering at the edge of a group from a coach party, to whom Erica was explaining some of the ballet background in the paintings of Degas.

'So you see these girls didn't have the benefit of our present-day knowledge of nutrition, so that's why some of them look so pale.'

'Poor little things,' murmured the ladies from the coach. Mr Dulliver signalled at Erica from behind them.

'Excuse me, I see someone else needs some information,' she said, and left them surveying the tired ballet-girls taking a five-minute break.

'Good morning, Councillor,' she welcomed him. 'Come to see how the Easter attendance is going?'

'Ah, yes, very nice, quite a lot in the special exhibition too. Er . . . Could I have a word, Miss Pencarreth?'

'Of course.'

'In private.'

'Oh.' That didn't bode well. 'My office, then? Would you like coffee?'

'No, no, I'll be having lunch quite soon. No, just a word or two, that's all.'

What could be the matter? She'd stayed within her budget, put on exhibitions that had attracted quite large crowds, the Christmas cards had made a surprising profit . . .

The councillor was an elderly man, broad and given to tweed suits that made him look broader. He sat down slowly, glancing about at her office as if to mark it for tidiness and efficiency.

'I had a telephone call from Willard Townley last night,' he began.

Erica's heart sank.

'If you recall, Miss Pencarreth, it was largely due to his recommendation that you were awarded the post of curator here.'

'Was it?'

'You don't remember that?'

'Well, I remember you mentioned him, but I had hoped my qualifications had more to do with it.'

'Well, you see – qualified – what does that mean, as a matter of fact? You had the necessary degrees and diplomas but this was a special gallery – devoted to one era of painting only – and it's been very disturbing to me to learn that you made a bad mistake over that Monet painting that was all over the papers last winter.'

'Is that what Mr Townley said?'

'He said he'd been badly let down.'

'What about all the other experts who agreed it was a Monet?'

'But you were the *first*. You set the tone. And since you manage a gallery that's entirely given up to Impressionists, your opinion counted for a lot. That's so, now isn't it?'

She nodded, understanding that she'd have a hard time

justifying herself to Councillor Dulliver. He had taken the recommendation of Willard Townley when he helped to choose her for her post. Now that same Willard Townley was expressing doubts, and apparently with justification. So Councillor Dulliver must look into it.

'I quite agree that I took the lead at first in judging the painting to be a Monet,' she said. 'I was also the first to think perhaps it was not.'

'But by then, my dear young lady, a great deal of money was involved. You've cost Mr Townley a fortune.'

'The sale had to be cancelled. That's quite true. But Mr Townley didn't really *lose* any money—'

'You understand nothing about business, my dear, if you think that,' Dulliver said in patronising tones. 'And that's where the town council has to take an interest. The Corie Gallery has to make money.'

'But it *is* making money!'

'Yes, yes, it does better than break even, I give you that, but you have the power to exchange paintings with other galleries or owners, and the question now is, whether your judgement can be trusted.'

'What?' Erica gasped.

'You exchanged a – a—' He got a piece of paper out of his pocket and glanced at it. 'You exchanged a Guillaumin for a Morisot last year, and when you first took over you exchanged two Pissarros for a Cézanne.'

'Well, we had too many Pissarros.'

'But now we have to ask ourselves, what is the authenticity of the paintings you acquired?'

'But – what are you saying? They were – they *are* well-known paintings!'

'But in view of this fiasco over the Monet, can we be sure of that?'

Erica drew herself up. 'That is an insult, Mr Dulliver.'

'It's a straightforward question,' he said, with a gesture of irritation. 'Are you sure you knew what you were doing? And another thing, you've put this request before the Arts and Leisure Department for special funds to buy a Sisley—'

'But that's the agreement – over a certain price, I have to get permission from the committee.'

'Well, I spoke to a colleague from the Arts and Leisure Department this morning when I'd thought it over and in view of what Mr Townley let us know I have to say we'll be thinking seriously about granting permissions of that kind.'

She was keeping a tight rein on her temper. This philistine seemed mainly concerned about money, but money *was* important in her work. She couldn't improve the collection without the right to buy and sell, barter and exchange.

'Councillor,' she said with cold politeness, 'I would find it very difficult to do my job if your committee took up that attitude.'

'Attitude? It's not an attitude, it's paying proper attention to the use of the council's money. That's rate-payers' money, young lady, and we have to answer to them. And what we in the Arts and Leisure Department are beginning to wonder is whether perhaps you're too young for the job.'

'You knew my age when you appointed me.'

'But we took a risk when it came to your understanding of how to handle funds. And now when we consider the apparently light-hearted way you let Mr Townley invest in a painting and then made him withdraw . . .'

'There was nothing light-hearted about it. If you're repeating remarks made by Mr Townley, I can only say that he's misrepresenting—'

'I wouldn't say that if I were you, Miss Pencarreth,' Dulliver interrupted. 'Mr Townley's firm has been established for well over a century and old Mr Corie bought many of his paintings from it. You can't accuse the head of a firm like that—'

'It seems to me that Mr Townley is the one making accusations.'

'Mr Townley has shown good faith in this matter. He's alerted us to a problem and when you look back he's honestly admitting that he perhaps made a mistake in recommending you in the first place.'

'I see. To make a long story short, Councillor, are you asking for my resignation?'

'I haven't said that, Miss Pencarreth. I leave that to you.'

'If I don't offer my resignation, do I take it everything I do will be subjected to intense scrutiny?'

'That would be good sense on the part of the Arts and Leisure Department, I imagine.'

'Well, thank you for this frank talk, Mr Dulliver. And now, if you don't mind, I have people in the gallery – rate-payers, Mr Dulliver – who expect my attention. So I must break off this delightful interview and get back to work.' She opened her office door. 'This is the way out.'

He trod heavily behind her, huffing that he would report this to the Arts and Leisure Department at the next meeting. She handed him over to one of the attendants for the last part of his departure from the gallery. But instead of turning her attention to the visitors, she went back to her office and sat down.

She hadn't the slightest doubt that this was a first salvo by Willard to defend his reputation. The Monet had been accepted back, the sale had been cancelled. News would leak out into the art world. Newspapers might take it up. So, he was ensuring that the blame wouldn't fall heavily upon himself.

He'd been misled, that was his version. Someone he thought he could rely on had made a bad mistake. There was a very good chance he'd be believed because, to the public eye, he was the loser. He'd been going to receive a small fortune for the painting but, honest man that he was, he had invalidated the agreement when doubts were raised.

Of course there would be some sarcastic amusement among his fellow dealers. He'd blundered, and the reason he'd blundered was because he'd believed the young woman he was – shall we say – friendly with. Well, well. The clever Mr Townley had been caught napping.

But that would pass, there would be other things for the dealers to smile over, and the story of the Monet that wasn't 'right' would fade away.

But the Arts and Leisure Department of Gratesford Council would not forget.

She sighed. There goes the job, she said to herself.

Twenty

The lunch with the American visitors was much more stately than Lisbet Pencarreth and her daughter had expected. It took place in a headquarters building in the City, on an executive floor where a private drawing-room offered wonderful views of London. Pre-lunch drinks were offered. Through an open doorway a dining-room was visible where stood a table laid with silver and crystal.

The hosts were two visiting vice-presidents from the parent company, one of whom appeared to be in charge of a department which acquired paintings and sculptures. 'At our headquarters office in Philadelphia we have mainly portraits,' explained Ms Zelminski, 'but elsewhere we like to have landscapes and abstract art. I may say that the board has been extremely pleased with our purchases from your studio, Mrs Pencarreth. And we look forward to more in the future.'

A beautifully produced volume was brought out with illustrations of the artwork installed in other headquarters offices throughout the world: Mondrian, Braque, Marino Marini, Emilio Greco, Ceri Richards . . . Lisbet began to think that being singled out by a company like this was no small thing. Her agent kept giving her meaningful glances which meant, Good things are coming.

At his request Lisbet produced a portfolio of sketches that she'd brought to the lunch. The vice-presidents hovered over the table on which these were laid out. Ms Zelminski would hold one out now and again, to study it at eye level. 'Yes, yes,' she murmured. 'I see. Will these be under-drawings for projected oils?'

'Preliminary sketches just to get the feel of the place. I

don't under-draw, it would mean using a fixative before I put on colour and that's not for me.'

'I understand. Very compelling. This is where you live? Fierce country, Mrs Pencarreth – or may I call you Lisbet?'

'Please do.'

'Well, Lisbet, what I want to say – and I'm sure Myron will go along' – Myron nodded eagerly – 'is that we would like to have first call on the finished canvases from this work.'

'Oh . . . well . . . I leave negotiations to Phil . . .'

'Quite, I expected that. May I just say that Zonal Power Mining looks forward very much to seeing the finished paintings.' They dallied a while, looking at the sketches and commenting in what Erica felt was a very knowledgeable way. Even Lisbet herself had to admit this pair knew what they were talking about.

They were ushered in to lunch, a simple but beautifully cooked meal. They'd been invited for twelve thirty and at two thirty precisely the vice-presidents rose, said that alas they had business appointments elsewhere, and left. A PR girl showed them out; Phil the agent promised news of vast sums of money in the near future, summoned a taxi and was driven away to his office.

'Well,' said Erica. 'Are you going to make critical remarks about being mobbed by Americans in your studio?'

'Who, me?' Her mother glanced about at the busy City scene. 'Let's walk,' she suggested. 'I feel in need of a little contact with the common herd.'

It was a mild spring day. Above the financial skyscrapers a blue canopy flecked with cloud could be seen. They were on their way now to the Mayfair Rialto. When Erica had rung Zan to give the date of her mother's lunch in the City, he had immediately suggested she should bring Lisbet with her to tea. There was plenty of time so they strolled along, pausing now and then to admire the well-tended flower-boxes outside office windows.

'One day I might paint this,' Lisbet said, glancing about. 'There's life on so many different levels, isn't there – the people, the flowers and plants, the life of the engines in the cars and buses, the life of the money flowing through it all . . .'

'Not your usual territory.'

'No, but change is good. I used to paint market scenes, remember – and then there were a couple of years when I was obsessed with railway stations . . .' She swung her satchel as she walked. Today she was well dressed in a fine wool suit instead of her usual paint-daubed slacks and shirt. Change indeed. Everything was changing, thought Erica.

They walked along the Thames Embankment to Charing Cross and from there up Regent Street and into Mayfair. The thought of a cup of tea began to seem welcoming. They went into the hotel, tidied themselves up in the handsome cloakroom, and then asked to be shown to the lounge for afternoon tea. 'Miss Pencarreth?' the desk clerk inquired. 'Mr McNaughton and his sister asked that you should be shown up to their suite.'

'Their suite,' muttered Lisbet as they were ushered into the lift. 'This is my day for the high life.'

Zan opened the door to them, ushered them in, calling, 'They're here, Nyree!' A door on the far side of the sitting-room opened and a slender girl came out. She was wearing a light blue jersey dress by Ben di Lisi and on her head a silk bandanna containing every colour in the rainbow.

'Hi,' she said. 'Excuse the headgear but I'm having a bad hair day.'

Erica laughed aloud. What a bright, resolute spirit! She shook hands, then introduced Lisbet who said, 'At my age I have bad hair weeks.'

'You're the famous painter. I bought a book about you,' said Nyree. 'I found some of the pictures a bit scary.'

'Bits of Cornwall *are* scary.'

'But here – this one, it isn't Cornwall,' Nyree insisted, picking up a book from a side table. 'That's a railway station, isn't it? What's that, over there at the side – what's happening there?'

'Someone's trying to catch a train when it's gathering speed away from the platform. Speed's awfully difficult to paint.'

'She's off,' Zan said to Erica. 'She's been dying to find someone who can answer all her questions. Excuse me a minute, I'll summon up the tea.' He went to the telephone.

The suite was at the back of the hotel so that it overlooked a pleasant garden. The open windows of the sitting-room let in the scent from the newly mown lawn, the first cut of the season. The furnishings were pseudo William Morris of good quality, and the painting on the main wall was a reproduction Hobbema. If you closed your ears to the hum of traffic you could imagine you were in an English country house.

Nyree was arguing energetically with Lisbet. Watching her, Erica thought how brave she was. It caused her a stab of shame at her own self-pity. Compared with what this girl had been through and was still facing, Erica's own troubles seemed tiny. What did it matter if she had been made a fool of, was losing her job, might see her reputation damaged? She was fit and strong, she could repair the harm done to her by Willard Townley. Her future would be what she herself made it.

Zan put down the telephone. 'How did lunch go?' he asked.

'Oh, very top-notch stuff,' she told him. 'Executive suite, silver forks, the vice-presidents both had Raymond Weil watches. I kept pulling my cuff down over my poor old Swatch.'

'And from the business point of view? Didn't I gather it was set up by your mother's agent?'

'Well, she showed them some sketches she'd brought, and they seemed to know what they were looking at—'

'Sketches?' Nyree chirped, turning from the book of illustrations. 'You've got some sketches?'

'In my carrier,' Lisbet agreed.

'Could I see them?'

'They're not much to look at,' Lisbet said, hesitating. Although this youngster seemed keen, would she be able to understand what she was looking at if it was only black lines on white cartridge paper?

'Please, if you wouldn't mind – I'd love to look.'

Lisbet unzipped her big satchel to produce the sketches

in a folio folder. Nyree cleared a space on the side table for them. Lisbet put them down one by one, in silence, waiting for comment before she herself made any explanation.

After a moment Nyree burst out, 'How do you *do* that?'

'What?'

'Here – this great rock – and then the land seems to go off into infinity – it's vast, you feel drawn into it, but it's all inside about – what – eighteen inches?'

'About that.'

'How do you do it? It's a sort of trick, isn't it?'

'It's an illusion,' Lisbet said. 'In a way, all art is an illusion. The artist is trying to put down on paper or canvas what he sees, or what he feels, or what he finds inside his head. In times gone by it might have been an illusion of beauty where nymphs and shepherds are dancing. Sometimes it's an illusion of grandeur, to glorify some old duke or king. This particular illusion you're asking about is just a part of technique; it's called perspective. It has rules, you can do it with set squares and things, but I just go by instinct. If you want a proper explanation, ask my daughter – she's studied all that sort of stuff.'

'That's your cue,' Zan said to Erica, laughing.

'No, no. This isn't the time or place for a lecture.' Happily the tea was brought in at that moment so that Erica was spared the need to embark on a technical subject that had been part of her studies long ago.

They settled themselves around the table wheeled in by the waiter. Nyree was hostess, poured the tea, handed it around, offered cakes. An occasional glance of encouragement from her brother told Erica that Nyree wasn't accustomed to this kind of thing.

'Do you have "afternoon tea" at the vineyard?' she ventured.

'Oh, we drink tea all the time, not just in the afternoon. Gallons of it. I get the impression that my forebears reached New Zealand on a tide of tea,' said Nyree. 'But it's nice having it all dressed up like this, in a fancy pot and things.' She sighed. 'When we go back, there's a lot I'm going to miss.' Then she added, with a laugh, 'How're

292

you gonna keep 'em down on the farm, after they've seen Paree?'

'You're thinking of going back soon?' Lisbet inquired.

'Well, we only came so that we could see this special doctor and find out why I was dwindling away. Now that's solved, and the specialist is corresponding with some other specialist in Wellington, so these dreadful pills and things will all be on tap back home and if anything else needs doing, they're all clued up. So we *should* be going back.' She was silent for a moment and then added, 'And besides, you don't think the wine will be any good unless you're there to supervise, do you, bro?'

'I *know* it won't be any good,' Zan countered. 'You can say what you like about the tricks of painting, but the trick of wine making is just as magical, and only a few extremely talented people – such as myself – have it.'

'Talking of tricks,' Nyree said, taking a nibble at a little iced cake, 'what was all this about the Monet? I got a sort of cut-down version from my big brother.'

Everybody looked at Erica. She nodded and braced herself. 'In my handbag,' she said, 'I've got the laboratory analysis from Kevin Cheffield. It proves that the so-called Monet has a charcoal sketch on the surface of the canvas.'

'What?' exclaimed her mother.

'You may well say "What".'

'I don't get it,' Zan said.

'Nor do I – and as everybody knows, I'm the brightest of the McNaughtons. What does it mean, Erica?' asked Nyree.

'It means it's almost impossible that Monet had anything to do with it. Most of the Impressionists used a technique called *"alla prima"* – and that means painting very fast, using your brush as the only tool. Everything we know about Monet tells us that he painted straight on to the canvas. He never sketched with a charcoal stick. Yet for this painting, on the fibres of the canvas there's a faint charcoal sketch for the bridge and a fixing agent over it . . .'

'So it's a forgery.' Nyree waited for her nod of assent.

'But Zan told me when he first saw it, a lot of big nobs in the art world were looking at it and saying how good it was.'

'Yes, they were. And some of them were considering chipping in with money to pay for the restoration of the burnt part, so as to get in with an early offer when the restoration was finished.'

'It must have looked awfully like the real thing,' said Nyree, frowning at the idea.

Lisbet smiled. 'We were talking about illusion. This painting is a lovely illusion – and actually a *good* painting,' she said. 'I only saw photographs in the magazines, but it has a lot of power.'

'So what's wrong with it, then?' Nyree persisted.

'It's not by Monet. It may look like what Monet saw, it may be painted the way Monet might have painted it, but Monet was an old man with cataracts. The illusion here is that you're supposed to think this is something seen through his eyes – but it was painted by someone else. There's no integrity in it. Although,' Erica added, 'I agree that it's good. Whoever he is, the forger has great ability if he would only use it for his own work.'

'It's a she,' Zan corrected.

'What?' cried Erica. 'How do you know?'

'I met her. On your Greek island.'

She drew in a breath, a bitter realisation dawning. 'Lottie,' she said.

'You *know* her?'

Erica felt herself colouring up. She picked up her teacup and took a sip. After a moment she was able to say, 'I've heard of her.'

'She's well known?' Zan asked in surprise.

'No, no, I just meant I'd heard her mentioned.' The last thing she wanted was to be questioned about Lottie Siegler. 'You actually went to Parigos?' she said to Zan.

'Yes, for a short visit, where I found this lady in the middle of painting a picture that she said was just "for practice". It was like something by – wait a minute, I wrote it down – André Derain.'

'Well, people do that, Zan,' his sister informed him. 'It's not actually forgery. You know we saw students sitting at easels copying things in the Louvre.'

'So we did, but this young woman didn't have anything pinned up to copy from. And she gave me an angry lecture on why people should think just as well of an imitation as they should of the original. Very huffy about it. I think she had a grudge against the world for not appreciating her.' He paused, looking back at the moment. 'An extremely forceful character.'

'But did she say she was going to put the painting on the market as genuine?' Lisbet asked.

'No,' Zan acknowledged with his brief smile, 'but that would have been admitting forgery, wouldn't it? Like Mr Spock, I used logic. Here she was, in a cottage owned by Willard Townley, who'd tried to sell me a painting with a dodgy provenance. She's painting something that looks very much like a real master work, and she gets angry when I say that though I'd like to buy it I'd expect to get it cheap because it's only an imitation.'

'Well, yes . . . But I'm talking about actual proof, Zan.'

'You've got me there, Mrs Pencarreth. I think that at about that point I leave logic behind and rely on instinct. I just know she painted the Monet, and to test that I sent it back to Townley.'

'So I heard,' Erica remarked. 'Willard was in a state of – well, I suppose you could call it alarm.' She forbore to mention the anger he'd shown, the ill will. She still felt the chill of that moment, the moment when she realised he actively disliked her.

'I'm sorry if it caused a problem for you,' Zan said in a troubled tone. 'But I was pretty sure it would cause a crisis for him. I wanted to see how he'd react.'

'What happened? Did he agree to take back the painting?' Lisbet asked.

'Yes, and the deal is officially off.'

'That means he's admitting it's a fake.'

'Or at least he's admitting there's enough doubt for me to cancel the purchase,' Zan said. He cast an anxious glance at Erica. 'Just as well. I didn't want to have to go to law about it.'

'But hey, listen,' cried Nyree, holding up a warning finger. 'What *about* that painting? He gets it back, what does he do – flog it to somebody else even more gullible than my brother?'

'Oh, shut up, minnow,' her brother replied in mock annoyance.

'He can't sell it,' Lisbet mused. 'It's too well known now. A reputed Monet with a burnt corner, which has had quite a lot of publicity? Its provenance is in doubt now.'

'But if he's got this tame forger at his beck and call, what's to stop him getting the burnt corner sorted out – what do you call it – restored, and selling it as a perfect Monet?'

'No, no,' Erica rejoined. 'How would he account for it? Where has it been all these years? No, he couldn't make it seem genuine because an undamaged Monet would have no background.'

'Well, then, what about this other chap – who was the painting by, Zan? Degas?'

'Derain, whoever he is.'

'How about if this crook Townley puts a Derain on the market?'

'Nyree,' Zan said sharply, 'mind your manners. That's a friend of Erica's you're talking about.'

'Not any more,' said Erica bleakly.

A sudden brief silence fell. Erica kept her gaze fixed on the tea tray, Zan looked at Erica, Nyree looked at Zan, and Lisbet looked at them looking at each other.

'I'll pass on what you've told us to Sgt Groume,' Erica explained, keeping her voice very calm. 'There's a lot of co-operation among national police forces when it comes to art swindles. I think if anybody starts trying to sell a "recently discovered" Derain, he'll find it gets a lot of hard scrutiny.'

'He might give it a go,' Zan commented. 'He's terribly hard up.'

'How d'you know that, bro?'

He shrugged. 'I've had this investigating chap taking a

296

long look at Townley's finances, and just in the last few days there's talk of Townley selling up.'

'You mean, selling his cottage on Parigos, or the cabin cruiser?' Erica asked, recalling that she'd recommended those very actions to Willard. It was too much to hope that he was actually trying to do the right thing about his debts, she felt.

'The cottage and the boat, and everything else as well. The business, the lease on the premises, his flat in Hampstead or wherever . . .'

Erica couldn't take it in. She sat looking at Zan in astonishment. He for his part was glad to see there was no regret in her gaze, no appearance of being stricken at the news.

It was her mother who asked the question. 'What on earth is he up to? That Mayfair gallery is one of the most prestigious in London. And though you say he's in debt, in the past he's handled some very good sales. He could get more.'

'The rumour, so Pleydell – my investigator – says, is that he's moving to Houston.'

'Houston?'

'There's a lot of money in Houston,' said Zan, who'd had time to think about it. 'And he's got a backer, so the gossips are saying. Some rich but empty-headed widow he met in New Orleans.'

'New Orleans!' echoed Erica.

'That means something?'

'He was in New Orleans over Christmas.'

'Well, this lady is sponsoring him to set up a sales gallery in Houston.'

'Americana,' she murmured. 'He said something about early American art when he came back from that trip.'

'What, you're thinking Norman Rockwell? Or Samuel Morse?' her mother reflected.

'More likely Primitives, Mamma. It might be very easy to fake Early Americans like Hicks or Kane, the sort of thing you could claim was done by an itinerant portrait painter in the early eighteen hundreds.' She was trying to follow

297

thought processes she knew only too well – the thought processes of the man she'd been in love with. 'Then when photography comes in these amateurish paintings get stowed away in the root cellar of a farm in Virginia or Mississippi. But hey presto – some friend of Willard's is lucky enough to find them.'

'We had artists like that in New Zealand,' Nyree put in. 'It's the kind of painting you see in our museums.'

'And worth a lot of money,' sighed Erica, knowing that that was what might be in Willard's mind now. 'Particularly to people who have a million or two to spare for something that might shore up their own claim to a family history.'

'Oh, that's cruel,' Nyree said, horrified.

'Should we be doing something about it?' Lisbet wondered.

'Such as what?'

'Letting someone know . . .'

'There's nothing to tell. All this is pure speculation, Mrs Pencarreth. And highly slanderous,' said Zan in a tone of warning.

After a pause, Erica said, 'I'm sure Sgt Groume will pass the word along. Unofficially, you understand.'

Nyree's mind had gone on to something much more personal. She shook her head at Erica. 'I think it's better to have stopped being friends with a fellow who might do that sort of thing,' she ventured.

'It would have been better not to be friends in the first place,' Erica said. Oh, if only she'd been less easily taken in, less ready to fall under the spell of someone who seemed to value her.

'Well, I *never* liked him,' her mother remarked with considerable vehemence.

'The thing that I noticed was,' Zan said, 'that *he* didn't like *me*.' After which he burst out laughing so that everyone else joined in and the look of regret on Erica's face was banished.

'He didn't like you because he was trying to do you down,' Nyree commented. 'I bet it's the same for anyone who's trying to pull a trick like that – they've got to persuade

298

themselves their target deserves to be swindled because he's
. . . you know . . . inferior, not worth bothering about.'

'You might have something there,' Lisbet agreed. 'But
Willard Townley has always thought himself superior to the
rest of us.'

'Well, he's clever, you've got to admit that. This scheme
of his might very well have taken me in completely if it
hadn't been for Erica.'

'Oh, yes, great work, Erica!' Nyree cried with enthusiasm.
'Willard Highbrow-Hotshot may be clever but you're even
cleverer!'

Erica was shaking her head. This public character-
examination wasn't much to her taste.

'Come on, let's drop it,' Zan said at once, 'we're embarrassing her.'

'Right, right. And it's my duty as hostess to change the
subject so here's something I wanted to ask. Would it be a
lot of trouble to you, Erica, to draw up a list of books for
me? I've read and reread the ones you lent me and they're
here, by the way' – she nodded to a pile on top of a little
bureau – 'for you to take home. And thanks a million for
the loan.'

'No, no, I don't want them back. I've got dozens more at
home and, in fact, I can lend you others if you want—'

'But if you'd make a list, I could order them and have
them shipped home.'

'Well, we could put our heads together and see what you
fancy. Perhaps you'll come to Gratesford and take a look at
what's on my shelves.'

'Could I? That would be grand.' She looked thoughtful.
'What your mother was saying – you know, about perspective – that's different from anything I've been reading so
far. Are there books about that?'

'Oh, that's very dry stuff,' warned Lisbet. 'It's much easier
if somebody's there with a pencil and a sketchbook to show
you how it's done.'

'A teacher, you mean? Zan, could I take lessons when we
get home?'

Her brother gave her a smile. 'Where are you going to

find lessons like that? The nearest is probably Christchurch and it's a long drive there and a long drive back.'

'Oh, well . . .'

'I could give you a few pointers,' volunteered Erica, 'as long as you're still in London, that is.'

'Would you?' Her face lit up. 'Oh, that would be *great*! I want so much to understand what I'm looking at, you know. I mean, some things are sort of easy – you look at a portrait and you realise the artist is trying to say something not only about what the subject looks like but about his place in life, or his character, or something like that. But how is it done? How do you make a face look as if the person behind it is thinking? Or is too stupid to think?' She chuckled. 'I'd like you to teach me all that in a month, if you don't mind.'

'Come on, Nyree, be reasonable,' her brother chided. 'Erica's got better things to do than spend hours teaching you the rudiments of art – she's got a gallery to run, for one thing.'

'Not for much longer,' Erica said.

'What?'

Her mother was staring at her open-mouthed. Nyree was surprised, Zan was concerned.

'My contract comes up for renewal in June. I've written to Gratesford Council saying I don't want to renew it.'

'Erica!' Lisbet was astounded. 'This is the first I've heard of it!'

'It's the first time I've said it out loud.'

'But when did all this happen? I've been staying with you for nearly a week and you never *mentioned* it!'

Erica didn't want to admit that she'd only written the letter the day after Dulliver's visit. She didn't want to say that Willard's manoeuvre had more or less forced her to this step. Instead she said, 'I've been there three years now. It was fun at first, getting the gallery up and running, but it's time to move on.'

'To what, for goodness' sake?' Lisbet demanded. 'Have you had an offer from somewhere else?' She knew that career openings were scarce in Britain for the likes of Erica. If she'd had an offer from elsewhere it almost certainly meant going abroad, and though Lisbet was quite prepared to accept a parting, it came as a surprise.

'No, I've got no immediate plans,' Erica confessed. 'I thought perhaps I'd take a bit of a sabbatical.' Leave Gratesford with all its memories of that dead love affair, leave England perhaps and start afresh . . .

'Now that's a good idea!' Lisbet was delighted. 'You've been under a lot of strain these past few months—'

'Mostly brought on by problems about that confounded painting,' Zan intervened. 'I should never have involved you in all that.'

'No, no, you couldn't possibly have foreseen—'

'But I should have realised what an ordeal you were going through.'

'None of it was your fault, Zan,' she said quietly. 'I blame myself, for letting myself be blinkered for so long. And it's true, I do feel . . . strange . . . disconnected . . . now that it's all over. But it's in the past, and I'd like to take a year or so, to think what I'd like to do. I've sometimes felt, recently . . . that I might try again . . . but that's silly, I expect . . .'

'Try again?' Her mother took it up. 'To paint?'

Erica sat silent for a moment. 'I don't know if I could paint. I mean, I *can* paint, but it doesn't seem to come to much. I was wondering if . . . I don't know . . . I feel a bit drawn towards something more – more craftsman-like . . . engraving, perhaps.' She became aware they were all watching her with concern, and smiled. 'It's all right, I'm not going to leap into a bath of black printer's ink. It's just a thought I've had. I want to take my time, let it sort of simmer a bit.'

'What you ought to do,' Nyree suggested, 'is take a long holiday and come to New Zealand!'

'Nyree!' her brother said despairingly. 'Will you just for once think before you speak?'

'I *am* thinking. I've been thinking quite a lot, Big Brother, and you should listen instead of always trying to squash me!' She turned to Erica. 'You know I've been seeing all these marvellous art things on our trip to the UK and it sort of opened up a new world for me. Where we live, we get people coming to the vineyard to talk business

301

or taste the vintage, so we have this building – we've made it quite nice, I admit part of it is just a restaurant but part of it is sort of a reception room, and you were saying that you'd had lunch with these people who want to buy paintings for their offices and I was thinking – well, I think it's a good idea, Zan, and you shouldn't just laugh it off, but why couldn't we have paintings in our business offices too?'

Everybody was taken aback. At length Lisbet said, 'I'll donate a painting to start the collection.'

'You mean you think it's a good idea?' Nyree asked, elated.

'It's a great idea. I'm all in favour of art being put on display wherever folk might look at it.'

Nyree looked at Zan. 'Well, come on. Speak, O Great Oracle.'

He gave a rueful laugh. 'You needn't think I'm going to try for another cut-price Monet.'

'Well, no, and that's a shame, but we could try for something different – couldn't we, Erica? We couldn't afford Monets or Cézannes, but there are good painters around now, as good as your mother maybe, and the sort of thing we could start collecting?'

'Oh, there's so much out there, you've no idea!' Erica cried. 'It would be great if you could do something to encourage young talent, and *local* talent—'

'But how would we know talent if we saw it?' Nyree interjected. 'You see, that's what I was getting at. We need someone to help us choose things.'

'What would be a help to you,' Lisbet suggested, 'is to see schemes in progress at all sorts of levels. I understand that on your way from New Zealand to London you stopped off and went into a lot of galleries and museums. But those show the artist's finished work and, in general, show only the very best. Now, where I live, in a little village on the moors, there's a community all around where people are producing things – oil paintings, watercolours, sculpture, pottery, collage, engraving' – with a nod towards her daughter – 'you name it, we've got it. Some

302

of it is good, some is bad, and a lot is in between. But it would give you an idea of how to compare, how to evaluate.'

'That sounds great! Could I come, and you'd show me around?'

'Nyree,' her brother intervened, 'people have lives of their own to lead.'

'No, no, I'd be delighted,' Lisbet assured him. 'That is, if you're sure the journey wouldn't be too much.'

'Oh, no, Zan will call up his chum Bert Allgood and his limousine, and Bert will wrap me in cotton wool and install me in the back and stop at every service station to ask if I need a cup of tea or to go to the loo, and we'd arrive as fresh as daisies.'

'Then I'd love to have you – there's loads of room.'

'Well, great, splendid! I suppose you'll want to come too, chief?' This was addressed to Zan, but she added in a loud aside to the others, 'He's such a tyrant! I have to ask his permission if I so much as want to sneeze.'

Zan laughed. 'I grant permission for this excursion but only on the grounds that as it's a little village, you won't be able to spend a fortune on designer clothes. But I won't come with you, thanks – I could use the time catching up with some business details.'

'Oh, come on, Zan, you're always saying you miss the hills and fields.' She turned to Lisbet. 'You do have hills and fields in Cornwall, Mrs Pencarreth?'

'Oh yes, quite a few. Do come, Zan,' urged Mrs Pencarreth. 'I think you'd like it. If you like open spaces, we've got plenty.'

'It's very kind of you, Mrs Pencarreth, but I do have some work—'

'This is Wednesday. I'm driving back tomorrow,' she went on, overriding his excuse, 'and I'd need a few hours to straighten things up, which would take up Friday morning, but if you could arrange to arrive about tea-time Friday, then Nyree could have a good night's rest and we could drive around to a few of my friends on Saturday. And Erica often comes down by rail on a Saturday evening so we could have quite a reunion on Sunday. Would you come down, maidie?' she asked her daughter.

'I'd love to,' said Erica. 'And nowadays I'm going to take time off when I want to – what can they do, fire me?'

'Oh . . . well . . . perhaps I could rearrange my business appointments . . .' Zan murmured.

Nyree exchanged a glance of triumph with Erica's mother. It was clear they were on the same wavelength.

When the plans were finalised Erica and her mother said they must leave. Nyree and Zan went down to the hall to see them off, and afterwards went out to the hotel's garden for a breath of air. Strolling among the azaleas, Nyree thought back over the tea party, smiling in satisfaction. Erica had turned out to be just what she'd hoped.

'She's nice,' she remarked.

'Erica? Or her mother?'

'Oh, very clever, bright boy. Of course, Erica. I thoroughly approve of her.'

'Who asked you?'

'I just thought you'd like to know. And I'm sure Jayce and Heck will like her too.'

'Nyree,' her brother sighed, 'don't interfere.'

'I'm not interfering. I'm just giving an opinion.'

'You're matchmaking.'

'Who, me? Perish the thought.'

'Because if you are, drop it. Erica's still in shock over that jerk Townley.'

'She's been hurt, OK, I grant you that. But I think it's more to do with ethics than emotion.'

'And you would know, would you, out of your long experience of relationships in the world of art?'

'The world of art, ha! This is a simple example of a chap being an all-round cheat – and let me tell you, Erica's come to terms with that. Of course, she's still shook up about the fact that she was innocently involved in a swindle. But as to friend Townley being important to her – no, no, that's in the past.'

'But she told me in so many words that he . . .'

'Oh yes? When was that? Today? Yesterday? Wake up, bro. Whatever she used to feel, it's all over.'

He studied her, half smiling and yet shaking his head. 'Even if that's true, it's no guarantee she wants to give up the world she knows and come to set up a petty little art gallery at the back of nowhere.'

'At the back of nowhere? McNaughton's Hill is a very desirable spot.'

'But she's used to cities, and conversations with Sir This and Lord That. Cocktail parties – that sort of thing.'

'Zan, talk sense. Her mother lives in a big old farmhouse in a village in the West Country. As far as I can gather, Erica was born and brought up there. She's a country girl.'

'Oh, dry up, minnow.'

Seeing she'd said enough, she obligingly did as she was told.

Twenty-One

The car journey to Cornwall was accomplished very much as Nyree had foretold. Bert Allgood fussed over her in a way her brother had learned to avoid because he knew it annoyed her. Nevertheless, the trip was made easy by their driver's good intentions, and they arrived as promised in time for tea on Friday.

As Bert edged the vehicle up the muddy unmade road, Zan was glancing about with interest at the cordylines and yuccas growing in Lisbet's garden.

'Quite a bit like home, isn't it?' he said to his sister. 'You could almost imagine the vines over the next ridge.'

'Oh, you and your vines,' she groaned. But she knew he was thinking about the pressing, which would start soon back home at the vineyard. And she felt a longing to be home again, to see her brothers and Cookie, to ride the hills . . . To come home to the familiar old house with its wooden floors, to hear the dogs bark a welcome, and . . . perhaps . . . to see Erica come out of one of the out-buildings, with printer's ink on her fingers and a smile on her lips.

Mrs Pencarreth was on the doorstep to greet them as the limousine drew to a halt. She ushered them in, anxious about Nyree but taking care not to show it. Coats and luggage were disposed of, the visitors were shown their rooms. Nyree exclaimed in delight at the fact that her windows had leaded panes. She stared out through them at the moors in the distance, untying the silk scarf from around her head and murmuring that she must find something less gaudy and more in keeping with the surroundings.

Lisbet had arranged for food to be delivered from St Ives. She therefore could offer old-fashioned scones, fresh farm

306

butter, locally made jam, and Cornish cream. Nyree, who had reappeared wearing a checked cotton kerchief as headgear, was delighted. Afterwards she was given a conducted tour. Accustomed to old buildings being made of wood, she was fascinated by the bulging walls of lathe and plaster, the faded bricks of the garden wall, the ancient stones of the out-buildings. She felt a sort of kinship with the people who had lived here, country folk, earning their living from the land.

Soon after dinner, she began to fade. She apologised and went off to bed. Lisbet and Zan were left to sit over coffee and the remains of a superb apple charlotte sent by the caterers.

'What do you think about Erica sending in her resignation?' Zan asked. It had been worrying him ever since he heard of it. 'I got the impression her work meant a lot to her.'

Lisbet nodded agreement. 'Yet you have to understand that she was quite restricted in what she could do. The Arts and Leisure Department of the council weren't exactly generous over funds. She has no second-in-command, you know, they wouldn't provide the salary. So it's meant that she's been very tied to the gallery when, in the usual arrangement, a curator has quite a lot of freedom to go looking for works of art or attending conferences, that kind of thing. No, I think she's right to go.'

'I didn't quite catch the implication when she . . . Did she say she wanted to do something more craftsman-like?'

Lisbet smiled. 'That might be in the air. You know, Zan, when Erica was a child, she was sure she was going to be a great painter. And everyone agreed with her. She did well in art as a school subject and was accepted for college – but she found out there that when she put oil on canvas, she wasn't saying anything.'

Zan was listening with keen attention. He allowed his hostess to take her own time before she resumed.

'It's hard, you know, being the daughter of a mother who's always had a reputation as a good painter. By the time she reached her teens, I was being singled out by the critics, earning very good prices for my work, asked to paint special pieces by city councils and the like. It's meaningless, really – a painter has to paint – but it can't help sounding *impressive*. I'm sure she felt she'd never measure up, and she went to pieces. It was a bad time. I didn't make it any better because I didn't know how to handle it.' She drew in a deep breath. 'Well, she got over it and found a career for herself. But now, I think . . . something's beginning to stir again.'

'There are lots of other things she could try?'

'Yes, she's realising that to be an artist doesn't necessarily mean being like her mother – there are arts other than painting, and sometimes it takes a while before you understand where your talent lies. Gauguin, for example – he spent years as a stockbroker before he cut loose and headed for the South Seas. Rodin was a stonemason for a long time before he became a sculptor. Erica may turn out to be an engraver . . . Or perhaps not – time will tell.'

'Nyree's determined to get her to McNaughton's Hill to set up this art gallery.'

Lisbet chuckled. 'I should think Nyree usually gets what she wants.'

'Mmm,' said Zan. 'When she was a kid, she was the one that started campaigning to get the Christmas decorations down from the attic while it was still November. She's always wanted to get going on things, you know? And since she's been ill, it's been even more urgent for her – she wants things *now*, in case it gets too late.'

'It's very understandable.'

'But it's no reason for hustling other people to do things they don't really want to do. She wants Erica to come to McNaughton's Hill, but I don't think she stops to wonder if it's what Erica would really like.'

'Oh, I think Erica's extremely intrigued with the idea, Zan. To help to start a collection – it's a very attractive proposition.'

'You really think so?'

Lisbet marshalled her thoughts. She was fairly sure she knew what her daughter wanted, but you couldn't go blurting out things about other people's feelings. She said: 'I think Erica is in the mood to make a big change. This disaster with Willard—'

'Oh, him,' grunted Zan. 'He wants his head looking at! To have a girl like Erica in love with him and not to understand what a marvel that is . . .'

'I agree with you. And I think my daughter – well, you know how that old song goes – "I'm gonna wash that man right out of my hair". So she's sent in her resignation and she's in the mood to make a big change in her life. This idea of Nyree's has a lot to be said for it.'

'You really think she'd want to do it?'

'Why don't you ask her?'

'Well, I would, but you see, I think she has a bit of a guilt thing over that stupid painting. I'm afraid she might feel she has to fall in with what the kid sister wants because she owes her something.'

Lisbet didn't know what to say. She honoured the man for being so considerate but she wanted to say, 'Be selfish for a change! Make a grab for what you want!' However, Lisbet wasn't good at giving advice so she contented herself with a sympathetic smile and a shake of the head.

Next morning, Saturday, was the day for Nyree's tour of the local studios. She rose rather late, to find that her brother had been up since six and had gone out for a walk. 'Oh, that's just like him,' she complained as she tackled bread rolls delivered fresh from the oven of the village baker. 'He just wants to get out of having to look at the paintings and things.'

'No, no,' Lisbet assured her, smiling at the thin young face under its bright little tied kerchief. 'I sketched him a map of where we're going and he said he'd join us at the Westmores. I hope he doesn't get lost!'

'Not him. He's got a bump of locality. And I suppose I'm a bit of a bore, dragging him round galleries.' She looked anxiously at her hostess. 'If Erica comes to McNaughton's Hill, I hope she won't find us a bunch of hayseeds. It's not that the boys aren't interested in things like painting and music – it's just that they've had to work so hard to get the

vineyard going and make it a success. Zan in particular –
he's the money-man, he's had to give up his time to studying
the markets, making investments . . .'

'I understand.'

'As a matter of fact,' Nyree went on, eager to make things
clear, 'Heck – that's my brother Hector – he's a pretty good
carver. Only things for the house, you know – salad bowls
and cupboard doors, things like that, but they're good, at
least I think so. Jason's married, and his wife Dorothy does
weaving – that's not particularly artistic, I suppose, but the
colours are sometimes lovely. My mother was keen on art, I
used to watch programmes on TV with her, about Leonardo
and people. And she'd take us to the local art shows and she'd
always buy something, just to encourage everybody.'

Lisbet nodded and offered the marmalade.

'Zan's always been an outdoors man – likes to be out by
himself among the vines, walks miles in the hills. He reads a
lot, though. And he's – he's . . .' She faltered into silence.

'I know,' Lisbet said, and patted her hand. 'Don't get
upset about it, dear. I think it may work out all right.'

'D'you really think so? Because I'd so much like him to
be happy.'

'And that's what I want for Erica, so let's just keep our
fingers crossed.'

Nyree managed an uncertain smile, then cut open a second
roll for a thick layer of marmalade. 'Perhaps *you'd* like to
come to McNaughton's Hill some time, Mrs Pencarreth?'

'One day, perhaps, maidie,' Lisbet laughed.

When soon after midday they reached the studio of the
Westmores, who were enamellists, they found Zan was
already there. 'Slowcoaches,' he chided. 'Where have you
been?'

'We've been to three other places, that's where.' She came
close to whisper, 'One of them was a dead loss.'

'This isn't too great either,' he returned in the same tone.
'Too fiddly for my taste.'

'Let's just have a quick look at their showroom and push
off. I'm getting hungry.'

He turned to Lisbet. 'Any good places for a bit of lunch?'

'There's a pub nearby. Erica and I often take guests there when we're giving them the studio tour.'

Zan gave Lisbet a little frown, to let her know he thought his sister needed refreshment and, though she couldn't know this, a chance to take her medication. He could see Nyree was enjoying herself yet he knew from experience that she would push herself too far if he didn't keep an eye on her.

Because the spring day was chilly, she was clad in a down jacket of silvery pink with a knitted hat of the same shade pulled well down on her ears. On her feet were pink socks and yellow Doc Martens and yet the *tout ensemble* was very smart. By comparison Zan was sedate in chinos and a green waterproof jacket over a flannel shirt. Lisbet surveyed them with pleasure. It would be so nice to have them as . . . well, as close friends, if not as relatives.

They all piled into Lisbet's Land Rover, Bert having been given the day off because his limousine was unsuitable for country tracks. Nyree was still asking questions about pottery glazing as they travelled, but Zan was silent. He was still wrestling with his problem.

Would it be right to urge Erica to come to McNaughton's Hill?

He was in favour of Nyree's idea about collecting paintings. On a small scale, of course, nothing like the mining corporation that was buying Lisbet's work. But Nyree wanted to do it, and looking back he could see that his mother would have liked it. But of course while she was still alive, they didn't have the funds because the vineyard hadn't come into profit yet.

If Erica would come . . . The idea of having a permanent exhibition of paintings was good in itself. And perhaps she needed the change, the chance to recover . . . But if she came, he would never want her to leave.

All through the morning he'd been going over and over it in his mind. If he had to go back without her, he knew he would be lonely. Never mind that he'd have his family around him, without Erica there would be an emptiness in his life. But was it fair to offer this invitation when she was in such a mixed-up state over that rat Townley? Nyree said

311

she was over that – but then Nyree was only a kid. What did she know?

But then, what did *he* know? He'd been too busy all his life to fall in love. Of course there had been girls – one in particular, Gerda, had seemed important at the time. But she got tired of waiting for the vineyard to come good and, looking back, he found it hard to recall anything about her except that she'd been a line-dancing enthusiast.

Not a bit like Erica. Erica, with her little cap of brown hair, her keen glance, her quiet smile . . .

'Wake up, bro, we're here,' chided Nyree, digging him in the ribs.

'Lord, what a bony elbow you've got,' he groaned, and helped her out of the Land Rover. He glanced at his watch. One fifteen. About eight hours until Erica's train rolled into the station.

But when they walked into the Red Lion, who should rise to greet them but Erica.

Everyone cried out in welcome. Zan's surprised delight couldn't have been more revealing. 'How did you *get* here?' he demanded.

'Drove to Reading and took the seven o'clock then bus from the station. I guessed you might be here about now – Mamma often brings guests here for lunch. And if you didn't turn up, I could always catch the bus again to the crossroads and walk up to the house.' She ushered them to where she'd been sitting.

'It's lovely to see you, maidie,' her mother said, 'but what about the gallery? Saturday's a busy day.'

'I just suddenly woke up in the middle of the night and thought, why should I wait till the evening to start out? Why should I struggle through another day with crowds of visitors when I'd rather be here? So I left a message on the gallery's answering machine for Suzi and they'll manage fine without me.'

'You're being very wayward,' her mother said in some surprise.

'Oh, yes, this is a hangover from my Dizzy Days.' But

Erica was smiling, feeling for the first time in months perfectly at ease with herself.

The innkeeper knew Mrs Pencarreth and drew her away to the kitchen to discuss what to offer for lunch. Nyree asked for the ladies' room and went off to take her medication. Erica and Zan were left alone at the table.

'It's really good to see you,' he said. Well, great, he said to himself, that's really descriptive of how I feel.

'I . . . I just had to come. I couldn't bear not to be here.' With you, she added wordlessly.

'I was talking to your mother last night after the minnow went to bed. She said that – at least I think that's what she said – she seemed to think you might really be interested in coming to McNaughton's Hill and having a go at Nyree's gallery.'

'Yes.'

'We'll probably be leaving in a month or so, once the doctors are happy to let her travel. We came by the east to west route, we thought of going home the other way round – Queen Elizabeth to New York, short hops across America taking in the Getty Museum, then on by ship via Hawaii. What do you think?'

'It sounds wonderful. I'm sure Nyree will enjoy it.'

'No, I meant . . . would you like to come with us?'

Her throat choked up, her eyes filled with tears. 'Oh,' she said helplessly.

'What's wrong?' He was scared at the reaction. 'Did I say something to upset you?'

'The only thing that could upset me is if we were parted, Zan.'

'You mean . . . you want to come?'

'Oh yes. Yes, yes.'

He glanced around. They were in a little dark inn with tables and chairs all round them. If he was going to ask the most important question of his life, he wanted it to be outdoors, under the sky and the clouds of heaven, where their words would float up and become part of eternity.

He reached out a hand. She took it, twining her fingers in his. He drew her to her feet and urged her to the door.

Across the narrow lane, there was a track leading up towards the moors, where a few stunted trees gestured with branches moving in the strong westerly breeze. Unspeaking, they walked up the track, Zan holding their clasped hands close to his side.

Lisbet Pencarreth came through from behind the bar bearing news about lunch. Seeing that the table was empty, she paused. At that moment Nyree emerged from a passage, about to rejoin the group. Lisbet intercepted her.

'We seem to have lost them,' she remarked.

'Lost? Where've they gone?'

'Somewhere where they can have a bit of peace and quiet, I think.'

Nyree's eyebrows rose. 'You mean . . . ?'

'Perhaps.'

Nyree moved past her, in the only direction in which her brother could have gone – to the doorway. Gazing up the track towards the moors, she saw Zan and Erica in a passionate kiss.

'No "perhaps" about it,' she murmured, turning back with a great smile to Lisbet. Together they went to sit at a table at the far side of the room, waiting and hoping for the news they longed to hear, that the two people they loved were entering into their time of happiness.

Quite unaware of their surroundings, wrapped up in each other, the two under the gnarled trees of the moorland never even noticed that anyone had come to the door of the inn.

They were a world away, seeing a future opening before them – a future that promised days of being together in a partnership of work and achievement, and nights of being together – together in joy, together in love.

X